NEIGHBOR RESURRECTED

ALSO BY CORDY FITZGERALD

SHOPPING CART ANNIE

A Thriller **NEIGHBOR RESURRECTED**

CORDY FITZGERALD

ARCHWAY
PUBLISHING

Archway Publishing books may be ordered through booksellers or by contacting:

Archway Publishing
1663 Liberty Drive
Bloomington, IN 47403
www.archwaypublishing.com
1 (888) 242-5904

ISBN: 978-1-4808-7777-1 (sc)
ISBN: 978-1-4808-7776-4 (hc)
ISBN: 978-1-4808-7778-8 (e)

Library of Congress Control Number: 2019907067

Print information available on the last page.

Archway Publishing rev. date: 6/10/2019

FOR ROSS, NOAH, TONYA, NYA, AND RONNIE,
MY FAMILY, MY TEAM

CONTENTS

CHAPTER 1

A BLAZING COLORADO SUN began its descent. Dried leaves played circular tag in mid air. Captivated, eighty-year old Gaelen Drisco turned the volume down on his country music station. Nothing he regularly listened to did justice to sunsets.

It was that time of day when he would cover his pink scalp with his Orange Crush cap, ignore his ever-present knee pain, hop down from the front porch, and squeeze his jelly jar of Glenlivet to inhale both his liquor and his blue spruce. All the while, he praised God for one more spectacular day.

His queasy stomach told him these pleasures were fragile. How long could he help his adult children financially and live where western skies resembled fresh paint? Often he'd remind friends to bury their parachutes in good times so's to dig 'em up in bad. But lately he wondered if he'd saved enough himself.

Screeching tires halted his reverie. A neighbor's car careened around the corner. Like a rudely awakened Rip Van Winkle, Larry Carmichael fought his steering wheel through his scraggly white beard to make a U-turn into his driveway across the street. Miraculously the car stopped an inch from his garage door while Arnold, Larry's English sheepdog, barked wildly from inside the house.

Tired of being a silent audience to Larry's downhill spiral, Gaelen reached for his cell phone, but stopped. A rattling mailbox distracted him.

"That you, Inez?" he shouted. Briskly, he jogged across two driveways, his malt scotch splashing over the edge of its jar. Parts of Park Hill had black neighborhoods, but Gaelen, living in the predominantly white section, happily enjoyed the company of the only black neighbor on his block.

Atop her porch, Dr. Inez Buchanan rummaged through her mailbox, wearing a full-length robe pinned at the neck with a rhinestone bauble. "Whoops. Ya' caught me. I come out here when the sun goes down so nobody'll see me," she said.

She never looked up, thumbing through a wad of envelopes. Gaelen knew her words, like those of all schoolteachers of a certain age, were meant to underscore *his* errant behavior. Poised at her bottom steps, Gaelen had a view of well-shaped coffee-colored legs and a round rump, breathtaking for a sixty-eight-year old woman.

"I got it! I got it," she said waving a medium-sized envelope in the air. "This year's invite to the China Scholars Dinner. It's in DC, ya' know."

Sometimes he felt sorry for Inez. She'd always get involved with some academic project or another until she was way too busy to take care of her own health. All of her family was dead she'd said. They'd all died of the same disregard for themselves.

"Don't forget," he reminded her, "you're a retired teacher now."

"Every child in this country needs to know how everybody else lives on this planet. It's the only way to get people to walk in the shoes of others. But I admit it. I still have that need-to-be-needed complex."

The look on her face was suddenly expressionless as she looked down at him, then stretched a concerned gaze across their driveways. "Hear that rustling?" she asked. "When you're at home like I am, you can hear slight changes in the air."

"It's the beginning of autumn," he answered. 'I make a great noise of rustling all day, like rabbit and deer running away.'

Her smile lifted both her face and her diaphragm. For a moment he stopped breathing. Her eyes had their own rhythm. She'd always be exotic to him. *Who but a black woman named Inez would wear rhinestone jewelry to get her mail!*

She rested one hand on her hip. "I just love a man who can fling his Robert Frost around whenever he wants."

… *That's not all this man can fling,* he mused.

"But I'll need more practice opening my mailbox," she continued. "Traveling unseen is supposed to be one of the perks of being black at sunset, you know."

He'd gladly shoot whoever convinced her she was good enough to do stand-up comedy. Looking at his feet, he said, "Don't you realize everybody notices you, Inez?"

But when he looked up, her door was shut. He knew she was busy. There was her research into education funding. Why was it that teachers could never get their hands on appropriated money to buy supplies for students, she'd say? She wrote newsletters to teachers from her basement. She'd had several successes too, stopping fraud in two different states. With no regrets, he walked back to his own front door, remembering the things he had to finish by nightfall.

Autumn brought silent anonymous advertisers to Park Hill. They taped their ads to screen doors. Most told of gutter cleaners or tree trimmers. The one Gaelen picked up as he walked praised cremation. *Odd!* Reading it prompted him to vow once more to add codicils to his will to make certain he'd be buried alongside his dearest Helen. He released the ad into the wind, content to finish his drink inside and wait for his youngest daughter to arrive. *Is she going to ask me for money, too?*

Gaelen stepped across his threshold, intending to set his jar down on the hall telephone stand. Both hands had to be free to pull the dead bolt shut. The jar shattered as it fell against the table's wrought-iron legs.

The speed with which the intruder entered made Gaelen furious. But spilling twelve-year-old scotch made him even madder! His left arm was forcibly twisted backward almost out of its socket, his shoulder shoved forward, and his upper body forced to swing forward and down.

His inverted diaphragm absorbed his scream. He couldn't hear. Had he gone deaf? In the time it took to blink, Gaelen had seen, from the corner of his eye, a head covered in black cloth and eyes staring back through small holes. It was an image of a robber or terrorist the likes of which he'd seen only on TV. But damn it, this was Denver!

The intruder was also bent forward, his elbow wrapped across the front of Gaelen's neck. Slowly the man squeezed inward against Gaelen's carotid artery. Familiar with the hold, Gaelen gingerly slid his feet further apart to brace against the additional pain that was sure to come.

His intestines rumbled. His head and abdomen throbbed. Sweat stung his eyes. Every nerve tingled as he fruitlessly tried to move a body no longer able to defend itself against a younger man's strength.

His feet might be an asset. Maybe he could dance toward the door to keep it open. Gaelen jerked his left foot sideways, felt his muscles strain along his quads. Just then the door slammed shut with the intruder's arms still surrounding him. Had it been a strong wind or another person? How many intruders were there?

"Where eez?" the man holding him whispered.

European? Middle Eastern? Gaelen couldn't pinpoint the accent. He was tiring. The man mashed spongy lips below the back of his ear.

"Pont wid free hand."

Was it lousy English or a killer who didn't care? For a moment, Gaelen's body shook with final doom. But he was still alive.

"What?" he asked, but he knew it sounded more like an escape of air.

Odorous exotic tobacco from further down the hall shut down his peripheral vision, turning his brain into a paperweight. Gauloises! His head smacked the floor as he recognized the smell of French cigarettes from World War II. Then there was the smell of freshly dug earth.

What had Inez asked? *Hear that rustling?* Arnold had only barked. Both Inez and Arnold had sensed the intruders.

"Come here," Helen whispered.

Nooo, I have promises to keep, and miles to go before . . . he answered.

Gaelen watched a forest of black pant legs tracking mud across the kitchen floor. Someone shouted "EBAEE! Ebaee!" near his head. But Gaelen's hearing ceased when his life ended.

SIX MONTHS EARLIER

CHAPTER 2

MARCH 2006   BEIJING BATHHOUSE

"SPYMASTER!"

He didn't move, although he clearly heard his great grandson Kee.

"Spymaster. It's almost time."

He kept his eyes shut, reasoning his joint pain would disappear as soon as he resumed his dream. The air that touched his face was heavy and moist. Dressed in street clothes, ninety-year-old Quan Yu lay across his favorite recliner, gently inhaling the smell of birch bath salts from the towel Kee had thrown over him for added warmth.

Quan easily returned to a deep sleep in which he high-stepped through blood- soaked torture chambers, places he had created and been tortured in himself. After an abrupt halt in his steps, he proudly saluted Generalissimo Chiang Kai-shek. Fast-forwarding through his dreams carried him across sixty-five years of public service, until Quan finally reached his most prized memory, a parade before friends and foe, while being hailed the Himmler of China.

"Spymaster. It's time!"

Quan opened and then closed one eyelid so quickly he was certain Kee had not observed him. Indeed, Kee's back was toward him, preparing the autoclave.

Confident he was unobserved, Quan opened both eyes and smiled at an unconscious man in his late twenties sprawled on his back atop a gurney. Quan was happy about his good fortune. He'd recruited this Chinese-American scholar on a trip years earlier to San Francisco, unbeknownst to the scholar himself. Within a few short years of that recruitment, Wren Xiao had become Stanford University's youngest doctor of bioengineering, dumb as dirt in the ways of his people, yet gifted around human engineering codes. Except for a pair of white socks, the young man wore nothing but a towel across his genitals. Having recognized in him all the ingredients of a future Chinese super spy, Quan continued to stare at this disturbed, antisocial genius with a certain pride.

Finally lifting himself from his leather recliner, Quan asked, "How much time do I have?"

Kee ceased his preparations and stood quite still. The gesture always endeared itself to Quan, who appreciated Kee's ability to concentrate on his master's words.

"Ninety minutes," I'd say, master. "Two hours would be dangerous."

"You are excited?" Quan asked.

"Oh, yes," Kee replied, while helping him into his surgical jacket. "There are times when I'm overcome with joy, working for you. Your name still carries much honor. Only you could have obtained such vast sums of money from the People's Committee, while providing so little explanation for its use. Your tenacity is incredible. What will the Party do when it discovers how much you've personally done to make China the eyes, the ears, and the voice of the entire planet?"

Quan was amused by his great grandson's astonishment. He would have thought it unusual if funding had been reduced or even questioned, such was his continued power. He maintained a league of supporters ready to defend his grandiose eccentricities whenever needed.

Lights in the lounging areas of the bathhouse had already been dimmed and heavy red drapes pulled across the front door. Clients had left for the night. How sad the plight of the bathhouse, bulldozed to make room for Olympic venues, no longer the central magnet of Asian life or the sophisticated business it once was.

"You've made sure no one has fallen asleep out there?"

"Yes master."

Once again, Kee proved how invaluable he was in managing the smallest of details while manipulating the larger needs of the man on the gurney. Yet Kee never seemed to quite able to grasp a larger view of life.

Quan stood motionless again remembering the repetitive nature of espionage. Only the higher echelons of any secret service grow old enough to retire. Spies are supposed to die young. They're sacrificed like dry twigs in their country's burning passion for power. Quan's body sometimes trembled with what he called ancient adrenaline. Having outwitted death numerous times, would he last long enough to see the success of a rapidly changing China he'd created?

Kee meanwhile fastened the buttons of Quan's jacket and helped him into latex gloves. When the old man felt his legs stiffen, he forced himself to walk toward a stainless-steel tray under a blinding array of ceiling lights.

He merely waved a gloved hand over each tool that sat on the tray, such was his complete faith in Kee: chisel, tweezers, clamps, puncture needle, threading needle, ice funnel, and his favorite customized cordless tattoo machine.

Quan then ordered Kee to turn Xiao over on his stomach before switching on the monitor with its 200X magnifying lens. Kee complied. Working quickly, Quan made a deep incision, using backward strokes with the edge of a blade attached to his tattoo machine. It was just below the young man's shoulder. The motor pushed tissue away gently as Kee cauterized small blood vessels and used clamps for larger ones.

Once Quan felt satisfied he smiled at Kee. It was time to insert the nuclear detonator, engineered specifically for this unusual mission. Sandwiched between two squares of cotton, which Kee held, Quan used tweezers to grasp what had the look and weight of a wireless titanium circuit board. He inserted it into the open wound behind an intact but exposed artery. With no exchange of words, they simultaneously flew into rapid activity, applying antiseptic and gauze before closing the wound. Using his own signature carrier to mix with a specially made pigment, Quan tapped the man's skin again and again until it blended exactly with the patient's surrounding skin tone.

Meanwhile Kee opened the nearest door. Behind it sat an elderly woman with a sewing basket over one arm and two milky blue marbles for eyes. Kee directed her steps toward the gurney. Pulling a stool closer for her to sit on, he placed a needle threaded with long gelatinous material into her hands and planted her long fingers on the man's wound. Quan and

Kee stood over her and said nothing as she worked. In twenty minutes she was finished. Kee escorted her wordlessly from the room.

The combination of the young man's tattoo and the old woman's stitchery hid all outward evidence of entry to the untrained eye. Quan tore off his gloves.

"Magnificent," Kee whispered, while Quan sank back into his leather recliner and reached for his now tepid tea. There was silence for some time before Kee spoke again. "I've been wondering, sir, how this man, Dr. Xiao Wren, could be taken seriously in your plan to outsource China's espionage activity. He looks Chinese, sir. He'd be recognized immediately. Possibly his height suggests an American, but who . . ."

"Kee, you could not have taken his place," Quan replied with deliberate slowness, verging on tenderness. "Dr. Xiao will have very special duties to perform, none of which I'm willing to divulge at this time."

"But have you read his medical report?" Kee continued.

Quan's face was suddenly stern. "Everyone has a line they must not cross. Be careful you don't trip over yours haphazardly young man."

"I beg your forgiveness Spymaster."

"Spoken like a true disciple," Quan replied. "Be careful never to assume more than you've been told."

"But," Kee continued, "Xiao himself believes he suffers from schizophrenia. That's no small defect. He says he hears the voice of his dead mother, telling him to kill people."

Exposing a lavish set of gold teeth, Quan laughed heartily. "And so he will kill people. I believe he killed his mother years ago. In fact, I'm betting on his ability to kill. She wasn't a very nice person. Did you bother to read that part of his medical report? She reminded me of your mother Kee. How dare she laugh and curse at you as you waved goodbye to her. You were merely a boy heading for Beijing, alone on a train, to come here and work for me."

Kee's eyes studied the floor. His face was the color of alabaster.

"Why do you look so sad Kee?" Quan continued. "You're not sorry I had to dispose of her, are you? Certainly you understood it was better . . ."

"Yes Spymaster. I do understand." He quickly lifted his head. "It's not that. I was jealous of this man's rapid ascent to your favor, while I have earnestly devoted year after year of my life to your continued successes."

"And I'm very grateful," Quan answered. "You should be a very happy young man tonight. We live in China, the most magnificent country on the planet, or should I say, in this universe! We live in a place where there *is* no "private sector," no capitalistic business model to take money from the people, no security corporation, or financial mega-institution working to exceed the power of its people. Soon we will conquer the entire planet by embracing only those organizations and other governments willing to become clones of our own. That's how we'll increase China's strength. It's that simple."

Kee began the slow process of cleaning up their makeshift surgical area and said, "I know you've already selected an American company for your takeover. And I know it's not Haliburton or Blackwater. But have you given this company its mission yet?" Kee asked.

A slight smile stretched across Quan's face. He enjoyed Kee and trusted him, but not deeply enough to unveil everything. He'd survived too long to have his dreams destroyed by an assistant.

"I have chosen a newly formed American-based conglomerate," Quan replied. "It has all the bells and whistles, as they say in America. As for its mission, I've already paid them to unleash several missteps throughout the world. Many of my schemes have already been initiated, each one designed to go unnoticed by global media, by the United States Congress, the House of Lords, and actually by every civilized nation, including even the Peoples Republic of China. But each one of these missions, when taken as a whole, well . . . we'll see, won't we? And here lies a naive unconscious member of the proletariat, a young man useful for as long as he continues to ingest the appropriate medications we serve him. Soon he will have absolutely no choice but to add his miserable life to our cause."

CHAPTER 3

A FTER TWELVE LONG years Inez Buchanan still winced in front of mirrors. She washed her hands quickly under the automatic eye mounted in the head of one of the faucets in the ladies room. With wet fingers, she pulled up her bra strap. Lopsided was never okay. To the tune of *This Is the Way We Wash Our Clothes* she sang, "A radical mastectomy is a good thing, is a good thing, is a good thing. A radical mastectomy is a good thing, at least I'm still ali–ive."

She stared at her reflection then turned the light out. In darkness she liked the way she looked in black skin and a black muumuu, hated ultra-modern bathroom fixtures, and wanted to kick herself for not keeping her mouth shut when Miriam Garfield suggested they go out for drinks.

It had been a friendly gesture, Inez thought, from a woman not known for her friendliness. Yet Miriam's snide remarks seemed never to end. While the neighborhood was still mourning her father's sudden death, it seemed going out for drinks now was just too soon. Inez yanked the door open and marched out of the ladies room with a newly refreshed can-do attitude.

Nuova Paesana was practically empty. *The Denver Post* said it was the best restaurant to be seen in at midnight. It was now three thirty in the afternoon and deader than a King Soopers during a Bronco game. From nowhere, a tall man dressed in black, like herself, brushed hard against her shoulder on his way to the restrooms. Certain that chivalry was dead but determined not to let it die in peace, Inez turned her head and shouted,

"Excuse me," loud enough for him to hear, because that's how teachers teach.

When he made no change in his movements, she continued to walk past a wood paneled bar with overhead ferns hanging under artificial lights. A customer, could he be anything else, in a dark gray pin-striped suit, loudly conversed with a balloon-faced bartender wearing a large button earring. Suddenly the bartender seemed familiar. She tried to imagine him without his day old whiskers and his past-puberty paunch. Walking up to the bar, Inez placed one hand flat on the counter and smiled.

"Excuse me," she said. "Was I ever your teacher? Do I look familiar to you?"

The bartender paused in mid sentence, irreverently leaning over the counter to look her up and down from her loosely pinned gray hair to the mid-heeled sandals on her feet.

She was reminded how cruel young kids and impolite old men can be. No, he was no past student of hers. She would have rid him of those little behaviors he was using to show disrespect.

"Where are your manners?" she asked.

The man appeared to push back slightly. Finally he answered, "No, ma'am."

Quickly she turned into the dining room, telling herself she would never go out for drinks again just to be sociable. Her home was a much friendlier, safer, stimulating place than this bar.

Inez continued toward her table, with a waiter gaining on her heels. She deliberately slid into her high-backed Queen Anne's chair at a table where two filled wine glasses sat on a white linen cloth. Pleased with herself for not causing them to spill, Inez smiled at Miriam Garfield who sat across from her in a couture suit.

"Thought you got lost," rebuked the woman. "So I sent a waiter to look for you."

Inez placed her napkin back in her lap and answered, "Could have sworn we were around the same age. Oh, I may be a bit older. But do *you* ever get lost in empty bars?"

"Touché," Miriam answered. "Guess my eye was drawn toward your telltale strands of gray. Made me feel for a moment that I was out with a much older woman. Oh, I know you don't follow trends or care what other people think. Dad told me that years ago when he described you to me."

Inez pressed her lips together as a reminder to keep her mouth shut. She didn't believe her dad had said any such thing. How easy it would be to call attention to Miriam's spider-webbed skin, dusted with what looked like baking powder under bleached hair.

Gossip on the block was that Miriam and her husband were hired to manage a posh American restaurant in Italy. That was all Inez really knew of Gaelen Drisco's oldest daughter, Miriam. Inez had lived next door to Gaelen, for close to twenty-five years and he never once mentioned his eldest daughter.

For a solid twenty minutes, they exhausted the topic of Colorado weather and sipped wine, an activity Inez had practiced over the course of her career to make herself amiable to her white colleagues. They hadn't planned to have dinner and Inez was quietly giddy over returning home soon to eat her own gourmet concoction alone. Establishing a friendship with a catty woman would require decades of gentle management and Inez had no time for that nonsense.

Just then a new waiter emerged. His smooth strides were suggestive of wearing roller skates. A black eye patch covered his left eye and his white sleeves billowed in the wind he created as he moved. They both stared at him, Inez hoping his mere presence would delay their volley of mean-ingless chitchat. He carried a new bottle, which he opened and offered to Miriam to taste. Why had he picked her to do that, Inez wondered? Once Miriam nodded, he refilled each glass.

"Interested in menus, *signore*? Antonio is here to assist."

Inez stared at him with unabashed curiosity. This waiter's black vest and shirt were unbuttoned over a bare chest, like a costume. The black hair that fell past his forehead had white roots. And although his chest size said he pressed iron regularly, brown spots on the back of his hands said he was in his seventies, maybe older.

"*No, mi dispiace,*" Miriam replied. "*Aspettiamos per le mie sorelle. Grazie.*"

"*Prego. Benissimo, signore.*"

Inez hadn't understood what Miriam said, but hearing her say "no" was reassuring. The two must have exchanged pleasantries earlier, while she was in the ladies room. That's why he let her taste the wine first, Inez presumed. Surely he wasn't racially prejudiced.

As soon as Antonio left, Miriam pulled her chair closer to Inez and in her ear said, "So did you and Dad have sex?" Miriam then rested her eyes on the table, as if observing a pseudo form of quiet politeness, as she waited for Inez to answer.

Inez raised her eyebrows. "Flighty, shallow people have affairs," she answered. "So why are you . . . " she suddenly rose from her chair taking a hurried inventory of what she needed to go home . . . "asking me such things?"

Miriam had driven them to the restaurant however Inez was sure she could get the bartender to call a cab. She could have call one herself *if* she had thought to bring her cell phone with her.

"I'm so sorry Inez," Miriam interrupted. "I didn't mean to offend you. I was just relating what some people thought at the time. I didn't expect *you* of all people to have such a chip on your shoulder."

Inez looked down her nose at Miriam before resuming her search through her purse for the phone. The dining room lights had been dimmed. More people were in the bar now. A glance at her watch told her rush hour had begun. There'd be no available cabs. She flopped back into her chair and said, "Of course, I have a chip on my shoulder. I'm black! I was born having to prove I'm human, intelligent, and a moral person every minute of every day. Does your skin color do that?"

Looking into Miriam's eyes she asked, "Is the issue that you were never taught manners or that you feel using your manners with black people isn't necessary? You don't have to answer that. It's a rhetorical question."

"Forgive me," Miriam pleaded. "I don't make friends easily. In the restaurant industry I'm called the 'bitchwalker.' I'm normally hated. Male chefs get away with that all the time. But let me set the record straight. I'm no racist."

Inez looked into a face as anguished as she imagined her own to be. "Well, I'm no racist either!" she responded. "Maybe I'm just being assertive or aggressive. Maybe I should work on my manners so that no one will ever think I'm just a hateful bitch with no good reason for being that way. That's better than being racist, isn't it?"

Miriam didn't hide her look of disgust. But Inez didn't hide her fatigue over the situation either.

I should have known better than to visit this woman's dystopian world where bitchwalking is acceptable. How different Miriam's father had been!

Suddenly Inez felt the urge to talk about him. "It took months after I moved in next door before I could talk to your dad," Inez said, "much less trust him. But he turned out to be kind, all the time. In less than a year Gaelen became my very best friend. He helped me laugh during the dark days of my divorce. During both our bouts with cancer, we gave each other courage to stay the course. So how could he die and leave me alone on our block? Except for his brief scare with prostate cancer, he never got sick! And he never talked about his heart. I heard that you warned some of the neighbors about his heart problems one day, and the next day, he was dead from a heart attack."

Inez hadn't realized she was crying until something wet hit the back of her hand.

Miriam looked agitated once she noticed Inez's tears. "It's all my fault," Miriam said. "I was . . ."

Inez interrupted and waved her hand at her. "It's nobody's fault Miriam. I practically ignored Gaelen on the very day he died. After his death, I didn't answer my phone anymore. After his funeral, a construction crew tore down his house and framed in a three-story monstrosity that even covered his pet cemetery, and I cried again."

Inez wiped her eyes with the back of her hand. "We'd laugh and say that's where he must have buried his parachutes for the hard times to come. It would be wrong to think Gaelen was just an old ordinary white man. Gaelen was a man all of his neighbors respected."

Suddenly standing over them at five feet eleven inches was Sheila Drisco, who had already snatched a Queen Anne's chair from another table and pulled it over.

"Daddy would tell you two to go whine in the ladies room and you know it," Sheila said.

Though unexpected, Inez was happy to see the most glamorous of Gaelen's daughters, a professional model and over a decade younger than Miriam. Nuova Paesana had become noticeably louder with crashing dishes and shouting waiters. But Sheila's movie- star composure and resonant voice were quite distinctive over the din.

Inez watched Sheila accept a glass of wine from an anonymous admirer, brought over by yet another waiter. Inez known Sheila since she wore braces and ragged tennis shoes. Inez beamed with something akin to parental pride. "Gosh, you're looking good."

"Right back at you," Sheila answered.

Miriam had put on pince-nez. She was fumbling with a day planner as she spoke. "Sheila and Karen said you could be trusted. I asked them both here, but I'm too excited to wait for Karen. I believe Dad was murdered because of something he knew or for something he had, or maybe even for something he was."

Happy hour created a sound barrier between the older women. Sheila sat between them and watched the chaos of the evening around her. Inez watched Miriam's lips move, uncertain of what she'd just said.

Did she say murder? Oh, please! I've saved enough money to live where people don't get murdered. Nobody on my block earns enough money to turn murderous. She's crazy!

Miriam twisted a small strand of bleached blonde hair between her fingers and read aloud from papers in her planner. Sheila flirted with a man across the room. Inez was sadly reminded of classrooms where teachers had no control over their students but would continue to read while no one in the class listened.

Miriam suddenly shouted, "So maybe you weren't as close to Dad as I thought you were. And obviously you're not a trained investigator either."

Are those all the put-downs she can think of?

Italian folk music blasted throughout the restaurant.

"Nonetheless," Miriam continued, "we'll still need your help to find his murderer."

"Stop!" Sheila shouted at her sister.

Inez viewed the scene at her own table as bad theater. She glanced at tables across the entire dining area, performing imaginary triage by noting where emotional hotspots, and enjoyable socializing were likely taking place.

Miriam was in the process of turning her fantasies into soap opera. If

Inez could add a small amount of her own melodrama maybe she could manipulate Miriam into taking her home.

Miriam continued her theorizing, "There's a lot we didn't know about Dad. He may have been a spy during WWII."

Sheila gave a mocking grunt, while Inez, without fanfare, turned her wineglass upside down, emptying its contents into her lap.

"Oh, my!" Inez shouted, as she jumped up and pushed her chair back. "I'll have to go home right away."

Sheila leaned closer, dabbing her cloth napkin on Inez's dress. "That was so whak!" she whispered to Inez.

"You see," Miriam continued as if nothing had just happened, "the night Dad died, Karen collected several things from his home, including his medals. I've since discovered that some were awarded for code breaking."

Inez stood marveling at Miriam's hutzpa. *How could anybody be so self- absorbed? Gaelen's heart attack must have devastated her, but learning that he'd kept secrets must have hurt her even more.*

"It was news to me, too," said Shelia, as she continued dabbing away at Inez's dress. "I thought . . ."

Miriam interrupted as if her sister wasn't there. "Dad apparently knew several languages, German, Yiddish, Gaelic, and English. Makes me wonder if he had a Jewish parent. He had to have been an asset to our military. Before Karen was born, he once told me he'd met . . . of course, I didn't know who these people were at the time . . . Dwight Eisenhower, Marshall Montgomery, and who was that other guy?"

"Zorba, the Greek?" Inez mumbled. She finally sat down and decided to pour herself another glass of wine before embarking on yet another strategy to get Miriam to take her home. Slowly she realized Miriam was glaring at her.

When she spoke, her voice was calm, but her eyes mounted their own attack. "You don't believe me?" she asked Inez.

Inez took a deep breath before answering. "I knew Gaelen the practical jokester and the neighborhood peacemaker. He was everyone's friend, spy or not. You think somebody from as far back as WWII hated him enough to kill him now?"

Miriam looked pensive at first, then exuberant.

"That's why we need to join forces," Miriam replied. "You're not a real special investigator but certainly smart enough to edit your own newsletter. You're neither gullible nor related and so we don't have to pay you anything. What we need is your ability to . . ."

"No matter how much more we learn about Dad," Sheila broke in, "it won't prove he was murdered. He was cremated, for God's sake! All the evidence is gone. Police would laugh at us."

Inez raised her glass into the air in a silent toast.

Miriam spoke slowly and deliberately. "I was going to wait until Karen got here. But I'll burst if I have to wait any longer."

Suddenly her speech was faster than a cattle auctioneer's.

"Just before Dad died, I told him I was getting a divorce. Jack was sleeping with every waitress in the place and threatening to take custody of our son. I contacted an international lawyer who said I needed two hundred thousand dollars to buy his services."

Her voice cracked. Inez pushed a glass of water toward her, which Miriam sipped before continuing.

"Dad said not to worry, that was the price his house had just been appraised for. He'd sell it," she continued, "and go into a veterans' home."

Both Sheila and Inez gasped out loud and in unison.

"I know, I know!" Miriam shouted. Several people at other tables turned to look. Somebody, mercifully, had turned the music down.

"I told Dad I couldn't accept his sacrifice," Miriam whispered. "But he said to remember that Xavier was his only grandchild. He told me to call neighbors long distance and tell them he had a bad heart and needed a smaller place to live. We'd made the whole story up! And in less than forty-eight hours he was dead."

She cupped her hands over her mouth to muffle her sobs.

Inez suddenly realized the financial pressure Gaelen must have endured in his last days. She couldn't help taking a quick peek at Miriam's diamond stud earrings.

An anorexic young woman wearing a hairnet and the white uniform of a busboy appeared. She took an eternity to refill water glasses.

"Looks like a slow afternoon," Inez said to the woman with mild sarcasm.

"HA!" said the waif. "Waiters say this table's so emotional y'all probably missed the commotion entirely."

"What do you mean?" Inez asked.

"Police say a car got highjacked out front. Management doesn't believe it, but Antonio *is* missing. Police are in the back questioning staff. They finished with me, so I had to come out here. They're gonna pay me extra for this."

Inez cringed as she watched her pick food from between her teeth while pouring water. Miriam ignored her, using a gold compact to repair makeup. Now was as good a time as any to press ahead, Inez thought.

"We should leave," Inez announced. "You could drop me at my house and then go talk about these issues with your sisters. Sounds like decent bar service is over for the evening."

"No!" Miriam shouted. "Karen's late, but on her way. And I'm not leaving here without your commitment, Inez. I've got a plane to catch for Rome later tonight."

What commitment?

As if reading Inez's face, Miriam continued. "Karen was laid off. The Red Cross made budget cuts. She'll be looking for another job and Sheila's career is just picking up in the States. I'm working seven days a week until I sort out my legal situation. We'll all be too busy to give this the attention it deserves."

Inez was determined to tell her "hell no" without actually saying it. "I'm so sorry to hear Karen isn't with the Red Cross anymore," she answered. "It was the kind of job made for her talents. She still visits neighbors when they're ill. Maybe she could make a few phone calls for you as well."

Inez stared at Miriam, hoping she had successfully changed the subject from any talk of commitment.

Sheila kept the chatter going. "Karen's changed," she said to both of them. "It must have been terrible for her to find Dad's body. She seems more grown up now. Actually . . ."

Breathing deeply, Miriam interrupted her sister once again. "So, are you telling me, Inez, that you just aren't interested in finding Dad's murderer?"

"By your own account," Inez answered immediately, "you and your family have way more pressing priorities. And murder is a bit over-the-top for me to believe. To be honest, your sudden interest in your dad surprises me."

"How very perceptive you are!" Miriam shouted back. "Okay, so I hated the man! Is that what you've been waiting to hear me say?"

Her face was red and she looked directly at Inez.

"He thought he was the only one who had the right to mourn Mom's death. I wasn't even permitted to attend her funeral. My job was to raise his children, pick the girls up from school, and do the wash. He let me know I was too stupid to go to Catholic school. I cleaned his house and had to pay my own way through culinary school. He bitched about it every day. So when the first man came along, I married him to escape."

Sheila's face was distant as she played with her cell phone. She'd likely heard Miriam's story before. But Inez was surprised to hear that Gaelen had acted that way.

Suddenly Sheila broke the silence. "What I was about to say, before I was so rudely interrupted, is that Karen didn't come home last night. Now don't anybody get shocked. This isn't the first time our goody-goody-girl stayed someplace else over night and forgot to let me know."

The two older women remained silent.

"Wait a minute," Sheila continued. "I just remembered. Karen said the only reason Dad didn't have an autopsy was because she had tearfully explained to the rookie cop that Dad had a heart condition . . . a heart condition you now say," and she turned to Miriam . . . "didn't exist!"

Miriam quietly looked at the two women. Her eyes were glassed over again.

"Okay," Inez said. "It's *possible* that Gaelen did not die of a heart attack. But, it's still very *probable* that a heart attack killed him."

Through tears, Miriam found her phone. "I know Karen planned to be here. We talked this morning, or was that last night? I don't . . . " Her face shriveled. "It says her phone's been disconnected."

"That's nothing," said Sheila. "She hasn't paid the bill. As her roommate, I can tell you that's not uncommon either."

Miriam threw her phone into her bag. "Your place is close by, isn't it?" she asked Sheila.

"Not exactly, but follow me."

Inez couldn't help smiling at both of them. While Sheila and Karen's place in the new Stapleton area wasn't close to the restaurant it was close to Park Hill. Inez was finally on her way home.

Miriam pulled out a wad of money. Without counting it, she threw the cash onto the hostess station, the way Inez imagined spoiled rich kids would. Apparently Miriam didn't need money anymore.

They exited the dark restaurant and were greeted with harsh crime lights and yellow tape. All three walked cautiously in sandals between parked police cars. Only Inez walked through the parking lot. She let the wind touch her face and remembered parts of the busgirl's story about a carjacking.

It had been a warm December day in Denver with the kind of wind Inez cherished. It was so easy for her to believe that warm Chinook winds came down off the Rocky Mountains from time to time to purposefully kiss her face and run through her hair. After all, only God could make a mountain and push air over and around hills and canyons to reach her. Inez leaned back against the leather of Miriam's rental, while Sheila roared ahead of them in her own red sports car.

Murder and spies were the stuff of movies, Inez thought. Miriam's fantasies had nothing to do with ordinary people. But a short stop at Karen's place to say hello would be a fine way to end this silly evening.

As a four-year-old, Karen once asked Inez if she could change her into an angel. Karen had reasoned that as an angel she could see her mom every day. Of all Gaelen's daughters, Karen was the one Inez loved like her very own.

CHAPTER 4

T RACE MITCHELL STOOD beside unopened boxes of raw spinach, which exuded an aroma of freshly tilled soil inside his family's grocery store. His smartphone was wedged between his scrunched shoulder and left ear. Perturbed over trying to conduct surveillance across two continents and set out produce at the same time, he finally gave up and shouted, "Ma, I gotta go!"

He yanked his stained apron over his head. Like everything else in life, he should have started an hour earlier. "Ya' hear me Ma?"

She was in the back stacking inventory and if she'd gotten into her zone, she'd never hear him.

"Ya! When Harry's finished here, he'll go there to stock. Be fine."

Never too busy to use her "proper lady" voice, still tinged with faint echoes of Romania, she continued to yell. "See you soon, hon."

Trace handed his apron to his young nephew Harry while squeezing past him. At seventeen the boy had transformed into a sumo wrestler before the family's disbelieving eyes. Touted as East High School's only lettered vegetarian, he had yet to lose a wrestling match.

Their store hadn't always specialized in organic vegetables. When Trace left home to become a SEAL, the store, in a neighborhood of Greek, Ethiopian, and hippy restaurants, was known for selling anything to anybody. But with Mom still wanting to work after their dad died, the switch to a more genteel product and retail model was a necessity.

"Protect your grandma," Trace said, forcing his arm into his leather

harness. Harry understood. The gun Trace had trained him on was attached to a trick-release mounting under the counter. Tiny cameras captured all sides of the cash register, while the dummy cameras were five
times larger and in plain view.

"Chill," Harry replied. "Dad's taking my place soon as he gets off work.
I got homework due tomorrow."

Trace didn't smile. He couldn't tell him his real worry *was* his dad;
the eternally cocky older brother, who, as their mom put it, was good with
money. Well, maybe that was his greatest asset, but it didn't make him
more mature.

By the time Agent Trace Mitchell exited Organic Mercantile at York
and Colfax, he'd begun his own transformation. One hand smoothed
back a head of unruly dark blond hair against December's Chinook winds,
while the other hand buttoned his jacket to better conceal his .40-caliber
Glock 22. By the time he slid behind the wheel of what he lovingly called
his Batmobile, he was no longer the thirty-five-year-old son of a working
mother, but an agent employed by the Colorado Bureau of Investigation.

Rush hour had a half-hour jump on him. His red Saturn crept south
on Colorado Boulevard with no siren until he couldn't stand being motionless any longer. He pulled out his flasher, attached it to the roof, and
switched on the noise.

It was a crazy business. The promise of additional Federal money
had enticed Colorado to utilize CBI to track terrorists across the Rocky
Mountains. The man he had under electronic surveillance arrived in
Colorado two weeks ago. Although suspected of being a gun for hire,
he'd committed no crimes here. Then suddenly he poked his head up in
real time on two separate continents.

Agent Mitchell was hoping his man in Denver had been misidentified.
Interpol claimed he was in Paris last night, where he killed a Nigerian
chancellor. But his man's green card placed him in a newly opened Denver
restaurant, Nuova Peasana, working six days a week for the past two weeks.

Mitchell hesitated before getting out of his car. Tiffany Plaza was a
very large strip mall glued to the side of a big hill. It had somehow survived
the froufrou elegance of the fifties and was only now being taken over by

upscale retail stores and restaurants on three sides of a normally packed parking lot.

Denver police were everywhere. Trace had to put his eyes on the man in question, but CBI had no jurisdiction over anything. This was supposed to have been an electronic surveillance job.

Mitchell adjusted his Ray-Bans against what had earlier been a burning winter sun and slowly meandered to the quarterback position in a cluster of four Denver policemen he knew personally from previous overlapping cases. They were huddled in front of the restaurant.

"Sup?" Mitchell asked. Had they been briefed on CBI's terrorist tracking? He'd find out quick enough.

"*Nada,*" said Sergeant Ryan. "We got no vic, no car, no plates. All we got is two couples, that's four credibles. They don't know each other but swear a waiter from here carjacked a woman, teenager maybe, who was driving a beat-up dark-colored Camry, Nissan, or Rav."

Ryan pulled a pair of tarnished wire-rimmed glasses from his breast pocket and began reading from a ragged spiral. Mitchell was relieved. Ryan wasn't going to hold much back.

"Female inside the car," he continued, "screamed or said nothing then slid over from the driver's side, because, witnesses say, the man in black and white, same as what these waiters wear, pulled out a highly reflective gun. Our credibles do agree the female was alive when the car left the lot."

"No casings or tire marks?" Mitchell asked.

"Right."

"Could a bullet have lodged in the side of a car that left the lot already? That could explain the lack of casings in the lot."

"Well," sneered Ryan, "anything's possible."

Mitchell took out a notebook himself. "What about security cameras?"

"None here," Ryan said pointing a beefy thumb at the restaurant beside them. "However, as we speak, officers are trying to find the company handling the one camera at that realty company." His index finger pointed above their heads.

Mitchell had another question. "Any customers inside missing somebody?"

Ryan wrenched his spectacles off his face and said, "That's where we got stonewalled. Our credibles are from out of town, Nebraska and Wyoming, and they're way over fifty. Management claims the kidnapper was just a waiter doing double duty as a valet with his girlfriend inside the car. Owners sided with management and stood their ground; even had their lawyers meet us here. They don't want cops in there or the place closed down because of nearsighted boomers. They're at the precinct recording their statements now."

Mitchell knew why Ryan was pissed. Ryan had been over fifty for a long time. Why the Department kept him on was no mystery. The guy obviously either knew somebody or filled some politician's racial quota. And if there was one thing Trace Mitchell hated about law enforcement, it was having to work with soon-to-retire personnel, though he had to admit, being around Ryan was more like having the Dean of Cops looking over your shoulder.

"However," the Sergeant continued, "We managed to interview staff in the kitchen, where they wouldn't be seen by the public."

He stopped his recitation to stare at something behind Mitchell's head. Mitchell could hear the flippity-flop of several pairs of high-heeled sandals running across asphalt but didn't turn around, since his colleagues had beat him to it.

"Wow, three of 'em in two flavors," Ryan mumbled. "Too high maintenance for my salary. Did you see 'em?" he asked Mitchell.

Mitchell turned slightly to see the back of what looked like a model getting into a red Alpha Romero, while two older women got into a sedan. Ryan, Mitchell thought, was trying to convince others he was still young enough for the job.

"Being unobservant is gonna cost you one day," Ryan said to Mitchell. "Mark my word. One waiter's gone," he continued. "Employed two weeks. Put on an eye patch today and disappeared."

Mitchell involuntarily cringed. He hoped no one noticed. Sounded like his man. But he knew he'd have to provide information in order to get more significant stuff.

"Your missing man," Mitchell broke in "may be the man I'm after. I need Antonio Dante's fingerprints. Interpol believes he's a gun for hire, who killed a man last night in Paris. We need to know if he flew back to Denver in time to kidnap your vic this afternoon if there really was a kidnapping."

Ryan pulled a stark white handkerchief from his pants pocket and wiped away his perspiration. Mitchell had already seen his Louis Armstrong impersonation. "Betcha fi' pesos our man's from Mexico with no papers," Ryan chuckled.

Mitchell didn't laugh. A CBI truck pulled up. A man and woman jumped out wearing business suits, tipped their heads deferentially to Mitchell, then entered the restaurant with gear bags. Mitchell had requested them while still at his family's grocery.

"Ain't no fingerprints of that guy," Ryan railed. "We've already covered that ground. Everything gets washed the minute a waiter collects it. You think the menus will tell ya' anything? Besides, won't you have to shut that place down to get your people in? You got warrants already?"

"I will have," Mitchell fudged. He turned on his heels to size up the spot where the alleged kidnapping took place and to avoid Ryan's whining. From out the corner of his eye he could see Ryan was already on his phone to see if Mitchell really did have somebody's okay to bring technicians in.

Mitchell hung outside eyeballing distances before turning back to Ryan. "Just a heads up," Mitchell shouted. "Forecasters say it's going to snow tonight!"

Ryan rolled his eyes and resumed his phone conversation. Mitchell felt an urgency to collect evidence before the storm. His knee injury was better than any meteorologist.

Mitchell stepped inside the restaurant, leaving Ryan to simmer in his own chaos. He stopped next to a hostess stand where a barefoot woman twirled to Musak, in a flimsy Italian folk dress that continuously slid off her shoulders.

She smiled and asked, "Smoking or non?"

When he flashed his badge, her twirling stopped.

"I hope you don't close us up early," she said. "I need the money. The bathrooms are crawling with investigators. And Mr. Alport wanted to avoid all that. I don't think *I'd* feel comfortable eating with police everywhere."

"Ma'am, if you suddenly went missing, we'd be doing the same thing for you right now."

"Would 'ja?" Her smile took years from her face, as she leaned against her podium, giving him a full view to her navel. His job, he realized, was to look, and he did so dutifully.

"Well, Mr. Policeman, this may be your lucky night, cause I don't want to say the same things I've been saying for the last half hour. You want the names of the people missing some of their party, right?"

Mitchell was speechless as she kept on talking. "Only one group like that. Three women left their cash sitting right here. Their reservation, however, had been for four."

"Thanks. Can you give me their description?"

"Nope. Wasn't here when they were seated or when they left. Try in back. And don't be such a stranger next time."

Mitchell walked to the kitchen and began questioning. One waiter used the term "theatrical beauties" to describe all three women. One was black and described as being somewhere between twenty-five and seventy-five years old. The oldest was a platinum blonde, who was past the age of counting wrinkles. Two waitresses swore the youngest had been on a recent magazine cover.

Mitchell had already initiated a warrant for Antonio Dante. Now he pulled an agent off another case to search newsstands and the internet for a particular woman's face. He wanted magazines delivered to the restaurant, sirens blasting if necessary. Mentally he kicked himself for not turning to look at the three women Ryan had pointed out to him.

Meanwhile, investigators found a treasure trove of fingerprints on all the toilet levers, giving them little optimism over finding a match with fingerprints from Paris.

Mitchell finally stepped outside under the parking lot's crime lights, his earpiece squawking at him. It was Ryan. While Ryan spoke, Mitchell followed several men in uniform, all swarming the storefront windows of the Athens Realty Company.

"That restaurant manager," Ryan explained, "claims Antonio sometimes covered an artificial eye with a patch. Credibles saw no patch." Ryan paused. "Say, are you on your way here? Cause if you are, we're in the back storeroom area where this realty company keeps its sale signs and such."

"Yup," Mitchell answered. He wondered if Ryan had heard his heavy breathing as he walked uphill. Time to get back into the gym.

"It's a recent crime scene," Ryan continued. "Not a mark on him. Today's video is missing. Wanna know what I think?"

"Nope," said Mitchell, who was now standing beside Ryan, staring down at a dead white male his own age, wearing a knit shirt and no tie. With his blue eyes open, he looked as if he might suddenly sit up and talk.

Mitchell knew Antonio Dante had no false eye listed on his official documents. His gut told him Dante wasn't working alone, that the possible abduction outside Nueva Paesana was likely a real thing and that the murder was no less real.

CHAPTER 5

DECEMBER 2006   BEIJING, NEAR TIANANMEN SQUARE

A MORNING DOWNPOUR SCRUBBED Beijing's streets. Vendors huddled beside narrow carts to burn large circular pieces of charcoal. They grilled mouth-sized morsels of anything that once crawled or was dragged into captivity. The mouth-watering smell of seasoned crustaceans and pork bellies hung suspended like hazy umbrellas in the air.

Both vendors and clients took shelter under the smoke-filled awnings and listened to raindrops sizzle like oil on the grill. By late afternoon, continued rain prevented work at most construction zones. For Dr. Wren Xiao, it was time to return home from a dismal day at his downtown university lab.

He descended the marble steps in front of his building, as if making his way down the face of Mt. Everest without the ropes. Having lost his footing several times before, he traveled on all fours, head first, to keep his eyes on each step's unique characteristics. Women and men stared at him in that position, and yet because of the rain, larger groups failed to gather as they sometimes did.

Lingering headlights at the curb distracted Xiao. Perhaps it was too wet and cold for Kee and his great grandfather Quan to venture out. But an invitation to their bathhouse would certainly have been an enjoyable end to the day.

And while Xiao relished their attention, such unannounced visits were sometimes unnerving, particularly after discovering their true identities within the party. Fellow exchange scholars had taken Xiao aside and told him in secret that these were more than mere businessmen. They spoke of warnings they had received from Embassy personnel. Xiao had even sat through the boring movies that showed several ways in which unsuspecting students were solicited by Chinese nationals. But he'd fallen asleep though them, as had so many. His inner voices would reverently whisper or sometimes disappear whenever he was inside government office buildings.

Nonetheless, Xiao was excited over Quan's invitation to join a special program, The Friends of the Chinese People's Republic. Participants learned how to repay their host country for all it had donated to the Scholars Program. He felt membership was an honor.

For years, stories of ancient China had seduced Xiao. He forgave the country all its sins. Xiao believed his father had died from the futile jobs he'd endured in the United States. The entire family washed and ironed clothes in order to live in squalid apartments near San Francisco's wharf. His parents and relatives continues to blame Mao Tse-tung's re-education centers for their hardships and praised America for welcoming them.

As a boy of nine, Xiao took long walks, some lasting all night to avoid his parents and the jobs they'd assigned to him. By eleven those walks carried him through places his parents never went, like Stockton Tunnel into the Tenderloin District where day or night jazz blurted through the streets filled with one sleazy bar beside another. Criminals killed there with enough frequency that Xiao had observed it more than once.

He continued those walks at age fifteen from his college dorm whenever he suspected his mother might appear. Similarly, in Beijing, after work he walked to places that reminded him of his past journeys. Tonight he headed toward Tiananmen Square. At the ripe age of twenty-four he was obsessed with the denseness of China's fog and its ability to squash recurring voices in his head for several minutes at a time. Xiao yearned for the comforting, salty smell of San Francisco coffee and the sounds of rushing steam.

The bell on the door of Starbucks was comforting. He stood in line, arms folded, waiting his turn to admire the case of scones and small sandwiches, eager to impress the barista with his own knowledge of the menu. A warm hand touched Xiao's cold fingers. He snatched them away, thinking for a moment that his mother had finally found his only sanctuary.

"You look pale, my friend. Have you been ill?" Quan asked.

"I'm sorry?" replied Xiao as he jerked backward, reluctant to return to the real world. Quan was seated at a booth beside the very spot where he stood. Wearing a pin striped suit and a smile that revealed gold teeth, Quan appeared dressed for a major event. Unable to return the smile, Xiao finally emerged from his personal reverie. "I'm fine," he said. "And yourself?"

"I'm doing well," Quan said, "but I confess. I wondered whether you would continue to frequent this place, now that I've taken it over."

Suddenly dumbfounded, Xiao scanned the room, noticing the preponderance of men in business suits. The starry mermaid had disappeared. In its place was a circle with two fierce-looking fish, a ying and yang symbol of an eternal chase. On the wall, he noticed that the menu was almost the same, still written in Mandarin. He also noticed the smell of tea. Why hadn't he noticed the distinct whiff of star anise earlier? He was devastated, yet determined not to reveal it.

"You may not have realized," Quan said, "that you don't have to stand in line to be waited on anymore. Come. Sit with me."

A rush of inner voices told him not to, but anything else would have offended the man. As soon as he sat down, a woman in a black apron brought over what Xiao thought, from its appearance, to be brown sludge. She placed the small cup in front of him.

"I took the liberty," Quan explained with his head held high, "of having her bring what you usually order. You see, your frequent trips here made me realize how important such an enterprise would be for visitors during the Olympics."

What disturbed Xiao most was his own apparent loss of precise observation skills. "How did you know I come here, sir?" he asked. "I guess that's a stupid question for the head of the Secret Service."

"Ah, I see we have both used our resources to investigate each other. That makes me very happy, Xiao. That means I won't need to start from the very beginning with you. But I am in some ways, partially retired from that position."

"So you and Kee have been following me?" Xiao asked breathlessly, his growing anger interrupted by men in suits and two women in satin gowns.

They surrounded the table along with several waitresses, who brought chairs for them to sit on. Their focus was Quan.

"So," one woman said, a little too loudly, "we now have an answer to our question, 'Where in the world is Quan Yu?'" Manicured fingertips squeezed Quan's prune-like cheeks.

"And can we also assume," said a man in the group, "that you've already sold your bathhouse?"

Quan smiled. "I prefer a business that attracts younger clientele. The bathhouse will be closed for as long as it takes to find a buyer. Real estate in that part of the city has become deliciously desirable."

"I see your great grandson isn't here," said the other woman, who fixed her eyes squarely on Xiao. "At least I don't see him anywhere. You don't have any of those very private rooms like the ones you had in your bathhouse, do you?"

Xiao thought her modulated laugh, directed at him, was unnecessarily provocative. She spoke only to him, but he had no idea why. And he never saw any private rooms when he was at the bathhouse.

"Kee has work to do," Quan answered. "He'll attend our Grand Opening later."

"You Chinese-Americans do grow quite tall, don't you?" the woman finally said to Xiao.

Quan raised his hand signaling the end of conversation. The two women got up with only a hint of resentment and moved toward tables at the far end of the room. The men followed. Waitresses carried their empty chairs behind them.

Quan snapped his fingers, and Xiao thought it signaled that he too should leave. He pushed his chair back to get up. But before he could stand Quan reached out and touched Xiao's hand, assuring him he was to remain seated.

The choreography was impressive. Had it been rehearsed? Xiao vowed never again to underestimate Quan's powers. He bemoaned the loss of Starbucks silently, while voices in his head cheered. A waitress twisted the string on a hanging sign at the door. It read "Closed" to anyone wanting to enter.

Quan smiled at him and held an index finger across his own lips. "I shouldn't say such things in public," he said, "but decades ago, we would be lying across couches to share an opium pipe. I'm sure my little indiscretion will be safe with you, will it not?"

"Of course," Xiao answered.

"In modern times I can only offer you an aperitif with your coffee. Would you care for one?"

"Oh no," said Xiao. "I don't . . ."

"Perhaps you should this time. It will help you sleep better at night."

Not only was he being followed, Xiao realized, but the Peoples Republic of China also observed him as he slept. How else could they know of his nighttime fits?

"Leave everything to me," Quan continued. As he held his index finger high in the air a smartly dressed woman appeared holding a tray. Both the shape of the glass and the color of the liquid made Xiao assume it was either cognac or urine, neither of which he had tasted before.

"Go on," Quan prodded.

After one sip, Xiao still had no idea what it was. But the warmth as it eased down his throat was memorable. He thanked Quan profusely for his wise choice.

Xiao emptied his glass and studied the faces of people around them. Were their faces really that long? Were their ears that pronounced? The same woman appeared again, this time with two full glasses. Or maybe there were two women with one glass? Xiao couldn't be sure. Quan took several small sips of his own drink before speaking.

"Even though this is no longer an American-owned business, I hope you will still feel you are among family. Perhaps you will find that what you missed in the States can be found here."

Xiao said nothing but wondered if perhaps he should have been more guarded around host country nationals. The U.S. State Department had warned him but he hadn't paid attention to bureaucrats at that time; his excitement over receiving a grant and an opportunity to work and study in China had overwhelmed him. He remembered meeting lots of people, all with obvious agendas. One woman in particular seemed just as excited as he'd been. She was black and had passed out business cards in the shape of tiny human hands. He smiled, wondering if he still had that silly shaped card.

"Are you anxious," Quan asked, "to know how you might best serve China? It is not through those human cloning experiments that you waste time conducting. Our own scientists will soon catch up and surpass everything the U.S. has done."

"I'm not at all certain of that," Xiao began.

"Well, *I am* certain."

Quan paused, while Xiao wondered if he'd heard rumors about his blackouts and lapses of memory. He was becoming more worried daily that his schizophrenia would be discovered.

"So are you eager to know how you can balance the cost of your expensive research grant against your notion of being charitable to your host country? Or are you one of those young American geniuses bored with the notion of charity, having achieved success all by yourself?"

Xiao began breathing deeply. He didn't enjoy Quan's accusations. "No, no. I'm not bored at all and yes, I am anxious to serve China. I mean, I would be honored to help China." He felt flustered over his use of the word "serve". It sounded more committed than he wanted to be. Yet, the room's temperature made him feel cozy and even safe. Wasn't this why he'd come to this establishment in the first place?

"Then let me talk softly," Quan said, "so that no one else hears. I recently sent several valued operatives abroad to . . . to learn more modern techniques of spy craft. Three were sent to the United States on a dangerous mission. One of them returned to China too soon and became dismembered, recycled, you might say, part of our organ donor program. Another, who does not speak English well, remains in the States with yet a very capable spy trained entirely in the Chinese Republic. These two remaining operatives have access to an international company I recently acquired that strategically places spies throughout the world for me. I'm ready for another drink. How about you?"

"Yes, thank you." Xiao knew his head sat on his neck, that no one had removed it.

Quan motioned to the elegantly dressed woman again.

The room had become surprisingly crowded, for a place that was closed. Quan continued to speak of his spies, while Xiao continued to watch the constantly morphing faces of people around them. They stared back from behind folded fans and over the edges of menus. Xiao's internal chorus suggested that only those people who required Quan's friendship got to stay alive. No, Xiao thought. That was paranoid thinking. But his voices made it clear that he too needed Quan's friendship to stay alive.

Nervously, Xiao asked, "Could I have a glass of water, please?"

"Certainly, you may," Quan answered. "Now, let me continue. The operative who returned to China too soon brought back an American woman, her vehicle, and assorted equipment which we will use in our science program. The woman is being held in a secret location. The car was destroyed and the equipment . . . let's just say it won't concern your grant any longer."

Once Xiao drank his water, he began to awaken to Quan's words. "I don't understand," he said. "Why did the operative bring her back to China? Couldn't he have killed her in the United States?"

Quan laughed loudly. "You adapt to my description of this mission like water to rice. Since when have you been so callous about life?"

Xiao was startled; his face burned as he heard Quan's laughter above all other sounds in the room. Someone had turned up the volume.

Quan cleared his throat several times and continued, "The woman was interrogated. Later she was deemed useful if kept alive longer."

A waitress put a tray of steamed sweet buns in front of them. The word "interrogation" had made Xiao remember an old war movie he'd watched in his dorm with other geeks at Stanford when he was too young to get real dates. The smell of the sweet buns made him nauseous.

"I've given much thought to how you might fulfill your commitment," Quan said, as he tore open the white fleshy dough to let steam escape.

"How may I help?" Xiao asked, looking away from the deep red sweet-meat inside.

"See how easy it is to destroy something beautiful?" Quan asked, staring at the bun. "Chengde," he continued, "where the summer palace is located, is a beautiful tourist attraction, is it not? You may stay there for the next thirty days with this woman."

"But . . . " Xiao objected. He could barely catch his breath. "My research project, my grant. I'm so close to . . ."

"Call it a vacation. My personnel will handle your research with gentle fingers. Or They can begin a new line of research using preserved DNA from historically significant people of interest to us. My people will take care of everything: your work, your apartment. But understand this. On the thirtieth day, the woman dies. She will help you relax, to sleep better. But I want her dead. I want you to kill her."

Xiao felt dizzy. Quan was not unclear. Had Quan discovered his mother's body? Did he think he held something over his head to make him do such a thing? Xiao wondered if he'd called out his mother's name in the night. Part of his brain screamed to be let out of its skull, to be allowed to voice some resistance to Quan's order, but he didn't dare. What if he didn't do what Quan ordered?

"What's the matter?" Quan asked. "You're a doctor, aren't you?"

"I have a PhD in biophysics from Stanford University. I'm not a medical . . ."

"The Palace like everything else here, belongs to the People," Quan interrupted. "There will be plenty of employees around to help you. There's a clinic, a museum, even a cemetery. And I hear she's pleasing to look at.

"Take one day, two, but no more than thirty. Contact me when it's done. My driver is outside. He'll drive you to where the girl is located."

Confused, Xiao imagined that he'd be rid of his dead mother for at least thirty days. He watched Quan suck on and eat one piece of the bun for what seemed an eternity.

"What if I fail?" Xiao asked.

Quan poured himself more urine-colored liquid from the bottle that had been placed on the table.

"Then you die," he laughed, his gold teeth sparkling under ceiling lights. "But you won't fail. You have many skills, a long life ahead of you, and much to contribute. Assistants will help you with anything you need." Quan continued to chew between his words.

Xiao pushed himself up from his chair with his wrists, looking for the energy to go home, but found it difficult to stand. His legs were like rubber bands. Cigarette smoke clouded his vision. From nowhere, a uniformed man steered Xiao through the back door to a waiting limousine, where he lost consciousness.

CHAPTER 6

A S MIRIAM GARFIELD drove northeast on Interstate 225, she continued to babble to Inez about her dad's murder, as if it were fact.

"Inez. I'm not making sense to you am I?"

Without looking at Miriam, Inez replied, "Who'd murder someone who was always eager to earn your respect?"

Inez had hoped for a quiet ride to Sheila and Karen's townhome in contrast to the noisy bar scene they'd just left. At least she was getting closer to her own home. Staring out the side window, she had hoped to appear preoccupied with Aurora's suburban sprawl. It didn't work. Miriam hadn't shut her mouth once since they left the restaurant. And as she talked, she followed close behind Sheila's sports car.

"Maybe you didn't hear about the sale of Dad's house," Miriam prodded.

Finally Inez tore her gaze away from the strip malls that lined the highway to watch Miriam's profile. "What is there to hear?" she asked.

She and her neighbors were still angry that Gaelen's home was torn down and another built on the old foundation in only thirty-five days and at double its original size. Most assuredly their own taxes would increase.

"Before Dad's memorial service," Miriam went on, "I got a call in Rome from a lawyer in Cherry Creek. His client wanted to buy Dad's house and its contents. Remember, Dad told me his house had been appraised for $200,000, and I needed every dime of that for a divorce lawyer."

Inez began to watch more carefully out the front windshield as

Miriam's speed and speech increased proportionately. The sun was going down fast.

"So I threw out a number," Miriam continued, "thinking he'd hang up. I told him I wanted $600,000. I simply multiplied what I needed, you see, by three people. Damned if the lawyer didn't say yes."

Disbelief griped Inez in the face. "What! Nothing on our block has ever sold for that much. Gaelen told me he paid $15,000 for his home in the late sixties. So what did you think when you . . ."

"No! No! No! No!" Miriam interrupted. "I *didn't* think. My dad had just died. Sheila and Karen wanted me home to make arrangements. My son had to stay behind. I didn't know whether my husband intended to take him from me while I was gone or not. I didn't think! I jumped at it."

A black pickup truck suddenly edged in between their car and Sheila's. Its cab windows were open, and the two people inside were animated, waving their arms as they spoke.

Miriam seemed unfazed that the truck was tall enough to block her view of her sister's car and kept on talking. Obviously she knew where to go without having to see Sheila at all.

"Still not convinced he was murdered?" Miriam asked. "Then listen to this."

Inez grabbed the edge of the seat. She wasn't used to these speeds and wanted Miriam to focus on her driving. Finally Inez interrupted her and said, "I don't know why you're telling me any of this. I don't even read mystery novels. I could never figure out who did it, even after the writer would tell me by the last chapter."

Miriam merely cut her eyes at Inez and continued talking. "According to Karen, Dad's insurance papers were in plain view the night he died, as if he'd been looking through them," Miriam continued. "A prepaid cremation plan with Dad's cancelled checks and phone numbers of people to call sat on top of the pile. Of course, we realized later that he'd never have changed his mind about being buried next to Mom." Miriam paused, her eyes tearing. "But there it was, in the living room with his signature. Karen noticed the document right away and had him cremated before my plane landed at DIA. Dad already had a burial plot next to Mom's!"

Inez felt her heart jump to her throat. Something about Gaelen's attitude toward religion had made her believe early on that Gaelen wasn't the Catholic his wife had been. Although he sent his children to Catholic schools, he never went to church. And then there was that story he'd told her years ago. He'd been so poor growing up in Ireland that he stole the birth certificate of his dead friend to get into the States. What if he belonged to another religion, a religion opposed to cremation, like Judaism? In Ireland? At the end of World War I? Why not? She decided to research the possibility on the internet.

Just then, Miriam swerved to get onto an exit ramp. She'd given the truck a fair amount of distance in front of her. They were speeding at over 65 miles per hour, and by inference, so was Sheila. The roadway seemed otherwise deserted and appeared to wind through the remains of the old Lowry Military Base. Funny, Inez thought. The three vehicles seemed to form a fast-moving caravan. In less than a mile, Sheila pulled her car to the curb, while the black truck drove off. Miriam came to a stop a few feet behind her sister.

"This is it!" Sheila hollered. She'd already jumped out of her car to run ahead and into the house. Inez walked slowly, still pondering all that Miriam had said.

It was dark now. An icy wind swept across her open-toed sandals, reminding Inez that snow was in the forecast and that being sixty-eight meant wearing granny shoes for just such eventuality. *Yuck!*

No more homes had been built across the street from Sheila and Karen's place in this part of Stapleton. It was too new and too open to be haunted. Yet Inez had a sense she wasn't alone. Perhaps she felt the ghosts of Native Americans who once roamed these lands.

The young women's townhome sat perpendicular to an alley lined on either side with garages. Only the first house in the row had an attached garage. Inez thought houses were much too close together here. It was reminiscent of Park Hill, a much older neighborhood. Only Park Hill was a place of hope for people like herself, willing to save pennies and to go without food in order to move up to a peaceful existence.

Before going inside Inez watched prairie dogs scamper from one hole to another. Miriam stood at the bottom of stairs leading to a loft. Inez hadn't expected to inhale incense as she entered the house, but easily identified it as frankincense and myrrh. A counter and two barstools near the front door separated the tiny kitchen from a living and dining room area. Furniture throughout was the kind you take out of a box and put together with screwdrivers. Opposite the kitchen was a door that led to what Inez suspected was their attached garage.

Sheila came downstairs flipping the pages of an appointment book.

"I would have freaked," she said, "if I'd found Karen's wallet upstairs in her bedroom, but I didn't. Her passport isn't there, either. There's nothing written here for the last two weeks, and I'm not sure whether her clothes from yesterday are in the closet. She wears such plain stuff." Her lower lip quivered when she reached the bottom. "See you've got me scared with your talk of Dad being murdered."

Miriam wrapped an arm around Sheila's shoulders. They sat that way on the living room futon for some time. As an only child, it was the kind of bliss Inez had never known and didn't spend time thinking about.

Inez mentally toyed with Miriam's story about Gaelen's cremation. It added more pathos than credibility to Miriam's murder theory. Making certain the body was cremated would have been clever, but doing so would also have required an army of coordinated agencies to produce installment plan coupons with cancelled checks and receipts all brought to Gaelen's home by the murderer before he murdered him. Also, there had to be lots of additional accomplices ready at the other end of a phone to verify to Karen that such a plan existed and would be honored by a particular crematorium where a container for the ashes could be selected.

Inez sat on a stool and with 360 degree vision she could casually observe the habitat of two sisters. She surmised that they'd lived here for less than a year. There were still empty packing boxes and no books. In one corner, fashion magazines were stacked four feet high, and atop the coffee table were Red Cross leaflets scattered in abundance.

The kitchen was spotless, not even a crumb on the counter. That could mean the two women were rarely home or that one of them was able to afford a cleaning service.

A giant poster of children playing in Kathmandu was centrally hung on the wall at the very top of the stairs. It reminded Inez how often she'd thought Karen would become a great teacher someday. Larry Carmichael had said the same thing. He'd been her third- grade teacher at St. Anselm's and spoke about her maturity even then.

"Well?" Inez asked, feeling she'd waited a respectable amount of time. "When are you going to call the police?"

Sheila looked drained. She spoke as if reading a prepared statement. "Dad thought you were one of the smartest people he knew. I don't know anybody else with a PhD."

Miriam added, "Don't you still publish that underground newsletter for teachers he told me about?"

"It's really about school finance, isn't it?" Sheila added. "Asking teachers to follow the money to make sure it's spent on kids? You do a lot of research, don't you? That's the same as investigating, isn't it?"

Inez took a deep breath, knowing where this was headed. "What I do isn't really related to what you need. You need to call the police about Karen. Now. Put your dad aside for a moment."

Sheila jumped up. "Maybe Karen left town." She ran to the closet. "She could have left with friends and forgotten to leave me a note. Maybe she took the luggage in here. I'm sure that's it."

She opened the closet door. From where Inez sat, she saw nothing inside; not even a coat hanger.

"Oh, my gosh!" Sheila cried out, then rushed past Inez to open the garage door. This time both Miriam and Inez were on their feet following her.

A very old canister vacuum cleaner stood against a wall with a metal attachment propped next to it. Not even a speck of oil was on the garage floor.

"What's *supposed* to be in here?" Inez asked.

"For one thing," Sheila replied, "Karen's car is gone. The night Dad died Karen brought home his old vacuum cleaner and two suitcases filled with odd things: a laptop, a camera, and military medals. It was all stuff that fascinated her. She put that vacuum cleaner in the closet along with the suitcases, not out here in the garage. And I have no idea how long her car has been gone. I park out front." Tears streamed down her face. "I didn't do a good job of taking care of her, did I?"

Inez grabbed hold of Sheila's arm to steady her. "Call the police. Now," she insisted.

"Could you?" Sheila pleaded.

"No," Inez answered. "You have way more information about your sister than any of us."

Miriam handed Sheila her cell phone. Both sisters trembled.

Meanwhile, Inez meandered through the living room repeating statements to herself that Miriam had made earlier. She stopped her meandering long enough to ask Miriam a question. "Did you ever meet the buyer of Gaelen's house?"

Miriam had seated herself on the futon again, preoccupied with Sheila's phone conversation.

"No," Miriam finally answered. "The lawyer, who represented the buyer, took care of everything. I don't even know who the buyer was. I suppose his name appears on papers I have in Rome. But the lawyer was part of a large company on the top floor of one of those office buildings in Cherry Creek. I think I've got his card still in my purse. Yes, here it is. Keep it." Miriam flicked her wrist, as if she was about to throw it, then thought better of it. "I'm sure I have his address elsewhere."

Inez reached for the card and put it in her pocket without looking at it. Then she stared out the picture window through sheer curtains that gave the construction zone and sidewalks to nowhere a hazy picture-book quality.

She still yearned to go home to a warm cup of pecan coffee. But this time was different. Inez never really wanted to socialize. When she was with a group it was always a temptation to leave early before anyone discovered she had only one breast. However, this time she wanted to leave in order to organize her thoughts into manageable categories of information. Because that's what teachers do. And once done, events would fall into a sequence revealing the logic of what had happened to Karen and maybe even to Gaelen.

"I'm going to call a cab," Inez announced to no one in particular. "Your local police department will help the two of you with the things you need done."

There, she'd said it. These two women weren't concerned with friendship. They treated her like a valued employee, someone who was *supposed* to be there to do the work set forth by the entitled. Inez felt like their doormat, their speechless maid-in-waiting, ready to take on their responsibilities as well as her own. And if Gaelen was murdered what was there to investigate anyway without a body?

She finally found her cell phone in her purse while Sheila was reciting her address over her own phone to the police. All Inez had to do was repeat that address to the cab company. As she stood at the window to do so, what she had been staring at across a vacant lot suddenly came into focus. It was a black pickup truck, a tall one, like the one that had been in front of them earlier. Now it was parked with its front hood facing Sheila's townhome.

Two men sat in its cab. One man's shirtsleeve rested on the open passenger side window; a slight breeze made it billow, as it had while they drove here and, as Inez suddenly remembered, as it had in the restaurant. The man had black hair that drooped over his forehead. But it was too far away to swear it was Antonio the waiter. More importantly, what did those two men in the truck want?

CHAPTER 7

INEZ STOOD PERFECTLY still, her breathing quite shallow. She remembered the anorexic busgirl from the restaurant who said, "Antonio *is* missing." Was this that same Antonio sitting in the black truck? Why? Initially, Inez was too shocked to move, but she had to speak up at some point and *soon*.

"Miriam," Inez finally called out, "if you were a pair of binoculars, where would you be right now?" She hoped her voice sounded calm and disinterested, clever even, because the last thing she wanted was for anyone to rush toward the window.

"Oh, I don't know," Miriam answered. "The girls may not have binoculars."

Sheila was still talking to the police on the phone.

"But if they did," Miriam continued, "they'd probably keep them where we kept them growing up."

Inez listened as Miriam's heels clicked across the wood floor. In less than two minutes, she cried out, "Success!"

Inez realized she was still holding her phone. Had she completed her call for a cab? She couldn't remember as she put her phone back in her pocket and took the binoculars Miriam had walked over to give her. What Inez saw made her shudder. The streetlight cast few shadows. It was indeed the Italian-speaking waiter from the restaurant. She'd never seen the other man before.

"When are the police coming?" Inez asked Sheila with a false sense of strength. All the while, she feared the occupants of the truck might realize they were being watched. From the corner of her eye, she saw Sheila put her hand over her phone.

"They're not," Sheila answered. "They want me to go there tomorrow and file a missing person's report."

"Tell them the waiter from Nueva Paesana," Inez replied, "is parked outside your place in a black pickup truck. Tell them he followed you home, that he's with another man at the wheel."

Miriam's heels started clicking toward her again.

"No, don't!" Inez said. "They may not realize anyone is looking at them."

Miriam stood still, listening as Sheila explained all of it to the police. It was a lengthy story, but she told it with remarkable speed.

Finally ending her call, Sheila said, "They're sending a car."

"Let's hope it gets here soon," said Inez. Her arms were tired and her fear mounting.

Three minutes later a police car drove behind the black truck with its rooftop lights blinking, its siren off. Inez couldn't help but relax. The sisters yanked the curtains all the way back, acting as if the Marines had landed. Miriam suddenly grabbed the binoculars from Inez.

"Yes, that's him," Miriam confirmed. "I was sure he was Sicilian when I first heard him speak. Of course, that doesn't mean anything now."

Sheila snatched the binoculars out of Miriam's hands and stared out the window. Miriam, with no hesitation, snatched them right back. "You weren't even in the restaurant when Inez and I talked to this man."

Something about Sheila's heavy breathing and the look on her face told Inez this was no normal fight between sisters.

"How do you *know* that?" Sheila asked. "I may have seen him when I came in." And with that, she snatched the glasses out of Miriam's hand again.

"Grow up, why don't you!" Miriam shot back.

Sheila moved even closer to the window. A policeman walked toward the driver's side of the truck while a policewoman, her hand on her holstered gun, walked to the passenger side.

Both officers fell to the ground like rag dolls in a silent movie. The women at the window didn't speak or move, unsure at first of what they'd just seen. There'd been no sound, no doors on the truck opened, and the officers didn't get up.

Then, an engine roared, scaring them so much they jumped away from the glass. Sheila dropped the binoculars. Headlights suddenly lit up the entire living room. The truck lurched forward over first one curb and then the open field. All three women ran in separate directions. Miriam and Inez flattened themselves against the farthest wall, while Sheila crawled on her stomach until she found her phone and punched 911.

"Somebody just shot two policemen," she yelled, her voice shaking. "Stapleton neighborhood near Bluebird Lake. Two men in a black truck shot 'em on a vacant street facing my house. I don't know. I don't know the name of that other street. I don't even think it has a name yet."

She spelled out her own address as the sound of a loud crash jolted all three of them. It had to be the truck crashing into something metal; like the garage door?

"Hear that?" Sheila screamed into the phone.

Like silent robots, Miriam and Sheila took off their shoes and crouched on the balls of their feet. Inez stiffened against the far wall, then removed her shoes slowly as well.

The voice on the phone yelled loud enough for all of them to hear. "What was that?"

Nobody answered. Miriam and Sheila motioned to Inez as they scurried past her to the loft. She watched them ascend the stairs, heard Sheila whispering into the phone again, but Inez feared the loft offered no way out.

Even with her heart pounding so loud her eardrums vibrated, she thought of Tisley Mott, called Tizzy for short. He called himself a gangster transplant and attributed his longevity to what he told his favorite teacher, "When in doubt," he'd said, "play dead."

So Inez stayed put, prepared to play dead as soon as it was necessary. Surely the police would send reinforcements she reasoned.

Another loud boom produced a deafening sound that continued to ring in her ears. Each time the truck rammed the house, the walls shook. Inez bent down and ran past the picture window to reach the light switch.

She thought she'd have a better chance in the dark. She dragged a stool across the floor and wedged it under the doorknob to the garage.

People in the neighborhood had to hear the truck's tires screech backward and forward. She counted on it. How thick could these new walls be? She went to the bottom of the stairs and looked up at the loft. Miriam and Sheila must have turned the lights off up there as well.

From the garage came the sound of a truck door opening. Was someone getting out of the truck? Inez froze, her ears trained to the garage. Who were these people? She could hear Sheila still talking into her cell.

"I don't know what they're doing. Yes, they're in the garage." She gave directions to the house again.

Screeching tires suddenly drove away from the house. Sheila stopped talking. Quiet followed. But like a dirty tub follows draining water, Inez knew something could have been left behind in that garage.

Was it a trick? That's when they heard it. A crashing and then mashing of metal on metal, bricks and concrete falling and smashing. Sheila still held the phone and whoever was on the line kept shouting, "What's happening? What's happening?"

Anxiously, Inez ran to the garage door, pulled back the stool, and opened it slowly. A second later, Miriam and Sheila stood beside her.

Sheila cried softly, "Our house. Our new house."

Once again they paid no attention to the voice on the phone in Sheila's pocket but held hands to slowly step down into the garage.

Shredded metal parts from a battered and folded garage door lay scattered throughout. Wires and cables dangled from the overhead motor and frame.

Through what was now an opening to the outside alley, they saw occupants from surrounding homes running toward the next street over, some screaming as they ran. Like zombies, careful not to step on metal fragments, the three women, still hand in hand, followed behind the runners.

It was night, but something lit up the sky. The strong odor of gasoline fumes surrounded them. A crackling sound, like a bonfire, intensified as they traveled further away from Sheila's house. Police sirens heard in the distance now grew unbearably loud. The women didn't speak but took baby steps over the increasing debris at the end of the alley. Careless runners, anxious to see something, kept bumping into them.

Once they turned the corner onto the next street, one panoramic view told them what had happened to the black truck. Miriam, Sheila, and Inez stood and watched. They seemed to be the only people aware of the tragedy in two separate places. No one else seemed to know about the two dead police officers in the opposite direction. The three women couldn't help turning their heads to look back over their shoulders even though they faced a newer horror in front of them.

The black truck was now on vacant land upside down and buried under displaced dirt that made a mound around it. Parts of a sedan, the same color as the one at the end of the alley laid on top of the truck's upside-down bed which pointed high into the air. And propped against the overturned truck was a mangled yellow taxicab, its entire front half engulfed in flames.

The three women were at least one hundred feet from the crash, yet the heat was stifling. Two shirtless teenaged boys wrapped their arms in their shirts and darted in and out of the lapping tongues of fire, trying to see inside the cab, or touch the door handle, or drag the cab driver outside to safety.

They couldn't see the driver inside. No one had to tell Inez that the man was probably driving the very cab she had requested. She dropped to the nearest curb and faced the inferno, trying to listen over the crackling fire and police sirens for a voice inside. Tears covered her face. Miriam and Sheila sat beside her, their arms wrapped around her shoulders, their eyes glued to the funeral pyre in front of them.

Inez's head swam in circles. Someone's son and daughter lay not far from Sheila's townhome, killed doing what police normally do. And in front of her was another son or daughter who, only moments ago, had been searching for the house from which she was to be picked up. Inez had stood outside the gates of hell before. And here she was again.

She began mumbling prayers she knew by heart, while the sisters followed as best they could. Crowds of people and flashing lights slowly began to block their view. Children cried out loud over the noise of sirens.

Several adults dropped to their knees to sob aloud with them. Not until heat began to singe their feet did the environment change.

Occasionally someone screamed, "Get him out of there," or "Help him," or "Where were you guys?" Policemen and women pushed bystanders away gently at first and then with clubs. Miriam and Sheila yanked Inez up from the curb just in time to avoid the potent swing of a policeman's baton. Other uniformed officers forcibly attacked spectators, as they yelled through loudspeakers to move back. Though several onlookers cursed the officers' zeal, flames leaped onto the asphalt street. Fire trucks soon blocked the entire collision.

The three women turned their backs on the scene, arms locked together for support and began the walk back to Sheila's townhouse. The dead police officers were on the next street over. As the women approached the alley, they could see a line of police barricading the entrance. Dressed in black SWAT gear, in Inez's mind the men represented a fearsome statement of fact: two men in a truck, one man in a cab, and two police officers, totaling five people dead and Karen perhaps abducted, all within a three-block radius. And then, of course, there was Gaelen.

The entire blockade of police carried assault guns that were aimed directly at them. Electricity in the air spoke to Inez. As a black person, her statistical chances of staying alive in the midst of mayhem were far lower than those of the white women beside her. And she knew it.

Gaelen Drisco had shown Inez kindness in Park Hill. He'd kept her safe from statistical mishaps, cruel daily oversights, deliberate injustice, and social humiliation for the twenty-three years she lived next door to him. Her knees buckled slightly and she almost fell. Gaelen's daughters clung to her arms. Sheila sobbed loudly and slid in slow motion to the ground, still holding onto Inez's hand.

I'd rather be shot standing up, a voice inside Inez said and, as scared as she was, Inez instantly understood how her death couldn't possibly be worse than her own fear of it. At that very moment, Gaelen's voice or something like it, yelled in her ears from across time and the din of the mob. *"You bet I was murdered! Remember that evening, Inez?"*

Was it his breath she felt across her face or the chill of naked truth? She owed Gaelen Drisco a lot. But how do you help a dead man? To find answers she'd need to survive this night. Inez felt Sheila's body shake against her leg. Yet their tightly clasped hands remained steadfast as Inez pulled her up from the ground.

The armed police officers grunted like bears, while some made football signals in what had suddenly become bitter cold air. The women could barely make out the words being uttered through a bullhorn; the noise from fire trucks and emergency vehicles was just that loud. "THIS IS YOUR LAST CHANCE. GET YOUR SKINNY ASSES DOWN ON THAT GROUND. FACE DOWN."

A lone man emerged from behind the human barricade of police, wearing a construction helmet, a clear facemask, and a black vest with CBI printed across the front and back in neon yellow letters. He used his back as a shield to help three bedraggled and scared women through the smell of testosterone and gasoline, until they reached the steps that led upward to safety inside a large UPS truck.

CHAPTER 8

DECEMBER 2006   CHENGDE, THE SUMMER PALACE

XIAO WOKE IN total darkness, his head throbbing. Finding nothing to brace his body against, he rolled over the edge of the mattress where he must have fallen asleep, and onto the floor. He reasoned the mattress had been on the floor. Still in darkness and now on a hard floor, he felt mashed against something big and leathery.

"Good morning," said a cheery male voice with a British accent.

Xiao opened his eyes and still could see nothing. He rolled back onto the mattress. A swooshing sound could be heard to his right and then sunlight blinded him. Raising his arm to cover his eyes, he squinted until his eye sockets hurt. A musty odor of death seemed to grow in intensity. He opened his eyes only slightly to see the silhouette of a man wearing traditional Chinese robes, arms folded and hands hidden under flared sleeves.

Back and forth, the costumed man traversed the room pulling drapes away from giant windows and then smacking dust from pillows. Diffused sunshine, muted by dust, poured across lavishly decorated sleeping quarters. Though captivated by the sight of everything at once, the man's movements made Xiao cough continuously from the dust. As his coughs subsided, Xiao realized his nakedness and wriggled under thick bedcovers.

"I'm sure I've already seen everything you've got under there so you'd better..."

"I was doped, wasn't I?" Xiao blurted from beneath the blankets.

"Yes, you were. Someone in Beijing must have thought it necessary. Come now, Master Xiao, don't you want to ask me questions about my surcoat and the meaning of its court insignia while you're getting dressed? You've got to be out of here before the morning tourists arrive."

Xiao kept his head covered, preferring to sink into a warm bottomless mattress. Who was this man, anyway, to address him as Master? But when he heard nothing but the voices of his relatives berating him, Xiao pushed away the covers.

He sat up to find the man gone and the door through which he must have left wide open. Through that doorway he could see the curvature of the earth in the distance and what looked like the Great Wall of China, only smaller. So this was the Summer Palace!

It was freezing. Xiao grabbed a quilt from the bed and ran to the door, anxious to see more. Making certain not to trip over the blankets in his arms, he pulled up the longest quilt, holding all the rest high off the floor as he ran. His bare feet smacked the cold wooden floor. Still wrapping the quilt around him, he failed to notice the raised threshold. He tripped, jerked forward in a somersault and fell over the low railing of the narrow outside balcony in front of him. Like a movie running on fast rewind, his life sailed by. One of the blankets ripped from his arms as he was jerked backward. He landed on his back with a thud. He screamed. The skin on his back tore off as he slid down the clay tiled roof. Only the roof's upturned edge and the heels of his feet stopped him from falling to his certain death, several meters below.

Precariously, he stayed where he was, propped up on the very tip of the roof. Any realization that he had stopped was slow in coming. Hyperventilating, he desperately tried to slow his breathing even as he heard a muffled scream above his head and the crashing of porcelain dishes.

"Oh, Master Xiao! Don't move! Don't do anything! I'll be right back."

Xiao made no attempt to move. He lay very still, listening to his voices in Cantonese, once again berating him for being too stupid to go to work, for getting his brother and sisters into trouble, for getting the family thrown out of their apartment, for having to study home alone. Too afraid to move, he held onto his breath for as long as he could before daring to take yet another breath. In the distance he could see people parking their cars and going to work. Could they see him?

"Master Xiao, Master Xiao! Hold onto this blanket. Grab hold of the end that I'm throwing at your head. Master Xiao, listen to me!"

Feelings of shame made him believe he might disappear, if he willed it so. But gradually the voice of the man from this morning surrounded him. Was he using a loudspeaker? Xiao could hear that voice over the other voices that taunted him. Slowly he rolled onto his left side, almost slipping in the process. Looking up at the balcony he'd fallen from, he saw the man with the loud voice standing far away.

The man leaned over the railing as if he too might fall. In his hands he held a long twisted rope of blankets, maybe two or three tied together.

"Xiao! You must do this now before we're found out. Tourists will be here soon. Can you hear me? Grab the end of the blanket I'm lowering down to you. That's right. Keep looking up at me. Don't look down."

Xiao mulled the words over in his mind. These were directions he could follow without injuring himself further. The man at the top pulled on the blankets until Xiao could feel himself being lifted up the slope of the roof toward the balcony like a helpless piece of raw meat.

His shame increased the closer Xiao got to the narrow balcony. Yet he noticed the man's eyes. Who was this man who stared back at him with what Xiao knew was fear? His own breathing was under control now as the man helped him over the railing.

He sensed the man's fear strengthening. Xiao asked, "Where are you hiding my clothes?"

"Your clothes are beside your bed," the man replied, trying to hold one of the blankets around Xiao's shoulders as he walked back into the room. "One of Quan's men packed that bag for you last night," he continued, "at your apartment. I heard him say so. Everything you need should be there."

Once he spied the satchel, Xiao paid no more attention to the man but sat on the floor and pulled the satchel closer to him in order to search through it. He was surprised to see his rugged boots and hiking clothes, new purchases he'd made but never worn.

"What was it you dropped on the balcony back there?" Xiao asked without looking up at the man who stood over him. "Sounded like dishes."

There was no answer for a long time.

Finally the man said, "I dropped the antidote."

"Antidote for what?

"For . . . for the drugs that rendered you unconscious last night." The man had begun busying himself again by returning the blankets to their original place over the mattress.

"You're lying, aren't you?" Xiao responded as he laced up his shoes. "Your voice isn't as confident as it was earlier. I was given urine to drink with opium in it, right? Or was that cognac with some other chemical? Where can I get decent coffee around here?"

The man continued to straighten the artifacts in the room and said, "If you're wondering where the American harlot is that you'll be tending . . ."

Xiao didn't like this man and concluded he had no more authority than what Quan had given him.

". . . she has been moved to the Mulan Forest, Master Xiao, where she is being held by a family employed by the Peoples Republic of China to handle just such emergencies."

Why was this man telling him this? Xiao wondered. Were the emergencies he referred to all kidnapped Americans?

"And what will happen if we are discovered by tourists?" Xiao asked.

"Your driver is downstairs," the man continued, "where he preferred to sleep last night. You must have misunderstood me in all the commotion of getting you back up here and off the roof."

It was obvious the man was not going to reveal anything more. Having been close to death, Xiao was now sensitized to everything around him that threatened his existence. "Where do I stay for the next thirty days?" Xiao asked. "Do I stay here?"

"Someone will give you those instructions before the day is over. For right now, however, bring your satchel with you and be very careful. Follow this balcony to your left. It leads to a stairway. Keep going down until you see giant stoves at the bottom. If you insist loud enough, someone there will give you coffee."

"Wait!" Xiao shouted. The man was already out the door and bending over to pick up pieces of porcelain, placing them on a tray that was also on the stone floor of the balcony.

"Does this woman know why I'm here?" Xiao asked.

The man was silent as he stood up with the tray in his hands. He looked past Xiao to the treetops in the distance, and then back to Xiao. "I'm sure I don't know." With that, he turned his back on Xiao and walked away.

"I don't know your name," Xiao shouted, but the man was gone.

Xiao hurried back into the room, closing the door behind him. The chill was too much. Hurriedly he finished dressing while remembering the night before. He had been carried across the back of a soldier in the middle of the night. He felt certain of it. His back was in pain and probably bleeding, but he refused to slow down and attend to it. Would Quan have cared if he'd fallen off that balcony and died?

CHAPTER 9

JANUARY 2007   CHENGDE

X IAO'S LIMO DRIVER was dressed in the uniform of a soldier in the Imperial Guard. He explained his job to Xiao as he drove. In Mandarin, he said he was to drive him to the woman then take the two of them wherever they wanted to go and return to Beijing by nightfall.

Only when they had driven off the grounds of the Summer Palace did Xiao, seated in back, feel comfortable enough to open one of several tins of food the man in traditional garb had prepared for his adventure. That man wasn't so bad after all. Or maybe the man felt sorry for him.

Xiao pulled the lid off one of the tins and found octopus in its own ink over saffron rice, a far better meal than the previous night's steamed bun. The nameless man had also packed a thermos of coffee, but Xiao didn't touch it. The highway was full of ruts making the limo bounce frequently.

He kept his head down and slurped his food like a man just rescued from days at sea. He realized that one of the driver's duties was probably to report whatever he saw back to Quan. Xiao bent down more, hoping the driver couldn't see him in his mirror.

After traveling an hour outside the city, the driver pulled off-road, waking Xiao from a fitful nap. They were stopped in front of a small farmhouse. The driver backed the vehicle up ten feet then drove slowly onto a stone-covered driveway that ran behind the house and beyond. Further from the highway were other buildings all in need of repair. Overgrown vines covered most windows.

A filthy woman sat on a stool used for milking cows. She directly behind the house and dressed in oversized peasant clothing. Around one ankle was a metal chain that reached down an embankment to what Xiao knew must have been an outhouse. Though dirty, her hair was an unusually light color. Was this the woman? Far into the distance were several more women wearing colorful scarves and carrying long sickles in their hands to hack down what Xiao guessed was wheat.

People in the fields stopped to stare at the vehicle. The woman with dirty tangled hair turned toward the limo. Her left eye was bruised and her mouth sagged. Through the dirt Xiao could see she was plain and skinny.

He swallowed hard. He had hoped the woman would be handicapped in some way and, therefore, thankful for an early death. The driver looked stoically ahead and said nothing. Still chewing his meal, Xiao finally packed up what remained, putting lids back onto the tin boxes. Then he slid across the back seat and got out.

Leaving the car door open, he took his time trekking across the uneven ground toward her. A middle-aged matron finally came out the back door of the house. She wiped her hands on a cloth tied at her waist.

"You're from Beijing?" she hollered in Mandarin.

"Yes," Xiao answered, suddenly aware that much was expected of him.

"She's chained because she runs away. We did not beat her as you asked us to, but we had plenty of trouble. Are you here to take her? We could use the money now. She refused to eat or drink. How could we make her do chores, if we couldn't beat her? We should be compensated for the indignity."

Xiao said nothing but made certain he'd wiped the sauce from around his mouth as he continued to slowly walk toward the woman on the stool. The older woman walked with him and talked incessantly. Obviously, he was supposed to be the Red Chinese Government's representative and *had* to act like it. But what money was this woman talking about?

As he got closer to the younger woman, she stood up. Neither attractive nor unattractive, she smelled like the outhouse she was chained to. If he had a gun, he thought, he could shoot her where she stood and return to Beijing with the driver.

Defiance was written in lines around her mouth as she stared at his clothing. Filthy fingernails on both her hands rested on her hips while she looked him over.

"If I didn't know better," she said, "I'd think you were related to Doc Martin and Eddie Bauer."

"Yes, I'm American," Xiao nodded.

She quickly approached him, breathing hard. "You're from the Embassy?", she asked reverently. Without waiting for an answer, she stretched her hands out to touch his arms. He instinctively drew back. She grabbed his flannel shirt around his neck, pulling his face closer and kissed his face over and over again.

"I'm not from the Embassy!" he shouted, pulling her arms off of him.

"But you're an American. You can't leave me," she hollered. "They beat me. Only God knows why. I don't know what they're saying, even when they think they're speaking English. Last night was the first time I was scared for my life. They used a rubber hose."

With no hesitation, she flipped up her cotton jacket to reveal a bruised stomach, rib cage, and small breasts. He could easily count her bones.

The old woman began yelling in Mandarin, telling him she'd made those bruises herself when she tried to escape.

Tears rolled down the young woman's face in torrents before she flipped her jacket back down. In a haughty gesture she flung her head back high without a sound. Xiao thought he could even hear her tears trickling, then realized she was peeing on herself. He pushed her away from him. Inadvertently, he looked sidelong at the outhouse.

"You're crazy if you think I'm going in there," she shouted.

"This woman claims she didn't beat you," Xiao responded. Even as the words escaped his mouth he was embarrassed that he'd uttered them.

"Yeah?" the younger woman yelled. "And she probably said she had nothing to do with kidnapping me, either. That your car?" The woman didn't wait for his answer but started walking towards it, only to be yanked back by the chain on her ankle. She landed face down in the grass. "Come on," she said. "Help me up. We've got to get out of here before the men return."

Xiao stared at the old woman, knowing she'd lied about the beatings and that she would never have dared to lie to Quan.

The old woman began her angry tirade again. "You can see we had to restrain her. We need more money. We buy American food from Chengde hotels because she won't eat our food and threatens to starve herself. One person must stop work in the fields to sit with her; otherwise she'll try to escape. She's very expensive, this one."

So there had been others? Xiao nodded in acknowledgement and looked around to marvel at the strangeness of it all. He'd prepared himself to do anything in order to be considered Quan's trusted employee. Deep in his soul, he had accepted China's invitation to come to this country with no desire to ever return to the United States. But how in the hell could he kill another human being with or without a weapon? Quan had said there'd be plenty of people to help him. Were these the helpers? He didn't think so.

He turned to the American woman lying helplessly in the grass and asked, "These men you spoke of, where did they go?"

"You think they told me? PLEASE, let's GO! Those men have guns."

Xiao turned to the old woman, whose eyes seemed glued to the dirt-encrusted woman. In eloquent Mandarin he said, "I must take her now for interrogation, but I will bring her back here when I'm done; if not today, then tomorrow, if not tomorrow, then the next day. I understand your need for more money, but first I must get authorization."

The old woman grunted, as if it all made sense to her. Xiao was relieved. He was digging deeper into his reservoir of late-night dorm movies, where he had taught himself his first few phrases of Mandarin. She pulled a set of keys from her dingy apron and unlocked the chain around the young woman's ankle.

Large patches of skin around her ankles had been rubbed entirely away, and for one small moment Xiao felt pride in American endurance. Without thinking, he gave her his arm as they strolled up a small incline toward the limo, then snatched it back when he saw the expression on the face of his driver. Quan's driver continued to watch them as they approached the vehicle.

"Let's hurry," the young woman said. She was limping. "I don't trust any of these people."

Xiao began to laugh.

"These people! Really!" he said. "You'd actually say that to me!"

She looked up at him. "You're not like them. You're an American."

"A more accurate statement would be, I *am* an American and I am also like these people."

He'd left the back door of the limo open, and she jumped inside hollering the entire time. "We don't have time to preserve your racial dignity here. You've got to get inside this car and get us out of here! Quick! They're white slave dealers."

Her words stunned him and slowed him down. In the twenty-first century? But which would she prefer, he wondered, slavery or death?

"What's wrong with you?" she asked. "Get in here!"

He took his time, wondering if the driver spoke English too and wondering what that man would tell Quan upon his return to Beijing. All the while, he searched for the button to put the back windows down. Her odor was horrific. She'd need a bath. Once in the car, Xiao's first directive to was to find a hotel in Chengde. The driver quickly backed the limo around, but a rickety wooden-sided truck pulled off the road and blocked their way. All three limo occupants looked out the rear window at five men with rifles standing on the bed of the truck.

"Oh no," she whispered and slid to the floor.

Xiao spoke to the driver in Mandarin, careful to hide his own sudden fear. "Why do they carry guns?"

"They're government employees. They have permission to hunt these forests and sell whatever they catch."

In a voice as calm as the driver's, Xiao asked, "What do you suggest I do to get them to move their truck?"

"They're waiting for traffic to pass before they back up and let us out."

Xiao closed his eyes with relief and turned around in his seat. It was the same quiet queasiness he'd feel every time his mother would reappear. Luckily he had already lowered the windows. He stuck his head out and threw up his entire breakfast of octopus and rice. He eased back against the leather of the seat and let out a mild scream, as the pain from his back raced through his body. He had forgotten what happened on the roof of the palace and closed his eyes for a moment in spite of the pain.

When he opened them again, they were speeding along the highway.

The young woman stared up at him from the car's floor like a cocker spaniel, waiting for its master to tell it what to do.

"I see you're awake," she said. "Who the hell *are* you?" The look on her face told him she no longer trusted him. But her arms were around the calf of his pant leg.

"Come on," he said, patting the seat farthest away from him. "Sit there." The wind had taken some of her stench with it. "We'll go to a decent hotel," Xiao continued. "You can clean up there and get something to eat. We'll talk then, or not."

Up ahead, however, he saw a helicopter hovering over the highway and something told him it had something to do with him.

CHAPTER 10

AGENT TRACE MITCHELL couldn't believe his luck. There they were, the three women he'd been searching for, standing out in the open, performing what looked like a passion play at the end of the alley. Sheila Drisco's photo had been found on *Maxim's* website at about the same time 911 received her second call. By the time Mitchell arrived in the Stapleton area, he knew exactly what he was looking for unlike the SWAT team which was answering the "officer down" call.

The unlucky part of the scenario was the weather. After a seventy-degree day, an Arctic storm was already dumping snow in the Colorado mountains. Meteorologists were confident it would arrive in Denver in less than five hours.

All three women were filthy, dazed, and required assistance to climb the steps of what appeared to be a UPS truck but was the cleanest of CBI's surveillance trucks. They'd all been crying, but none of them spoke as they climbed inside through the sliding door. Only the youngest continued to sob. They nestled atop swivel stools attached to the floor in front of a bank of TV monitors. Mitchell, meanwhile, switched on a light that swung from a short chain over those monitors.

Observing their soot-smeared clothing, Trace wondered why they stood so close to the fire. Could that car accident be related to their missing person report or his search for Antonio Dante? Situating himself against a cabinet less than two feet away, Mitchell realized their smoke-laden clothes might eventually overpower them all.

"I'm agent Trace Mitchell with the Colorado Bureau of Investigation," he said, while he removed his helmet and facemask. "For the past two hours, I've been looking for you, so we've got to talk quickly. When Denver police realize who you are, they're going to take you away from me. They have jurisdiction over the crime scene at Tiffany Plaza."

They whispered among themselves before the black woman asked, "What crime was committed at Tiffany Plaza?"

"Maybe it has nothing to do with you," he answered cleverly. "I'll let the police talk to you about it specifically. But weren't you missing a person in your party?" he continued.

"What are you saying exactly? You don't know much about the crime at Tiffany Plaza?" the black woman asked again.

Agent Mitchell stared back at her, knowing she wasn't going to let him conduct his interview his way. She'd already proven herself capable of self-martyrdom. They could all have been killed out there by SWAT for not following directions. She'd be damned, dead, or tazed before she'd be willing to lie facedown on the ground, he figured. And he'd seen enough people get shot that way at close range to know it wouldn't have been pretty. There was such a thing as too much pride, he thought.

"I'm asking," Mitchell said, "if you all were waiting at the restaurant for someone who never showed up?"

There was a moment's delay.

"Oh, my God," whispered the platinum blond. She ran her dirty fingers through matted hair. Her diamond stud earrings, however, still sparkled in subdued light. The youngest woman put her head in her hands and sobbed loudly.

The black woman again spoke. "Yes. I didn't realize it when we first arrived, but these two women were waiting for Karen Drisco."

Trace wrote it down and said, "The police are investigating the possibility that a young woman, maybe this Karen Drisco, was kidnapped in front of Nueva Paesana. Didn't you know that?"

"No. I mean we didn't connect it to Karen," she continued. "I don't think Sheila and Miriam were listening when a girl who usually does the dishes told us about the commotion outside." She looked at the other women for agreement.

Mitchell took note of their concern and asked, "Are any of you related in some way?"

Miriam spoke up. "All three of us are sisters: Sheila, Karen, and myself. I'm the married one with a different last name and Karen didn't show up."

"I don't suppose any of you knew Antonio Dante before tonight?" he asked, as he continued to write.

No one responded, as Sheila's sobs grew noticeably louder. Both women took turns rubbing her shoulders and back.

"Is that the name of the waiter?" the black woman asked. "Is he supposed to be the kidnapper, too? Is he the same one who shot the police officers outside Sheila and Karen's townhome?"

Mitchell suddenly sat up straight. It was like being stabbed in the heart with information he should have already connected. The relationship between the police shooting, not the truck accident outside, and the man he was tracking suddenly made sense. He couldn't answer her questions and decided to shift gears.

"Is she going to be alright?" Mitchell asked, pointing his pen directly at Sheila. "I'm sorry I can't offer you water," he went on. "Our tank hasn't been filled in God knows how long."

"Should I repeat my question?" the woman asked. He'd felt her eyes on him the entire time.

Actually," he finally said to her, "I'm not trying to avoid your questions, Miss . . ."

"Doctor Buchanan," she stated flatly.

He wrote it down and repeated it, "Doctor Buchanan." Okay. He had pissed her off. "I don't have any answers yet. We'll know more when that fire is out and we can examine those bodies in the truck and the cab. I *can* confirm that the name of the missing waiter at Nueva Paesana is Antonio Dante," he said. "But you probably know better than I whether he pulled the trigger on those police officers."

The two older women looked at him quizzically and then at each other. Maybe they were hoping for more information.

"Antonio Dante," he continued, "is considered an assassin for hire, currently wanted in France for a murder as recent as yesterday."

The women were still silent. Even the sobs from the youngest stopped abruptly.

"Did any one of you actually see this Antonio guy fire a gun at the police officers?" Mitchell asked again.

Finally Miriam said, "Sheila may be able to answer that. She had the binoculars at the time they fell to the ground. But the peculiar thing about that is there was no sound of gunfire. Could he have used a silencer?"

Although she was no longer sobbing, Sheila quietly rubbed her eyes.

Thinking she was probably in shock, Mitchell didn't wait for her answer but asked, "Do any of you have a picture of Karen? I know the police will ask for the same thing. Hopefully you've got more than one. How about her car? Do you have pictures of her car as well?"

He wanted to kick himself as soon as he'd said it. They had no wallets or shoes.

Sheila finally looked up to speak between gulps of air. "My pictures of Karen are at home."

Mitchell expected to see mascara down her cheeks and smeared lipstick. He at least expected to see the overly made-up face that was on *Maxim's* cover. Instead her face was clean-scrubbed. Not even splotches of soot took away from her inner glow. Her shimmering blue eyes stunned him, even pushed him back slightly. He hoped she hadn't noticed.

"You will find Karen, won't you?" she pleaded.

He struggled to find words. "The FBI doesn't have the case yet. Neither does CBI. If Denver police need help, we'll be there. But a lot needs to be determined first. Police have already entered your home." He pointed to a single monitor behind them showing the front door of their townhome. As the women turned around on their stools, his own eyes remained on Sheila.

"None of you can go inside until they've finished," he added. "And if they determine it was a crime scene, there's no telling when you'll get back in."

He reached up and opened several drawers mounted over the top of the monitors until he found a box of tissues. All three women grabbed at them, thanking him profusely.

"Miss Drisco, I have lots of questions," Mitchell said. "But they're the same questions you'll have to answer for the police. You'll be speaking with them before the night is over, so I'll wait until tomorrow to ask mine. Do you know where you'll be staying?"

"With me," Inez announced, never taking her eyes from the screen. "I live in Park Hill, not far from here."

"Mr. Mitchell," Sheila said yearningly, "is it possible," . . . she put one of her hands on his knee while staring up into his face . . ." I mean, could Miriam possibly catch her plane back to Rome tonight? Her son is there and, well . . ."

Trace watched as her voice trickled past moist lips. She was pleading from inside her soul, he thought. Denying any request she made of him was not going to be easy.

Both Inez and Miriam now turned away from the monitors to watch him.

Miriam broke the silence. "I'll be back in the States soon anyway, Agent Mitchell, the first of next month. I promise."

He shook his head without smiling. "I've got a date for the prom tonight, but I can't go either, not until I've finished my report to my boss." Their eyes never left his.

Exasperated, he asked, " Are you crazy? You're all eyewitnesses to police killings."

Miriam sat up straighter on her stool then reared her head back. "But we all saw the same thing," she declared.

"That's not possible," he quipped, then continued his interrogation. "And what happened after the police officers were killed?"

"We thought they were going to come through the living room window!" Dr. Buchanan answered. "Instead, they rammed the garage door. Which proves this Antonio guy couldn't have kidnapped Karen in front of the restaurant. He and the man driving were too busy following Sheila's car to her townhome. Maybe there're more assassins."

Sheila inhaled audibly with fear, but Inez suddenly swiveled around to face the TV monitors.

"Can you get these cameras to move?" Inez asked. "How do they work? What do I push?"

"Don't push anything!" Mitchell barked. "My tech guy'll be back soon and . . ."

"Can we see the garage?" Inez yelled. "Bet it's not there."

"Bet what's not there?" Miriam asked.

"There was only one thing in that whole spotless garage; the vacuum cleaner, the one Karen brought back from Gaelen's house. It was so old, its only importance had to be what was inside it. It must have been used to clean up after they'd killed Gaelen."

"WAIT A MINUTE!" Mitchell said. "Killed who?"

Inez ignored him and turned toward the sisters. "The other things Karen took from her dad's house must be important too. Maybe somebody broke into your house while we were at the restaurant. Anyway, I think this theory fits with what we know so far. On the night Gaelen was killed, Karen shows up shortly after."

"Now you're convinced he was murdered, aren't you?" Miriam said smugly.

"Yes, I am," Inez said. "The murderers may still have been in the house when Karen arrived that night, but in their haste, they left behind incriminating evidence, like dust, blood maybe. But that's okay, they think, because . . ."

"STOP!" Mitchell shouted. "What the hell are you talking about, lady?"

"Miriam can fill you in. Just let me finish," Inez answered. "All they had to do was buy the house and retrieve the contents. They were after something that remained either inside or underneath the house itself."

Sheila suddenly sprang to life. "Wait. You're saying Karen's kidnapping and Dad's murder are connected? That can't be."

They were all silent. Even the noise outside seemed to disappear.

Inez deliberated. "I agree it's weird," she finally said. "Why would somebody like Antonio want to kill somebody like Gaelen?" She seemed to be asking everyone in the truck. Turning to Mitchell, who had been writing madly in his notebook, she said, "You've got to look for that vacuum cleaner. If I'm right, it's underneath the truck out there."

Sheila began to sob and shake.

"You need to rest, don't you?" Inez asked.

Sheila nodded yes.

"One more thing," Inez continued. She was speaking directly to

Miriam. "Earlier tonight you said you thought your dad might have had a Jewish parent. Did you ever think he could have been Jewish himself? That would explain why he didn't want you in Catholic school with Sheila and Karen. It would explain why he never wanted Karen to become a nun."

Mitchell found it hard to write it all down and had no way to capture the pained look on Miriam's face.

"Mrs. Garfield," he said, noticing tears running down her face and not knowing why, "what time does your plane leave tonight?"

"Midnight," she said softly. Sheila rested her head on Miriam's shoulder, while Mitchell checked all the monitors. He felt sorry for all of them.

"I'll drive you to the airport," Mitchell said. "But you've got to answer my questions before you board. Do we have a deal?"

Sudden pounding on the side of the truck made the women jump.

"Yes," Miriam answered quickly.

Mitchell checked the monitor before getting to his feet. "Good." He stood beside the door across from the driver's seat and tapped his mouth with his index finger signaling all of them to be quiet. Tossing a quick look to Miriam, he nodded and slid the door open just a little.

"I was expecting you officers," Mitchell shouted to the people who knocked. "Here they are, Inez Buchanan and Sheila Drisco."

Miriam gave Sheila a momentary squeeze before she scooted under the counter that supported the monitors. Without speaking, Inez and Sheila hopped off their stools and grabbed each other's hands. Mitchell opened the door wider. Very large flakes of snow fell sporadically as they hurried down the steep steps in dirty feet.

Two men in dark suits, one middle-aged the other a whole generation younger, held out blankets for them to use as they all stood on the bottom step. "I'm Detective Logan and this is Detective Ryan. We'll get you some coffee before we head to the precinct. I'm afraid we've got to get your statements tonight."

Mitchell stood just inside the truck, listening as the two women complained about the cold air, not having decent shoes, and needing a restroom. He watched them press the blood out of each other's hands in the headlights of the UPS truck and knew they were gaining strength from each other in the cold. Unobtrusively, he closed the door, hopped into the driver's seat, started the ignition, turned on the heat, and slowly backed the vehicle away from the crowds.

"I don't know how I can thank you," Miriam shouted from the back end of the truck.

"Don't thank me yet," he answered. "If a police officer stops us, I'm going to have to . . ."

"I understand, Agent."

Mitchell now eased the truck forward between pedestrians and parked vehicles. The front side door suddenly slid wide open. In jumped a young man with an opened flannel shirt, wearing short brown pants, cowboy boots, and a ten-gallon hat. An assortment of digital camera equipment hung from his neck.

"Man, have I got some fab photos." He walked to the back as he talked. "I've even got meat sizzling on that poor man's bones." He shivered audibly. The sight of Miriam's protruding knees made him stop abruptly.

"I don't know you," he said to the woman on the floor and then reached for the overhead light switch. "Cam's already on," he said to Mitchell.

"Leave it running, Enrique. And that's Miriam Garfield," Mitchell hollered over his shoulder. "Mrs. Garfield, this is Enrique, the tech guy from hell, a wanna-be agent-in-training."

She simply nodded. Enrique nodded back.

"Listen up, Mitchell, there's a snowstorm headed here. I've got to get my long pants on. I wanna know how these UPS guys do it." Enrique flipped on more TV monitors as he spoke, being careful to let the camera Mitchell had running continue. "What'a ya' know. Police are scrambling to get everything covered up."

Mitchell hollered to Enrique, "Did you happen to see an old vacuum cleaner in the wreckage? It would have been on the black truck, a metal canister, I think they said."

"No. But I'm gonna' need lots of time examining these blowups. That fire was hot! Melted everything. What's a vacuum cleaner got to do with us?"

"I'm about to find out from this lady on the floor," Mitchell answered. "And I'm about to find out about another murder. Well, Miriam, you might be staying in Denver overnight after all."

"Please don't say that," Miriam cried out. "All I need is my bag out of the trunk of my rental car and a lift to DIA. Maybe there'll be an earlier flight. I'll start talking right now about anything you want, including my dad's death, which we believe now was really a murder. You heard Dr. Buchanan's theory. She's a lot smarter than she looks and certainly more observant than anyone else I've ever known."

Mitchell laughed. "Like Miss Marple, only different." He glanced in the mirror at Miriam, who was still on the floor. She looked worried and much older than she had before. After all, he thought, in the midst of this, her baby sister was gone.

CHAPTER 11

NEZ MADE SURE her rhinestone brooch tightly closed the lapels of her robe. With a little more confidence, she sat at her kitchen window, praising God for his gift of shelter. Snow blew sideways in her backyard. Typical of Denver, yesterday had been summer like. But during the hours police had questioned them, the temperature dropped by thirty degrees.

When uniformed officers finally deposited both women beside Sheila's sports car, it was after two o'clock in the morning. Miriam's rental car was gone and yellow tape could barely be seen above the snow, although a white canopy stood above where police officers had fallen. As Sheila drove to Inez's house, she anxiously called Miriam, but the older sister's phone was turned off. Had she caught her flight to Rome or was she sleeping inside a closed airport?

Inez now listened to the snow laden hundred-year-old spruce tree scrape against the kitchen window of her house. The ringing of her land-line that morning had gotten Inez out of bed at six o'clock. Unfortunately, the ringing stopped the minute she reached it. Since it was likely a wrong number, she set the machine to take messages. By seven o'clock, she'd showered and made coffee.

Gaelen's snowblower no longer purred outside as it had in past storms. The silence spoke to her. It told her what she had taught to her students so many times, that she could become anything if she put energy into it; a decent investigator, a detective, or even a spy. She'd learned how to follow the money in her research for the newsletter she created. But could she get an attorney to tell her who bought Gaelen's house?

Inez sat quietly and listened as a phone message was automatically recorded on her machine. After the message was over, she enjoyed the return to peace and quiet, knowing Sheila slept upstairs. But a voice startled her.

"I'm following that marvelous aroma," Sheila announced from the stairs.

When had Inez last heard another voice in her home this early in the morning?

"You couldn't sleep?" Inez hollered back.

Sheila was quick on her feet. Already in the kitchen, she had grabbed the percolator, taken a cup from the overhead cupboard, and was pouring coffee as if she'd lived in the house for years. Sheila had been one of several kids in the neighborhood who'd made Easter eggs and Halloween decorations at Inez's house during their school-aged years.

"I don't even remember getting into bed," Sheila said. She sat in the chair across from Inez, wearing a robe that looked overly large belonging to Inez. Without warning she said, "Karen's dead, isn't she?" Her voice broke into sudden sobs.

Applying her fist to the edge of the kitchen table, Inez boldly declared, "I believe with all my strength that as long as the police haven't found her body, Karen Drisco is alive and well! I don't need to know from where she's coming back; I don't even need to know when or how. And I certainly don't want to dwell on anything negative about her absence."

Sheila took a deep breath and reached for the box of tissue on the counter. "I'm glad to hear you talk like that. I just . . ." Her face wrinkled and she stared at the table. "Inez, I want to apologize for the way Miriam acted last night. I thought we were going to the restaurant so we could get to know one another better. She'd gotten married and left home around the time you moved in here. We were going to seek your advice, at least that's what she told me, not give you an ultimatum to launch an investigation."

"You and your sisters are separate and independent women now," Inez replied, her eyes skimming the top of snowdrifts in her yard. "You have nothing to apologize for."

"Guess you figured it out," Sheila said. "I'm the one in the family who cries."

"No shame in that. Every family's got at least one of those. What do you want for breakfast? You haven't forgotten that awestruck CBI agent, have you? He left a message just now to ease your fears about Miriam. He got her to the airport in time to take the last plane to New York before DIA closed."

"Oh, thank God."

"He also wanted to remind us he'd be here by nine this morning. It's you he wants to see, I'm sure, even in this storm."

"Coffee's enough for me, thank you. How should we handle this guy? I mean, shouldn't we have a plan?" Sheila asked.

Inez took note of how astute that comment was from someone whose job was to look nice all day. She replied. "If last night taught us anything, it's that the police aren't going to consider any possibility unless they think of it first. And if we don't use Agent Mitchell to get information about this investigation, we won't find out anything at all."

The doorbell rang, and they both jumped.

"That can't be him," Inez ventured. She got up to answer it.

"I'll get dressed," Sheila announced, rushing past her and up the stairs.

Inez cracked the door open slightly, leaving the chain attached. Howling wind carried snowflakes inside to melt on her wooden floor. Larry Carmichael stood outside, shivering in his neighborhood uniform, a bleached denim shirt over threadbare jeans.

Not wanting company, Inez removed the chain and opened the door only an inch more. He'd left his dog Arnold at home, but Arnold wanted Larry to know just how angry he was about that. His loud barking from across the street told everybody on the block how he felt. At least Larry had trimmed his beard.

"How's Sheila? Saw her car out front. Thought I'd wait till after seven to come calling. How are you, for that matter?"

Begrudgingly, Inez opened the door. "How should I be?" she asked. "We're not hippies anymore, eager to rise and roam the world."

He hopped inside and she slammed the door shut. There he stood, a man over sixty, slouched like a teenaged boy who was looking for some-body to play with. Inez feared he'd still carve his initials into anything if she didn't keep an eye on him. Larry had avoided Vietnam with a reason Inez had never been privy to, and he had become a teacher for no other reason than that he could.

"It's all over the news," he said. "I'm surprised there's no reporters outside. Maybe nobody knows where you live."

"Why would anyone care?" Inez asked. "Want some coffee?"

"Sure. Is Karen really missing?"

Was "missing" the word used on TV? Inez wondered.

"You know," he said anxiously, "I saw Karen yesterday, or was it the day before?"

Inez cringed. She'd seen his performance of an ignorant bystander before.

"What time was that?" she asked calmly.

"Noon."

"Where?" Her eyes drilled a hole in the side of his face.

"My house. She gave me back a book I'd loaned her. Thought her intent was to go back to school. Sheila up yet?"

"Probably."

Inez poured coffee for him as he reached across the counter to the television.

"Actually," Inez said firmly, "I'd like to keep that off. Makes me mad when I know what's happened and they get it wrong. So did Karen say where she was going after she left you?"

"Nope."

"Have you talked to the police about it?"

"Didn't know she was missing until I turned my TV on. Anyway, TV's full of those cops that got shot. I could see it was near Karen and Sheila's townhouse."

"When was the last time you were at their townhouse? How about some toast to go with that coffee?" Her chest got bigger with her new opportunity to be a detective.

"No thanks. Had breakfast."

He turned from the blank TV to the hallway and then back again. Finally he said, "Must have been not quite a year ago, when I helped Sheila move into her place. Karen didn't move in with her until Gaelen passed away. That was just before she lost her job."

Inez hadn't put events into a time frame before now. Karen lost her job, then her dad, and then moved into a new home in a short span of time. And where was her friend and neighbor Inez during this time? She sat down, crushed under the weight of her own guilt, then realized Larry was still in her kitchen.

"You may want to call the police," she advised. "Help them establish a time line. In fact, if you hang around here till nine you'll meet a CBI agent. You could tell *him*."

"Oh? I might just come back then." He put his cup down and sprinted toward the front door. "Tell Sheila I was here."

"Sure thing," Inez replied.

As soon as she heard the door shut, she put her hands on the TV remote. She felt better not having to explain anything to Larry. A loud bang against the back door made her put it down. It had to be Billy Needham, her nineteen-year-old former student to whom she happily paid money to mow, shovel, install software, answer email, write newsletter articles on the sorry state of public schools, and scan correspondence. Attending community college without a car meant he'd walked the eighteen blocks from his house to hers.

"I'm here to shovel," he shouted through the closed door, while Inez fumbled with the lock and chain.

"Bless you," she declared, the minute the door was opened. "How about coffee and a muffin first?"

"How come your TV's off? Aren't you interested in those dead cops? If you ask me, police already have a bro' picked out for those murders."

Inez purposely ignored his comment and busily found a small plate for his muffin. She threw out Larry's untouched coffee and said, "Haven't had time to turn it on. But listen, I think it's time we put aside our focus on the newsletter. What if I told you Mr. Drisco, next door, was really murdered? It was no heart attack. Wouldn't you want to find out who did it? I think if we put our heads together we might find out."

With muffin crumbs around his mouth, Billy started laughing. "All I know Dr. Buchanan is, that

You got somethin'
buzzin' in your brain.
So you thought you'd call my name
I'm always ready
to go side by side,
for the ride,
'cause the only time my brain expands,
is when you's draggn' it,
kickin' it cross the sands.
Hey only you can
stuff it, pound it, and damn near drown it
full a yo' academic ideas.
Yay beyond the . . ."

"Quit!"

"Yes, ma'm."

"Hey, Billy!" Sheila said, as she pranced into the kitchen. Dressed in false lashes, jeans, and a sweater, there was no way to mistake her as anything but a professional model.

Billy looked her over from her shoes to her hair before giving her a giant bear hug. "I thought you'd gotten too big to come back to Park Hill," he said.

She took a bite of his muffin and with a full mouth said, "You're the one who's getting too big around here." She rubbed both sides of his waist as she spoke. They both laughed.

To Inez, she said, "Hope you didn't mind me staying upstairs while you talked to Larry. He gives me the creeps."

"Really?" Inez was surprised. "What did Karen think of him?"

"Karen suffered from broken wing syndrome."

"Meaning?" Inez asked.

"Sounds like you women are about to have a chic chat," Billy interjected. "I'm gonna' go shovel." He released Sheila and gobbled the last of his muffin. "How long you stayin'?" he asked, before opening the door.

"She's moved in for now, Billy, so you can talk to her later."

"Yes," Sheila confirmed, "and I do want to hear more about this

underground newsletter for teachers you and Dr. Buchanan work on together." Sheila winked at him and poured herself another cup of coffee.

"Great!" Billy said, "Maybe you can take me out to dinner or something before you go back to wherever it is European models go." Then he
quickly opened and closed the door behind him.

"Okay," she said sitting across from Inez, "this is how I define broken
wing syndrome. Remember when Larry's wife left him and took their kids?"

Inez nodded, though she had only a vague memory of it.

"It was when St. Anselm's was investigating allegations of sexual abuse
made by two students Larry had taught a year earlier."

Inez was struck dumb.

Noticing the look on her face, Sheila added, "If you'd been a member
of the St. Anselm family, you would have gotten a letter in the mail from
the Denver Archdiocese. Don't look so shocked. Anyway, Mrs. Carmichael
left him, he lost his job, no charges were filed, and he was almost immediately hired by the public schools because St. Anselm's gave him a letter
of recommendation. Karen knew the sister of one of the girls who'd made
up the whole story about Larry because he was going to flunk her for cut-
ting school. Anyway, over the years, Larry became an alcoholic, and by
the time Karen was in community college, she had taken him under her
wing. His was broken so to speak. To her credit, she got him into AA. It
seemed to me that from then on she was attracted to drunks, the disabled,
or anybody else with a broken wing."

"Wow," Inez said. "To think I lived across the street from all that and
didn't know about it." She couldn't help feeling dejected. Her fear of having one breast lower than the other had reduced her to such reclusiveness
that she'd missed out on what was happening with her neighbors.

"Inez, I know Karen was seeing somebody. You don't suppose it was
Larry, do you? Larry's a dirty old man. Surely Karen understood that
much." Sheila's words shook Inez out of her self-analysis. She'd always
trusted Larry Carmichael. She didn't like him, but they spoke the same
language. They were both teachers.

They continued to quietly sip coffee, Inez realizing she should pay
more attention and at least be present in Sheila's life.

Suddenly Sheila's words gushed out at once. "Actually, Karen saw a doctor. I may as well say it. I suspected Karen was pregnant and was surprised when Miriam didn't mention it last night. The two had gotten close after Dad died. They hadn't been close before. They fought constantly when we were young. Karen wasn't about to let Miriam take her mother's place, and Miriam wasn't about to treat her like a baby."

Sheila took another sip of coffee and started again. "I hate to say this, but neither of my sisters loved Dad as much as I did. Dad was furious with Karen and threatened to pull her out of Catholic grade school if she kept talking about becoming a nun. As far as Karen knew, her Dad never loved her. Anyway, Karen told me, the very morning she later found Dad dead, that she had something important to announce. She said she would announce it to the rest of us after Dad heard it first. But of course, he was dead when she got there."

"Maybe I should write this down to tell Agent Mitchell," Inez said reaching for her laptop.

"You're not suggesting," Sheila asked, "that we tell that clown about any of this? Those police detectives thought you were crazy last night when you tried to tie everything together for them. Maybe you don't care what people think about you, but I care. I care a lot. Models care what people think about them. You should start caring about things like that yourself."

Inez's eyes narrowed. She hadn't realized the extent to which Sheila had become her own woman since leaving home. What was Sheila trying to tell her?

"I'm merely suggesting," Inez explained, "that Agent Mitchell is our only link to people like Antonio Dante. He'll give us information if he thinks we're giving him information as well."

Sheila wilted into tears. Seconds later she asked, "You really think these incidents are all connected?"

"Yes."

"Then, we've got to find Karen, because I'm sure the police won't."

Inez got up and opened the back door wide to inhale a refreshing blast of cold wind and snow. Somehow the morning was turning into more excitement than she was used to. But Sheila was right about finding Karen. In less than a minute she was freezing and shut the door hurriedly.

"Billy can't shovel snow. It's still coming down," Inez said. "If he's around front, I'll tell him to stop and come inside."

Sheila followed. When Inez opened the front door, she could see lights flashing from police cars at Larry's house across the street. Had Larry called them? Inez closed the door, leaving a slight crack. She'd wait until the police left before phoning him. A second later she heard Larry's voice. Two officers hurried out his front door with Larry between them in handcuffs.

"Inez!" he shouted. "Tell Hank or Billy, whichever one you see first, to find Arnold and feed him for me."

"Okay!" she hollered back.

Her heart fell to her stomach as she closed the door hard. Why arrest Larry? One look at Sheila's face and Inez seriously thought about crying herself. Everything Sheila had just told her about Larry muddled her brain. Arm in arm they slowly retreated toward the kitchen, when they heard banging at the back door.

Inez opened it, and there stood Agent Trace Mitchell with Billy beside him. Mitchell's hand was firmly on the shoulder of Billy's jacket, a jacket soaked in blood.

"Says he works for you," Mitchell said, as he pushed Billy inside.

"What did you do to him?" Sheila cried out. Startled, Inez sat down immediately to catch her breath.

"Nothing!" Mitchell shouted.

Sheila, meanwhile, pried Billy's jacket away from each of Mitchell's gloved fingers. Mitchell stepped back against the door he'd just closed, watching her.

"You pigs are all alike," Sheila huffed. "Give a white man a badge and he believes he's privileged enough to make the whole world his plantation. And yesterday, we thought you were our savior."

Inez wondered where the blood on Billy's jacket came from, but she was also struck by Sheila's attitude. Where had this young woman been modeling? She needed to remember to Google Sheila Drisco's name as soon as she had the chance. Mitchell however, stood staring at Sheila with his mouth open.

"No, no, no," Billy pleaded. "This isn't my blood. This man here was only helping me stand up in this blizzard. It's brutal out there. This is Arnold's blood. Arnold's dead. Somebody slashed his throat and buried him under bushes on 17th Avenue Parkway. Arnold dashed out of Larry's house the minute the police came. He chased some man in a hoodie. I didn't want him to get lost, but I couldn't catch him. When I didn't see the man or the dog anymore, I came back here to shovel. Then I realized how dumb that was. So I decided to make one last search for Arnold and that's when I found him under a bush. How could anybody . . ."

"How, indeed?" asked Inez. "It's obvious Arnold knew something we didn't know he knew. Makes me wonder how much more Gaelen's killers have on their to-do list."

Billy looked tired and drained. "You think," he asked Inez, "there was more than one murderer?"

"Ha," said Mitchell rudely. "I don't know what murder you could be referring to, young man, but I just stopped by to say I'm no longer on this case. The police have taken over the investigation of your sister's disappearance, Miss Drisco. And I'll be closing Antonio Dante's case soon. Although he was parked in front of your townhouse, it turns out his death has nothing to do with any of you." He turned around and left through the back door, slamming it shut on his way out.

If there was one thing Inez knew for certain, it was that Agent Mitchell was dead wrong. She even had her doubts that this agent was your average arrogant white man.

"Yes," Inez said to Billy. "I think there were at least three men, and one of them may have died in the truck accident last night."

CHAPTER 12

X IAO'S DRIVER SLOWED to a complete stop several meters from where the helicopter landed beside the road. Its blades slowed, and the wheat in the field on which it landed was beginning to stand upright again.

"Did you know this was going to happen?" Xiao asked the driver.

The man in front was hesitant and didn't turn to face him. Finally, he answered, "I knew an interception by officials was always possible."

A man dressed the same way as the driver climbed down from the helicopter and ran toward their limousine. When he stood beside the vehicle's door he shouted to the driver to get out and run to the helicopter with all due speed because his orders were to return to Beijing with Commander Kee. Xiao had met Kee only once, by accident, at his great grandfather's bathhouse. Although they were around the same age, Xiao thought they'd never be friends. Kee moved his body like Jackie Chan, but it was a body strengthened through weight-lifting.

The driver continued to sit and look straight ahead. The new man then grabbed the door handle and immediately opened the car door, almost yanking the door off its hinges. Xiao was impressed with muscles that were obviously hidden under the new man's uniform. This time he ordered the driver to jump whenever spoken to by someone higher in command. The driver awkwardly turned out of the seat and quickly ran all the way to the helicopter.

Even as the driver was running, the new man bent down and introduced himself to Dr. Xiao Wren in fluent American English.

"My name is Bohai, and I will be your driver. Commander Kee wants to speak with you personally beside the helicopter. You see, there?" He pointed a beefy index finger at it. "Please, you go now. My orders are to wait here inside the car with the girl." As he sat behind the steering wheel, he once again said, "Please, Dr. Wren. Please go."

Xiao had seen the small section of a dragon tattoo that ran out from under his jacket sleeve to the man's index finger. He knew that tattoo continued under his shirt and around the man's entire arm just as it did on all the members of the Pacific Avenue Boys, a San Francisco gang named for the street on which its founding members lived. That gang in particular, consisting of Cantonese and Vietnamese boys eager to demonstrate their manhood, was the major reason Xiao had been home schooled. Any male or female who crossed its members was summarily raped or vivisectioned into large pieces. Xiao turned to the young woman beside him, wondering how he could warn her. She spoke before he could say a word.

"It won't do me any good to be afraid," said the woman. "So I won't."

Xiao said nothing and got out of the car, slammed the door shut, and walked with no particular speed toward the helicopter. Once again he began listening to a chorus of voices cursing him into damnation for all he had done wrong so far that day. Yet he'd done everything he'd been told. He turned his head around quickly, thinking he'd heard his mother's voice as he walked, but instead saw the young woman in the car leaning forward to watch through the front windshield.

To Xiao's surprise, when he turned back around, Kee was walking toward him with one hand extended to shake his hand.

"My great grandfather wishes you well, Xiao. But unfortunately, Quan has very pressing events he must attend to immediately. Therefore, I have come to explain that you no longer have thirty days before you must kill the woman. Quan says it must be done in seven days. Unless, of course, you want to kill her now. All you need do is turn around and point your thumb down so your driver sees it. He will very efficiently put a bullet through her skull as we stand here."

Xiao was speechless, his mouth dry. He couldn't turn around or force his body to move a single muscle. His body felt like stone or maybe he wished his body would turn to stone. Breathlessly, he stared at Kee's eyebrows which didn't move at first. His breathing became more labored and louder, until the ground came up to meet his face.

When he awoke, he was standing, but his clothes were caked with dust and he couldn't feel his feet. Kee held onto his arms.

"What happened?" Xiao asked.

"You fainted." Kee's whole face turned into a giant smile. "It's okay though. I caught you before you did too much damage." He wrapped his arm around Xiao's shoulder. "Didn't think you'd pass that test. Come. Walk with me awhile."

Both their backs were toward the limousine. They headed toward the helicopter. The ground had been tilled into deep ruts and it was difficult for both of them to walk without stumbling. Xiao was surprised at how large the aircraft looked as they got closer. It had been landed on the smoothest patch of ground for several kilometers in all directions.

Kee was only a half-inch taller than Xiao, but Xiao knew he wouldn't be able to overpower him. All the ads he'd ever seen about pumping iron came to mind, as Xiao lifted one heavy foot in front of the other. Maybe if he'd tried working out before now he wouldn't be in this predicament.

Xiao asked, "Did you fly this helicopter yourself?" It was not an entirely stupid question. The cab of the helicopter was so high off the ground it required steps to reach it and Xiao couldn't see inside. Maybe there were other people who couldn't be seen from his angle.

Kee smiled menacingly. "We can stop walking now," he said. "No one can hear us out here. I understand you had some trouble this morning. Almost fell off the roof of the Summer Palace. You damaged your back. You may need to return to Beijing sooner than seven days for a complete medical examination. We'll let you know of our decision."

Kee was treating him like a child. "Did you finish drinking that thermos of coffee the tour guide made for you this morning?"

Xiao was taken aback by his detailed knowledge. The man with the British accent certainly was Quan's employee. Xiao explained that the thermos was still in the car and expressed his sincere gratitude for all that Quan was doing for him, deliberately leaving Kee's name out of the equation.

Kee pulled out a stainless-steel flask from his back hip pocket and gave it to him telling Xiao to throw out the liquid in the thermos because it was cold. Kee then reached inside his suit jacket and pulled out a gun from its underarm holster and handed it to Xiao. He explained that there were three bullets in it, certainly enough to kill the woman. Xiao stuffed it into the waist of his jeans without thinking. He'd never been a boy scout or joined the ROTC. He had no idea how to put the safety on a gun. Everything was happening too fast.

Kee then handed him two passports. "From time to time you may be questioned by government officials who might not have been briefed on what Quan is undertaking for the benefit of China. You may be asked to produce these items."

Now that was an interesting statement, Xiao thought. And where did Kee get his passport? He didn't bother to look at the second one, assuming it belonged to the young woman in the car. She was as good as dead anyway. The last items Kee handed him were a credit card and a cell phone.

"All businesses in China will honor this card," Kee explained, "but its life span is short, as is your mission. And the phone is for communication with only one person, Quan. It will not permit other calls."

He asked if Xiao had any questions, and Xiao wondered for a moment why he was standing in a wheat field beside a highway with a helicopter nearby on a sunny day. He wondered if he couldn't shoot this man Kee with the loaded gun in his pants and fly that helicopter back to America. It was worth a try. But his voices kept telling him he was too stupid to do anything like that. And for what, they asked? He looked long and hard at the helicopter. Who besides Kee could fly it?

Kee never stopped talking. He explained that the new limousine driver would drop them off at a hotel near Chengde and return to Beijing immediately. If he needed transportation after he'd killed the woman, he was to call a number written on the credit card, but not with the phone he'd just been given, unless he wanted to talk directly to Quan.

Without saying goodbye, Kee quickly climbed up the steps into the helicopter, closed the door, and started its loud motor and whirling blades.

Xiao stood very still, letting the dust swirl around him. He didn't want the blades to slice his head off and refused to let his knees buckle under him. He wondered if he could ever become like Kee and dominate others in the way Kee and his great grandfather did. Xiao was too ill, he thought, to ever become as mean as the two of them.

Xiao walked back to the car as slowly as he had walked to the helicopter.

"This driver pitched your thermos out the window while you were gone," she screamed, before Xiao reached the side door.

"It's okay," Xiao responded calmly. But it wasn't okay. He told her he had a new one which she could see for herself now. It wasn't okay to feel downtrodden. Yet there he was with blue sky overhead and Kee, Quan, a driver named Bohai from the streets of San Francisco, and a British-sounding spy all holding him hostage.

No sooner had he closed the door behind him than the driver sped away. He caught the young woman staring at the handle of his newly acquired gun. It protruded from the waist of his pants. He had a gun alright, but he was just as powerless as she was.

**

The hotel manager reminded them they'd be without electricity for several hours each night. Xiao needed no verbal confirmation that this was not the kind of hotel he thought he'd be staying in. The driver pulled money from his pocket and paid the manager. He then explained to Xiao that they were not to return to the Summer Palace even as tourists. He left the hotel without another word.

Though small, their room had two beds, a bedside table, one upholstered chair covered in what looked like bleached cheesecloth, and a wooden stool, on which he now sat. It was the hotel's attempt to imitate what American tourists were accustomed to. He speculated that a family of farmers had left behind the stool on their way to Beijing. Sitting on it placed him in a direct line of site to the bathroom.

The young woman bathed by candlelight. Xiao thought her no more than sixteen as he watched her for several minutes. He was confident he could stop her from escaping through the door and satisfied that she hadn't seen his embarrassment over the quality of the room. Occasionally Xiao shut his eyes only to see a recurring nightmare of himself naked on the edge of a roof with a mob of country peasants carrying rifles. They dared him to leap. Then he'd wake up.

Why not rush in and hold her head under water? What was there to stop him? Had she figured it all out, that he was there to kill her? Or had she fallen asleep while she soaked?

Suddenly her head was gone. He kept blinking away the sleep from his eyes. Had he fallen asleep? Had she drowned or escaped? He stood up, ready to do anything necessary, when just as suddenly, her head reappeared out of the water. Slowly, with only her head above water, she turned her body to face him, her hair dripping in ringlets down her face.

"You thought I drowned, didn't you?" She laughed, but he was sure they both recognized the sound of her false bravado. She stopped her laughter abruptly, and Xiao sat back on the stool again. He stared at his satchel, wishing he was in his own apartment, but he knew the previous driver had packed every piece of clothing he owned. Quan had not intended him to return to that place. Xiao couldn't help feeling disturbed, queasy about everything around him. To calm himself, he though about Kee's new driver, who had undoubtedly reached Beijing by now.

Xiao covered his eyes with his hands and pretended to strangle her with both of his thumbs against her larynx, no need for a gun. Yes, he could picture himself killing her now.

"I feel a lot better." It was her whispered voice above his head. He opened his eyes to total darkness. She'd blown out the candles. Her hand took hold of his hand and placed his fingers between her legs. She stood beside him.

"See," she said. "I'm all clean."

He snatched his hand back, stood up, and the lights suddenly came on. They flickered on and off until they stayed on. She wore no clothes. One thing he knew for certain, her taunting would stop once she was dead. Only then, if she was anything like his mother, could he expect her to begin using her unleashed anger.

Xiao put his hands on her shoulders and pushed her backward onto the bed.

"If you're hungry," he said, "you'll need to get dressed." It had been a couple of years since he'd seen a live naked girl. The coed dorms had been full of them; girls who pretended not to know he was studying.

She made no move to get up but said, "I don't suppose you've got anything I could wear inside that suitcase?"

"What happened to the clothes you took off?"

"Those dirty, smelly things?"

"Then wash them."

"I have. They're hanging over the tub."

He leaned sideways to confirm her statement, then opened his mouth as if to speak but couldn't think of anything that would show enough disdain. He fiddled with his satchel's lock, then reluctantly pulled out a white tee shirt and tossed it at her head. Like all his roommate's girlfriends, she stood up to angle her bare butt toward him, hoping his erection would embarrass him more.

She'd need more clothes, he thought. And what about food? He was hungry himself. And where would he find a store that sold what he'd need over the next seven days? Seven days! It was all a game, and he knew it. He was certain Kee would return tomorrow and say, "Quan needs her killed today."

Even before her head reappeared through the neck of his tee shirt, she began questioning him. "How long have you lived here? Do you daydream a lot?"

Once her head was through the neck of the shirt altogether, she hollered, "HELLO, can you hear me? Who was the Chinese man I flew to China with? Why did they put my car on that plane? I'd only owned it a few hours. God, I loved that car. Were those people on that farm working for you? Am I your slave now?"

Xiao's mind was elsewhere. He stared without actually seeing her.

"Are you really an American?" she continued. "Let me see your driver's license."

He paid no attention to her words or her extended hand, but eventually took out his wallet to see how much cash he had. She grabbed his license when it fell on the bed. Without thinking he raised his hand to smack her, but her voice stopped him.

"California." She read it slowly, as if the word itself was a ball of soft-serve ice cream. She sat on the bed with her legs wrapped under her, not caring, Xiao thought, that her pubic hair showed.

"My license is from Colorado," she said, smiling back at him. "But I don't know what happened to it. I think it fell out of the car when that man got in. He looked for it, because he didn't believe me when I told him my name."

Xiao said nothing but finally ripped his license from her fingers.

"Tell me," she asked, "why is it nobody cares to know *my* name? It makes me think I'm as good as dead."

She chuckled in that false high school way he'd heard earlier, then fell back against the headboard before Xiao realized she was crying.

"Don't cry," he heard himself say from his position on the stool. "You're just hungry."

"No, I'm not!" she said. "Tell me! Do I belong to you now? I ask because you're not so bad. I mean I just want to know."

Xiao was thinking of his own voices, which sounded like a low-pitched static now. He worried what his growing hunger would do to the chorus of voices. Her questions annoyed him. Maybe he would kill her now or better yet, ask her questions to see how *she* liked it.

"Did you go to college?" he asked.

She sucked in air, as if the question held some significance.

"No," she said, leaning forward. "I went to work right after my high-school diploma. I got a job with the Red Cross until they let me go."

"I like the Red Cross," Xiao said modestly. "It helped my family when I was younger."

"Did you grow up in a large family?" she asked.

"Yes. How about you?"

"Yes. And is your family still in California?"

"I don't want to talk about them," he said sullenly.

"I don't know where my family is anymore," she said. "I ran away from home when I was fourteen, hitching rides West till I was fifteen. I've never seen any of them since."

Xiao's eyes grew wide. He was very impressed. She'd led the life he'd wanted. He'd read every "running away" novel he could find before age eleven.

"Why did you run?" he asked.

She shrugged her shoulders. "Nobody was going to miss me except Pa. He had no one else left to beat up. I was the middle kid and I don't want to talk about that, either."

Xiao was quiet. He could have listened to her all night if she was going to talk about her family.

"Ask me something else," she said. "Ask me anything. Make me think you care. I thought maybe somebody was looking for me in particular. But I'm nobody. So I don't get why I'm here. I'm alone in the world. Are you alone, too?"

"Yes." He thought of his mother.

"So what did you study in college? I can tell you went."

"Bioengineering, I have a PhD."

Her eyes widened in what Xiao could only assume was admiration. What the hell was he doing, basking in her attention? He stood up suddenly, tired of his own naïveté. He was supposed to be fucking her brains out before he killed her.

"I'm so sorry," she cried. "Have I embarrassed you? I never want to do that."

"Shut up!" he said, pacing the small amount of floor space available to him. "Stop sucking up to me. You sound so . . . so Asian."

Suddenly he darted toward her neck, grabbing it, pushing her shoulders down against the pillows, his knees on both sides of her chest. He heard his zipper, felt her fingers entering his pants and stroking his penis. Though her eyes were tightly shut, she continued to pull at his pants. Scooting forward, he prepared to squeeze her neck harder.

"Wait a minute!" she managed to say, letting go of him to pull up the tee shirt she was wearing. "Remember, I'm a virgin."

Both her hands reached between his legs, gripping him firmly, her jagged nails scraping his foreskin. Pain tore at him from the inside out. He screamed as he released her neck, then rolled over on the bed in a fetal position holding himself as he groaned.

"I'm so sorry," she said. "My nails keep breaking. I didn't do it on purpose. You've got to forgive me."

"Quiet," he mumbled.

"You will forgive me, won't you?"

"It's a bad dream," he said.

"Hey, it's no dream. It's your back. It's bleeding. It's bleeding through your shirt. That's one of those Eddie Bauer shirts, isn't it?"

He lay motionless, realizing the pain snaked through his entire body. He was certain he was drowning in his own blood. He was dying.

"Can you hear me?" she asked. "I know about such things. I was with the Red Cross, remember?"

CHAPTER 13

SUNLIGHT THROUGH HIS only window in the hotel room made Xiao's eyelids pop open. Blurred images made him wonder where he was. He tried to wipe his eyes and couldn't move his arms. Wrapped mummy style in sheets on the floor, he blinked continuously and rotated his head until he saw a blond woman on the edge of the bed, eyes shut, breathing rhythmically, wearing nothing. Some of the sheets on the bed and around him were bloody. Why was that? He noticed both the curvature of her hips and the warmth he felt for her. Her eyes opened, startling him.

"C'mon," she said. The rest of her hadn't moved.

He continued to stare.

"Are you still in pain?" she asked. "Is it your back? You slid to the floor an hour ago. C'mon."

She pushed herself backward across the bed, beckoning him to lie down beside her. He was quite satisfied to remain where he was. It was like watching an exquisitely sculptured statue slowly come to life.

Hours passed, he thought, as he began to walk off the edge of the roof and into a pool of mud. But when his eyelids opened again, he gradually began to unwrap sheets from around his own naked body, until he was standing upright. His back was stiff and it throbbed.

With her eyes closed she said, "Just because the sun is up doesn't mean *we* have to get up."

Xiao gently flung the stained sheets over them both. Whatever had happened last night made him feel connected to every part of her, even her skin, which he touched above her elbow.

She opened her eyes. It surprised him again and his own eyes expanded. She laughed in his face, but it wasn't like the falsetto she had attempted yesterday. She put her hand over her mouth and said, "I'm sorry. But you are so good looking even when you wake up. I guess all women tell you that."

Her face glimmering with speckled sunlight mesmerized him. He paid no attention to her words, which he hadn't understood anyway.

"You are very pretty," he said, realizing he'd never uttered those words before.

She continued to smile. "I'm nowhere near as pretty as you are handsome. Haven't women stared at you before?"

"Yes, but that's because they . . . they read my secrets."

She rolled onto her back laughing. "Xiao, where have you been all your life?"

His back stiffened. It hurt. How did she know his name? What else had he told her? He was about to get up, certain he'd feel more comfortable pacing the floor. But she stopped his movement by simply putting her fingers on his nipples and pressing down gently until he fell against the pillow.

"You don't remember last night, do you?" she asked.

He was slow to speak, feeling the tingle of her fingertips throughout his body.

She took her hand away and said, "You told me about the voices. That they started in your first year at college."

He turned his face away from her and anxiously looked at the ceiling. He felt her fingers slide around his bicep to gently message it. "It does sound like schizophrenia."

How would she know? He sighed?

"But couldn't it also be a brain tumor?" she asked. "Anyway, you're the doctor, aren't you?"

"I'm not that kind of doctor." He stared at the ceiling as he spoke. "And whatever it is, it's not information I could share with just anyone. I could have lost my scholarship, my job, been sent home, been disgraced."

"Bet you've had blackouts before," she said.

He turned his face toward her, his bewilderment flooding his eyes. "Is that what happened last night?"

She was quick to respond. "Everything's okay," she said, while continuing to rub his arm. "I'm no expert, but I'd say it was more like a seizure lasting twenty or so minutes. If you see a doctor, I'll go with you. Your symptoms are milder than those of people who rant and rave in public parks and subways. I've read about such people shoving, beating, even killing strangers and not remembering it."

He sat up shaking his head. "I'd know if I'd done stuff like that. Besides," he ventured, "I work hard every day in a very competitive environment. I have a grant. I'm improving humanity by using valued genetic material from historical leaders."

She smiled. "If your lab is as competitive as you think it is, who would dare to tell you that you've blacked out or that you sat for hours speaking nonsense?"

He didn't look at her but remembered Quan's insistence that his research could go on without him. If Quan had hidden cameras he might have seen him black out. What else had he said last night? He sat up in bed waiting for her to say more.

She yawned before she said, "Maybe we should be going soon."

What was she talking about? Go where to do what? He said nothing, confident for the moment that no matter where he went Quan would find him.

"Don't be afraid, Xiao," she said. "I'll take care of you. I promise. We'll start today, as if everything is brand-new, as if it's our first day together." She moved closer. "Still think I'm pretty?"

"Yes," he said, though he looked at the window across from them.

"Good," she said, "because I need to confess something before another minute goes by. Remember when I said I was a virgin last night?"

"No." He put his head back on the pillow.

"Well, I did. But it wasn't true. I just didn't want you to think I was bad."

Xiao sighed, preoccupied with Quan.

"So you *do* think I'm bad," she said.

"No. I don't." He watched her pale freckles wrap across the bridge of her nose. "I'm glad you're not a virgin," he said. "Because one of us needed to know what to do. I'm the virgin, you see."

"No you're not. Not any more."

Xiao laughed. "Wow! You'd think I'd remember that."

She propped herself up on her elbow to laugh with him. They continued to laugh in each other's arms.

"I know I've laughed before," he said. "I just don't remember when."

He enjoyed the feel of her body against his, but gradually felt awkward for not remembering the night before. "We really had sex last night?" he asked.

She pulled away slightly, but they still held on to each other.

"I'm not at all offended that you don't remember," she said. "I was afraid when you blacked out the first time. That's when I gave you that liquid from your flask. I thought it might be medicine, since that man on the helicopter brought it to you. I was surprised at how lucid you became after drinking it. After that we made love—had sex, I mean—and you said we had to hide, that both of us could be killed. So I didn't think it wise to go to the lobby to get help for you. Last night you said we could live together happily in the forests of China. We could become farmers and live off the land. During the night I dreamed about it. And this morning, I admit I don't think it's such a bad idea."

Xiao released her, sat up, and swung his legs over the edge of the bed. The reality of his situation returned to him in full force.

"Last night," she said, "I told you my real name, and I'm glad you don't remember it because people always laughed. But since we're starting a new life I should have a new name as well. I never liked my name. The name I really like is the name of my very best friend in all the world. Her name is Karen, and she's one of God's angels." Her eyes teared up and she wiped them with her hand. "So my new name from now on is going to be Karen."

Xiao shook his head and said, "Karen, I don't know about this."

Suddenly she began crying. "Oh, Xiao, I've saved the most ridiculous thing about last night for last. I think, I mean, I believe something was put inside your back. I tried to remove it last night, but it's too deep. It was placed there surgically. That much I know. You bled a lot. What I don't know is what it is."

She pulled open a drawer in the table next to the bed. "I used this sewing kit to sew you up after I cut you open a little to see better. I don't know why you didn't feel any of it. I do know that whatever was in that flask was potent. Obviously, it didn't kill you, and so after you drank some of it, I used what was left to wash your wound. You passed out. Don't look at me like that. No, we didn't have sex. I lied. I've lied about a few things. I didn't run away from home. I wish I had, but I didn't. You were unconscious and somebody kept trying the doorknob all last night. I was so scared, but I jammed the door with the back of the chair. I'm telling you the truth now! Honest!"

A knock on the door made them both freeze.

"Who's there," Xiao answered in Mandarin.

There was no answer, but the next knock was louder.

"Scoot down," he whispered to her. "Cover everything but your head," Xiao demanded, as he jumped into his jeans. "Pretend to be asleep."

"Dr. Wren?" asked a timid voice through the door.

Xiao flung the door open wide and saw the driver from yesterday sneering at him. The man tried dodging around him, rising up and down on the balls of his feet to get a better look over Xiao's head.

"Remember Bohai? So sorry to disturb you, but I wonder, is she dead?"

"No." And with that, Xiao tried to slam the door shut.

Bohai's beefy arms held the door steady. "Do you know me?" he asked. I thought I saw you look at my tattooed hand yesterday."

"No, I don't know you?

"But you're from San Francisco. You know who I represent."

Xiao said nothing.

"If you are ready for breakfast," Bohai said, "I am to drive you to a place nearby for a meal. The management here must clean your rooms in the meantime."

Taking note of Bohai's strength, Xiao became less aggressive. Graciously, he said, "We have to wash and get dressed first. Come back in an hour and we will be ready, thank you." The two men smiled insincerely at each other.

"You must be ready in thirty minutes," Bohai said, still smiling.

Xiao closed the door behind him with a full understanding of the man's dominance. He remembered that Kee told him the driver would return to Beijing. Why was he still in Chengde? Did he work for Quan or Kee?

"We've got to get out of here in fifteen minutes," he said turning to Karen. "Bohai must report his findings. That means Quan will shorten the length of time you have left again. Get dressed."

While she did, he opened his satchel and began looking through the pockets of each article of clothing until he found what he searched for. It was a weird-shaped card of a miniature human hand, which he took to the phone on the bedside table. Would the government let his call go through? Several clicks and static sounds later, Xiao finally hung up. He was wasting time. He reached for the credit card and gun given him yesterday, both resting on the other bed where the woman could have easily reached them during the night.

Karen stood near the bed, fully dressed, watching him. He noticed her trembling.

"You must never touch this credit card," he said. "It says the bearer is employed by the People's Republic of China and that it can only be used for emergencies: clothing, food, and shelter. Every time we use it, they will know where we are.

"We'll need to get bicycles. We'll ride to Yunnan Province as soon as we can. We're far from there now, closer to Beijing," he said. "From Beijing we'll take a bus. We'll need bedrolls and down jackets. We have to work fast."

"Why don't we go to the American embassy when we get to Beijing?"

Xiao looked at her sternly and said, "I can see you don't have a healthy respect for Chinese people. We'd never get inside alive, much less get sent back to the States. The Chinese will do anything to save face, and if that means killing both of us, they will. I may look and act stupid, but I'm not. I know you're likely to tell me anything you think I want to hear in order to stay alive. You're like everybody else in my life so far. You lie and you'll lie often if need be."

She said nothing but watched as he put his shirt and shoes on as he spoke.

"I don't know when I'm me or not me. I'm always occupied with the me inside me, but remember this," he continued. "You've got to throw that credit card away when we have what we need. That card was given to me to help Quan track us.

"This is crazy. I'm crazy," he continued. "Would you really take care of me?"

Karen put her hand on his arm. "Of course I'm going to take care of you. I said I would, didn't I? I'm taking a chance on you and your health, too. What's in Yunnan Provence? Are we going to be farmers there? What made you want to live there?"

"Have you ever read anything by James Hilton?"

She shook her head no.

"I'll tell you about him as we travel. Will you really take care of me, even if I've done something bad? Will you make me your only lover?"

"Of course I will, of course I will. I'll say it over and over again until you believe me."

Wearing his gun at his waist, he carried his satchel in one hand. Holding Karen's hand in the other, they tiptoed down the hall and out the back door of the hotel. He hesitated for only a moment, thinking that he had just seen the driver's face in the crowd near the hotel's door.

CHAPTER 14

DECEMBER 2006   DENVER, NEXT AFTERNOON

B Y TWO O'CLOCK in the afternoon, Chinook winds had returned and
eaten yesterday's entire blanket of snow. It was as if the blizzard had
been a Denver-wide hallucination. Only sand remained to swirl its way
down the nearest sewer. Mountain towns reported record powder and
record crowds were still on their way to try it out.

Having finished her grocery shopping, Inez drove into her driveway,
singing at the top of her longs along with Aretha Franklin. She relished the
whole idea of preparing spaghetti with a well-seasoned white clam sauce
and a great Caesar salad for dinner with Sheila. When her phone rang, she
stopped the car in the driveway next to her house.

"Hello?" Inez hated phones and felt her calls were usually not worth
answering.

"Aye, Dr. Buchanan, it's me."

"Oh, Billy! Wha'd ya' find?"

"A lot. I was talking to the head custodian as I filled out his application,
and he's telling me I won't need to clean the whole building right now
because the top floor is vacant. Says companies come and go so fast in
Cherry Creek you'd think they were being paid to leave. Actually, he was
wondering if it was the same company coming back after each bankruptcy
with a different name or something."

"Now, that is interesting."

"There's no trace of the company you're looking for. And I didn't ask
him about it because I knew he'd get suspicious."

"Okay. Good job! So you know where to go next, right? The Office of Records."

"I'm on it."

"Oh, and Billy . . . hello?"

He'd already ended the call when her phone rang again.

"This is Sheila," said the voice. "I'm so sorry, Inez. I just couldn't stay at your place another night. Your house is marvelous, but it's too close to where Daddy died. There're too many memories there. And when Arnold was found dead so close by, I knew I couldn't bear staying another night."

Inez inhaled. "I understand." She hoped her voice hid her disappointment. Inadvertently, her eyes flashed to her rearview mirror and all the bags of groceries bought for what she thought would be a chance to have a young roommate for a while. "I should have been more sensitive," Inez continued, "but I was hoping it would work out for you here."

"I know Inez, and I'm so sorry. Your keys are on the kitchen table. I didn't know when you'd be back. You've got a ton of messages on your machine, by the way."

Realizing it was getting dark, Inez responded, "Well, I'm still inside my car. And you must have left a light on in the dining room, right?"

"Yes, I did. I wasn't sure what time you'd be getting home and . . . and I just want you to know that I'm still close by," Sheila added. "I'm staying in Capitol Hill, 14th and Emerson. The apartment belongs to a friend, an airline stewardess, but she's gone most of the time. Anyway, I wanted to tell you what I found out about Larry."

Just then a tall figure—Inez couldn't see the face—opened her passenger side door. Inez was ready to scream into the phone. The man bent down. It was Larry Carmichael.

"HUH! You scared the hell out of me!" Inez shouted.

"Inez?" Sheila asked on the other end.

"That's Sheila, isn't it?" Larry seemed overly calmly as he got inside and slammed the door behind him.

Inez put the phone against her ear again. "The police must have released him; he's sitting beside me now."

"That's what I wanted to tell you," Sheila said, laughing.

"Well then I'll give you a call tomorrow and see how you're doing," Inez said. "You take care now."

The minute she ended the call, Larry began talking.

"That was the dumbest advice you've ever given me! Remind me never to listen to you again," he said. He turned sideways to see her better. His mouth curled up at the ends. Inez could tell he wasn't as angry as he sounded.

"I'm sorry," she answered. "I had no idea the police would think you kidnapped Karen."

"Everybody's a suspect including you," he pointed out. "I don't know how many times the police repeated that yesterday. They're investigating everybody. I was just somebody they started with, 'cause I CALLED THEM. Can you believe it, Inez, 'ole buddy? I stupidly called them!"

"They kept you all day?"

"And all night," he said. "I'm not upset. I was at first, but it was like the good old days, in a way. This is more serious, but with all my practice from the sixties, I didn't really give a damn."

Inez didn't believe him. His face looked terrible.

Someone suddenly banged a rock or a fist on the roof of her car. Both Inez and Larry jumped as if they'd been caught in some clandestine activity.

"Hey, you coming in or going out?" somebody yelled.

Although her heart was in her mouth, she and Larry quickly got out of the car.

Hank Jeffrey could have been Larry's twin brother if each man's physical build was compared. But they were as opposite as any Republican and Democrat, liberal and conservative, could get.

"I hope I haven't broken up any neighborhood hanky-panky," Hank said. "After all, I'm usually the very first to know these things so that I can repeat it around the neighborhood." He laughed so hard his Orange Crush cap slid off.

"Glad you're still able to stimulate yourself," Inez said angrily.

"I, for one," Larry said, "am glad to see ya'. Thought I was going to be buried alive in the belly of the Denver jail and never see anybody ever again." Larry pumped Hank's hand up and down, as if he truly meant it.

"I'm so sorry for your loss," Hank replied, still holding on to Larry's hand. "How'd it happen? The missus and I had just gotten back into town and listened to Inez's message on our phone."

The street was deserted as the three of them stood under a much darker sky. Inez could see glistening signs of tears welling in Larry's eyes.

"Nobody knows," he said. "Billy found him for me."

"You mean that colored boy that's always hangin' round here?"

"No!" Inez answered quickly. "He means Billy Needam, the African-American young man who I've employed for the past two years as my IT guy. You've met him on several occasions."

She hoped the poison in her voice matched Hank's poisonous rhetoric. If the sneer on his face was intended to scare Inez, it didn't work. She knew Hank kept his brain hidden in his biceps and was glad Hank hadn't ever stooped so low as to spit his tobacco onto her property because Inez didn't know what she'd do to him. He was like the Marlboro man, with a lynch rope visibly attached to his waist, never intended for cattle.

"Billy's okay," Larry said to Hank. "He buried Arnold where he found him, up under a bush on the Parkway. But I dug him up a few minutes ago and put him in my own backyard, where he belonged. Billy told me he'd seen Arnold digging in the Parkway before the blizzard, as if he was trying to dig something up. Arnold kept little stashes of stuff buried all around here. He got out of the house the minute the police came. Billy's a good kid, if you ask me."

"Well, I am sorry, too, Larry," Inez added.

"I know it's a hard thing to get over," Hank added. "But actually I've been trying for months to talk to both of you."

"Then let's go inside," Inez suggested, "and do our talking over a cup of coffee. I need help with all these groceries, and I can pay both of you with a decent cup of my favorite pecan coffee."

"That's not a bad deal," Hank said.

Inez paused behind her car to single out the front-door key from the others, while out of the corner of her eye she noticed a car in the street slow to a crawl. Was it slowing to look at Larry's place or hers? Its windows were dark, but a small emblem near the license plate told her it was a rental. As quickly as it slowed down, it sped up again, disappearing around the corner.

She looked at the two men, who had also stopped to look at the car. "Did we scare off a suitor Inez?" Hank asked. "Must be the person all these groceries are for. Agnes and I don't eat this much in a single month."

"Let's get inside," Inez said, ignoring his comments. She suddenly felt a chill at her neck. Were Gaelen's killers still around? But why? And if they used a rental car, were they from out of town or from a different country?

She was happy to have company and as soon as the coffee was made the three of them sat around the kitchen table to drink and talk. She told them what had happened two nights ago at the restaurant and about what happened at Sheila and Karen's townhouse. They were reverently silent through her entire recitation.

A long time passed before Larry spoke. "I told the story about the night Gaelen died maybe a hundred times yesterday, but I didn't tell it all. I was too scared. I was drunk that evening. You see, two months earlier, Karen told me she was pregnant."

He stopped talking and looked at Hank and Inez, as if asking for help. But there was a long silence again, until Hank suddenly understood the connection and Inez could only glare at him.

"Aw naw, naw," Hank finally said, pushing his chair back, raising himself up from that chair, and then sitting back down again.

"She could be your daughter," Hank pleaded. "If Gaelen had known, he'd a' killed you. Don't think he wouldn't have. That's the kind of man he was."

Inez nodded in agreement, sickened by what Larry was saying.

"Anyway, she wasn't," Larry said. "I collapsed and fell off the wagon. I had successfully talked myself into wanting that baby. That was the day Gaelen died. That day, Karen found me in a bar on Colfax, poured coffee down my throat, and said she'd made some decisions. Said she intended to tell her dad about those decisions. But the more sober I got, the more I wondered if she wasn't pregnant after all. So I intended to stand up to Gaelen and tell him what I'd done, because as God is my witness, I love Karen Drisco."

"Shut up, man," Hank shouted.

"Instead, I came home and passed out. When I woke up, a police car was across the street. I ran over there and found Gaelen dead and Karen claiming he'd had a heart attack."

Hank looked at his empty coffee cup and shook his head. Inez hurried to fill it in order to keep this politically incorrect cowboy seated and listening in the name of righteousness to Larry's tired urban tale. She felt some part of Larry was hoping his neighbors would say, 'That's okay, Larry, we understand.' But Inez didn't understand, and bless his rednecked hide, neither did Hank. Larry was maybe sixty years old. And Karen couldn't have been much over twenty-four.

Like dark clouds, their thoughts hung over the kitchen. Inez finally looked at Larry and asked, "So what did you see when you got inside Gaelen's house that night?"

"You mean did I see a crime scene?" He took a gulp of coffee, perhaps wanting Inez to fill his cup too, but she didn't move.

"Like I told the cops," Larry said, "I didn't think so at the time. There was no blood. I figured it had to be a heart attack. I was hung over anyway. I remember Karen packing some of Gaelen's belongings into one of his suitcases. That's why she didn't want to talk to me, I guess."

"Geez, her father just died," said Inez.

"What things?" Hank asked. Both Larry and Inez were surprised by the question.

"Things she must have wanted," Larry answered.

"That's just it," Hank said. "That's the reason I've been trying to get hold of one of you. About a month before Gaelen died he asked to borrow my camera. Well, I've got several. But I'd just purchased one with exceptional resolution. I paid two-thousand dollars for it. And that's the very one Gaelen wanted to use, because he was trying to sell something on eBay. He wanted people to see its quality magnified."

"eBay? What did Gaelen know about eBay?" Larry asked.

"A lot," Hank replied. "He'd been learning how to upload photos and answer email. I helped him buy a laptop the year before. Told me not to mention it to anybody."

"Why that old mule!" Inez declared. "Gaelen swore he was going to live out his days without ever receiving or sending one piece of e-mail."

"Surprised me, too," Hank said. "But Gaelen claimed getting on eBay would solve all his problems. I asked him what problems, thinking if it was money, I could certainly loan him some. And he said it was nothing he couldn't handle."

"So you loaned him your two-thousand-dollar camera?" Inez already knew the answer and felt sorry for Hank as she asked him.

He sighed deeply.

"I'm sorry, Hank," she said. "According to Sheila, there was a camera in the luggage Karen took away from his house. I can only assume it was your camera."

Hank smiled.

"There's nothing to be happy about," Inez insisted. "That suitcase, with the camera inside, went missing from Karen and Sheila's townhome along with Karen, her car, and Gaelen's old vacuum cleaner."

Inez felt she'd just told Hank that John Wayne had died. His whole body shriveled. But she didn't care. She had more questions to ask.

"Did you see what Gaelen was hoping to sell on eBay?" she asked.

"That's funny," Hank finally said. "I followed him around his house, set up his laptop in a downstairs bedroom, and peeked in all his closets. Even asked him straight out, but he said he wasn't free to tell me."

"I wonder," Inez said. "Maybe you've discovered the motive behind Gaelen's murder."

Hank reared back in his chair and asked, "You believe he was murdered for my camera?"

She didn't say anything but shrugged her shoulders.

Larry banged his fist down on the table. "Get this straight! Gaelen was not murdered! And the police don't think so either!"

"Really?" Inez asked sarcastically. "So what *do* they think? That you murdered Karen?"

Larry didn't answer at first, then looked up at the ceiling, as if to prevent tears from rolling down his face.

Hank reached across the kitchen table and smacked Larry's shoulder hard. "We know you didn't kill Karen. Why, you couldn't kill the Vietnamese. You can't even kill that swarm of ants that keeps coming back on your walkway every year. Arnold had to do that for you. You pussy! Think you're gonna be indicted for murder? In your dreams."

Before Hank could stand up, Inez interjected, "And Karen isn't dead. At least I don't think so. Don't ask me how I know. But I know that she's like so many girls I've taught; she's simply trying to find her way in the world."

"I don't know what you're talking about, Inez," Larry said, "because Karen is no little girl anymore. But I sure hope you're right, because there's a big black detective downtown, a former Vietnam veteran, who claims he knows I killed her and that it's just a matter of time till I'm on death row."

Larry put his hands over his face while Hank and Inez sat in silence for a long time.

Finally, Inez spoke to Larry just above a whisper. "I know you understand this better than Hank. We've marched in the same civil rights demonstrations. If you were black, you wouldn't be here in my kitchen now, black detective or not. You should at least be thankful you're white. Otherwise you'd be in jail. The FBI would have been called in on this case and a court date would have been set. You'd be lying on your cot trying to heal from wounds a judge and lawyer wouldn't be able to see through your clothing. You've got a lot to be thankful for."

Hank stared at his coffee cup.

Inez continued talking. "There are too many moving parts here for you to be considered the lone perpetrator of a kidnapping, and there's an ambiguous cluster of activity, suggesting that several things may be related."

Hank finally stood up and pushed his chair in. He turned to Inez and said, "I don't think Gaelen ever had anything worth as much as my camera."

"I'm sorry, Hank," she said. "So what *were* you going to do with a two-thousand-dollar camera, anyway?"

"Gather optronic intelligence. Private militaries occasionally ask me for help. That lens could see a bead of sweat on a mouse."

Inez sat up tall in her chair, surprised by both his answer and his knowledge.

Hank then turned to Larry and said, "You get yourself a good lawyer. He'll get you off."

Inez stood up slowly saying, "Arnold was killed because he smelled, heard, or saw something we humans missed around here when Gaelen was murdered."

Hank took one step back to sneer at her. "You've got quite an imagination on you girlie."

Girlie! How could I have taken Hank's side on anything? But who gathers intelligence "optronically"?

Eventually the men stepped outside into the cold night air. Only then did Inez ask Hank the question she yearned to know about. "Why are you gathering intelligence?"

"Used to be Military Intelligence before I retired. You probably paid it no mind when I mentioned it at one of those block parties of ours. I also did a few rotations as a soldier of fortune. You knew that, didn't you?"

Funny how your mind shuts out what you hear from someone you don't trust.

She nodded and quickly shut the door behind them. Inez had learned a lot. It never made sense that Gaelen, a man of modest means, already knew the appraised value of his house before he'd been asked for money. He must have gotten something appraised, and if it was worth the value of his house, two-hundred-thousand-dollars, he could sell it, give Miriam the money she needed, and stay out of a retirement home.

Yet why couldn't Gaelen tell anybody about it? Was it stolen? Then how could he sell it on eBay? She'd need to learn more about his war record and his years as a young man.

Inez remembered Shakey Martin, a former student who told her, "If it came from my neighborhood and it looks like marijuana and heroin, it's more likely to be oregano and salt. Those things can make you just as dead. Like holding a toy pistol at a cop."

Maybe this wasn't about the theft of an expensive camera. Maybe this was about the thing the camera was supposed to take a picture of.

And then there was Karen. Inez wanted to see local Red Cross financial records to verify her hunch. She wondered if Billy would come over at short notice to help with research. Was the predominantly white section of Park Hill really any safer than his? And who had been driving that car out front?

CHAPTER 15

HARRY MITCHELL'S TOOTHBRUSH was in his mouth, but he paid no attention to its vibration. He stared into the mirror, hypnotized by his own image.

His eyes were suddenly important. Yesterday Jaime Howard told him so—that his eyes were beautiful, the color of honey, that they looked as if they could see inside a person's soul. The longer Harry stared, the more he wondered if she'd been making fun of him.

What was she really telling him? He'd known her since elementary school. She didn't make fun of people then. That's what made her special. Maybe high school was different.

Maybe having beautiful eyes wasn't a good thing for a guy anyway. Was Jaime telling him she knew he liked her? No secret there. Was this her way of telling him she liked him back, liked him better than a friend maybe? He finally turned his toothbrush off.

At five in the morning, his house was dark except for the bathroom he'd occupied for the past hour. After switching the light off and opening the door, he tiptoed past his parents' bedroom on one-hundred-year-old floorboards.

Had Jaime noticed his eyes last year when he was a sophomore and just hadn't said anything until now? If he had learned anything last year about girls, it was that his lettered wrestling jacket caught their attention more than his eyes.

Moonlight streamed through his bedroom curtains while he pulled up his raggedy jeans over raggedy briefs. Cleaning refrigeration units was filthy work, requiring filthy clothes. He'd done it before, so he knew how to dress. If he started early enough, he'd have the rest of the day to himself. Almost forgot his Wellingtons. He'd need them, even if they were getting snug.

So, would his eyes ever get bigger like the rest of his body? He was pumping iron daily. Would Jaime think his eyes were expressive next year? Enough! He'd call her later and ask her straight out if she wanted to be his girl.

He put on his jean jacket, the one with extra fleece, before locking his sleeping parents safely inside their Capitol Hill home. Holding his Wellingtons against his chest with one hand, he grabbed his skateboard off the front porch. A cold wind told him to button up. But a closed jacket said he was a prick. He sailed across Vine Street till he reached the alley.

Purposefully, he stepped off his board and carried it down the entire alley because old lady Shepherd would call his mom, even in the middle of the night, if he made noise passing her bedroom windows. Even so, he couldn't resist throwing a pebble against her fence. When he reached the sidewalk, he dropped his board, flipped it over a curb, and began his cruise down Colfax toward Downing.

An early morning wind against his face made his ride crisp and satisfying. Through squinting eyes against the wind, he watched the steeple atop East High School get closer, letting his thoughts veer from urban legends about that tower to nearby busboys singing a Spanish rap.

It was 5:35 a.m. Call him crazy, but he was looking forward to being alone, music blasting, doing a man's heavy work, building more muscle, and getting paid for it. He could see his uncle's car parked out front before he reached the store. Police never ticketed it, out of courtesy. It was also a warning to thieves that someone could be inside the grocery. To Harry it simply meant his uncle was driving one of CBI's undercover vehicles. Yet he half hoped his "Unca Tray" would be inside, crashed out on the cot in the back room to keep him company.

He was coming up quick into the back alley. He'd perfected a swift maneuver to get in through the back door after using the keypad and before the audible alarm went off. On the edge of his wheels, he sped around two corners of Organic Mercantile, flipped the board up with his toe, wrapped it under his left arm along with his Wellingtons, punched in the code with his right hand, opened the door with his left, took a giant step inside, all the while turning to the right to snatch the inside handle and shut the door behind him. But in those last few moments, as he pivoted to pull the door shut, he shuddered.

His short-term memory told him he'd just seen, in one nanosecond, the eyes of a man in a black ski mask, looking dead into his eyes, from about nine feet away. It was cold, but not ski-mask cold. The man had been close, but apparently not close enough to get inside behind him. Or had he imagined the whole thing?

It was dark out. Harry faced the door he'd just closed. Without his hands touching it, the latch was rocking, as if someone on the other side was pulling it to determine if it had caught. Or had the wind pushed it? Harry's heart leapt to his throat. He could open it and find out, or he could look out the plate glass side of the store.

He rushed through the back office past the empty cot, to the front. There was plenty of glass to see both ends of the street. More than a few people were running to catch the number fifteen bus. Would the masked man be one of them? Had he removed his mask? Was he still behind the building? There were no windows back there. Damn.

Dull lights had been left on in the store all night, as they had every night, so police could see inside as they drove down Colfax. The sun would be up soon and he could turn them off. Maybe the masked man decided not to break in after all.

Harry shifted his eyes instinctively to the counter where the rifle was hidden. His tension subsided. No one, not even a professional sprinter, could beat him to that gun. Anyway, a full ten minutes had passed. He was ready to start work. All he needed to do was take his jacket off.

An ear-deafening crash of falling glass from the skylight above pressed down on him, knocking him to the floor spread-eagle. Jagged pieces of glass and plaster surrounded him. He was in a position a champion wrestler couldn't accept for long. Quicker than he could spit, he humped up on all fours, forcing the object, whatever it was, to slide off him.

The object, a medium-sized man wearing a black ski mask, jumped to his feet and grabbed him from behind with a head hold that Harry knew could kill. Harry's back was arched and immobile, his chest thrust forward by the force of the man's arm on his neck.

An instant message pulsated through his brain: not a tournament, win to live, live to win. His jacket minimized the man's hold, protecting his neck from the full grip of his arm. Harry knew he'd need to jerk into, rather than away from, the intruder's hold before the man contemplated using any of the pieces of glass strewn everywhere.

He hurled himself into the man's chest, then bounced off to complete a rolling somersault down the aisle of broken bottled salad dressing. Unfortunately, the intruder traveled the distance with him. Harry grabbed the man's throat in the same way he'd been grabbed. Forehead to forehead, the two squeezed hard against the other's windpipe till each could feel the pain. Neither would let the other move back to head butt; thus they created a deadly dance back and forth against pickle barrels and crashing produce bins.

Harry caught a whiff of something strong, like a tobacco smell oozing from the intruder's pores. The smell increased his pain. Simultaneously they released each other's neck and pushed back off the other's shoulder blades.

With distance between them, Harry scampered on all fours toward the checkout counter and the rifle behind it. But the man was just as quick; scampering with him, pulling at Harry's shoes first, then his jacket, till he was on top again.

It was a bad move, Harry realized too late, and if he ever got this man off him again, he vowed he'd stand his ground rather than try to reach that gun. It was no slogan. He was in a fight for his life.

Desperately, he tried to move, but in vain. The man's arm length, he was guessing, was at least a half-inch shorter than his own. Again, an odor from the man's clothes and skin made Harry dizzy. But he could taste his own adrenaline and knew he had it in him to conquer the bastard no matter how bad he smelled.

The man's hold, though not life threatening, continued to mash Harry against the floor while slightly pushing him forward. He spied a broken shard on the floor to the side of him, halfway hidden under a mound of mayonnaise. The man, Harry supposed, was trying to slide him away from it. Perhaps he too had noticed the difference in their arm lengths.

The floor was slippery. Harry's Wellingtons could have given him an advantage, if only he'd put them on. Maybe his rubber-soled shoes would work just as well. He shot his left arm out toward the shard, hoping for a similar move from his assailant. Instead the man used his fist to pound Harry's left kidney. Sharp excruciating pain spread through Harry's body, taking his breath away and giving his opponent an opportunity to get a death grip on Harry's neck. His eyes teared up from back and shoulder pain.

"Where eez Meetchell?" the man whispered in his ear.

Harry's heart muscle froze. He couldn't have answered if he wanted to. He could barely swallow and the man must have sensed it because he let up very slightly on his hold so that Harry might speak. Fear turned to action. That one move gave Harry the fraction of an inch he needed.

Twisting with lightning speed, but only moving an inch, Harry faced him. With a freed left fist, Harry sent a blow as hard as he could against the man's skull. The man's muscles shrank, which again gave Harry a looser grip and he was able to turn completely around. The positions had reversed now.

Harry got up on one massive and squarely balanced knee, as he held the intruder's head between his muscular hands and nailed his body between his legs. The intruder slapped wildly at Harry's pants and then his testicles, a feeble last move from a man with a shorter arm length. Harry barely felt the cold wet swipes across his own lower body. Swiftly and with every ounce of his strength, he twisted the man's neck until it cracked. He jumped up, letting the intruder's listless body smack the wood floor as dead weight, the sound of cracking bone still resonating in Harry's head.

With hands over his ears, he stood over the body, shutting out a ringing sound that wouldn't stop. His heart pounded against his entire frame. The store spun. He stared at the impossible position of the man's neck. The contents of Harry's stomach, in one painful hurl, splattered across the floor. He fell to his knees and shook uncontrollably. Only then did he see his waist, his pants, his thighs, drenched in blood. And then he noticed the shiny blade near the dead man's hand.

Fighting wooziness, he went flat onto the floor, as if some large hand mashed him down. He slithered on his back, barely lifting his head, to reach the landline in the back room. His opponent's last goal had been to gut him. That much he understood, as he cradled the receiver to his ear. Looking at the ceiling, all he wanted to do was sleep.

CHAPTER 16

JANUARY 2007   CHINA, YUNNAN PROVINCE

OR DAYS, XIAO and Karen pedaled over rocks and climbed mountains
with their bikes on their backs. At night they slept on roads that, in some
places, held boulders over a meter high. Xiao's body hurt, particularly his
back shoulder area. There was nothing he could do about whatever had
caused his back pain. It must be connected to what happened on the roof
of the palace. His lungs burned as well. He'd been off his bike for the past
half hour and stretched out on dry grass.

Two expensive all-terrain bikes lay in a heap beside them. Karen slept,
her body tucked into a ball of scorched skin covered in the same dusty
frayed cotton outfit she'd worn when they first met. Xiao had traded his
satchel for a huge backpack, while Karen carried a smaller one. They were
not going to make it to Lijiang by nightfall as planned.

Fear of everything kept Xiao awake more than he slept. They were on
a frontage road about forty meters from a six-lane highway. Weary drivers
with huge night beams on cargo trucks were headed for Vietnam and Laos.
Xiao fought back images of being turned into road kill.

Karen's hair, now dyed as black as his, blew gently across her face. He'd
wake her soon. Though her skin had peeled around her nose and forehead
and her bare arms displayed bug bites and bloody welts from low-hanging
branches, he still found her pretty.

They'd been extra cautious, Xiao thought. Using the credit card, they
rented a car and left it outside Erinhot, hoping Quan would think they
were traveling in the opposite direction. Xiao wanted him to believe they

were crossing into Mongolia. Flat on his back, he stared at Jade Dragon Snow Mountain and smiled at its illusion of snow hanging suspended in air. He'd seen photos in *National Geographic*.

Xiao was in a part of China he'd longed to see ever since watching a snowbound Ronald Coleman trudge across the Himalayas on late-night TV. Shangri-la would never look anything like Hollywood's version. But he longed to see an entire ancient village hidden in the mountains away from civilization.

Noise and wind from the highway were constant, but a loud pop from what Xiao thought was a gun made him sit straight up. It was a backfiring vehicle, a rickety putong che with a surprise in front, an empty bicycle rack under its front windshield. Could he entice the driver to stop? He was just as slow standing up as the bus was in its travel down the road. Xiao fell, his knees collapsing under him.

Karen woke with a groan and was slow to move, still partially asleep. The bus, which had slowly passed them, came to a complete stop about sixty meters away. The driver jumped out, hollering that his passengers were treating him like a fool. They wanted him to see what was the matter with the two people on the ground. But when Xiao explained that he could pay for their ride to the nearest major town, the driver suddenly became gleeful and helped them lift their bicycles onto the rack.

The ride to Lijiang was long. They sat on wooden seats with no padding. There were constant stops through towns on the sides of mountains with no guardrails. Karen stayed awake, entertained by a chubby, pink-cheeked baby boy whose mother bounced him on her lap. Satisfied Quan wouldn't have put spies on this particular bus, Xiao fell into a coma-like sleep for the first time since their journey began. When the bus finally spurted to a stop at the Lijiang station, Xiao woke disoriented and embarrassed that he'd permitted himself such a dangerous luxury.

"C'mon," he told Karen. He grabbed her arm while jumping to his feet.

Why was she still holding that baby, even as he shoved past passengers to get to the door? Wanting to get to their bikes before anyone could steal them, he finally snatched the baby from her hands and tossed it over the heads of the other passengers. He had thrown the baby suddenly and silently in mid-air toward the biggest woman still seated, near the middle of the bus. Karen gasped. He squeezed both her arms and literally carried her off the bus.

Much relieved, he released her arm and stood in front of the unmolested bicycles. Some time passed before he realized she was cursing him, in public, as other people, some of whom spoke English, gathered around. He listened to the tone in her voice as he drank water from the canteen attached to his backpack. She sounded like hundreds of his relatives engaged in what they did best.

After he lifted the bikes from the rack, he led both of them away from the bus to the far side of the station, saying nothing. Karen followed, continuing to rant, sometimes pacing back and forth around him until she plopped to the ground, lotus style, and sobbed loudly into her hands.

Xiao put the bikes down in the dust beside them and quietly sat next to her. He had no idea how long she cried, but the sky was preparing for nightfall. Had he fallen asleep? Karen had sprawled across the ground, still crying. He finally took off his pack and dug inside it. Eventually, he pulled out two granola bars and dangled one in front of Karen's face. She stopped crying and sat up. Grabbing it, she ravenously tore the wrapper off and ate.

When they'd both finished eating, Karen said, "You could have killed him."

Xiao's face twisted as if in pain. "I don't really care for children. I'd never thought about it before today, but I don't like them. They're mean and require constant attention. My brothers and sisters, all except my oldest sister, were very mean when we were children. They . . ."

"How can you *say* that," Karen asked. "He was just a baby! What will you do when you have babies of your own?"

He looked at her, not comprehending her words. She stood up to blow her nose into a piece of toilet tissue she'd taken from her pack. He stood up, too.

"I don't ever want babies!" he said sternly. "I want you!" He drew her close to him and kissed her passionately.

She kissed him back with gentle affection. "Silly," she said. "I want you, too. But we can have it all. We could live well here. I know. Let's splurge tonight. We'll go to a four-star hotel to soak away the dirt and heal our wounds."

"That works," he said eagerly. "Oh did I forget to tell you? We have nothing to splurge with." They laughed together and walked arm in arm, their bicycles beside them, unsure of where they were headed.

Even in this remote oasis of spectacular views and preserved shops, China prepared for the Olympics. Hotel construction was everywhere.

Xiao felt comfortable here. There were far fewer people around in late evening. Xiao and Karen felt they looked and dressed the same way the villagers did. Only a few wore colorful native costumes, and no one stared.

Maybe Quan had given up looking for them. Just how important could they be? They were separated from Beijing by kilometers of difficult terrain, mostly traveled by China's indigenous people.

The couple found a very small place to eat at the corner of what looked like a merchant's house with his lights left on. The merchant was eager to cook for them and refused to take money until they had eaten. Behind the house, the man said, were rooms he rented to good people for a modest price. No coaxing was necessary. After their meal, they did not awake until late the next afternoon.

**

Xiao rose suddenly. He'd been troubled during the night by a dream with a chorus of voices that spoke a nasal language he didn't understand. A giant calendar, not quite as tall as Mt. Everest, withstood strong, cold winds. Its monolithic pages hung like a Salvador Dali painting. Instead of a large number, a giant snowflake took up most of the calendar's page, and Xiao felt compelled to count the number of spikes in the snowflake to determine the date. But he didn't want to know the date. Finally, he ran away from the giant calendar.

Now awake, Xiao sat on the side of the bed and began counting everything in the room. He counted each item on their bikes as well. An hour passed, and Karen had not moved. He wondered how she could sleep through all the noise from the voices in the room next to theirs, as well as his own counting.

A sudden curious feeling made him decide to search his backpack for the passports Kee had given him. How peculiar, he thought, that the name on her passport, Karen Drisco, should be the very name she had changed hers to. How would Quan have known? The photograph was also strange. It must have been taken when Karen was asleep, making her look more dead than alive.

He walked to the other side of the bed and stared at Karen to make sure she wasn't dead. Her chest moved slowly, and he began imitating the rhythm of her breathing. Gradually, he felt at ease again and put the passports back into his pack.

The gun Kee had given him was still there. Carefully, while the gun was still in his pack, he pulled back its trigger housing, noting that it was indeed loaded. Today was the seventh day since he'd seen Kee. Was Quan waiting until her last day before looking for them? Was their verbal contract still in effect?

Nervously, he put the gun away and slid the backpack under the bed. Not wanting to wake Karen, he dressed quietly. While his voices questioned him. How could he stay alive? Who would care if he shot her as she slept? He sat on the edge of the bed and looked at her.

If he could survive his own family, surely he could evade Quan. He reached across the bed and pulled back the curtains at the only window in their room. Faces passing by on their way to and from work were faces that looked like his. If they could find a place to live among all of these ethnic minorities, the Naxi, the Masu, and the Dong, many of whom questioned the authority of the People's Republic with regularity, then maybe he and Karen could flourish here. But to survive he'd need Karen's strength. He put his hand in his pocket and felt the business card in the shape of a human hand. He'd also need the help of the woman who gave him that card.

Karen's eyes fluttered open.

"Get dressed," he said. "We'll get something to eat and talk about the next ten years. We'll turn ourselves into impoverished but colorful local inhabitants. Right now the locals look as if they eat better than we do. Like Sichuan, Yunnan province is known worldwide for its cuisine. And yet . . ."

Her head lay on a cotton pillowcase. Tears rolled down her cheeks and onto the cloth beneath her.

He stopped talking when he saw the stains. "What did I say?"

"You goofball." She cried and laughed at the same time, then sat up in bed with her arms stretched out to wrap around his neck. "You're such a handsome devil."

Did she really mean it? He didn't care. She couldn't see him beaming while they embraced and that was just as well. He'd do anything to keep her feeling this way. He'd be fine if he could hide his voices, his lapses of memory, his confusion over little things.

"Why don't you take a walk around the village? See what there is to see and I'll wash up and get dressed before we have that talk. Take a long walk because I think I may have to pump the water and heat it, before I can wash with it," she said.

He wondered for a moment. She knew he'd return to her, but would she be here when he got back? He could hear confidence in her voice. Wouldn't she try to leave? She hadn't tried last night.

"Okay," he said. " In an hour I'll meet you in front of that place around the corner where we ate last night."

Xiao left out the back door of the place after saying good morning to the owner and thanking his family for their hospitality. They smiled in return.

He was curious about the entire village, and the day was warm. He'd only taken two steps outside when he noticed he was surrounded by a large stone courtyard with a stream of rushing water at the far end of it. It was like standing inside a picture postcard.

There were tourists at the stream, most likely from Beijing, who stood arguing over whether the water was clean enough to drink. About fifty paces across from him stood an elderly man dressed stylishly in a brown cap and the blue jacket of the Naxi people. His neck and mouth were wrinkled, making him appear somewhere between fifty and one hundred years old. The man looked at Xiao for some time. Xiao turned away to walk through the nearest butong. The man followed, calling out to him in English. Xiao quickened his steps.

"Sir," the man yelled. "I was afraid you were going to sleep away a second day. I want to introduce myself. My name is Meng, and I want to be your guide."

Xiao was almost running. The man's English disturbed him. It was not a British accent. He turned his head and called back to the man. "We don't need a guide, thank you."

"Please excuse this humble servant. I do not wish to tell you what you need. I simply . . ."

Xiao stopped in his tracks and asked, "Where did you ever learn English like that?"

The man was beside Xiao now. Silver-gray hair jutted from beneath his cap and yet he was not out of breath. "I sound like I'm from the Library of Congress."

"What do you mean?"

"*National Geographic* came here, several years ago. Ten years ago, I believe. They documented my people, kept track of our growth, brought books and a teacher who stayed in the mountains with us."

"Quan sent you here, didn't he?" Xiao began walking again, trying to decide when to begin to run.

"I know nothing of this Quan. I am no man's emissary."

Something in the light in his eyes told Xiao the man was speaking truth. Yet the intensity of his brow could also mean he was a gifted liar. There was no doubt he was an educated man and physically strong. Xiao inhaled uneasily, realizing his quest was as much to stay alive as to find happiness. He stared back into the elder's eyes. There was no smile and no anger in him, only confidence.

"Tell me," Xiao asked, "where could I find the meal of a lifetime? I have little money." To prove it, he pulled nuts and bolts from his pockets that he'd used to fix his bicycle. There were no coins in his hand.

Clouds intermittently hid the sun, while the man spoke with clarity. "In two hours, I will bring horses straight to the place where you slept last night. Our journey to a lodge in the mountains is only one hour away by horse. But I must get there and come back for you. The people of my village are famous for their cooking. I will leave you now in order to return quickly. You will tell your grandchildren of this meal."

"I will never have grandchildren," Xiao remarked. "How do you know of me?"

Meng turned toward Jade Dragon Snow Mountain and jogged slowly in order to speak to Xiao. "I know you because I'm the baby's uncle."

"What baby?" Xiao hollered back. There was no answer. The man was jogging faster now and had traveled farther away. Xiao turned to walk back to their room, when he suddenly remembered what baby the man must have been referring to. Immediately, he switched his direction. He began searching for the most expensive hotel he could find.

CHAPTER 17

W IND PUSHED AT Xiao's back, helping him to increase his speed. He ran from one hotel to another, realizing that the baby's uncle might intend to do him harm. What if this Meng was also one of Quan's agents? Yet babies were evil. He spoke aloud in English as he ran. Babies robbed families of all affection. Babies demanded everything. And those demands helped them stay alive. No one had ever paid as much attention to him as Karen and no infant would ever take that away from him.

Breathing heavily, he stopped running. What he wanted was in front of him, a hotel with an unusually large lobby. Against one wall were computers and telephones that were wired in straight rows across several tables. Tourists were seated in front of some of them. As he entered, he noticed two people had their suitcases with them and appeared to be making travel arrangements. Xiao purposefully sat down beside a man who had a briefcase on the floor and a small leather case on a table beside the computer he was using. The case was filled with what Xiao could see were USB drives. He sat beside the man and turned a computer on in front of him. A glance at the front desk told him he would have to hurry because one person behind the counter eyed him suspiciously—or was it his own paranoia?

One of the man's plugs had the words Magik Jack on its side. What a great idea, Xiao thought. When no one was looking, he put it into his pocket. He then rearranged the wiring at the back of the computer in front of him. When he rebooted, he was able to get online without the hotel's password. Shortly, the man next to him got up and left.

Xiao pulled out the unusually shaped business card of a woman named Dr. Inez Buchanan. She'd offered a helping hand to scholarship recipients on their way to China. This time she said hello on the second ring.

"I'm Dr. Wren Xiao. You won't remember me, but three years ago you handed me your business card. It said I could call you about troubles a friend back home in the States might understand. At first, I thought you were there just for the African-American students, but you handed me a card, too."

"I'm not sure I remember *you* in particular, since I hand them out to anybody that might need one, regardless of race. But you obviously have such problems now or you wouldn't have called. Hope I can be of help."

"That evening, years ago, I told you that a doctor at my university said . . ."

"What university was that?" she interrupted.

"Stanford. Dr. Jab said I displayed a subtype of schizophrenia. You said —"

"Yes, I remember you now. I said you looked like you were handling it well. I remember because you said nothing more to me after that. You wouldn't even look me in the eye again that evening. That was my first indication that the campus doctor could have been correct in his diagnosis, not that I'd know, mind you. Is that the trouble you've called about? Your schizophrenia?"

"Maybe . . . maybe it's at the heart of the matter. I'm not sure. I'm calling because Quan Yu is going to kill me if I don't kill an American girl he gave me. One of his agents kidnapped the girl while he was in the United States. Quan then sent a messenger to me named Meng. I think it's because I threw his grandson in the air through the bus. This man Meng will kill me if he has the chance."

Xiao paused and listened attentively to the silence on the other end. "Hello?" he finally asked. "I won't be able to call you again, so I must know what to do now."

"Who is Quan Yu?" Buchanan asked. Her voice was firm yet comforting.

"Head of the Chinese Secret Service, or he used to be. I thought it was an honorary title at first, but former colleagues tell me he still operates out of his old office."

"And who told *them*, I wonder?"

Xiao had no answer.

She was quick to continue talking. "I can tell by your voice that you're making yourself upset. Since childhood, I've always wanted to be a spy. As a teen, I read the exploits of the Office of Strategic Services, the CIA's predecessor. Ordinary people like our parents did very dangerous things in those days to preserve democracy. I'm a little jealous of your opportunity. Maybe you'll wind up working for the CIA. Maybe the CIA told your colleagues to stay away from this Quan. Can you go to the American Embassy?"

"No."

"I can contact the Embassy from here on your behalf, if you'd like. Shall I tell them you want to return home to the United States?"

"Yes," he blurted out, "and with the girl I'm supposed to kill."

Again, Buchanan was slow to answer. "Tell me. Did you find out you weren't Chinese enough to call China home?"

Xiao was surprised by her question.

"I'm sorry if I offended you," she added. "Africans from African nations don't always look at African-Americans as if they trust us. After all, we're Americans now."

"No," Xiao answered. "I'm not offended. I know I'm more American than I thought I was."

"If this man Quan wants you to kill for him, he must want you to spy as well. Should I contact the CIA, too? The agency exists to protect American citizens. And yet I confess that I haven't heard anything about its black, Asian, Egyptian, Indian or any other minority agents. But there must be such people. How else could this country survive assaults from other countries outside our borders? Has Quan asked for your research as well?"

"Not exactly. China wants to create a super race. Such projects abound here. But that was not the reason I passionately studied DNA. Quan's agents have taken over my laboratory to give me time to kill this girl. They could be using it for their own experiments."

"Is there an address where you can be rescued?"

"No."

"Then head for home. Walk over mountains, if necessary. Work for passage on a freighter. Try to cross friendly countries. That way the CIA or any other U.S. intelligence agency has a chance to intercept you and bring you home.

"And I'm worried for you and the girl. Like all of us we wear our race. I wonder how easy is it for someone in your profession to show that you are *not* a spy for China?"

"Don't know. Never had to think about it."

"Seek help from Chinese-American social groups. I'll ask them to look out for you. Freedom isn't free," Inez continued. "We'll always have to fight for a place where the government works for the people and not the other way around. I wish I had more common sense to share, but all I can remember is Paul Laurence Dunbar. 'We wear the mask that grins and lies, it hides our cheeks and shades our eyes—this debt we pay to human guile; with torn and bleeding hearts we smile.'

"You'll have to wear such a mask to get home. But know that whole races and cultures of men and women have had to do the same thing, and many succeeded. There's no reason to ever think you won't."

"I must go." Xiao watched a woman walk toward him. He placed the phone down and walked out the side door of the hotel lobby. He was just about to run when he spied a reflection in the glass window of the hotel. The face watched him exit.

Was he hallucinating? Was it really Bohai, the limousine driver? Was his anxiety controlling his brain? Xiao quickly turned his head around to be certain. But the man was gone, so he ran.

Only a well-trained spy could have followed him, Xiao decided. He began to slow down so as not to create unwanted attention. But what about Meng? Was Meng a spy too?

He'd been gone for not quite an hour when he pulled back the curtain that served as the door to their room. Karen sat on the side of the bed staring out the window. She smiled at him and stood up to greet him.

"I was just about to walk around the corner to meet you," she said.

Xaio fell to his knees beside the bed, his hands frantically searching under it for his backpack. "Good. We'll leave soon," he said.

Finding it, his fingers fumbled with its zipper. Inside a secret compartment was the gun, which he pulled out. She stood directly over him.

"What are you doing with that?" she asked.

He didn't turn to look at her, but swiftly inserted the gun into the back waistband of his pants, hoping its disappearance would make any questions she had disappear just as quickly.

Her nervous eyes targeted him.

"It's insurance," he explained further. "It'll make me feel safer."

"They don't like guns in this part of the world," she ventured.

He lifted his backpack onto a nearby chair, all the while noticing the fear on her face. Her bottom lip trembled and she bit down on it.

"I don't want to frighten you." He placed both his hands on her shoulders.

"Who said I was frightened?" Her chest heaved rapidly, her nostrils widened.

"I'm not going to hurt you, Karen. Ever! We made a deal." He placed the palms of his hands on the side of her breasts. "You said you'd stay with me. You said you meant it."

"I do, I will, I promise."

"Then we have a lifetime of adventure ahead of us. All I ask is that you stay with me no matter what."

Staring into her eyes, he felt her nipples harden under his touch. Would her passion last? She pulled him toward the bed, and his doubts subsided.

But suddenly remembering Meng, he pulled her up and said, "I met a man who says he's the uncle of the baby on the bus."

Her eyes became bigger. Was that a faint smile he saw?

"She's a marvelous woman," Karen said, "the baby's mother, I mean."

"How would you know?" he asked.

"Women know these things."

Her answer ran contrary to the voices in his head. They told him to get away from her and the room they were in now.

"Dress warmly," he said, pulling his own down jacket out of his backpack. "I don't trust this Meng. We need to be gone before he returns."

"Why would he return?"

They heard horses' hooves on the stone walkway outside. Suddenly in the doorway stood Meng with furs wrapped over his shoulders. They were tied with a braided leather cord at his waist. His girth appeared enormous. Xiao slowly eased from the bed and toward the bicycles hoping to reach behind his back unnoticed, for his gun. Karen stood behind Xiao as her cover from this strange-looking man.

"I returned," he said loudly in English, "because you have been invited to the meal of a lifetime. But, what I heard just now tells me you misunderstand my intentions." Meng's eyes rested heavily on Xiao's face, while he made no attempt to come closer.

"Luckily," Meng continued, "I didn't have to go all the way to the top of the first ridge. I caught up to a caravan headed for my village."

As Meng spoke, two other men joined him in the doorway. "That caravan had enough horses for all of us to ride. We breed Himalayan mountain horses because they know these mountains better than those of us born here. These particular horses have been trained to bring you to our village whether you participate or not." Meng smiled, as if he had made a joke.

But Xiao spoke up, "We've changed our minds about tonight. Perhaps you'd like to join us in a meal at a nearby restaurant?"

Meng was cunning, Xiao thought. No man and certainly no horse could be as smart as the horses he described. The loud voices in his head agreed. Finally, Xiao was doing what his relatives wanted. That gave him a bounce to his step as he pranced from one side of the small room to the other.

Meng took two steps into that room, while a tearful Karen grabbed onto Xiao's shirttail. Frantically, she hid behind his constantly moving body.

"I insist!" Meng said to both Xiao and Karen. Meng's smile made Xiao's heart pound faster.

To get a better look at the young woman, Meng leaned sideways. To her, he said, "And your name is …"

"Karen," she answered.

"You, my little one, shall ride with me," Meng announced. "Xiao will ride with my nephews. That way we will travel quickly through terrain that would otherwise be difficult."

"How long will we be gone?" Karen asked.

Meng laughed aloud, obviously pleased with her trusting curiosity. "If we leave now, you'll see the sunset atop our ridge."

Karen smiled warmly at Meng as Xiao looked on, confused by their behavior. He slid back and forth between the two of them, his color turning deep red. But he needn't worry, he told himself. He had a remedy, and he intended to use it.

Finally Xiao pulled out his gun, while two younger men dashed inside their room. These men too, wore furs, and with a quick yet purposeful demeanor, lunged at Xiao. One of them smashed his fist against the young man's chin, sending him backward, and instead of the other one catching him, Xiao's head slammed against the nearest wall. Karen screamed. Still mashed against the wall, Xiao slid to the floor unconscious or dead, leaving a wide trail of blood along the wall. Karen trembled.

Meng approached her gently. "There's nothing to fear," he said. "We will attend to both of you."

The two men picked Xiao up and carried him outside.

"You have my word you both will be safe," Meng continued. "The baby's mother has smiled upon you. She's our matriarch. I know you aren't able to understand or speak our language, but surely you must have known she would send someone to fetch you, my dear?"

"Yes. Somehow, I think I did know," Karen replied.

CHAPTER 18

"TRACE MITCHELL, LINE one," shouted a male voice over rows of desks.

"Yeah?" Mitchell hollered into the receiver.

"Unca Tre . . . ?"

Mitchell jumped up from his swivel chair and reached for his jacket the minute he heard his nephew's voice.

"Where are you, Harry?" Using sign language in front of office staff, Mitchell got someone to get a car ready.

"Store." The boy's whispered voice spoke volumes." . . . killed a man. Jumped down . . . kill me . . . but . . ."

"I'm on it. How bad ya' hurt?"

No answer.

"Harry!" Mitchell shouted. "STAY AWAKE!"

Mitchell dropped the receiver and shouted orders to a room full of CBI investigators as he ran to the elevator. By the time he hit the bottom floor he'd found a driver. By the time they pulled out of the parking lot he'd notified Denver Police and organized a tech team from CBI to meet him at his family's store. Who'd tell his brother? He'd rather eat shit.

All the while, Mitchell replayed Harry's voice in his head. It was tiny, like the little guy Trace used to carry on his shoulders. Organic Mercantile was history, Mitchell vowed. All that self-defense training for Mom, all that weapons training for Harry, and for what? Suppose Mom had been there. Could the world get any nastier? He finally called his brother.

**

Yellow tape at a bus stop across the street meant gawkers had caused a traffic accident, he told himself. A flotilla of police cars surrounding the store meant every Northeast policeman knew a crime had been committed against the family of someone in law enforcement. Officers on foot literally created a blue wall that opened as soon as Mitchell dashed from the agency's car to the front door.

He half expected to see a four-year-old splayed across the floor. Instead he found a broad-chested state high-school wrestling champion, stripped to the waist, revealing a huge patch of bruised blood around his rib cage, a pile of what looked like sawdust covering his abdomen, a neck brace covering his chin, and an oxygen mask hanging near his mouth.

Paramedics raised his gurney. "He shouldn't talk," said one of them. "Vocal chords are damaged, there's extensive internal bleeding. But he'll be fine. It's the dead guy who met his match and then some."

Mitchell tried to smile, but his lips trembled. Even so, Harry motioned to him with his free hand. Tears rolled down the older man's cheeks before he had a chance to turn away. He glanced out the front window in time to see his brother, dressed in pajamas, hop inside the back of the ambulance as Harry was carried out.

Mitchell refused to let himself get emotional again. He scanned the floor for the body. The eyes of three uniformed men, including Ryan, were nailed to the floor in front of them. As Trace approached, he could see the sprawled torso of a man with a broken neck.

Without looking at Trace, Ryan said, "I was about to call you CBI people."

Trace squatted down to look at the body up close and waited to hear Ryan explain why.

"He's got no identifiable clothing labels, no wallet, no gun, no trash in his pockets, no watch, no phone, but he does have a wad of American money—tens and hundreds mostly, totaling two thousand dollars." Ryan kicked at the ball of the dead man's shoeless foot. "He's also got a pedicure and an otherwise Middle Eastern flare to him. Oh, and I almost forgot, a ski mask made out of linen. They don't wear these in Vail, do they?" He didn't wait for an answer. "Naw, I didn't think so."

Another officer held the mask up on the end of a pencil.

"They tell me you can get em in Iraq."

Still squatting, Trace didn't speak. He felt the need to compose himself before he tried.

"Did you notice what happened across the street?" Ryan continued. "Our best theory is a second man was there. Must have noticed the woman seated at the bus stop. She could see directly inside the store from where she was sitting. We think she reached for her cell phone, but maybe not. Anyway, her throat was slashed, and nobody waiting with her saw who did it."

Mitchell stood up to watch outside activity through the windows. Detectives were interviewing witnesses.

"Remember our realtor in Tiffany Plaza?" Ryan asked. "He didn't have a broken neck like this guy. No, he'd been strangled, carotid artery crushed. Only his eyeballs told the story. Anyway, that realtor had similar bruising around his kidney area, like your nephew's wounds. Your Harry fought for his life and won using the same trick. Somebody in Special Forces must have taught him. Good thing, too."

Trace looked at Ryan appreciatively. The aging veteran detective was justifying Harry's barehanded killing. They both knew that nobody at Harry's high school had taught him how to break an opponent's neck. Trace cleared his throat and said, "Thank you. I'll be at the hospital. Keep me posted, will ya'?"

Trace exited the store without a thought about the keys to the front door. The grocery may as well have belonged to the police. They could board it up, leave it open, or burn it down for all he cared.

He got behind the wheel of his car, still parked out front where he'd left it two nights ago. His cell phone vibrated and wouldn't stop. He wasn't about to let anything keep him from driving to St. Joseph's Hospital. A quick look at the caller, Enrique his tech freak, verified that it could wait. But as he pulled into the hospital's parking lot, his personal fear of hearing bad news inside, made him pause for a moment before taking the call.

"Eh, my man," Enrique hollered. "I know this ain't the time, but ain't no time gonna' be the right time." Trace said nothing. "Interpol faxed me photos you need to see. They had that Antonio Dante dude under surveillance all year. Photos show him meeting people in outdoor cafés, soccer games. You name it."

"You're right, Enrique, this isn't the time."

"More than one photo," Enrique continued, "is of one of the chicks you had in the van two nights ago. Remember? You switched on the camera when you switched on the overhead light. Recorded the whole thing. What was her name? Not that old one we took to the airport. Sheila something, wasn't it? I swear Interpol has pictures of she and Antonio lookin' at each other like they need a hotel room. Mitchell you still there? Another thing, Antonio Dante was just one of his aliases. I don't know what name she knew him by, but I can find out."

Mitchell felt like a cream-filled doughnut that had just been squeezed. Sheila Drisco! He looked at the hospital. If Harry died in there, he wouldn't be able to talk or walk for weeks. Maybe he needed to do his job before he found out about Harry's condition. He made a U-turn with enough anger to propel the car into the air.

With the phone still at his ear, he shouted, "I'm headed for Dr. Buchanan's house! That's where Sheila Drisco lives now. Send somebody there to meet me, so I don't beat this chick to a pulp."

"Hey, man," Enrique hollered, "don't make me hate myself."

"Just talkin' trash," Mitchell answered.

"If you want, I can tag the place. We'll get every sound from any part of the house."

"Call you back on that."

CHAPTER 19

M ITCHELL USED HIS fist on Buchanan's front door, bracing himself in the event Sheila opened it. Inez greeted him with a smile and stepped aside for him to enter. He hoped his anger wasn't immediately apparent.

"I thought," Inez said, "you weren't involved with Karen's investigation."

"Where's Sheila Drisco?"

As soon as the door clicked shut, the doorbell rang. Mitchell, who was standing closest to it, yanked it all the way open.

"Hi, everybody." A familiar-looking black boy about eighteen or nineteen took a giant step inside.

Ignoring the young man, Mitchell turned to Inez and shouted, "WHERE IS SHE?"

Both Inez and the boy stood as straight as soldiers. Mitchell could read the surprise and fear on both their faces, their eyes tinged with anger. Worse yet, he recognized that fatalistic disposition in the way Inez slightly tilted her head. Having seen her in action before, he knew she was prepared to die in the foyer of her own home at the hands of a white out-of-control cop. He could already hear it on the ten o'clock news and took a deep breath, wondering if he had it in him to stop himself. But Inez spoke first.

"I've got her new address in the kitchen," she said, turning her back on him in slow motion.

"WHAT NEW ADDRESS?" Mitchell took a long look at the stairs, deciding whether to run to the second floor to see for himself.

Inez froze where she was.

"Oh, that's right, you didn't know." She had turned her head to answer. "Sheila said my house was too close to where her dad died." Again, Inez headed toward the kitchen.

"Is that what she told you?" Mitchell knew he had no reason, other than anger, to talk so loud, but he couldn't calm down quite yet. He followed her.

"Hey!" the boy said. "I've seen you before. It wasn't just on the morning of the snow. You remember that, don't you? You pulled me in here to get verification that I worked here. But haven't I seen you at East High? You've helped out at the wrestling tournaments. Aren't you what's-his-name's...? Yeah, I didn't recognize you the other day. I'm Billy." He put his hand on the agent's elbow to slow him down.

Mitchell swung around, pulling his gun from its shoulder holster with his opposite right hand, wanting to stop, but deciding not to, and knowing he'd better be prepared to use it once it was drawn.

At once, the boy stood motionless, his back against the wall of the dinning room.

Mitchell zeroed in on Billy's face, then read the boy's entire rigid body. Mitchell relaxed his arms slightly. This kid had done nothing more than what any young man might do. But Mitchell could feel the youth's hatred in his tensed muscles, particularly around his mouth, as he kept his face taut. Quickly Mitchell said, "Didn't recognize you at first, Billy," then holstered his gun.

"You look terrible." Inez said. "Coffee?"

It was the voice of a stern schoolteacher, at full throttle. He deeply wanted to apologize but instead said, "Sounds good." He reached out to put a hand on Billy's shoulder but the young man's body bent ever so athletically backward to avoid his touch.

They slowly walked into the kitchen. Billy sat at the table across from him, and leaned in, almost daring him with his eyes, to hurt Inez.

"Could you use a couple of aspirins?" Inez asked.

"I'm good," Mitchell answered too quickly. He unbuttoned his collar and loosened his tie.

Billy started talking. "Dr. Buchanan, you remember Harry Mitchell, don't you? Went to Park Hill Elementary."

Mitchell swallowed hard.

"Naw, second thought," Billy said, "maybe he transferred out before he got to your room."

Mitchell stared up at Inez and asked, "You taught Harry Mitchell?"

"His name sounds awfully familiar," she said, pouring his coffee.

"I may have killed him this morning," Mitchell replied.

Billy shot Inez a quick look and Inez almost let the coffee overflow out of his cup.

"No," Mitchell added, "I don't mean literally." He continued to explain what had just happened to Harry in the early hours of the morning.

"WAY TO GO, HARRY!" Billy shouted, then slapped Mitchell's shoulder hard. "You *know* he's going to be okay, don't you? That champion wrestler's got grit. I've seen him compete at East several times."

Mitchell's shame overwhelmed him. This outburst, from a young man he'd just pointed a gun at, made Mitchell's lips quiver until he quietly lost himself in that kitchen, not caring who saw or heard him. Eventually he gulped coffee, letting his tears flow until he felt Inez Buchanan's hands rub his shoulder and saw Billy nudge a box of tissues closer to him.

Mitchell finally said, "Thank you. Both of you. I'll be okay now."

"I know what it's like to feel naked in front of your neighbors," she said. "It's nothing we don't understand."

To Billy, he said, "I'm sorry, man."

"Sokay," Billy replied.

Mitchell didn't look away, keeping him in his sight to assure him that everything was, in fact going to be okay.

"Almost forgot," Inez said. She got up from her seat, went to what looked like a recipe box and returned with an index card. "Here's Sheila's address."

Mitchell didn't touch it right away but let her place it on the kitchen table. "They were lovers," Mitchell said quietly, "she and whoever Antonio Dante turns out to be."

"WHAT!" Inez shouted. She plopped into the nearest chair, her mouth wide open. The agent's cell phone rang and he answered it.

"Enrique here. We've been trying to determine when Sheila Drisco last talked to Dante. There's no record of a call for the past month. Her last call in the U.S. was made yesterday evening to Dr. Buchanan from DIA, where she boarded a plane to Rome, Italy. Thought you ought to know, since you're with Buchanan now."

"Thanks," Mitchell replied.

Mitchell took out his notebook and searched his pockets with one hand, for a pencil.

"Also," Enrique continued. "Interpol took her into custody as one of Dante's possible accomplices in the Nigerian's death. They didn't know Antonio was dead until today."

Mitchell said nothing during the conversation. When the call was over, Mitchell turned to Inez and spoke decisively. "Sheila called you yesterday. Whatever she said was a lie."

Inez wrinkled her forehead as Mitchell continued, this time picking up the index card from the table. "Sheila boarded a plane for Rome about a minute after talking to you."

Inez pursed her lips. He could tell she was playing chess inside her head, not wanting to incriminate a woman who was like family to her.

"In light of what I just told you," Mitchell said, "you think she killed her father, or had her sister kidnapped? If she wasn't working directly with Dante, when do you think she recognized him? What do you think was going through her head when I interviewed all of you together? Was she crying because she was mourning Dante's death?"

Billy kept shaking his head. "We are *not* talking about Sheila Drisco! She's my homie! She is not involved in anybody's international intrigue. Sheila's just a damn good model, another East High School graduate. Catch her on YouTube."

Inez stared for a long time at both her hands, which rested in her lap. "And what about the vacuum cleaner? Have you found it yet?"

Mitchell chuckled with a haughtiness he immediately regretted. "CBI is pondering Sheila's affiliation to terrorists and you're asking about a vacuum cleaner. Interpol needs to know what to do with her: put her under surveillance, ship her back to Colorado, or make sure she stays locked up in an Italian prison."

Billy was very quiet. The sides of his jaws moved as he clenched his teeth.

Inez sat back in her chair and said, "Sheila didn't kill her father or kidnap her sister. She's no more responsible than you are for what happened to Harry. Last night I investigated local Red Cross financial statements on the internet. They took two female employees off their payroll at the same time. That's right, two! What if the other woman was a friend of Karen's and what if she was the one kidnapped? And what if . . . ?"

"Can't use what-ifs." Mitchell interrupted. "I need evidence. You got proof of anything you're saying?"

"No. I don't yet know why Gaelen was killed," she said, "and I don't know what Gaelen wanted to sell on eBay. But Billy and I intend to visit a man I found on the internet who may have fought with Gaelen in WWII. He lives in the Veterans Home near here."

"Listen!" Mitchell announced. "Here's what we know! Sheila's father died of a heart attack and Karen Drisco is missing. Sounds as if you're playing detective. There's nothing worse in my book than an untrained meddler playing detective because it's a surefire way to get innocent people hurt, if not killed. I have a ring of terrorists to stop and Sheila may damn well be mixed up in it."

"Police," Inez said belligerently, "should stop looking at Larry Carmichael as if he murdered somebody. And if you can do anything to help Sheila, I beg you to try. She's young, naïve, from a supportive neighborhood, and she lives vicariously, not understanding how truly ugly life can be. Can't you bring her home, where her sins aren't going to be life altering?"

"How can you be so confident about her moral intent? She's a grown woman." Mitchell stood up and pulled his phone out of his jacket.

Inez put her hands over his. "You're not listening. Anytime you can forge papers for cremation; buy the victim's house and tear it down overnight; kidnap the victim's daughter, even make her car disappear; kill police officers as if it's nothing; and slit the throat of a dog that may have seen, heard, or smelled something it shouldn't have; then you're big, really big. You're as big as Denver, if not the whole state of Colorado. And when you're as big as a state or some business conglomerate you're not committing murder. You're accomplishing missions, you're reinforcing what you believe. It's your cultural destiny! Who do you know that's that big?

Somehow, Gaelen came to the attention of some large industrial complex, some municipality."

Mitchell took a deep breath. "You're creative. I can say that for you. But you need to leave this to professionally trained people who can sort out the relevant from the irrelevant; people trained to collect and measure physical evidence. Hopefully you can see that all the things you mentioned can't possibly be related."

"Well, I've got your evidence," Billy said. "And I think it's all related."

While still seated, Billy twisted around in his chair, grabbing something out of his jacket pocket. It was black and wet: a mask hung from his fingers, like the one Mitchell had just seen on the end of a pencil inside his family's grocery.

Mitchell sat down under the weight of his thoughts, his phone still in his hands.

"Where'd you get it?" he asked calmly.

"A bone was sticking up where I buried Arnold. Larry must have dug him up after he got back from the police station. When I pulled on the bone, before coming here this morning, this cloth came up with it. I'm sure Arnold buried the bone some time ago, then buried this with it later. I almost forgot I'd brought it with me."

"Put it on the table," Mitchell instructed. He turned to Inez and asked, "You have a plastic bag I could use?"

"Certainly," she answered, getting up and bringing it to him.

"The man Harry killed," Mitchell sighed, "wore one of these."

"Well," Inez said with a huff, "it's that man's employer I'm describing to you."

Billy stared at the thing on the table and said, "Dr. Buchanan's got eyes in the back of her head, you know. That's what they used to say about her when she taught school," Billy warned.

"I believe it," Mitchell answered. "I'm going to take this with me, and if you two don't mind, I'll be back for another cup of coffee soon." He stuffed the mask into the bag and put the whole thing into his breast pocket.

"When you come back," Inez said, "I'll tell you about a young man in China. I could kick myself for not remembering to ask the girl's name but his plight might relate somehow to these incidents. I've already reported it to the CIA. And now I'm not sure I did the right thing."

Mitchell watched her eyes drift into her own world. He felt sorry for her. Sometimes the elderly yearned for the attention they received earlier in life. Perhaps that was why she needed to create bogeymen.

Suddenly his phone rang again and he was thankful. This time he read the text aloud. "Harry's out of surgery. Bleeding stopped. Not as serious as first thought."

"What did I tell ya?" Billy said, with a hard slap on Mitchell's back that sent him an inch forward.

Mitchell grinned, first at the good news and then at Billy's enthusiasm. But as he left Inez's house, he was happy about his newly found freedom. He was now free to convince CBI, the Denver police, and the FBI if need be, to send him to Rome to retrieve little Miss Sheila Drisco, whoever the hell she turned out to be. It was personal now.

CHAPTER 20

MARCH 2007   ROME

MITCHELL BUCKLED HIMSELF into his economy-class seat on Alitalia, wondering if he'd been played, not by one but two masterful women. People seated around him prepared to sleep their way across the Atlantic. It was one in the morning in New York, but he couldn't force his eyelids shut. What did Inez Buchanan really know about damsels in distress? And how could he ever care about an accomplished liar like Sheila Drisco?

As the pilot soothingly entertained passengers over the speakers with small talk, Mitchell replayed the harsh words his boss had used to explain to him that the United States government had no use for the Sheila Driscos of the world. Her return to the States on the government's dime was absurd. The whore of a dead gun-for-hire was old news. Given the opportunity to speak up, she hadn't. Let her rot in a foreign jail, he'd shouted.

Denver police and a district court judge, however, saw it differently. She had, at the very least, become a person of interest in the death of two Denver police officers. And of the three women who witnessed the killings, she was the only one using binoculars. Mitchell had successfully convinced the D.A. that he was the best agent to go get her.

He felt reassured when a CIA agent calling himself Mendalson had, at the last minute before his departure from Denver, presented him with a very small gift, a cardboard box containing cuff links. The agent explained in very direct terms to Mitchell that none of his questions would be answered, but that he could use the cuff links only when he was alone and only in a dire emergency.

Upon landing, Mitchell retrieved his bag from the baggage carousel in Fumicino and walked toward the airport's main lobby. He'd swear, if he needed to, that three out of the last four underwear advertisements along the concourse had Sheila Drisco in them, but that couldn't be true.

He was in a hurry. Which was why he couldn't stop to examine the ads and why he hadn't bothered to carry his gun on this trip. The bureaucratic red tape would have delayed him another whole day. This assignment was supposed to be simple: pick up a cooperating person of interest and escort her back to the appropriate jurisdiction. In no case was this a matter in which he'd need a gun.

Because of the briefing he'd listened to at the office of Interpol's National Central Bureau during his one-hour stopover in Washington DC, it didn't take long for Mitchell to locate the Interpol office inside the airport in Rome. Three men in blue uniforms were waiting for him. The mutual exchange of credentials took place as well as polite introductions inside the outer office. Mitchell was then led through a long corridor to the office of a man in his fifties. He wore a well-made Italian-cut suit, and his name and title were engraved in bronze on his desk. Inspector Vitale Falvo.

When they had finished shaking hands and were both seated, Falvo explained that Sheila Drisco had been interrogated yesterday by Carabinari concerning the depth of her involvement with Antonio Dante, a man born in Greece and old enough to be her father. He explained that Dante used several aliases, passports, and apartments around the world. In the end, her story was convincing; she knew nothing of his life as an assassin and knew him by one name only, Pater Konstantinos.

"She continued to refer to him as Pater. Quaint, no? Says she had no idea he was also this Antonio wanted in Denver until she looked at him through binoculars out her front window in Denver."

Inspector Falvo trilled the only "r" in Colorado, as if it was a talent he'd been born with.

"It won't be the first time a woman was misinformed by her lover. In this case, however, because she is so famous . . ."

"How do you mean, famous?" Mitchell interrupted.

"*Di fama mondiale. Famoso.* Oh, you make a joke signore."

Mitchell waited for an answer in English and when it didn't come, said, "She is not famous in America."

The inspector laughed and leaned forward. "Here, you can see her in her underwear anywhere. Lovely, isn't she? But I don't want you to think we are blinded by her charms. We are not signore."

That was exactly what Mitchell thought.

"She has cooperated with us fully," Falvo said, "and for the time being resides in one of our safe houses across from the Spanish Steps. She is not being held here by any government. Please don't get an idea that is wrong. But you see, though she knows nothing of this man's past, the organization he worked for knows of her well.

"I want to show you something," Inspector Falvo continued, as he took a photo from a folder on top of his desk. He twisted it upside down for Mitchell to see. It was an X-ray of the inside of a handbag. A marker had been used to make a circle around the figure of a key.

"Sheila Drisco rents a small apartment in Paris," Falvo said. "She's lived there ever since she came to Europe five years ago. She showed me pictures of the place and the keys to her apartment there. But she did not go to Paris. Pater Konstantinos, on the other hand, had several lavish apartments. We have accounted for four of them, even the one in Paris. Our intelligence tells us there's maybe one more. We think it's in Rome. It's possible that key in the photo opens it. We have just confirmed that this key does not open his apartment in Paris."

Mitchell continued to stare at it, then said, "I don't know what you're asking here, but as you know, I have papers from a judge in Denver wanting..."

"Yes, I know. Let me continue. She came to Rome in a wig and dowdy clothing, saying she was here to visit her sister. But as of an hour ago, she has made no attempt to reach her sister by phone or in person. We think Konstantinos's apartment is somewhere in the vicinity of the Spanish Steps, which is why we chose a safe house near there. As I said before, we have no reason to keep her here or to confiscate her belongings. Besides, the paparazzi would demand an explanation from us if they knew who she was. We are not prepared to give them such information yet."

"I was hoping," Mitchell explained, "to get back on a plane with her in a few hours because nobody in Colorado wants to pay for my room and board in Rome overnight."

"Oh, signore, we would gladly take care of such a thing, up to a point. I only ask for a reasonable amount of time, say the time it would take to complete the paperwork for you and Miss Drisco to board that plane to return to the States."

"Now you've made a joke."

"Perhaps, but you understand, don't you? We don't know if Konstantinos's apartment is in Rome or that it will reveal any more information than the others. Some of them have held great treasures. We simply need time to . . ."

"I'm sorry," Mitchell said. "If the shoe was on the other foot I'm sure I'd be arguing the same points that you are, but . . ."

"In the last two months, major cities in Europe, North America, Japan, and Istanbul have reported unusual spikes in the numbers of murders committed there. Are you aware of such things from where you sit in Denver? We believe Pater, or Antonio as you call him, has been responsible for hundreds of these murders. We're not used to this many homicides. The company Antonio worked for last year was taken over by an international conglomerate. In the past, Antonio's pay was enormous. But we don't think he has been making anywhere near the money he did before. Now he must travel more and kill more people to make up the difference, to feed his lifestyle. But how does he pick his victims and why are they being targeted?"

There was a long silence between them. Mitchell was recalling Inez Buchanan's look of certainty as she described a large organization.

"Here, Signore Mitchell, you keep this. It's research we have done concerning this conglomerate so far." Falvo hand him the entire folder.

Mitchell glanced through it quickly, then said, "When can I see Sheila?"

Falvo reached across his desk and pushed a button on his intercom. "I can have someone drive you there in minutes."

"Listen," Mitchell said reluctantly. "You want two things. You want to know where this apartment is and you want to enter without breaking down the door or disturbing the place once you've found it. I understand that. All I want is to get Sheila back to Denver as quickly as possible. I need you to have those exit papers you spoke of by late this afternoon. I may not get you everything you want, but if I don't, it's because Sheila doesn't have the information. Are we clear? Do we have an agreement? If I'm not on that plane for the States by midnight tonight, something terrible has happened."

The inspector got up from the chair behind his desk, his face plump with excitement, and extended his hand to Mitchell. "We have a deal," Falvo said.

Just then a man about Mitchell's age stepped inside the office. He was tall and handsome, wearing a much more expensive suit than the inspector's.

"I'd like you to meet my son, Luigi," Falvo continued. "He has been reading about this case. I'm very proud of him. He has worked his way up the ladder to assistant inspector."

Not in that suit, Mitchell thought.

"He will accompany you to the safe house. And your papers will be ready when you and Miss Drisco return to my office later today."

Mitchell put the folder that the senior Falvo had given him under his shoulder and shook his hand. Before leaving, Mitchell reached for a business card on the inspector's desk. "I'll need your phone number to stay in touch," Mitchell said as the two men left the office.

**

"I didn't realize you were so high up the chain of command that you'd be the one sent here to bring me home."

Mitchell could hear the venom in Sheila's voice. But nothing in her face told him she was as angry as her voice implied. He looked around the flowery, pillowy parlor, trying to find a real chair for himself. The smell of overly sweet perfume was no invitation to stay. If he didn't get out of this place soon he'd sneeze. Luigi, by contrast, had immediately found a place on the love seat next to Sheila.

"It's the other way around," Mitchell answered. He continued to stand. "I have absolutely no status on the food chain. I had to convince people you were worth bringing back."

She searched his face, while he stood motionless, hoping she'd see nothing beyond a clear-headed professionalism. As for her own looks, she was deliberately dressed in a frock that said Little Miss Office Librarian. No one would have mistaken her for a model.

"And I'm certain," said Luigi, "you remember me from yesterday, no?"

Sheila turned to look at the man beside her, as if looking at a stranger.

Finally, Luigi answered his own question, sounding a little disappointed he hadn't been found memorable. "My name is Luigi. Inspector Luigi Falvo."

"Oh, yes, now I remember." She turned away quickly and looked at Mitchell. He was certain her eyes were pleading with him, so he looked away, knowing he wouldn't be able to resist her for long. He'd been observing the lush interior of what the Inspector had called a safe house and it bothered him along with the perfume. It was more like an over-the-top expensive brothel.

"You've got a key in your purse," Mitchell suddenly blurted out.

"Signore," Luigi interrupted, "this is inappropriate to divulge."

"And if it's the key to Antonio's apartment," Mitchel continued, "we've got to go there now and open it up for Luigi. Otherwise, we'll have to stay in Rome longer than I think is safe."

She hopped up from the love seat and in two giant steps reached the bag on the other side of the room. "I'm ready. Let's go," she said. "But first I must tell you that some of my own personal belongings should still be there and I want them. They're mine!"

The two men exchanged looks but said nothing and followed her out the front door.

"You know, there's a safe in this place," Sheila announced casually as they walked outside, "and I think I may know the combination."

"So where are we headed?" Mitchell asked.

"It's on the corner." Turning to Luigi, she said, "Pater would point to that safe house we just left and tell me stories about the Resistance housed there during WWII. He knew lots of things." Turning back to Mitchell, she whispered, "You think Pater kidnapped my sister or killed my father? I had to come to Rome to find out. I just had to."

"I hope you're not going to cry again," Mitchell answered. "I may puke.

And you shouldn't volunteer information in front of foreign policemen, that is if you want to go home any time soon."

They walked past the Fiat he and Luigi had arrived in, with its Official Police Business sign in the window, until they reached an unremarkable building less than a block away. Sheila did not take out her key but pushed a heavy ornate door to no avail. Mitchell and Luigi gently pushed her to the side and it opened.

If this was how Sheila had lived in Rome, Mitchell was never going to be in her league. Luigi, on the other hand, seemed right at home against the marble floors and walls of what could have been a lobby in a medium-sized museum. There were no windows. Ceiling spotlights fell on various small paintings and glass-enclosed objets d'art.

"These things look expensive," Mitchell said, standing in front of an ornately framed oil painting, "so why wasn't the door locked?"

"It locks from the inside," Sheila replied, "You can come in, but you can't leave. And there's video."

Reaching for the door before it closed behind them, Mitchell asked, "You have a pencil to prop this door open?"

"My key opens it," she answered.

"Oh," Mitchell said sheepishly.

Luigi took his gun out of its holster and called out in Italian, with something Mitchell figured was "Come to Papa." No one responded. It was like closing the barn door after the horses were gone thought Mitchell.

An electronic eye told the stainless steel elevator doors to open and, following Sheila, they got onboard. Mitchell watched Sheila wave her hand over a steel panel that had no buttons to push. There was no sound as doors closed and carried them up.

"How many apartments are in this building?" Mitchell asked.

"One," Sheila answered. "Pater has offices with very high ceilings on the second and third floors. His living quarters are on the fourth where we're headed."

Mitchell and Luigi exchanged looks again. Interpol would be interested in the entire building.

When the elevator doors opened, the lights on the fourth floor turned on. A heavy scent of cinnamon greeted them as she led them to the left along a short hallway that opened into the kind of enormous bedroom photographed in magazines. To one side was an equally huge bathroom.

Sheila hurried past them to a glass-enclosed shower stall, large enough to seat ten people. Pulling back the top lid of one of the built-in marble seats revealed a ceramic handle, which she unscrewed. The two men watched as a canister rose automatically from the seat.

"This was his personal safe," she said. "Actually, I'm not sure what to do now. Pater would take something ordinary-looking from his bathrobe pocket, like a small wrench or a . . ."

"I'll go look," said Luigi. "I saw clothes hanging in the closet."

"Some of those are mine, remember!" Sheila yelled to Luigi as he walked away from her and into a closet.

Mitchell leaned against a far wall and watched as Sheila rapidly opened dresser drawers in the bedroom, supposedly looking for her possessions. He'd already noticed mirrors, lights, and built-in speakers. From his vantage point, this top floor was a theater with two stages: a large bedroom and a glass-enclosed spa and shower area with a long marble latrine on the side.

"Why don't you say something?" Sheila asked. She had taken a small bag from her purse and stuffed it with lingerie from a drawer. "Why don't you tell me how shallow I am; that I was impressed with all the wrong things, for all the wrong reasons."

He smiled at her politely, then looked at the walls with more concern. "I only hope we're not streaming over the Internet right now," he said.

She walked closer to where he stood and stared at the walls, too.

"You mean . . . anyone can see . . .?"

"Yeah. That's what I mean."

She followed his gaze to the bed, watching him stare at tiny holes in the ceiling overhead, before she screamed, "Oh, my God."

Mitchell pulled up the bed skirt to reveal computers and cords on a Lucite trolley under the mattress.

"Luigi," Mitchell hollered. "Hurry up. We may be playing somewhere in cyberspace."

"*Scusi, un momento,*" Luigi answered. "I think I found it."

Mitchell followed Luigi into the shower and began interrogating him.

"Did your tech people disconnect the cameras at Antonio's other apartments? Did they shut down his website? He must have had a website. Did you track the cameras back to this guy's employers?"

Luigi had found a special wrench and was applying it to the canister inside the shower seat. "I speak very bad computer," Luigi answered.

"Luigi, don't you get it? Mitchell asked. "There are computers under the bed. Didn't you know about them before coming here?"

"I've got to go to the bathroom," Sheila said nervously, then disappeared behind a marble wall. Her splattering urine echoed loudly across the entire shower.

Meanwhile, Luigi grunted and hissed at the unyielding lock. Mitchell watched the man's anger increase and began to back away.

When Sheila emerged from behind the wall, Mitchell spoke slowly, continuing his conversation with Luigi. "You've got a forensic team coming soon, right? What's their ETA? Sheila, have you got everything you wanted? Sheila and I will call a cab. We'll go to a hotel and freshen up."

Sheila gave him a look that said, poor baby.

"Luigi, are you listening? We'll call your dad from the hotel and make sure our exit papers are in order. We don't want to be in your way here."

Luigi said nothing, continuing to attack the lock. Mitchell beckoned Sheila to come closer to him. Luigi then pulled his gun from its holster with his right hand. With his left hand, he continued using the wrench.

"You're too smart to die here Mr. Mitchell. Stay where you stand," Luigi ordered, without looking at them.

Mitchell had no intention of underestimating Luigi's peripheral vision. Sheila trembled, yet backed away.

Luigi's back was toward her as she mouthed the word "stairway" and pointed for Mitchell's benefit. His forehead furrowed deeply. Mitchell even shook his head and looked as perturbed as he possibly could, hoping to convey strong disapproval. But too late. They were suddenly in total darkness.

A gun fired and with it came a sudden flash of light. A second bullet echoed off a tile surface followed by the sound of a falling body. Sheila screamed in the dark, and for a moment, Mitchell wondered if he was unconscious or dead.

CHAPTER 21

JANUARY 2007   YUNNAN PROVINCE

XIAO AWOKE TO the noise of family chatter in a language that sounded similar to Cantonese. However, he could not make sense of it and kept his eyelids closed. A warm crackling fireplace was on his right side; the other side of his cheek felt like ice. A long swishing skirt brushed against his forehead from time to time. The sound of liquids being poured came from further away. He sensed a great deal of moisture in the air. And with that moisture came an intoxicating smell of ginger, fermented plums, and fatty lamb, making his eyelids finally pop open.

He lay atop a fur blanket and was covered by yet another. Precocious toddlers crawled around his head and infants were propped against his legs. He closed his eyes again. The humiliation was too great. He had obviously been relegated to a corner of the room with all the less important things.

A woman with an exceptionally long face wore a red peasant blouse and leaned over him. Her skirt brushed his face. She spoke to others he couldn't see from his vantage point. Two big teenaged boys pulled a few of the children away and squatted on either side of him to lift up his back and slide him against a footstool. They weren't gentle, only strong.

His head throbbed and flopped over his chest. To help him see the full length of the room, one of the boys propped his head back, resting it upright against a folded blanket. Focusing was difficult, but eventually he saw one man, Meng, who no longer wore his furs. The rest were mostly women and children. Only three other men sat on the floor with what he assumed were their families. He didn't see Karen. All the women were dressed similarly and had jet-black hair surrounding their faces.

"Where, where is . . ." Xiao unknowingly sputtered aloud.

"Ah," said Meng. "I think he will stay awake longer this time." He walked toward Xiao, carrying a steaming bowl. "Take this." He handed it to one of the two young boys, who put it up to Xiao's lips to drink.

Xiao was ravenous. The soup had small bits of lamb, goat, herbs, rice, and spices. It was better than anything he'd eaten in weeks.

"The rest of us are full. If you can stand later, you'll feast upon a plate of assorted meat, ripe fruit, and cheese you'll never forget." Meng then hurried back to the women he'd been seated with.

Xiao's eyes grew accustomed to the sparse light. Between sips of soup, he noticed a quiet woman at Meng's side. That woman wore what the other women wore. But there was something different about her hair. It was lighter. Maybe it was Karen. The woman's skin was also whiter than the others, like Karen's. If it was Karen, why wasn't she beside him, feeding him?

He felt dizzy as he let his eyes carefully search the room. The voices inside his head mumbled. On the floor in the distance his eyes found what he thought was his own backpack opened, its contents strewn across a pile of blankets. Curtains hung by ropes around the pile. Similar blankets lay in other corners of the exceptionally large room. Why had Karen brought their backpacks along? Had they paid for their hotel rooms, or had they been kidnapped?

After finishing the soup, the huge boys helped him stand, then just as suddenly kicked his feet from under him. They quickly stood over him, covered his shoulders with one of the fur blankets, and then stood him up again. It had all happened so quickly, Xiao wondered if it had happened at all.

"Come join us," Meng said.

The women slowly moved away from the table, gathering their children into their laps to sit with others already seated at the far corners of the room. Karen grabbed her down jacket from the back of a chair and pulled it over her red blouse. That was when Xiao recognized her.

She stood beside Meng at the table and smiled at Xiao, who took his time selecting a seat across from them. Additional food was brought to him with chopsticks by one of the women. Another woman cleaned pots with several young children. Still others lay quietly staring back at the people at the table. Some breast-fed their young in front of the fireplace. Xiao made certain the fur blanket never slipped from his shoulders for continued warmth.

"Xiao," Karen said, "they want us to stay here with them." Her face glowed as she said it. There was no mistaking the excitement in her voice.

Xiao gulped down large bites of food. "Why?" he finally asked her. As he ate, he glanced at one person and then another.

Meng spoke with authority, "I think you don't want the government to find you. Karen tells me I am right. Communists leave us alone. We share a healthy respect for each other. Our people have learned impressive and highly useful skills over the years. From spy craft to making soap, we excel."

Xiao looked into Karen's face and said nothing. He continued to eat, still not understanding her jubilance but marveling over the blend of spices used in the meal.

"This *is* a memorable meal," Xiao acknowledged. "The women are very good cooks here."

"Only a few of them had anything to do with this meal," Meng said. "Their men did the killing, the skinning, the seasoning, and the roasting. Naxi women basically take care of everyone's children. They may tend to the farm areas. But men and women here are free to form relationships with anyone they please. Here, a woman decides what man will live with her," Meng explained politely.

The three of them sat quietly while Xiao ate. He did not intend to leave anything uneaten. Meng poured three cups of a fermented drink, but Meng was the only person who drank it.

After a long while, Xiao asked, "To what do we owe your desire to take us into your community?"

"My niece is greatly respected. She's the matriarch of a sizable group residing in this valley. She and Karen, without the assistance of language, became friends on the bus and when Karen said she might be with child, my niece was happy but also concerned."

Xiao's whole body stirred. His brain ached. What exactly did "might be with child" mean? "How in hell . . ." Xiao said aloud.

Meng interrupted him. "Might is a complex word, is it not? Karen also used the English word 'slave'-a word my niece understood well from my readings to her. Although she does not speak English as I do, she does understand several words."

With his face burning, Xiao pushed back from the table, his eyes buried in Karen's face. There was much he wanted to discuss with her, but he wanted to be alone with her. He watched as her hands covered her mouth and tears ran down her face. Xiao knew Meng was talking but had no idea what he said. He didn't care. Meng's simple sentences had just destroyed the world he had hoped to build.

". . . so you may wish to ponder all the things we've talked about," Meng continued. "Spend your days here recuperating with us. We've made a place for you. My nephews will come and apologize for their earlier behavior. They should not have hit you as hard as they did. As terrible as their actions were, however, I could not permit you to kill them. They are my brother's sons, after all.

"If there is anything more you require," he added, "someone will see to it immediately. Tomorrow we can speak more on these matters."

Xiao made no sound but looked straight ahead, as if observing the intricacies of another world that no one else could see. His voices continued to speak to him in hushed mumbling sounds as if they too wanted to listen.

"Concentrate on my words, Xiao. It is important for you and Karen to give our way of life a chance." Meng got up from the table, as if to leave, then sat back down.

"I've . . . I've changed my mind. I think you may want to meditate on the matters we spoke of. There is a better place for meditating. My nephews are both trained to carry people over mountainous terrain. They will take you to a lodge high in the Himalayas. It is beautiful there. You will need to get started very early in the morning. They will leave you at a lodge in those mountains. Plenty of food and fuel will be brought up to you during the following day. Your provisions will last a month. That's when my nephews will return to bring you down safely.

"It is a place of continued healing. Karen feels certain you may have had a serious concussion when your head hit the wall. Let your mind and body grow still. I will see you again upon your return. That's when we'll speak of your gun. Be ready to leave with my nephews in a few hours." He then got up and without looking back, left the building.

Karen ran to the other side of the table to sit in the chair closest to Xiao. She took his hand in hers and lifted it to her moist face.

"I didn't mean to worry you. I don't know if I'm pregnant or not," she cried. "But when you said you didn't like children, I couldn't even talk to you about it, could I?" Her tears made the back of his hand wet and he pulled it away. "But look," she continued, swallowing back more tears, "we've got what you wanted, a group of people to blend in with. You thought it would take time, years, you said. But it won't."

He didn't face her but was hidden in shadow when he spoke. "Whenever any of these villagers need money, medical attention, or they feel you have something they don't; whenever you piss one of them off, they'll turn you in to the Chinese government without hesitation or they'll force you to do whatever they want most."

Karen said nothing at first but put her hands in her lap. Minutes passed and they still didn't move. He listened to his voices repeat the words he'd just said with more emphasis.

Finally she spoke. "I don't think they'll turn us in to this Quan man you spoke of. They aren't friends of the Communists. They actually *want* us here."

"Right now, they may need our hands to help work," Xiao explained. "But as Americans, they may never trust us entirely. As an Asian American, I know the truth in what I'm saying."

A few women, too far away to hear anything, moved to the enclosed mattresses with their children. Some had already left the building.

Karen reached for his empty plate and bowl, but Xiao grabbed her wrist.

"Don't do that. It's not fitting. You were never my slave."

"What *should* I do?" she asked.

Unable to prevent his grief from spilling into his words, he remained silent.

She stood up quickly. "Come, we can go to mattresses they've assigned to us." Grabbing the kerosene lamp from the table, she darted to where he had seen the strewn contents of his backpack. The few women and children who remained were now completely hidden behind cloth drapes that hung above the fur piles on the floor. He saw only two men resting beside their women and children.

Reluctantly, he got up and followed her, noticing his headache was less severe. She knelt on a fur blanket and set the lamp on the floor beside her. Karen reached up and grabbed Xiao's jacket, pulling him down on top of her. Fiercely, he rolled off her body, forcing his back against the wall of the building.

"You don't want me now. And that's okay, I understand," she said. "I'll be with you for as long as you want me."

"You lie," he said, pushing himself away from the wall and from her. He felt only a slight pang of anger. "You'll be emotionally and physically tied to a community you think you can trust. By the way, did you see what they did with my gun?"

"Weren't you listening? Meng has it," she said. " He believes he should keep it until you show that you want to live here, that you don't mean to hurt anyone with it."

No, he hadn't heard Meng say very much. He'd been preoccupied with his own loss and grief. Karen sat up and pulled the curtains across the ropes to conceal them both.

"You'll feel much better," she said, "when you've gotten some sleep. It will help your voices relax as well. I'll be here to help, too. Remember that." She began to unbutton the embroidered shirt the women had given her. He watched her in the light of their kerosene lamp.

Suddenly she looked at him and said, "I found this U.S. passport." She held it up. "I've never seen it before. It expires soon. Where did you get it? It makes me look like I'm dead or something. I was waiting for the right time to talk to you about it."

He marveled at the fact that she had searched through his belongs like a nosy wife, but she hadn't found his secret compartment where he kept his personal credit card. He intended to keep the card for the day they escaped China together.

The one thing Xiao understood plainly was that he needed to stay with these Naxi people long enough to get his gun back. He needed to wear the mask of a spy, the mask Dr. Buchanan had described, before he could eventually head home to the States. Not home in China, where he had earlier dreamed of living with Karen. He couldn't live with Karen because she now belonged to a community, not to him. She had removed all of her clothing, clothing the community had given her.

"Where do they keep their horses?" he asked. A sudden memory of being thrown across the back of a horse came to him. That was how they came up the mountains. Maybe he could leave the mountains that same way.

Karen piled her clothes and shoes neatly into the corner of their enclosed area. She looked bewildered by his question but scooted down under a fur blanket to lay flat beside him, the passport still in her hand.

"We left them in stalls behind this building," she answered. "They're lovely animals, so intelligent. Meng trained them to always return to this lodge. But we don't want to leave, do we? We just got here. Don't think about the horses. We won't need horses if we stay here."

His upper back began to throb around his shoulder. The fur blanket he'd had around his shoulders became his pillow as he lay down beside her. His eyes closed immediately, letting the sound of her voice talk in hushed tones with his other voices. Over it all, he heard Karen's voice speak louder.

"Meng wanted very much to keep your gun, but I begged him to let me have it because I trust you," she said. "I told him we both come from a country that believes in gun ownership for everyone, so having a gun is not such a bad idea for us. Meng suggested a compromise. He suggested that we both lie to you and tell you that he would keep your gun. I agreed. But now that we're alone, I know we shouldn't ever lie to each other, ever."

Xiao opened his eyes and felt the gun against his side. She had placed it on the blanket between their bodies. He looked across at Karen's face. She was smiling in the glow of the kerosene lamp. He sat up, picked the gun up, wrapped the fur blanket that he had used as a pillow around his hand and the gun twice, then pressed the nozzle against Karen's temple and fired.

He continued to hold the gun while he listened intently to the quiet of the room around him.

CHAPTER 22

FEBRUARY 2007   DENVER, VETERAN'S HOME

ACCORDING TO AN attendant at the Colorado Veterans' Home, eighty-
nine year old Abraham Wallace just had his diaper changed and was
unusually irritable after that indignity.

Inez and Billy tiptoed into his room, having called ahead to explain
they'd be late. It had been a rare morning. Trace Mitchell's unplanned visit
had thrown them off schedule. Still, they anxiously hoped Abraham could
unlock the mystery of what Gaelen intended to sell on eBay.

Wallace had meanwhile, fallen asleep in the only armchair in the room.
Inez sat on his bed while Billy leaned against the door of his wardrobe.

"I don't understand," Billy whispered to Inez. "Why are you so interested in finding justice for that white man who lived next door to you and
now here's another white man who probably never comes in contact with
black people unless . . ."

"Haven't you ever bought something or applied for something and just
when you were about to deliver your hard-earned money or your best effort to people in authority you felt them laugh or thought someone behind
you laughed? You later found out that what you thought was important to
you was more important to whoever manipulated your thinking. Well, I
think something like that happened to Gaelen, and if something like that
could happen to a nice man like my neighbor, white as he was, it could
happen to you and me both without our ever being the wiser.

"I think we're so busy trying to survive that we can miss certain un-
derhanded dangers to our surroundings and to the very way of life we're

trying to achieve. There are people who don't want governments that protect individual freedoms and a diverse population."

Wallace suddenly snored, then caught himself and sputtered as he woke to find visitors staring at him. Immediately Inez explained who she was and that their mutual friend Gaelen had died without recording his testimony of the war. She hoped Abraham could tell her everything he could possibly remember for the sake of future generations. She and Billy wanted to record whatever Abraham could remember.

Billy had his own reasons for participating in this venture. He'd never met a WWII veteran and had recently read accounts of two major battles in that war.

"I appreciate this Mr. Wallace," Inez shouted, aware that he must have been turning his good ear toward her. She hoped to be heard over the construction work going on outside his window. It was otherwise a well-maintained single-storied nursing home on grounds that sprawled over a half acre.

Wallace nodded his head and then turned drooping gray eyes toward Billy, who placed a cassette recorder in front of him and then took Wallace's picture with his phone. "Was that okay, Mr. Wallace? Did I scare ya'?" Billy asked.

"Whatda'ya' think, I'm feebleminded or somethin'?"

"No, sir. Take a look." Billy brought the phone close to Mr. Wallace's face. Then he asked, "You need your glasses? Here," he said, reaching for them and placing them across the old man's nose.

Wallace smiled at the picture, and Inez was grateful for Billy's people skills.

"Yes, indeed, Gaelen Drisco," Wallace finally said. "A handsome boy. Course we were all handsome then. Too poor to know it though. We had nothin' but what the military put on our backs. We were proud of that uniform, those of us that got to wear it a while."

She quietly turned up the volume on the tape recorder she'd brought. Wallace's voice sometimes vanished into hoarse whispers.

"So he's dead? Well, how do you like that? My turn's comin'. I'm probably the only one left who knew him. He had special skills. I'm not telling this to create bad feelings. But Gaelen was a thief, ya' know."

Uh-oh. Inez felt her eyebrows furrow. Were the old man's memories gone? Was he describing another soldier? She'd been sitting near his bed, but now she moved closer to his chair.

"Oh, he never stole money, far as I know," Wallace continued. "He wasn't like that. That's why those of us who knew him never told anybody. He lied about his age. I remember that. But so many boys lied to get in. Nobody could have been poorer than Gaelen. Gaelen ate tubers, any tuber, even ate the dirt and insects right along with 'em. That's how poor he was. And that's why he could survive behind enemy lines and live to tell about it."

Inez embraced each word, feeling she was one tissue away from a good cry.

"Chaplain finally had enough. Nobody wanted Gaelen to get into serious trouble with . . . oh, I don't remember names anymore." He kept shaking his head back and forth, as if being tortured by some monster attacking his brain.

A cement drill outside his window started up. Abraham Wallace didn't blink, but shook his head more. Inez leaned over him and whispered, "What was Gaelen stealing?"

Wallace turned his head to get a decent look at her whole face. "Clothes were important to a man then. Clothes kept you alive against the cold. Uniforms turned you into respectable people. Gaelen stole uniforms. Can you understand that? He didn't steal enlisted men's uniforms. And he never stole new ones either. He only stole from high-ranking officers. And that wasn't smart 'cause they'd have shot him for less than that during the war. They might figure he was working for the enemy and trying to fool somebody. But Gaelen was a God-fearing man."

Wallace reached for a carafe of water on a side table and Billy rushed to pour the water for him. Inez was restless. She had lots of questions and bit her tongue rather than interrupt. She wanted to be sure he was talking about Gaelen Drisco.

"You see," he continued, "Gaelen thought, if he stole their old sweaty, bloody, filthy uniforms and kept them in a vault somewhere, he could sell them later, when he needed money, and they'd be worth a fortune."

Inez sat up straight to listen better.

"Everybody would want clothing from the liberators of the free world. Clothes made you who you were in those days. People don't think that way anymore. Wonder what he ever did with them things 'cause he was too scared to get them cleaned anywhere.

Inez was deep in thought by the time Wallace finished talking. His eyes closed. She put her hand on his arm very gently and asked, "Mr. Wallace, whose uniforms did he steal?"

Slowly he opened his eyes again and scanned the room. When he found Inez's face, he took his time answering. "Gaelen was a genius. He could decode anything. Nobody knew how he did it. Which, if you ask me, is why he never got court- marshaled. I was a typist. I was faster than a damn bullet," he said, bringing his left hand close to his face for his audience to examine the swollen joints of his fingers. Then he let his whole arm drop to the side, as if he didn't want it anymore.

"They'd send me with him sometimes to type up what he decoded. That's how I come to know him. We'd sometimes parachute into enemy territory. The British had their Bletchley Park, their Enigma, but Gaelen was portable and funnier than hell. He could crack any code the Germans threw at us. It usually took minutes, but sometimes it took a few days.

"It took a while before Field Marshal Montgomery and Eisenhower knew their uniforms were missing. I thought for sure MacArthur was going to nab him."

Wallace's voice began to lose its volume. "Only person who thought that stuff was worth more than trash was Gaelen."

"Mr. Wallace," Inez said softly, "do you know if he was Jewish or not?"

His chin slowly fell to his chest and even the folds of his eyelids drooped. "He warn't nothin'," Abraham replied. Then his head reared back suddenly. "I take that back. I did see him sneak inside a synagogue once, maybe twice. Gaelen said I was mistaken, but I knew it was him. It sure looked like him."

His eyes closed and his chin stayed propped against his chest for a long time.

Inez finally whispered to Billy, "Let's go. I think I've got what we came for."

"Really? You think he was talking about Gaelen?"

"Yes, I do."

Billy packed up Inez's recorder into his backpack. She followed behind him, deep in thought. They walked slowly down hallways toward her car, which was parked beside orange plastic barricades and a pile of sand connected to construction around the nursing home.

Where would Gaelen have kept those uniforms, she asked herself? Hank had looked all over Gaelen's house for whatever he intended to sell. Finally the hills and valleys of her brain began to tingle.

"Gaelen's murderers didn't find the uniforms the night of the murder," she said. "That must be why they had to buy the house."

She and Billy stood beside her car as Inez remembered back many years ago when she had eavesdropped on two students in her classroom. They talked about digging a hole in the ground behind their apartment building to hide their stash.

"Gaelen," she said, "must have wrapped his stash of uniforms in plastic bags and placed them underground in his pet cemetery. Nobody knew about DNA in those days, so unwittingly he preserved the DNA of heroes for all these years."

Having solved one puzzle, she became quiet, reflecting on how DNA echoed throughout Dr. Wren Xiao's dilemma too.

What had Xiao received his grant for? Something to do with DNA she remembered. How important was human DNA to producing a Chinese superhuman? Very! And Gaelen's uniforms, presented on eBay, were full of DNA.

She then wondered about the girl Xiao spoke of, the one he was supposed to kill for a man named Quan. And worse yet, she wondered just how a Chinese American could ever prove to CIA that he wasn't a spy for China? For that matter, she pondered, with America finally realizing its numbers of homegrown terrorists, how could you tell which Americans could ever be trusted? These issues consumed her while she paid little attention to Billy.

He was loading the back of Claire's car, as a UPS truck drove up close behind them.

"HEY, WATCH IT," she heard Billy holler to the driver.

Inez looked up to see a door slide open, which disclosed four young men standing inside the truck wearing dark suits. Two of them held badges out for her to see.

"CBI! Get in! HURRY!" they shouted.

"Wait a minute," Billy yelled to Inez, who was already walking toward the truck.

"It's okay, Billy" she shouted back. "Let's get in. C'mon."

CHAPTER 23

MARCH 2007   ROME

M ITCHELL TRIPPED AND fell over a body. A second later the lights came
on. He knew it would turn out to be Luigi's body and that he would
be dead. Stunned by the rapid succession of events, Mitchell didn't move
from where he fell, staying atop the body long enough to see that Luigi's
eyes didn't close and that his chest didn't move.

When he stood up, Sheila asked, "You all right? What about Luigi?"

Luigi's gun, Mitchell noticed, was on the other side of the shower
stall floor.

Suddenly Sheila was hysterical. "He's dead, isn't he? You shot him?
What the hell happened? What were you thinking? You were supposed
to follow me. I was going to lead us down the back stairs. Why didn't you
follow?" She was bouncing up and down on the balls of her feet, as she
spoke. Her voice, likewise, bounced off the walls of the shower.

"Shut up and let me think!" Mitchell shouted. He bent over the body
for a second, then walked to the gun. "I cannot tell a lie. I didn't kill him."

He took a handkerchief out of his back pocket, picked up the
nine-millimeter Beretta from the tile floor, and waved it under his nose.

Sheila yelled, backing away as she spoke. "They're never going to let
us leave Rome, are they?"

"Well, running down the stairs was a stupid idea," Mitchell quipped.
"Could have gotten us both killed. I intended to get the gun from him
first; otherwise he'd have shot us. I thought I may have killed him in
the struggle, but I didn't." He slowly walked in circles around the body,

attempting to grasp some perspective on where the fatal shot had come from. Suddenly he stopped moving. "Someone must have been on those back stairs."

They were both silent, letting the realization sink in.

"Whoever shot Luigi is probably still here, unless that person has a key like yours."

Sheila started making weird noises again, while Mitchell released the clip from Luigi's gun. He let it fall into his hand, then jammed it back into the gun. No bullets were missing.

He grabbed Sheila's hand and whispered, "Lead us out of here."

"Let's go!"

"Wait." Mitchell kneeled over Luigi's body, searching until he found car keys. Sheila squirmed and made noises again as she looked away. Luigi's phone fell out of his pocket and Mitchell grabbed that, too.

"Look, look!" Sheila cried.

Mitchell got up to see the marble receptacle Luigi had been madly working on. The man's personality had changed under the stress of getting it open. Its top had now been twisted off, and whatever had been inside was gone.

Both of them leapt down three flights of circular iron stairs, Sheila leading the way. On the ground floor Mitchell grabbed her shoulders, pulling her behind him so he could peek through an entryway door he hadn't noticed when they were downstairs. Holding Luigi's gun chest high, he nudged the nozzle through the narrow opening. No one was there, and the front door appeared to be closed.

Wordlessly, they both tiptoed, one behind the other, to the door where Sheila was ready in a flash with her key. As soon as they saw daylight, they ran to Luigi's car. With the keys Mitchell had taken off Luigi's body, they opened it and quietly sat scrunched together inside before either could talk.

"I wonder what will happen when I use my own phone here in Europe?" Mitchell was talking to himself and staring at his phone, not expecting a response from Sheila.

"The Italian government will know where you are. That's what will happen."

"Then it doesn't matter," Mitchell replied. "I've got to notify Luigi's father that his son is dead."

"Use Luigi's phone."

Mitchell couldn't believe he hadn't thought of that first.

People strolled past them wearing warm jackets. The overhead sun was bright and warm for winter, but there was still a chill in the air. Young and old sat on the steps across the street.

"For God's sake," Mitchell exclaimed with the phone at his ear, "it's Interpol! Why doesn't anyone answer?"

"Maybe you have the wrong number."

"I've tried it twice. You don't suppose Luigi's father ... No, I'm getting to be like Inez Buchanan."

"Why do you say that? You don't look anything like her."

Mitchell took a good look at Sheila. There he was in romantic Rome with the immature little girl Inez said she was. He smiled at her, and Sheila smiled back.

"So what are you doing that's like Inez?" she asked again.

"I'm beginning," Mitchell explained, "to think everything is connected to everything else. That's how conspiracy theories start. I was about to suggest, just because he hadn't answered the phone, that Luigi's father could be a private contractor like Antonio, I mean Pater. Actually, I'd prefer to think Luigi was moonlighting, that he knew he could confiscate any money found inside that safe as easily as he could rise through the ranks of Interpol to become assistant inspector."

Sheila sighed, "Maybe you're right."

"There's one thing I am certain about. We've got to get to the airport. Interpol's office is there and so is Luigi's dad. We've got to get back to the States."

"But I can't go right away. You've scared me now, Sheila said. "Miriam and I were never close. I never contacted her whenever I'd come to Italy. But I can't help thinking she may be in danger, too. I've got to find out before I leave. Please."

"Call her. Meanwhile, I'm going to hop out here where I can get more bars to call the police. I'll give them the location of Luigi's body, but anonymously."

Meanwhile, two smiling female tourists, dripping with expensive cameras, jewelry, and clothing, stood about ten feet in front of Luigi's car, holding colorful shopping bags. They stared and pointed to the Fiat, as if Sheila was someone they recognized. Mitchell kept one eyeball on them as he made his call.

He wanted to be somewhat ambiguous about street names so the police would believe the call came from a tourist. The last thing he wanted was for one or both of them to be held in Rome for questioning.

The women began barking at each other in a Slavic-sounding language and Mitchell assumed the women were inebriated. He watched as Sheila got out of the car to exchange pleasantries with the two, who gasped admiringly. By the time Mitchell finished his call, Sheila stood beside the driver's side door.

"I'll drive," she said. "You're not used to European highways."

"Okay, officer," Mitchell responded happily. "I'll go peacefully." He ran around to the passenger side. "You can take me anywhere."

"Good, because I couldn't reach Miriam. She left a message on my machine in Paris. She moved to an apartment in Tivoli and believes her ex-husband is traveling to South America. She didn't say whether her son Xavier was with him or with her. But she claims someone has been trying to kill her and the police won't do anything."

Mitchell was pensive. He didn't like complications. One of the two women in the street waved to them before Sheila made their tires screech as she sped away.

"Good God!" she shouted, looking through her rearview mirror. "Duck!"

Rear window glass blew through the car like splintered daggers. Mitchell had raised his arms, which shielded his face, but the back of his head was hot with pain. Sheila shook debris from her hair and shifted gears, continuing to drive straight ahead. The headrest protected her.

"You okay?" she asked breathlessly, her eyes never leaving the streets in front of her.

"I'm okay," he said after a minute, still bent over. He rubbed his neck and the side of his face before giving out a quick yelp. Blood stained his fingers. Pieces of glass dropped from his head as he slowly straightened up. "How fast can you make this car go?" he asked.

"I'll show ya'," she answered.

She sat up straighter. Rushing wind took their breath away. Her speed reached ninety kilometers. He turned to look through the opening that had once been the rear window and the open window beside him, where the bullet must have exited the car. He knew he could have easily been killed. They must have used a rifle with a high-caliber bullet.

"Were you cut?" she hollered, still not turning to look. He liked that. She had good skills, even if her decision-making was horrible. Still, no one in his office could or would have had the balls to do what she just did.

"Not seriously," he responded. "I suppose you're headed for your sister's place?"

"It's not far," she shouted over traffic. "Maybe forty miles from Rome. We'll see a sign soon. Or maybe I should stop along here and take a good look at you."

"No, don't stop. I'll get checked out when we reach the airport. I'm still planning on us leaving Italy tonight! You realize I have no clout here. Nobody cares that I'm with CBI. I'm simply a man carrying a gun that I shouldn't have in my possession."

"Yes, but Miriam's scared. Her message said people have been shooting at her ever since she returned to Rome. She's staying in a renovated roadside chapel. It must belong to somebody she knows. Miriam hates to pay for anything. She didn't want to tell Inez about attempts on her life for fear she'd stop investigating Dad's murder."

Mitchell took a deep breath. "So why doesn't Miriam call the *Polizia?*"

"She's called them so often concerning her ex-husband," Sheila explained, "they don't believe her anymore."

Remembering something, Mitchell stretched an arm under his seat. He'd left the file folder Inspector Falvo had given him before entering the safe house. Finding it, he fingered through the packet of papers inside.

"What's that?" Sheila asked.

"It's research Interpol conducted on the company Pater worked for. It might give us some idea who's trying to kill us and why."

Sheila weaved in and out of traffic at breathtaking speeds.

"There's been a Mercedes, S Class, robin's-egg blue behind us, since we left Via Condotti. It drops back just when I'm convinced it's following us," she said.

Mitchell rotated in his seat and failed to see the car she described. Yet he had no doubt she knew her high-priced cars. He continued to sit so that he could look out the back and front windows of the car. Again, he read from the papers in his lap.

"Listen to this. French police said Antonio's most frequent employer was a company called Shockenaugh, Inc., a company hired by government military offices, energy installations, and financial institutions that purchase services ranging from altering evidence to kidnapping, assassination, and guerilla warfare. The short list of governments that have employed this company is impressive: England, India, Iran, North Korea, Dubai. Damn it! Buchanan must be psychic."

Mitchell punched buttons on Luigi's phone.

"Here it comes again!" Sheila warned.

Mitchell shut the phone off and looked at a blurred dot that quickly became a blue convertible with a dark-skinned driver wearing a black turban. If Sheila was doing eighty miles per hour, the other car was doing a hundred. In the lane beside their car was the type of truck that could have been hauling gasoline or milk.

Mitchell removed Luigi's gun from his pocket and held it close to his face. He had no desire to escalate the situation, but gambled that the driver would reconsider his options or at least slow down to unholster his own gun once he saw Mitchell's. The driver must have seen it, because he dropped back rapidly.

The truck next to them finally sped ahead while Mitchell hoped that its driver was too high off the ground to see him holding his gun or to call the Carabinieri to report him.

"We need help," Mitchell said.

Like clockwork the blue Mercedes appeared again, this time heading straight for the trunk of their car. Mitchell climbed into the back seat, propping his gun out the shattered back window.

"You're blocking my view," Sheila yelled. "I can't see anything out the rearview mirror."

"So, don't look!"

The Mercedes pushed forward and then slowed down. Mitchell took aim just below the man's turban. But a scraping sound distracted him as he pulled the trigger. The blue car began to swerve, trying to avoid Mitchell's bullet. The car drifted close into the lane beside it, lightly scraping the other car riding in that lane. The two cars suddenly locked door handles and collided. The blue Mercedes rose into the air with the other car beside it when they exploded. Both cars turned over backward several times.

The sound was continuous and loud, the flames far reaching. Sheila pushed the gas pedal to the floor and left the mayhem behind. Other cars crashed into the burning ones. Sheila and Mitchell continued on the autovia, carried along by pure adrenaline.

CHAPTER 24

JANUARY 2006   YUNNAN PROVINCE

X IAO KNELT ON one knee to peek through the hanging cloth surrounding the sleeping area he'd shared with Karen. For close to an hour he waited beside Karen's dead body. Meng's beast-like nephews were late. He'd never ridden a horse before; otherwise, he would have attempted an escape down the mountain on horseback.

Instinct told him to pack Karen's passport into his backpack again although he couldn't understand why the document had mattered to her. Already he was sorry he didn't have Karen to talk to about such things, but there was no turning back. His head throbbed; his voices had gotten louder with condemnations.

This was all Meng's fault. Meng said he needed to recuperate in the mountains, from a concussion. Xiao barely remembered the event. Meng's nephews were involved. Yes, they had thrown him headfirst against a wall. Yet he patiently waited for those same two nephews. He knew they'd expect Karen to be asleep when they arrived. Covering her body in blankets would fool them and anyone else who looked for her.

Finally, they appeared in the doorway of the lodge. Xiao jumped up and walked through the cloth curtain. He waited until they saw him to say good night to Karen and snatch up his backpack. He walked toward them before they came closer. Having brought snowshoes with them, they stayed by the door to put them on.

Cold air invigorated Xiao, who noticed that the little thermometer on his zipper registered only five degrees above zero, before heading out. The stars were bright with only a sliver of moon.

In their own language, the young men apologized for throwing him into the wall. But since Xiao could only translate a few words, he could only guess at their sincerity until one handed him a hefty piece of smoked pork and the other an even larger piece of fried bread. They all smiled at one another while Xiao packed the food into his backpack.

After an hour trekking uphill, Xiao felt exceptionally calm with these two wide-bodied young men on either side of him. His gun, stuffed securely in the back of his pants helped him feel that way. He had two bullets left in case these men did anything threatening. After the second hour, he realized they were repeatedly ignoring him and talked to each other as they walked ahead. Finding it hard to keep up, Xiao knew he could never be their friend. They had no common interests. But then, Xiao never had any friends.

It was only a matter of time before Meng would discover Karen dead inside the lodge. And then what? Would Meng wait until his nephews returned home before sending them back up the mountain to get him, or would Meng find a posse of other villagers to start the climb in order to find them immediately? Wouldn't Meng fear for the lives of his nephews, knowing he had his gun?

Just then snow began to fall. Several dried leaves fell around him. He suddenly realized he was alone. He looked up at tree branches and spied the outline, in darkness, of a red panda, its glistening eyes closing. Xiao stood perfectly still. The animal went back to sleep in the treetops.

Both nephews appeared from behind a cluster of trees and walked slowly toward him. One of the young men put his gloved hand inside his fur jacket and pulled out a long-nozzled revolver, the kind Xiao associated with Wyatt Earp movies. Xiao was impressed. Meng was shrewd. He kept his family armed.

The nephew with the gun pointed it at the panda and then tapped on Xiao's backpack. Xiao shook his head no. He had no need for panda meat to go along with the pork they'd given him. Lightheartedly, the young man put his gun back into his jacket and they proceeded up the mountain into heavy snowfall. The sky was much brighter, making their steps easier to see.

Along the way, the younger men pointed out one lodge after the other, showing off the growing wealth of members of the Naxi tribe. Each lodge, some occupied and some not, provided Xiao with landmarks on a mental map, in case he had to travel down the mountain the same way he had ascended. If he knew the route to the lodge they were headed toward now, he'd have no further need of them. As he climbed, Xiao began to favor the idea of killing both of them before they reached the top. He'd have more choices for escape without them.

After four hours, they stopped at the base of a steep incline. Xiao began to ask questions in Mandarin, which they appeared to understand. Xiao had convinced himself that Meng must have found Karen's body by now. How long before they reached their destination? he asked. Would they need to rappel up any of the mountains along their way? He had assumed it was a one-day trip. Their answers surprised him.

"We've never made this trip in one day," said one, "although it may be possible if there's a prize offered." They both laughed. "There are several unused lodges at the summit, as there are along the way. Many at the top belong to friends of our uncle, who prefer to live in the village during the winter months. Once we've reached a height not easily reached by the average climber, we'll simply pick one. Your woman told us that you shouldn't climb by yourself because of your head injury. We may decide not to go as high as the summit if you're not doing well."

Xiao felt his lungs and brain being squeezed. But there was no time to reflect on his weaknesses. A decision had to be made now. Could he make it from here to the top on his own? Did he really need these two? Would Meng send villagers to get him as soon as possible? He was certain Meng would send at least one villager. Maybe Meng would come himself.

As the young men talked, they took out water bottles from their packs and drank. They shared everything they had with Xiao, including food they brought for themselves. But Xiao gradually moved away and closer toward a boulder, behind which he could duck if he missed his shot. He pretended to casually seek a place to pee in private. In one swift hand movement, however, he reached under the back of his jacket and shot both in the neck.

It took longer than he expected to search their bodies, pull them behind the boulder, and cover both with ground debris. The air was thin. Between them they had binoculars, a wristwatch, and a cell phone, which he crushed into little pieces with a heavy rock. They had a flashlight as well as the gun he'd seen earlier. The gun was too big and cumbersome to take with him, he thought, and between the both of them, there was very little ammunition. He decided in the end to take the gun anyway only to make certain it wouldn't be used to kill him. Then, of course, there was the food. He was about to carry it all, then realized that if he left some of it on them, the animals would make certain they were never found.

His first steps without his two guides were arduous. He now carried nearly ten more pounds than before. To avoid steep terrain for as long as possible, he decided to trek sideways. But at this rate it would take weeks to reach the summit. Was fatigue the result of his concussion? At the next switchback he stood on the edge of the mountain expecting to look across a vast range of snow- covered peaks. Unfortunately, cloud cover made it impossible. Though disappointed, he decided to sit down where he was and wait for the clouds to move. Whoever was looking for him would have a similar problem.

He fell asleep under a vinyl thermo skin. The wristwatch he had taken from Meng's nephew told him three hours had passed. Blue sky was directly overhead, but the mountains and villages below were now covered by low-hanging clouds. The scene above him was inviting and clear. Glaciers dotted the sides of mountains above tree line.

Were there villagers in those forests, trying to follow his tracks under those clouds? He didn't need more voices condemning him. He needed to work fast, but that was difficult. Moving across the mountain had been no less tiring. He began to climb upward.

Suddenly and without warning, pain shot through Xiao's back shoulder like a flaming arrow. His upper body shook as if electrified. Would the pain ever end? Just as suddenly the sharp nerve-peeling pain stopped. He fell backward, sliding headfirst down the mountain. His total body pain distracted him from fearing where his head might finally land. Slowly, painfully, his body came to a complete stop, while something inside of him continued to burn. He could smell his own flesh burning as he lost consciousness.

When his eyelids popped open, an Asian man stood over him covered in a suit made of rabbit fur, the sky around him was dark, and he held a burning lantern close to his own face.

"Damn," Xiao heard the man say in clear English. "After all these years, the bloody thing still works."

Xiao's eyes closed on their own. He was still conscious. Fervently, he hoped he could stay alive. Yet he had no control over anything. He was totally numb.

Finally, somebody pulled up his right eyelid, blinding him with light. The same person probably let that eyelid fall and did the same with the left eyelid. Xiao knew he was breathing hard, but that was his last memory before finding himself in a bed that he knew was not sitting on the floor.

His vision was blurred. Blinking rapidly didn't help. Eventually he saw the outline of a window at the far end of a long room. It reminded him of the lodge. Could he have been brought back to the village where Meng lived? His heart almost stopped with fear.

A tall man in black wearing eyeglasses walked into the room and stood over the bed. Xiao didn't recognize him. With the exception of his height, Xiao thought he was Asian. As his eyes became less blurry, Xiao saw that he wore a black woolen sweater and pants. He blinked, and the man was gone. The next time he saw that man he carried a chair and sat down close to the bed.

"How do you feel?" he asked, leaning over Xiao's head.

Xiao discovered that even the slightest attempt to move was met with severe throbbing pain. Only his eyeballs moved freely without pain.

"I understand," the man said. "You are deciding for yourself if there is any pain and where. Can you speak at all?"

Xiao pried his dry lips apart. The man quickly got up from his seat and left the room. He returned shortly with a ceramic cup of cold water. One drop from the cup hit Xiao's forehead and made him try to inch forward with his upper body. The man helped by gently holding the back of his head. Xiao was so grateful and so thirsty, he cried.

The man rushed to refill the cup and gave him more. Xiao appreciated this man's kindness and his height. Xiao was usually the tallest Asian in most crowds.

"My name is Dr. Woo. And you are Dr. Xiao Wren."

Xiao's face must have expressed his shock and surprise because Dr. Woo laughed, taking off his eyeglasses as he did. Finally Woo said, "I can tell you're one of Quan's men."

"And you are not?" Xiao asked with a raspy voice.

"Ah, you are quick. I like you already. And I want to assure you your vocal chords have not been injured. Sometimes animals I've tagged and later caught in my invisible fence can no longer whimper or growl as a result of those radio waves out there. It's a long story." Woo sat quietly placing his eyeglasses over his nose and around his ears, then peered into Xiao's eyes with a light.

In turn, Xiao felt hypnotized by Dr. Woo's movements. Somehow he seemed like an older version of himself with glasses. Xiao could stand the silence between them no longer. "Where am I?" he asked. "What caused my pain? How do you know my name?"

When Woo finished examining Xiao's eyes, ears, and inside his mouth, he stared at him for some time. Xiao listened for other sounds around them and heard nothing.

Then Woo said, "Quan gave you no training to become his spy. You also were given some nefarious purpose other than spying, and yet you aren't certain what that purpose is. I don't know why you're here, either."

Woo continued to stare. "You're about twenty kilometers from the summit," he continued. "I'm an American citizen, too," he paused. "Recruited by Quan in similar fashion, I suspect. Regarding your second question, there's something buried inside your body. It set off the alarm in my fence and caused your pain. It's in your back. There's a scar there that someone tried to camouflage. Quan doesn't usually do such shoddy work, but he's no surgeon. You're lucky I found you. You could have died from exposure.

"I know your name because it was transmitted to me separately by both the CIA and Quan's men. I'm answering your third question, by the way. I'm supposed to be on the lookout for you, but no reason was given by either organization. That's common.

"If you really are a lucky man, my fence shorted out most of the components inside that device in your back. That would make you nearly inoperable as a human weapon. But I'm only speculating. Yet if you adhere to Chinese tradition, you may expect the sacred powers of these mountains to brush your body and drip into your eyes, gifting you with medicinal herbs, and the magical fruits belonging to any cave heaven."

Woo got up from his chair, as if he suddenly heard something. He walked to the far window and with one hand yanked it toward him, like he was pulling open a cabinet door. It was not a window after all, although it looked like a real scene of the outdoors where snow occasionally dripped from branches. Instead, it was a flat monitor. Behind that monitor were several TV images.

Xiao used his fists and arms to fight the pain in his neck and shoulders in order to sit up in bed. Woo's back was toward him.

"Are we . . .? Are we . . .?" Xiao became dizzy and fell back against the pillows.

"Underground?" Woo answered. "Yes, we are. I keep track of people who venture inside four different lodges in this area. I've also got outside cameras covering two more lodges. Tourists stay a few nights and leave. It's rare that I have to . . . Hey, what are you doing?"

Xiao had pulled his blanket back and was trying to slide one leg off of the bed.

"You've got to rest," Woo demanded, but he didn't rush to Xiao's side. "I think the three young men who walked inside the furthest lodge," Woo continued, "are very likely looking for you. You'll need your strength." Then he walked to the bed and pushed Xiao's legs back under the covers.

"Who are you?" Xiao asked.

"You know what a spy is and what they do, right?

Xiao nodded in agreement.

"Well, have you heard the term counterspy?"

"No."

"How about a double agent?"

Xiao shook his head.

"That's okay, Xiao. Hopefully we'll have more time to talk later. I haven't had the luxury of adult companionship for . . ."

"Daddy?"

It was the voice of a little girl. Xiao's eyes widened at the sound. He remembered the sounds of the baby he had grabbed by the feet and legs before throwing it. He remembered Karen's tears and her angry reaction. But most of all he remembered her betrayal. Tears rolled down his face, his eyes got bigger, his breathing quicker, and his whole face showed fury. He remembered Karen's change in allegiance. Slowly he remembered everything, including his gun. Where was his gun? No, he had more than one gun now. Or did he? Did he leave the gun he had killed Karen with?

Dr. Woo stared into Xiao's eyes. Very slowly he sat down on the chair beside the bed again. The space between Woo's eyes narrowed in wrinkles before he answered the girl, never once taking his eyes off Xiao.

"What is it, honey?"

"Oh, nothing," a sad voice answered.

"You go to bed now," Woo replied. "I'll be there in a few minutes to tuck you in."

"I just want to play another game of peek-a-boo."

"Maybe not tonight, I'm afraid," Woo answered.

The two men continued to stare at each other for a very long time.

CHAPTER 25

NEZ MOTIONED FOR Billy to follow her. She desperately wanted to talk to Trace Mitchell again. He'd be inside the truck with these men, wouldn't he? The four men helped her up the steps and inside.

They weren't waiting on Billy's reticence. From their height, standing just inside the truck, they lifted him off the ground and yanked him inside by every appendage, while Billy squirmed in midair until he leapt free of his coat.

Scurrying over the top of utility vehicles and hills of sand beside the construction zone, he reached the roof of the nursing home. Close behind him was a man built like a football player but dressed in a well-made suit. Inez caught a brief glimpse of Billy on the roof of the nursing home. Fear hit her just as the door of the truck slammed shut. She fell backward into a barrel-shaped swivel chair.

"Have a seat," said a big grinning man. "Oh, you're already seated." When he realized he was still holding Billy's coat in his hands, he balled it up and threw it forcefully to the floor. Then he walked to the barrel-shaped chair across from Inez and sat down.

"You do know how to scare a person," Inez said.

"Do we go get that clown?" the driver yelled back.

"Naw," hollered yet another man, already seated in another swivel chair. He held a half-sized computer in his lap and stared into its screen. "He's disappeared over the roof of the place. Gordon'll catch him."

"What are you talking about?" Inez asked.

No one answered.

She knew better than to let them see her fear. Were these people really from CBI? She glanced around, realizing there were no tables with monitors, and no stools as there had been in the truck she sat in before.

The closest man to her still wore a grin and continued to stare at her. "We brought this truck," he finally said, "hoping you'd recognize it and trust us, Dr. Buchanan. I'm Agent Parker and we don't have time to introduce you to everybody. The two of you," he said, glancing at an empty seat beside her, "have been under audio and GPS surveillance by an international private military company called Shockenaugh, Inc. We were unaware of it until Trace Mitchell contacted us from Rome. He filled us in on several of this company's attempts to kill certain targeted people in the United States and elsewhere."

She brightened at the sound of his name. "How is he and what . . ."

"Before I get to that," Parker said, "let me tell you that CBI does not look kindly on people stepping into their territory. You probably consider it amateur sleuthing. We call it obstruction of justice."

He was definitely the senior agent among them, flaunting gray hair at his temples as proof. An earpiece connected to a coiled wire disappeared into his clothing and the man with the laptop wore one too. She couldn't see the driver at all from her seat.

Inez spoke up. "Then shouldn't the FBI be sitting here instead of you guys? I don't pretend to know a lot about government, but I have read a few of Colorado's laws. I know there's nothing that says it's okay to snatch people off the street."

There was silence, as the truck moved through the streets at a constant speed, only stopping, she assumed, for the occasional traffic light.

"Stop!" hollered the man with the laptop.

The truck stopped abruptly. A moment later, a fist banged hard against the sliding door. "It's Billy Needham," the man with the laptop announced.

So, Inez noted, the truck had a camera mounted somewhere on the outside. She got up, holding her purse tightly under one arm, intending to open the door with the other. The man with the laptop, however, swiftly blocked her effort, putting his whole weight against the door's handle. The seated elder statesman of the group, Parker, nodded his decision and the young man opened the door.

Billy was briskly lifted up into the back area of the truck with the rest of the passengers and frisked from head to toe by the man holding the laptop in one hand.

"You okay, Dr. Buchanan?" Billy asked, as the man shoved him into a swivel chair on the other side of Inez.

"Where's Gordon?" asked Agent Parker.

"He slipped and fell," Billy answered.

"Did he now!" the agent said angrily.

Billy turned to Inez and asked, "Did you tell them you wanted to go home?"

"Shut up," said the young man with the laptop. He sat down across from Billy.

"It's okay," Inez said, smiling at Billy. She couldn't hide her relief in seeing him. "These gentlemen are with the Colorado Bureau of Investigation. She reached out to touch Billy's hand, who grabbed it inside his own with a worried look on his face.

Parker spoke again, moving only a few muscles around the corners of his mouth. "To get back to what we were saying, the State Legislature knows what we're doing, Dr. Buchanan. You might say it's a test to see if we measure up to what the twenty-first century throws at us. All intelligence contractors pose a possible threat to law-abiding citizens of any country."

Up until now, Parker had rested the palms of his hands on his thighs. But very deliberately he stretched his arms out as if yawning, letting his jacket open to reveal a gun and shoulder holster.

"You have no idea what Shockenaugh is capable of," Parker continued. "Your conversation with Abraham Wallace was definitely compromised. That's how we located you. We followed Shockenaugh's communication signals. The content of your conversation was of little value to them. They broke it off after ten minutes."

Inez found that interesting and listened intently.

The agent with the laptop added, "That's why we staged that makeshift construction site next to Wallace's window. We wanted to block anyone trying to eavesdrop on your communication with that guy."

Inez became baffled. Why were they telling her this?

Billy, however, unable to control his anger, bounced on his haunches and said, "You fuckin' with us, aren't you?"

Billy then turned to Inez and said, "Pardon my patwah, Dr. Buchanan, but do you believe this shit? I don't!" He stood up inside the moving vehicle.

"Please!" Inez said sternly. Billy sat down before an agent could grab him.

"Billy." She touched his wrist with her hand and ignored the presence of the others in the truck. "There are several reasons why we should believe them. Remember when I told you that from my investigations I knew that a large entity was behind this, a country, a giant business, or municipality? Well, a private organization like this Shockenaugh Company makes sense."

Agent Parker broke in, "Your investigation, as you call it, has put a lot of people on their hit list. There's you, Billy, Trace Mitchell, his nephew Harry, Mr. Wallace, Sheila Drisco, Miriam Garfield, as well as her son. All of them can become an immediate embarrassment to Shockenaugh. And the list keeps getting larger. You've got to stop your investigation or all of them are going to die, if they haven't already!"

Inez looked directly into the agent's face. She held onto Billy's arm tightly. "What's happened to them?"

There was a pause, as if Parker pondered something important.

"Oh, give me a break!" Billy yelled, then leaned back in his chair.

Parker said, "They may have been seriously injured in a series of attempts on their lives. I don't know what the most current reports say. I can only tell you that it isn't likely that all of them survived."

Inez was speechless. Billy squeezed her hand tighter.

"Doctors are doing all they can, but . . ."

"I get it. I get it!" Inez said.

"Do you, Dr. Buchanan?" said Parker, "because frankly, we don't have the manpower to keep you under surveillance 24/7. You really think you're going to be able to apprehend self-righteous members of a killer elite private military force on suspicion of murder? It's not going to happen. Besides, we believe young Harry Mitchell may have killed the last Shockenaugh employee sent here to kill on this soil."

Inez shivered. "Where are we going?" she asked him.

"We're going to drop you back at your car. But I need to give you a tip before we leave. Don't use your cell phone again. Put a hammer to it. Stay off the internet. However we need you to keep your landline. And never leave your car unattended again. You've got a secure garage. Use it and stay home."

He handed her his card. "Call us anytime. Our people finished an extensive examination of your car while you've been with us. It will be safe to drive home now."

She was breathing hard, but still had the strength to ask a question. "Do you have any idea why I was talking to Abraham Wallace?"

"I'm not able to share that informa . . ."

"Then tell me this. Why was Gaelen Drisco killed?"

There was no answer. The truck came to a complete stop.

"Karen Drisco?" Inez asked. "Do you know her?"

Parker exhaled loudly and slid the side door open. "She's in a better place," Parker said. "Watch your step."

Billy jumped down first. Inez grabbed hold of Billy's hands. Tears collected in her eyes. The second her feet touched asphalt the truck sped off.

"I'll drive," Billy said and opened the passenger side door for her. A nursing home attendant ran out of the facility and up to the side of the car.

"Glad I caught you," the woman said. "We wondered if you were still in the building. Several orderlies went looking for you. I see someone must have told you the surprising news. I say surprising because Abraham was in perfectly good health for an eighty-nine-year-old."

Inez realized her tears had been silently falling since she got out of the truck.

"It was so nice that he got a chance to speak to you about the war before he passed away. He never got to go to the memorial in Washington, DC and no one had ever asked him to recount his story before. If you call us in a couple of days, we'll be able to tell you about his funeral arrangements," she said. "I've got to go back inside now and help give comfort to those he lived with. Thanks so much for coming."

Inez couldn't find her voice. She watched the woman run back inside and swallowed hard. She turned to Billy, who sat behind the wheel.

"I think you were right and I was wrong," she said.

"About what?" Billy asked.

"I don't think those men were with the Colorado Bureau of Investigation. And it's possible one of them killed Abraham while we were in their truck. There were four men beckoning me inside through the sliding door. The driver makes one more. One man left to follow you, so there should have been three seated with me but there were only two: Parker and the man with the laptop. I didn't notice it till we were leaving."

Billy and Inez continued to sit in her car in silence as night made the sky darken and the outdoor lights of the facility turn on around them.

Billy spoke first. "Abraham was an old old man," he said.

"Which is why I'd be wasting my time bringing this to the attention of the police."

Suddenly Inez declared, "I'm driving! I'm going to get you away from this mess just as soon as I can. When I drop you home, you stay there and away from me. You hear me? I'm a stupid old lady who shouldn't be out this late at night."

She opened the passenger side door, got out, and slammed it shut.

"Aw, now wait a minute," Billy said, as he slowly got out from behind the wheel and stood beside the car waiting for her. "Why you wanna' kick me to the ground when I'm already down?"

Though he held the door open for her, she glared at him.

"You know better than that," she said, as he walked around to the other side. "People are getting killed!"

"I know I messed up in that truck back there," Billy said, "but I was only . . ."

"No, you didn't mess up," she said. "I messed up. I was too afraid to ask to see their IDs because I thought they might be phony after all and then they'd know that I knew they weren't who they said they were and then they'd have to kill us. And if they weren't CBI, who else could they be?"

Billy stared at her, waiting for what she'd say next.

"So the less involved you are," Inez continued, "the better off you'll be."

"So who were those guys?" Billy asked.

"They had to be employed by the very company they were talking about."

"No shit! You're givin' me goosebumps. But how do you know that?"

She started the car, as if she was ignoring him, but continued to keep the brake on. "I can't say I'm 100 percent sure. Trace Mitchell would point out that I have no evidence. I can't put my finger on the thing that told me they weren't CBI, but something did."

"I know what you mean," Billy echoed. "They looked like middle-aged Crips and Bloods to me. I'm saying I don't see any link between what Wallace said about Gaelen Drisco and this Shockenaugh Company those men were describing."

Inez looked into space and said, "Oh, I see the link, all right. You weren't listening to the right part of Abraham's story, about the sweat and blood and hair left on all those uniforms Gaelen kept. Those uniforms belonged to war strategists, the heroes of the Second World War."

"I still don't get it."

"Whoever hired Shockenaugh wants those uniforms for the traces of DNA on them. If Hank was right, his camera must have captured Eisenhower's dandruff and MacArthur's sweat stains in every photo he posted on eBay."

"No joke?" Billy was silent after that, but only for a moment. "Here's the thing though, I want to keep *you* safe. You need me. You know you do. And I'm not going home to wait for you to call me. Hell, I'm in danger whenever I cross Martin Luther King Boulevard. Every black man's in danger of dying from the day he was born. I'd like to think it's cause we're too busy fighting injustice. I'm in a better place around you Doc. I really am. Nobody's going to get murdered without paying for it on your watch.

"And I'm learning more around you. I feel like I'm doing something for the greater good. Like you said to me once, look five chess moves down the board before you jump. You're like my second mom, my Obi-Wan. Besides," -he pressed his back against the seat's upholstery and looked out the windshield- "I know something you don't know. I know who Gordon is."

She turned the motor off. "What do you mean?"

"I mean I took his wallet after I knocked him out. I meant to give it back once I was inside the truck, but somehow I didn't think that was wise." Billy began pulling it out of his back pants pocket.

"I was trying to catch up to the truck so I never had a chance to look inside it." He handed the wallet to Inez and sat quietly waiting for her to look through everything. As soon as she finished, she looked at him.

"I was hoping I was wrong," she said, "that I was jumping to conclusions, making associations where there weren't any. But there isn't anything here that says he works for CBI. There is, however, a business card belonging to someone in naval intelligence named Gerald Simon ... nothing in here with the name Gordon on it."

"Maybe we should give this to Mr. Mitchell," Billy suggested. "Oh, that's right, he's gone to Europe to bring Sheila back."

"Well, you're right about one thing," Inez said. "We should give it to someone who can help. I have no idea why we're still alive. Except the good Lord didn't want us just yet. So if you're going to be my sidekick on top of being my tech guy, my envelope stuffer, my snow remover, my grass cutter, and so forth."

"Yes ma'm, I got it. I've got to use my head more. I know that. I want to live, too. Honest to God I do."

Her eyes slowly lit up. "I think I know where to get the help we need. Now you put this wallet away and don't tell anybody about it until I tell you to, okay?"

Billy nodded in agreement before putting his seatbelt on.

Inez turned the ignition on and backed the car out of the parking space. She headed back to Park Hill.

CHAPTER 26

MITCHELL TWISTED AROUND in his seat to see Sheila's knuckle bulging through bloodless skin while she gripped the wheel. Like someone playing a video game for the right to live another day, she determinedly stared ahead.

"You're doing fine," he said. "Take it easy." He took Luigi's cell phone out of his pocket again to complete the call he'd started earlier. Mitchell spoke no Italian, but Sheila helped. The machine asked him to leave a message.

"Sorry for your loss Inspector Falvo, but we need your help," Mitchell said into the machine. "As you've heard by now, your son was killed inside an apartment occupied by Antonio Dante. We don't know who did the shooting, but Luigi was shot while trying to open a safe. When the gunfire stopped and the lights came back on, the safe's contents were gone. People have been shooting at us ever since.

"Sheila's sister, Miriam Garfield, has also been shot at since returning here from the States. We're on our way to Tivoli to meet her and . . . hello? . . . hello? . . . So much for cell phones and message machines."

"You summarize well." She laughed then shouted, "Hey! That's our sign."

He dug his fingers into the upholstered back of her seat as she swerved on two tires to cut across three lanes of traffic.

"We made it," she explained.

"We can't help her if we're dead," Mitchell exclaimed.

"Sorryeee."

They drove cautiously down narrow streets. "Now I understand why Italian cars are so narrow" Mitchell said. "Did I tell you this is my first trip to Italy?" he asked.

"Nooo, really? I'd never have guessed. Look for Via Sputelli. I'm sorry," she said. "I must sound horrible, but staying alive is much more important to me at the moment."

"I agree. I was just providing comic relief."

They both saw the sign at the same time. Sheila turned sharply and headed downhill. At the bottom was a small church surrounded by a narrow garden with statues. A forest of trees and low-growing bushes stood forty or fifty feet away from the stone building and continued up the sides of the surrounding hills. Only one car sat in a large car park, its windows broken out, its tires flat.

"Is she renting the whole building," Mitchell asked, "or has it been renovated into more than one apartment?"

"Her message didn't say. I can replay it for you, if you want."

"No. See if you can drive around at least the two sides of it that have no forest behind them." Mitchell directed.

Nothing looked good about the place. It was similar to a mid-sized fortress with miniature turrets around the roofline. They'd passed a small bed-and-breakfast hotel up the road with lights warmly glowing from its windows. This comforted Mitchell, who felt they hadn't left civilization altogether. However, the church Miriam lived in showed no signs of life. The windows on the lower level were frosted or painted. Sheila was about to make a U-turn and drive through again.

"Not so fast, Inspector Clouseau," Mitchell said to his driver. "Back up to those bushes and park. Turn off the motor. Guess you didn't see those two motorcycles hidden behind the bushes. Use your phone and call her. Ask where she is in relation to the front door and ask her something silly. See what she says."

Sheila pushed buttons again and again, but there was no answer. Turning to Mitchell, she finally said, "I can't drive away from here without knowing what's happened to her."

"What made her choose a place like this, anyway?" Mitchell asked.

"Don't know. We were never close. Give me the gun and I'll go get her," Sheila said.

"You're quite a piece of work, Sheila Drisco. I'll say that for you. You think I'm not in there right now because I'm scared. Bet you'd traipse up to the front door and scream her name," he said.

"What's wrong with that? You've got Luigi's gun."

"Why do you suppose she hasn't answered the phone?" he asked.

"Have no idea and don't want to think about it. Are you coming or not?" She opened the car door.

"Stop! We could be outnumbered. When *I* get out of this car, I want you to drive further up the hill to that little hotel we passed. Stay parked behind the trees so you can see who comes out the front door down here. Be as quiet as you can. Wait fifteen minutes and then call the police. Right now, I'm going to let air out of those motorcycle tires."

They stared at each other for a moment, but his reaction time was quicker. He grabbed her face with both hands, kissing her lips roughly. But before he turned to hop out, she'd landed her fist on the same side of his jaw that had been cut by flying window glass.

Though his intake of air was audible, it was his Navy Seal training that prevented him from hollering.

"You think I'm a whore, don't you?" she spit.

He kept his jaws locked, knowing that anything he did now, he'd regret.

"Well, don't you?" she asked again.

Maybe he did. He hadn't thought about it, and certainly this wasn't the time or the place.

"How's the gas?" he asked.

Her nostrils widened, her chest heaved in short, quick movements. "We're good," she replied.

Mitchell closed the door behind him quietly and dashed toward the motorcycles while she drove back up the hill.

There was a good chance Miriam was already dead, he told himself, particularly if that was her mangled car parked out front. An entire side of the building was covered in ivy. Gargoyles surrounded the roof and one turret grew out of nowhere. The sharp angles of the roof suggested the building's use at one time as a church.

A second-story door on a shallow balcony compelled him to try that first. He began climbing what appeared to have been a vine, which over the years had turned into something more like iron. He reached the upstairs door quickly. It was unlocked and heavy.

Mitchell eased it open only far enough to enter noiselessly. There he stood, in a hallway, listening for voices.

"Why're you still here?" a gravely voice said. "You should have been outside diggin' her grave by now."

"Gotta get this open."

Mitchell's heart sank. What surprised him were their accents. It sounded like cockney English, and he was suddenly reminded of the varied ethnicities of the people doing the shooting. Were they all members of Shockenaugh, Inc? How were they recruited to murder across the globe?

Mitchell tiptoed until he reached a stairway and could hear the men clearer.

"We gotta do somethin' 'bout her before the day is over."

"Keep your head on. I say we scrap this project. It's a mess we got 'ere. Too complicated for the likes of us, I'd say."

"Walk away from that kind of money?"

"Never sent body parts through the mail before, have ya'?"

"I don't see the problem. I could shoot that lock off with . . ."

"You don't get it. That door down there is part of a vault. Part of the . . . the reliquary, I think she called it."

"Don't act smart with me. You'd never heard of it before either."

"What do ya' say we walk away? Nobody's the worst."

There was hope yet, Mitchell thought. He realized Miriam was locked behind something that prevented her from being reached by phone. Maybe she didn't have her phone with her anyway.

"That broad's seen my face."

"Don't kid ya'self, Freddy. There's nothin' distinctive 'bout the way you look."

"I don't know. It's not your life bein' screwed here, is it? Besides, I think there's somebody in there with her."

Mitchell heard a gun being cocked, then just as suddenly, heard it resound through the walls.

"What's the matter with you! You think nobody'll hear that?" Mitchell worried. Would the shot bring Sheila running back?

"Yeah, well now we know, don't we, Fred?"

"Now we know what, ya' stupid arse?"

"No gun we got is gonna' break down that damn door. We gotta' get outa' here. There's other ways ta' get our hands on a million. He never really asked us 'bout it, said we was too dense to get it straight anyway, said this was the kinda' job he'd have to shoot us, if we botched."

"If you think Berini was offerin' us a part of his take, you're loonier than you look, I'd say!"

Mitchell heard footsteps as they climbed the stairs coming up from the basement. They must have walked down the hall just below his floor until they reached the latch of a door at the back of the building. He heard it break apart and then clamp shut again. Mitchell waited three minutes then hurriedly tiptoed down the stairs, across the hallway, and down the stairs into the basement until he stood beside the door with the bulletproof lock.

"Miriam! Miriam Garfield! This is Trace Mitchell! Remember me? I drove the UPS truck in Denver? Are you all right?" He stopped. Metal began to clank against metal on the other side of the door. The sound stopped.

"It's okay, Miriam," Mitchell yelled louder. "Sheila's getting help."

The noise of scraping metal started up again until he could see the stone door move slightly. Mitchell pushed on his side.

"Dear God," Miriam said, "I thought we were as good as dead." She pulled the door back just far enough to see out. Don't ever tell Inez this, but I too had my doubts that Dad was murdered. I don't have any doubts now. I just don't know why all this is happening."

"We aren't safe yet," Mitchell said. There was no time to process anything Miriam was telling him. "I haven't heard their motorcycles start up yet. Stay here and be ready to lock up again if you hear anything indicating trouble."

He crept up the stairs to the hallway and waited. Still no sound of a motorcycle's ignition. Mitchell had made sure not to let out enough air to be noticed. Worried, he headed for the double doors at the opposite end of the doorway. They weren't locked. The lights were on and magazines were on the floor, as if Miriam had only just left the place. Even messy, it had the look of a living room out of *Architectural Digest*.

Mitchell searched for a window that opened, as an alternative exit. These windows were exceptionally tall and, what the hell, he'd break one and tackle the consequences. He picked up a short but heavy figurine from the coffee table and threw it.

Large pieces of glass crashed loudly to the stone floor. He jumped into the gaping hole and landed on grass, when someone grabbed him by the neck and shoulders and yanked him across the lawn. His legs scraped against jagged pieces of window glass until a fist from nowhere socked him across his chin.

Mitchell was only stunned. From his position on the ground, he saw an overweight man standing over him dressed in ragged clothes and covered in black chimney soot. Had he entered the premises through the chimney?

"Look here, what I found," the man said to someone behind Mitchell.

Mitchell pulled from his groin to get up, but the man put a sturdy leather boot on his chest to mash him back down into the grass. However, it wasn't sturdy enough, and Mitchell twisted his opponent's foot forward over his head to get the fat man to fall. Stealing a move he'd taught his nephew, Harry, he leaped to his feet as soon as the man fell, but the man behind him had a weapon.

"Take two steps backward or I'll blow your head off."

He held a long-barreled rifle and Mitchell knew the man's threat was real. He took two steps backward toward the building.

"Cal, you get behind me."

The fat man on the ground couldn't get up and Mitchell's eyes darted from one to the other. He was making plans.

"Wait!" Mitchell shouted. "You know your friend Cal here is going to bleed to death if he doesn't see a doctor soon."

His words got the man with the rifle to take his eyes off of Mitchell and look behind him.

Quick as lightning, Mitchell snatched the gun away from the man who was standing, while he kicked the man on the ground in the face to keep him there longer. Although Mitchell had possession of the rifle, the angry big man tucked his head down and rushed Mitchell, aiming for his chest. They both landed inside the living room on the floor with the man on top of him. The rifle was in the grip of both men, Mitchell holding it over his head.

He barely saw the figure of a woman behind the man. He only knew something was moving. She must have been waiting by the broken window. Miriam hit that man hard over his head with a metal golf club. The rifle went off as he fell limp before falling halfway onto the floor beside Mitchell.

"That was close. Glad you didn't wait downstairs," Mitchell said. But as he looked up at Miriam, her face was ashen. She dropped the golf club. Mitchell sprung from the floor and grabbed her shoulders. "Miriam, what's wrong?"

"Xavier!" Her face slowly scrunched into a nightmarish jigsaw puzzle, forcing Mitchell to look where she was looking. Then she screamed. In front of her was a sprawled teenaged boy of about thirteen or fourteen. He must have been hiding in the line of fire. "Oh my God!" she cried.

Mitchell pushed Miriam aside, kneeled beside him, and felt for a pulse. He lifted him to the nearest sofa. Images of his nephew Harry stretched out on a gurney rushed through his thoughts.

"Is he all right?" Miriam shouted.

"That stray bullet must have caught him in the shoulder, I think. But I'm guessing. I'm no doctor."

Just then, the doors at the far end of the hall burst open. Men in uniforms, yelling in Italian, confronted Mitchell and Miriam, their guns drawn. Sheila broke away from the grip of a Carabinieri and ran out from behind him. She yelled, "I brought help. I brought help."

"Get an ambulance!" Miriam shouted back.

CHAPTER 27

FEBRUARY 2007 YUNNAN

XIAO COULDN'T REMEMBER whether the needle prick on the back of his hand came after his eyes closed or before. In any event, he'd been drugged. When his eyes finally opened, he noticed that the phony window showed the same outdoor scene, but at night. In an attempt to lift himself up to see better, he realized he couldn't move. He was paralyzed from the neck down. Xiao screamed. He wasn't very loud. His lungs barely moved. Was he dying or dead already? He tried screaming again. Where was his chorus of voices when he needed them?

Woo ran into the room and stopped short beside Xiao's bed. For a moment there was silence, until Xiao tried doing the one thing he knew he could. He screamed again.

"Xiao, you're okay." Dr. Woo put a hand on his shoulder. "It wears off. You're not in pain anymore, are you?"

"No," he said between longer breaths.

"See? Obviously, your vocal chords are better, too. I gave you something to repair your body. Try moving your extremities, slowly at first."

He did so, and his body gradually began to relax. He moved his arms and bent his knees before feeling confidence in Woo's words.

"What is your field of study, Doctor?" Xiao asked.

"Psycho-chemical engineering. And you, Doctor? You're very young to be a doctor."

"Bioengineering. Are you going to kill me?" Xiao asked. He watched Woo walk to the cabinet, not with a limp as much as a peculiar way of shaking one leg before setting it on the ground. It was done so quickly it could have been overlooked. Xiao noticed Woo watching those monitors inside the cabinet. "Quan has no reason," Xiao added, "to kill me, now."

With his back facing Xiao, Woo answered, "No one has asked me to kill you. But Quan is known for creating reasons out of thin air. Several men have been looking for you today. After you've eaten, I'll show you a few faces from the monitors. You may recognize who is searching for you."

What made Woo think they were looking for him? Xiao wondered. He decided not to ask, preferring to appear stupid. He also resented not being able to get Woo's full attention. Instead he asked, "I heard a child's voice last night, a little girl." Xiao busily flexed his muscles under the blanket as he spoke. He was determined to one day escape from this man. "Who was she?" Xiao asked.

"Last night?" Woo turned around to look at him. "That happened over a week ago. And when you became conscious the first time, you had been in a coma for two months. Your brain was swollen from the electrical shock my invisible fence gave you when it detected the device inside your body. I kept you in a coma until you showed signs of healing. I'm not a surgeon though. I didn't remove whatever it is inside you. I think it was meant to kill you, while it performed some other function. It could still be a booby trap inside you. Quan is known for his deceptions. That's why I didn't touch it. Unfortunately the invisible fence doesn't work anymore and I'm not able to get the parts to fix it."

A very delicate little black-haired girl pushed a tray mounted on wheels into the room. It was the right size for her dolls. On it was a regular-sized cup of coffee, a single slice of familiar-looking bread and two thin slices of smoked pork.

"You carried enough provisions," Woo said, as he held the food so that Xiao could take bites, "to last several months. Had you been traveling with others?" he asked.

"No." He knew he didn't have that much food on him, but he added, "I intended to walk back to the United States."

The middle-aged man held the coffee cup for Xiao to drink from and said, "How odd, that we should have the same mission. Let me introduce you to my daughter, Kaitlyn. She's four years old and I'll be taking her with me on that walk back to the States."

The girl said nothing but clung to her father's pant leg. Woo sat on the chair next to the bed and lifted the girl onto his lap. For some reason Xiao suddenly wasn't hungry anymore.

"And by the way," Woo said, "why did you keep that cell phone? Surely you knew it would track your movements. Were you trying to stay connected to someone?"

Xiao didn't know how to answer him.

"You're very lucky you're in this cave," Woo continued. "It blocks all such signals. But I took the further precaution of wrapping your phone in tin, just in case you forgot and took it out of the cave again."

Xiao said nothing. He wondered himself why he had been so stupid.

The child sat very quietly on Woo's knee and stared at Xiao. Woo said, "I must apologize to you. I know you have questions, but I have no time to answer them. I haven't asked you very much because I'm sure our stories are similar. For example, I, too, came to China on a grant, which I abandoned when Quan approached me with a deal to work for China. I realize now, it wasn't exactly working for China. I returned to the States to perform a mission that Quan blackmailed me into performing, whereupon the CIA charged me with treason. The CIA intended to send me to prison for life but decided to send me back to China, only if I swore to work for them upon my return. China doesn't tolerate double agents. Quan would have killed me on sight if he hadn't needed my help." He paused and spoke to the girl. "Go stand by your things. I'll be there in a minute."

She jumped off his lap and ran out of the room.

Woo leaned closer to Xiao and said, "Trust no one."

Sensing Woo's departure was soon, Xiao said, "You can't leave me here alone."

"Of course I can."

"What about my guns?"

"They're in the room beyond this one. These walls are merely the remnants of old cargo containers jammed into a natural cave. This shelter, as you see it now, was built decades ago

"But I can't even stand," Xiao pleaded.

"I know you can't. I planned it that way. Your legs and feet will be the last to regain their usefulness," Woo said.

Xiao ripped the blanket from his legs. He then twisted his knees to the side and flung himself over the edge of the bed. Woo quickly stood and moved his chair back. Xiao landed on wrists and hands that couldn't support his body. His feet and legs followed to the floor, bruising him.

"That wasn't wise," Woo said. "When the medicine wears off, your legs will feel the pain of that fall. Try not to make any more reckless decisions. There'll be no one here to patch you up. As a matter of fact, if I were you, I'd stay here for as long as I could."

Slowly and with little effort, Woo picked him up and placed him on the bed again. "You have irregular brain waves and inappropriate emotional responses. I'm sure a doctor has already given you his opinion. Perhaps living here will give you time to heal your body and repair your mental condition."

Woo covered the blanket over Xiao and said, "I'd better leave now. You know, I'd never have trusted you here around my daughter. Russian research suggests that fasting and meditating might be the cure you need. You'll find such articles and more in the makeshift library in the next room. The history of this place should interest you as well."

The more Xiao listened, the angrier he became. He noticed the room seemed to move again.

"If I hadn't decided to check the traps," Woo continued, "Kaitlyn and I would have been gone from here months ago and you would have died in the snow. Apparently, we both have important destinies ahead of us to fulfill."

Woo took out what appeared to be a map from inside his wool cardigan. "I'm leaving this with you and everything else that's here." He threw it on the bed, careful not to stand within Xiao's reaching distance. "There's oscillators, computers, filtered air systems, generators. I'm only the second owner of this valuable real estate. I took my stewardship of this place very seriously." He stood up suddenly. "My wife and son died much farther up the mountain to keep this place a secret. But in order to maintain Kaitlyn's safety we'll need to move."

Xiao's eyes closed. His head felt like stone.

"I put something in your coffee to make you sleep," Woo said. "It will lessen your anxiety over my leaving. Don't worry, Xiao. You've had the pleasure of meeting a good man who lost his way for a relatively short period of time in the scope of this planet's life. Perhaps one day you'll describe yourself in the same manner. Remember, people who have their mental health are always willing to help others. They're rarely consumed with, nor do they have time to dwell on their own problems."

**

The minute Xiao awoke, his eyes searched the room. He rejoiced. His movements were painless. First, he got up from the bed and opened the cabinet door that looked like a window. A single monitor displayed six stationary scenes. Did they represent six different lodges or several rooms inside one lodge? And where were these lodges?

There were four rooms, one behind the other. But not one metal wall had a door in it. There had to be an exit. He was sure Woo and his daughter were gone and that he had been left alone.

When he heard voices in the next room, he almost collapsed. It was the room where he'd been in bed. Slowly he crept to the doorway and peered inside. The sound came from the monitor, and he knew immediately who was speaking. Meng was inside one of the lodges with two other men. His face was drawn and he looked much older than he had when Xiao last saw him.

Xiao pulled the chair beside the bed, closer to the screen. Mesmerized by the thought that Meng couldn't see him, Xiao watched for most of a day as the men searched through furnishings inside the lodge. Whenever any one of them walked out of the line of sight, Xiao began to wonder about his own two guns.

But if he left his chair to look for them, he might miss something important. Just when he wondered how far away he was from Meng, he heard a noise overhead, like metal slowly and deliberately scraping another piece of metal. As he looked above his head, he saw a vent and an exhaust fan housed inside. The men on the monitor had not responded to the sound. Xiao felt some relief that he was not very close to them after all.

Suddenly he spied the papers Woo had left on the bed for him. He remembered Woo's talk of a map in particular. He grabbed them up and ran back to sit in front of the monitors again. The men hadn't moved. Were they preparing to leave or stay in the lodge? Was it morning or night? Xiao remembered the watch he'd taken from one of Meng's nephews and the food they'd given him. Where were these things?

Xiao slowly grew absorbed by the papers in his hands. Not only was there a map of the area, but a diagram of the shelter itself. Woo had left him a wealth of information. The map showed an entrance in the ceiling and a refrigerator was located there. A portable cookstove, with its own exhaust led outside the cave and a bathroom had been built around a hole in the floor. Woo had also drawn arrows showing where he had hidden the guns so that his daughter couldn't reach them.

Days passed while Xiao lay on the bed reading books, diaries, and papers. He began to breathe easily. This wasn't such a bad place to live after all. Woo had even drawn plans for running water. He also now knew that the closest lodge was about 3.5 kilometers away.

When a picture on the monitor faded away, he knew the cause was interference with the laser beam. Lasers carried data unseen across the mountain. Unfortunately, Xiao also knew that interference could be anything from fog, snow, animals, or humans.

The fence was another matter. It was entirely electrical with no visible metal parts, extending two kilometers in all directions from the shelter. That's how far away he had been when Dr. Woo found him. He also knew he would need more food once the pork ran out, but surely he could shoot something that roamed between the fence and the cave if he disarmed the fence at intervals.

Weeks later, a bright light came from the monitor. The screen was no longer a major distraction, since Xiao had found much more to occupy his mind. There was something familiar about this face on the screen though. He wasn't certain because the man had mashed his nose against the camera's lens. Was that to obscure his face even more? The man reminded him of the athletic-looking Bohai, and yet this man looked even younger. The screen suddenly went blank and Xiao later went to bed. In the middle of the night, he sat up in darkness, remembering that it was Kee's face. Could Quan be far behind? Just how safe was he? His fear, but mostly resentment, grew for both men from that night forward.

CHAPTER 28

NEZ HEARD TWO deadbolt locks turn before Hank Jeffrey's door opened about an inch. The eyes above Hank's weathered crow's feet looked stunned the minute they focused on her.

"I know we're interrupting," Inez said hurriedly, with her mouth near the opening crack. "And I'd like to tell you we'd be willing to come back later, but I'd be lying."

"I'm sorry," Hank said, opening the door wider and stepping back to let them in.

Inez knew his discomfort in letting black people into his home. Months ago she'd visited his wife, only once, when she was ill. Then, Inez had waited until he'd gone to the grocery store before knocking.

"There's a certain amount of urgency to my problem," Inez continued, "but it's going to take a while to tell it."

Agnes suddenly appeared from a dark kitchen like a cobra uncoiling its head, "Hello Inez," she said. "Billy, isn't it?"

"Yes, ma'm" Billy answered. "I'm surprised you remembered."

"Oh yes, I remember. You were so little when you helped me around the yard, but I never forgot you." Though she was smiling, Inez wondered who she was really remembering. The rumor on the block was that she was showing signs of dementia.

"You look stronger than the last time I saw you," Inez said. Agnes had always been fragile and now her gait was even slower. Age had not been kind to her. Agnes had contracted arthritis at a relatively young age. That was the reason the neighbors, including Karen Drisco, visited from time to time.

"How do you feel, Agnes?" Inez took hold of both her hands, trying to remember what she had heard about her last hospital stay. From the corner of her eye she noticed that Hank had retreated into the kitchen where he turned the light on.

"You people eat soup, don't you?" Hank asked.

"Not if I can get my hands on chitterlin's and hog maws," Inez answered quickly.

Billy grinned, but Hank never looked up. Inez was confidant Hank wouldn't understand her sarcasm anyway. He continued to examine his shelves of soup cans.

"No, no, Hank," Inez insisted, as she walked into the kitchen. "We aren't here for dinner. I was thinking we'd talk, while you ate your dinner and listened. We don't want . . ."

"Nonsense!" Agnes said. "You all go into the living room and . . ."

"Actually, I'd rather not," Inez said. "We're all better off out here in the back of the house where no one can see us."

Hank stiffened his chin as he watched Billy bring a chair from the dining room into the kitchen to sit next to Inez.

Finally, Hank said, "I don't mind a bit. Fire away."

"Before I do, do you have a cell phone anywhere?" Inez asked.

"I don't believe in them," he said. "Sorry."

Inez and Billy exchanged silent glances. "I knew we'd come to the right place," she said to Billy.

They all sat at the table except Hank, who busily attended to a pot of canned soup, adding spices from dusty containers.

"Billy and I want to tell you a story about Gaelen, hoping that your expertise on government conspiracies can help keep us alive."

"Wait a minute," Hank said. He poured soup into mugs, then put a handful of spoons in the center of the table with a giant saltshaker. After Inez and Billy thanked him for his hospitality, Hank took a long look at Inez. "Is this about somebody's civics homework?" he asked tilting his head toward Billy.

"No." And to herself, she said, *You stupid redneck, you! You think we'd come here where we're not wanted for that?*

She watched him walk away and into the dining room, stop at the sideboard, open a drawer, and pull out a handgun. He checked it for bullets. Inez cringed. Yet wasn't that one of the reasons she'd come to him? She knew he'd have guns. Weren't all conservative white men afraid to sleep without them? Her eyes stayed planted on the metal in his hands.

Returning to the kitchen again, Hank took a shawl off a wall hook beside the back door and placed it over his wife's shoulders before he sat down beside her. He gently placed the gun on the table in front of her.

"Go ahead now," he said to Inez. "I'm ready for your story when you are. You're safe here. Nobody can get a round off quicker'n Agnes."

Inez had entered a world in which she had no experience. But Hank was just as close to that gun as Agnes, and surprisingly, she still didn't feel safe.

Hank listened to Inez for fifteen whole minutes without interruption. Then he stopped her in the middle of a sentence, got up from his chair, and used the landline in his dining room.

"Nate, this is Hank Jeffrey. I've got a situation here. I'll need your help." He began to whisper and Inez couldn't hear anymore of the conversation.

He said the same thing to three more people he called, then returned to the kitchen and sat beside Agnes. Inez wondered what Hank was doing but didn't ask. She'd have to trust him, if she wanted his help. Then he asked her to pick up the story where she had left off.

After twenty more minutes, he interrupted again. "Before it gets too dark, Billy and I are going on reconnaissance to your house. You still got all that food you bought the other day? I ask because you need to stay here for a few nights. We shouldn't be out either, because Shockenaugh knows you're here by now. We're now on their hit list, too. If that doesn't make you feel guilty, I don't know what will."

Inez's face scrunched up under the weight of the day's trauma. She was not about to cry again. And she was not about to stay in Hank's house overnight either. But they were welcome to all the food in her house and then some.

Agnes looked like a blank sheet of white paper. Inez covered her own face with her hands to shut out Agnes and the world for a moment. She wanted to hide those feelings of guilt Hank mentioned. If only she had time to organize events into clearer sequential pictures. That's what teachers do, make sense out of life.

Hank knelt beside her chair and gently pulled her hands away from her face. Had he thought she was crying? The contrast of his large calloused and hairy white hands on her smaller brown fingers seemed to amuse him because he smiled, not at her, but at her hands. Inez pulled them back, suddenly uncomfortable with his touch.

"Don't worry," he said. "You made a good decision coming here." He stood up beside his wife and patted her shoulder. "But I am curious," he said, looking straight at Inez, "what made you think of me?"

It was a fair question, and she'd thought about it even before today.

"First, you have guns and you know how to use them. Second, I think rednecks want their friends' killers brought to justice as much as any liberal would. Third, during all the neighborhood block parties we had here, I listened to you give the most knowledgeable made-up explanation for almost every conspiracy theory out there. You, more than anyone else, may have an idea of what's behind all this. And last but not least, you recently told me you worked for military intelligence."

He laughed loudly, but no one else did. Billy got up and went into the living room, carrying the chair from the dining room with him. He flipped through magazines on their coffee table. Inez recognized his look of disgust.

"I think what I hear you saying is that I'm armed, honest, and almost as smart as you are. Well, I guess deep down I respect you too, Inez. A great many people helped me put aside my racist past. I'm just sorry you felt you had to wait so long to ask me for help. I had no idea the extent of your investigation. So brace yourself." Hank pulled his chair closer to Inez.

"Most people," he said, "assumed Agnes and I came from some cattle ranch in Wyoming that went belly-up. We didn't do anything to correct their misconceptions. All we wanted was a new life, one that bore little resemblance to what we did before we got here."

He got up to remove the last few empty cups of soup from the table and put them in the sink. If this was their dinner every night, Inez thought, she was certain no one else on their block knew it. She wasn't going to let any neighbor of hers go hungry as long as she could help it.

"You don't know how grateful I am to you, Inez," Hank said. "Remember the first block party after we moved in? You pegged me right away. Wanted to know how long I'd been a member of a militia. Wanted to embarrass me, I think. Wanted to call me out in front of my new neighbors. And at the time, I didn't know what the ideology of the word 'militia' meant in this country. Had to look it up in a dictionary when I got home to make sure."

"Hank, all I wanted to do was keep our neighborhood safe. I just . . ."

"Oh, I understand. But once I found out about the many kinds of militias there were across the United States, I joined one, right here in Colorado, started by a group of liberal hippies, if you can imagine it." Hank began to laugh loudly but no one else laughed with him.

"You see," he continued, "you were right. I thought you were one scary bitch, maybe even clairvoyant. Agnes and I were born and raised in South Africa. I worked in military intelligence, but not for this country, not in the beginning. We loved apartheid. Our homestead prospered. I confess we did some ugly things we thought we had to do to survive there. Guess you could tell. It was the constant hypocrisy that finally made us want to leave that part of the world. But the truth is, even when we first settled here, we were still people you would have hated."

Billy had put down his magazine and turned around on the sofa to watch Hank talk. Hank's back was toward him.

Most people accepted the lie that Agnes was originally from England, but me, well, I'm pretty good with any accent, even when I'm drunk, am I not? I've got that cowboy drawl down pat."

Billy listened intently but said nothing.

"You're full of surprises," said Inez. She was remembering all the camping and hunting trips Hank and Larry went on to bring elk back to share with neighbors. Her sudden disappointment in Hank was too big to hide, and she knew it was present in what few words she could manage to utter.

"Well, here's another surprise, Inez. After we sold our homestead, but before moving to the States, I made money as a member of a private army in South Africa called Executive Outreach. If you've done your homework, you've probably come across that name before. Some of my youngest recruits in those days have now become officers in several similar companies such as White River, Shockenaugh, and others. So you see, I'm your best bet. Not only can I get you out of this mess alive, I can probably find Gaelen's killer as soon as I know whose playground we're playing in."

He shot a quick look at Agnes, who stoically stared back at him.

"Right now we're in the middle of an overture," he said to Inez. "That's similar to a shift change at your local police station. There's a short interval when the right hand doesn't know what the left hand just did for the day. Only in security organizations it's unfortunately longer than a minute. Everyone slows down to listen to or read each other's reports until everyone's caught up. Shockenaugh was recently taken over by another company. That much I know. My guess is either CBI hasn't caught up with Shockenaugh's activities, or you and Billy were in a UPS truck filled with Shockenaugh operatives masquerading as CBI agents."

Inez stretched her neck back and with some astonishment said, "So why didn't they kill us?"

"If they'd wanted to, they certainly would have. And nobody would have ever found your bodies."

Fierce knocking at the front door made Hank switch off all the lights on the first floor. Everyone stood up in darkness, including Agnes, while Inez followed a few paces behind Hank as he walked to the front door. She looked back quickly and saw that the gun was gone from the kitchen table.

Hank eased the door open all the way, letting two huge men inside. One was white with black grease smudged over his face and hands. The other was a black man. Each carried camouflaged backpacks and large duffle bags they strained to lift. When they reached an open door to the basement, they stopped to place their heavy loads on the floor.

The black man said, "They spotted us under the only street light at the corner and shot at us soon as we got out of the car. The gun had a silencer."

"I think it's started," said the other man.

Inez noticed their body armor in a shaft of moonlight falling across the living room. Without fanfare, they lifted their gear and walked down the steps of the basement.

Inez found their words hard to believe. "Gunshots in this part of Park Hill?"

Just then, another fist rapidly pounded against Hank's front door. Everyone ducked behind the nearest piece of furniture because that's what Hank did. They waited, hoping in the darkness that the person would go away.

CHAPTER 29

MARCH 2007   TIVOLI

M ITCHELL HADN'T PEED since Luigi had led him into the men's room of the airport earlier that morning. He'd thought it was going to be a show of length. Trace was now thankful they'd made that sudden pit stop.

Mitchell and Luigi had gone to the safe house together, and now Luigi was dead. An Indian man wearing a turban was dead along with two men with cockney accents. If they were lucky, like his own nephew, Sheila's nephew Xavier was going to be fine. Medics had sounded positive. What the hell was going on?

As the ambulance drove away carrying Miriam and her son to the hospital, Mitchell bent over Sheila's moonlit-drenched hair and whispered, "Where's your sister's bathroom?"

She ignored him and watched the ambulance get smaller as it traveled up the road and finally beyond her line of sight. Turning her attention toward him she said, "How would I know? Never been here before. But I need to find one myself."

She grabbed his hand and they both turned to face the front door of the renovated chapel, only to find themselves surrounded by twelve Carabinieri.

"Oh, I forgot to tell you," Sheila said. "These men confiscated Luigi's car. I told them who the car belonged to and they said they've never heard of anybody named Luigi at Interpol headquarters and that they'd need to take us to their police station before we left Italy."

Mitchell stared back at each one individually and said, "Bathroom. Bathroom. Bathroom. Then I'll explain."

Two of the Carabinieri stepped just inside Miriam's place, arms extended. They pointed down the hallway, where Mitchell power-walked to a door with the universal sign for male and female clearly stenciled on wood.

Once inside the bathroom, he relieved himself of more urine than he thought capable of holding. A quick glance around told him there was nothing useful here for an escape. He let running water blast through the pipes for sixty seconds.

With his left hand, he formed a cup at the bottom of his nose, then whispered into his special cuff link.

"If ever the time was right, it's now. You wait any longer and we'll never get home." Trace spoke swiftly, but softly, as he watched the doorknob turn slightly.

Quickly, he turned off the water, opened the door, stepped outside, smiled at the men down the hall around the front door, and reached inside his jacket breast pocket for his credentials. An officer standing just outside the bathroom door and behind him grabbed his arm and forced it behind his back.

Another uniformed officer, clearly in charge, standing down the hall called out to him. "*Scusi signore.*" Unlike the other men, his tall black leather riding boots shined, and on either side of him there was more than one arm's length of space. "I must make sure," the man in charge said, "that we don't see more guns tonight."

"I don't want to see any either," Mitchell said with difficulty. He was bent over by the man behind him, who continued twisting his arm. "I was reaching for my papers of authorization. Signorina Sheila Drisco . . . by the way, where is she?"

"*Scusi.* No, no," the higher-ranking officer said to the man holding Mitchell's arm. Mitchell was immediately released.

"She is here," the officer said.

"I need to know where exactly," Mitchell explained, calmly stretching his shoulder back into its joint. He stood up straight and walked toward the man. "Your government and mine have assigned her into my custody until we reach Denver, Colorado, tonight."

The man said nothing but waited until Mitchell's papers were in his hands.

Mitchell continued talking as the man read them. "My name is Trace Mitchell, by the way. I don't think we've met." Quickly becoming anxious, Mitchell couldn't understand why he was unable to hear Sheila's voice anywhere around him.

After the man read the papers given to him, he said, "My name is Este. Just Este. Signorina Drisco tells a similar story. She says she spent last night in a safe house. But the address is a place owned by a wealthy Belgian industrialist. That man swears he has never given his house over to Interpol or any other government organization. And as for this father and son team of Inspectors named Falvo, ha! There are no such persons working for Interpol. You must admit it is a crazy story, is it not? What is that noise out front?"

Another Carabinieri raced inside. He pushed men aside who stood in his way in order to whisper into Este's ear. Trace caught enough English words to understand that the U.S. Airborne Brigade had finally arrived from Vicenza, a five-vehicle convoy that had apparently blocked roads as they traveled.

"Inspector Este," said a massive American soldier wearing army fatigues. "Glad we caught up with you." His insignia said he was a captain and his nameplate said he was Captain Herdstrom. He had stepped inside silently, as if trained to move as a deer over soft underbrush, and extended his hand to Este. He was taller than the Italian.

"Likewise," Este answered, unsuccessfully hiding his annoyance.

"And if I'm not mistaken, you've got my man, Mitchell, right here."

Mitchell was quick to speak up and extended his hand as he spoke. "Yes, sir, Captain Herdstrom. I'm Trace Mitchell. You were looking for me?"

"Almost since you got off your commercial flight. You and Miss Drisco are slated to return home on a military cargo plane that's already fueled and ready to go, by order of NATO command. That's why we started out so early today."

"I see," Este answered.

"And it was fortuitous that our roadblock up the way stopped a car carrying Miss Drisco to *your* headquarters. No telling how far out of our way we would have had to travel to pick her up. But your men kindly surrendered her to us and followed us back here to you. Why they couldn't have been more courteous."

"I'm so very glad to hear that," Este responded with a bitter flourish.

"Well, there's no time like the present," the captain said, as he grabbed Mitchell's arm and pulled him outside. Este followed. The captain suddenly turned to Este and said, "If you want to examine my papers, we'll wait, but as I'm sure you know by now, everybody from here to Vicenza has had a crack at 'em."

The officer in charge was slow to respond. He looked around at his men until his eyes landed on the captain again. "You're right, there's no need. Besides, I have Mitchell's copy. Where are you taking off from?"

"Can't answer that one, I'm afraid. Need-to-know basis and so forth. But thank you for your concern." And with that he turned on a dime and walked ahead of Mitchell up to a trailer with a shiny black exterior. Not quite the height of a double-decker bus, but just as long, it suggested superstar status. While swift- moving clouds covered the moon, the trailer reflected no light.

Once inside the vehicle, Mitchell was happily surprised to see Sheila seated at a built-in oak table with leather seats on all sides. What he frowned at was her drink in one hand, as she flirted with a soldier seated beside her.

The captain's presence, however, made the soldier jump straight up from his chair to salute. Sheila rushed to Mitchell's side asking him how he was and what had happened to him. Delayed exhaustion crept over his body. He was glad she was safe, glad they were both safe, and in the hands of the U.S. military.

"We don't have a lot of time," the captain bellowed to his sergeant. "Saddle up and get us out of here."

Mitchell noted that the sergeant had to step down from the trailer and climb into what seemed like a separate cab compartment. He'd never seen the likes of it and wondered if such a vehicle had been customized for a rock star.

As the trailer moved, soldiers outside hollered orders and trucks loudly screeched into gear. The captain closed a secret door to the driver's compartment and all outside noise ceased. Through blackened windows, Mitchell noticed the reaction of the Carabinieri. They looked as if they'd lost a soccer match. But Herdstrom was quick. He'd drawn the curtains closed inside and had switched on LED lamps throughout.

Then he turned to Mitchell and said, "Get yourself a drink. The bar's just behind that table. As you can see, everything in here is built for efficiency. Used to belong to some Arab potentate. His family assassinated him right inside the American Embassy here in Rome. And when we proved his own relatives were responsible for the murder, not us, they donated his vehicle to our military station here."

"I'm going to get a bottle of water out of this fridge for now," Mitchell answered.

Sheila sat at the table next to him, while the captain sat on a lengthy bench across from them on the other side of the trailer and pulled down a desk mounted on pulleys above his head.

"Miss Drisco," the captain said, "wouldn't you like to freshen up a bit?"

A puzzled look came over her, as her mouth slowly opened.

"Two reasons," the captain answered without hearing her ask a question. "This ride to our bomber will take about five hours; longer if we think we're being tracked. And second, I need to talk to Mitchell privately. He's a law enforcement agent, and we need to exchange confidential information."

"Then you must know how close we are to Fumicino airport right now, right?" Sheila asked.

The captain didn't look up, but continued typing on the laptop.

Finally, she got up and sauntered to the back of the trailer, as if she knew where she was going. Even as she walked away, Mitchell was aware that her feelings had been severely gouged, yet he didn't feel he could say anything in her defense without knowing more about the captain. He also noticed that the man was busy backing up both sound and image data before he disconnected the laptop on his desk.

When the two men heard a click, which must have been Sheila turning the latch on the bathroom door, the captain asked, "Is she somebody's little girl or just another Texas whore?" And with that, he got up from behind his desk and thrust the laptop on the table in front of Mitchell.

The question floored Mitchell for a moment.

"I already know *who* she is," Captain Herdstrom continued. "Her billboards are all over Europe. Didn't know she was from Denver though. Thought she was French. I'm asking if she's a terrorist or just another homespun whore."

"Given that choice, Captain," Mitchell replied, "she's somebody's little girl."

He thought of Inez begging him to help her and suddenly felt sorry for Sheila, who was no angel, but certainly no whore.

"Well, I take seriously the opinions of former SEALs."

"Thank you, sir," Mitchell answered. He ignored the captain's skeptical facial expression and lifted the top up on the computer. It was no surprise to him to see his resume had been examined and was on the screen. He knew when he received the cufflinks from CIA back in Denver that his savior, if he needed one, was going to come from the military.

Mitchell watched the screen dissolve to a grainy black-and-white movie. Sheila, the late Luigi Falvo, and his own figure could be seen from a camera focused directly inside the glass-enclosed shower room from somewhere near the ceiling. All the voices were inaudible even after cranking up the volume controls to the limit.

Mitchell was riveted. He'd had no reason to believe the equipment they'd found was still actually functioning, and yet there was no sign that it had been shut off, either.

"Keep watching," the captain said, "You'll see why you weren't charged with murder by the Italian *polizia*. Military intelligence has no idea how, or if, these murders today are related to each other, but I can tell you that this type of crime is happening on several continents simultaneously. My guess is we haven't finished counting bodies from today's murders. If the motive is to create fear in the hearts of ordinary citizens, as well as high-ranking government officials, it's working."

Mitchell glanced at him quickly, noting the deep lines around his eyes.

"Is it the work of one particular country," Mitchell asked, "a municipality, or a large corporate structure of some sort?" He was testing Inez's theory and thinking he should call her.

"When we find the source of these transmissions, I'm sure we still won't know who's behind it."

Mitchell had become more engrossed in the video than the captain's analysis. Whatever Herdstrom was saying, it had become too soft to be heard. The bright flash of gunfire on the computer monitor showed the existence of another person alright. But the image was gone the minute the flash was over. A technician could slow the video down, but would that be enough for an identification?

"You'll have to excuse me, Mitchell," the captain said. "I'm going to stretch out here and take a quick nap. I've been awake for the past thirty hours. There's a couple of beds in the back she can use. We'll continue our talk in, let's say two hours."

Mitchell continued to replay the part where he and Sheila left the room. He'd played it four or five times before he heard Sheila come down the hall to sit very close beside him at the table. She was wrapped in a white terry robe and smelled of Canoe.

"You took a shower, didn't you?" he whispered.

"Hmm," she replied.

"I think Herdstrom was offering you a place to wash your hands. Let's don't wake him."

She said nothing, but gasped when she realized what Mitchell was looking at. "Where did that come from?"

"Herdstrom," he whispered. "I knew there were cameras, but I had hoped they'd been turned off." Mitchell continued. "You were probably recorded every time you were there. I have the feeling Herdstrom has seen your bare ass before."

"Oh my God," she said and covered her face with her hands. "This would have killed Dad."

Mitchell screwed up his face. Was this underwear model serious?

"I'm afraid," said Mitchell, "that I'm too tired to wonder how you'll take this, but let's go to the back of the trailer and look at this video on one of those beds back there. I may doze off while I'm looking at this. It won't be anything you've said."

Very quietly they tiptoed to the back of the trailer and chose one full-sized bed on the driver's side. They lay on their backs and looked up at the monitor, which Mitchell held up high.

"The gun flash," he said, "makes it barely possible to see the gun, much less the person holding it. But if the shooter was a man of color, like the guy behind the wheel of the Mercedes, what would we see then? Shockenaugh, Inc. is definitely an equal opportunity employer."

They watched in silence, Sheila's body trembling slightly against his.

"What are you shaking for?" he asked absently, his eyes still fixed on the computer screen. "You know, this is the last leg of our journey home."

"Then I'd better hurry and get dressed."

"What did you come out of there undressed for anyway?"

She climbed over him, giving him a full view beneath her robe. He heard the bathroom door slam behind her and he shut his own eyes, hoping to memorize what he'd just seen.

"How sure are you," she said through the door, "that these soldiers are the good guys and that we're really on our way home?"

Mitchell didn't answer. He was busy playing with the computer again. Finally he said, "You're just pissed that we didn't go to the closest airport."

It didn't take Sheila long to open the door again and resume her place on the bed next to Mitchell.

"So," she asked, "how sure *are you* that these are the good guys?"

Mitchell turned over on his side and looked at her clean scrubbed face with its flawless texture and said, "Betrayal isn't a necessary part of life, you know."

"Yeah? Well, if you're wrong, I'll forgive you," she said.

He pushed back from her and asked, "Why?"

"Because," she said, while putting her finger over his lips, "whether you're right or you're wrong about these men, you, it turns out, are an exceptionally good man. You always ask yourself whether you're doing the right thing. Nobody will ever call you a typical white man. Your future neighbors will love the hell out of you."

"Sounds like you're crusading for somebody."

"Oh, I just remembered the way Inez described my dad. I'd always thought of him as being very ordinary. Turns out, I'm just putty in the hands of a really good man."

Her sudden long hard kiss on his mouth melted every tense feeling inside him.

"So why," Mitchell asked, "didn't you keep your clothes off?"

Mitchell let the laptop carefully drop to the floor beside the bed.

"Where's the fun in that?" she said playfully.

Their hands skimmed over each other, making certain, he told himself, that this was real, that she was really here. Eagerly yet silently, so as not to awaken the sleeping man in the front room, they removed clothing until nothing lay between them.

Mitchell smiled at her and whispered, "All the lights are off in the front part of the trailer. You want me to turn this one off too?"

"No," she said, "I want to see everything. I want a memory I won't forget." Gently he pushed her breasts up off her chest, cupping them in his hands before gently massaging her nipples with his fingers. Their hours together started slowly. He was showing off his acquired self-discipline. But when their breathing matched, nothing could contain him.

With an excited exhaustion, he finally lay very still beside her for several minutes hoping her memory was at least as good as his. The sound of jets circling overhead seemed normal to Mitchell at first, until he realized he was hearing them through a soundproof trailer. By the time he sat up, one bomb had dropped maybe half a mile away, vibrating the road they traveled. Abruptly, the trailer stopped, skidding a short distance.

"Get dressed!" Mitchell announced. When the second bomb landed, it was closer to the convoy, and he already had his pants on. He put his hand on the light beside the bed, wondering for a moment whether it had served as a beacon in the nighttime sky. He switched it off. The door to the driver's cab was open and he ran up front to look inside. This dashboard equipment resembled an NSA office. The sergeant and Captain Herdstrom were like pilot and co-pilot coordinating incoming intel until the captain got up from his seat and turned to face Mitchell.

"Whoever they are, they have us boxed in. We had less than eight minutes warning. We're being tracked by ballistic missiles. Run! There's no chance at all inside. Mitchell grabbed Sheila's hand, noticing she was almost dressed, as they descended the stairs of the trailer and ran into the darkness of an open field of alfalfa.

Teams of twenty armed soldiers from each of the four trucks on either side of them swarmed around them, as they ran across farmland. They needed as many meters away from their convoy vehicles as they could possibly create. A fire suddenly broke out less than half a kilometer from their first truck. A home beside the road went up in flames.

The next bomb hit the second truck in the convoy's line of empty trucks with tremendous force. Billowing smoke and flames reached the heavens throwing dirt, stone walls, and human bodies high above ground.

Mitchell felt nothing and then he awoke.

He'd been unconscious. Unable to move, he was reluctant to try harder. His brain was in a fog, and the sky hinted at the sun's arrival. He expected to hear screaming but didn't. Then everything went black.

Smoke enclosed his line of vision before trailing off. He lay on his back, not wanting to know if he'd been hurt. He was curious about the time but had no strength to lift his arms. When he turned his head to see how badly the convoy had been hit, it wasn't there. On his back, he could see no trace of a convoy. Another bomb must have exploded to do that kind of damage. Somebody, Mitchell thought, had called for a kill box carrying 105 mm shells. Who could do that? His mind was beginning to clear.

A soldier appeared on his knees beside him. Blood covered the front of his shirt. He could see that. The soldier stared at Mitchell's shirt, then ripped it open. His mouth moved rapidly, and other soldiers surrounded him on their knees as well. Mitchell felt a burning sensation along his left side. He could feel men hooking him up to something, strapping him down to something else. Then they disappeared.

Later, much later, he realized he was being lifted. It was the first time that he realized his frantic world of smoke and rubble had no sound to it at all and that he no longer held Sheila's hand.

CHAPTER 30

XIAO RELAXED ON the only bed elevated with bricks off the floor of the cave and reminisced about his past year. It was a year in which he had found his place among several decades of explorers. Three cave inhabitants had come before him. The first was an engineer, who had brought along several servants and student assistants. Decades later an anthropologist stumbled into the cave by following the oral legends told by nearby villagers. The last occupant was Dr. Woo, who had gradually brought his whole family inside.

Each man had built portions of the shelter separately: the first, out of intellectual curiosity during the middle of the eighteenth century; the second, for solitude and finally, Dr. Woo, for survival. Xiao was grateful and proud to have become a part of the shelter's stewardship, though very deliberately, he kept no diaries and had no desire to leave any trace of his existence.

Happily, his mother hadn't visited him once while living underground. Nagging relatives had stopped their cries as well. This achievement brought tears to his eyes, as he attributed their disappearance to his program of fasting and self-discipline.

A long time had passed since seeing a face on the monitor. But Xiao was confident that if Kee, a trained spy, couldn't find his way to the shelter, no one else could either.

On the other hand, he would not be surprised to see nearby evidence of his mentor and nemesis, the mountain ghost, the snow leopard who had left him deeply scarred. Nonetheless he regarded the sleek animal with quiet respect. Automatically, his hand touched the gash, the sunken hole that had been made in his left cheek the night the snow leopard's curled claw almost caused him to bleed to death.

From Xiao's first full day alone in the shelter, he had yearned to become as skilled and elegantly masterful as Dr. Woo. And in a way, Xiao's yearning, he felt, was slowly being fulfilled.

He devised plans of action, like those in Woo's psychology books, and devoted each day to achieving his goals. Xiao fasted for weeks at a time to rid his body of toxins and bad bacteria, part of a suggested remedy for schizophrenia found in a Russian research article among Woo's papers. Xiao lifted weights to strengthen self-discipline and build a respectable body of muscle.

By then, of course, Xiao knew where everything on the mountain was located in relation to the shelter. Dr. Woo left labeled diagrams showing every tree and rock in all four directions.

Xiao was building his own talent for stealth. He consumed very little but stole from other lodges and nearby villages to obtain the incidentals he depleted inside the cave. The pork given to him by the two young men who, he now was convinced had meant to kill him, lasted half a year.

Each time he traveled outside, he carried fire starters, a machete, a gun, and nonperishable provisions. He carried what Dr. Woo had always carried, a first-aid kit, and wondered if he'd ever meet anyone needing his help.

Xiao sifted through anything of note outside the shelter, looking for a single trace of men searching for him. And even though Dr. Woo left branches below the tree line to disguise his movements, Xiao never found traces of humans there. Animal tracks he discovered usually stopped at craggy rock formations or at smaller underground caves.

On one occasion, having read more extensively about animal tracking in snow, Xiao had differentiated a camouflaged snow leopard from its rocky background through his binoculars. It stood motionless as it stared at two young mountain goats further down the side of the mountain.

Xiao's heart pounded. He was thrilled to find protein. But his discovery would require another plan. He had no desire to skin, gut, and eat a whole animal. Sharing a portion of a mountain goat with a snow leopard would be the ideal situation, but not when Xiao first spied those animals. Such a mission would require cunning, strength, and speed, skills he had only recently developed. He returned to his cave that same day, knowing that the mountain ghost, with feet the size of human thighs, was unquestionably the better hunter. A month later, after rigorous aerobics, weight lifting, and the creation of an untested plan, he was ready to test his guile.

At the bottom of the rock-faced mountain, he made an inconspicuous camp without fire. His pockets were heavily laden with mid-sized rocks to throw at his target. Xiao was prepared to wait for three weeks if necessary for the snow leopard to attempt the killing of a mountain goat within his vicinity. He also brought a handmade long- handled torch and a can of butane with a nozzle he'd found in a chest of items in the cave. He assumed these were stolen items from a local vendor.

In his backpack were several balls of surgical gauze stuffed with dried leaves and wet twigs, food he hoped would lure goats closer to his location. After ten days, he began to wonder if he could survive another night in the cold. Two goats suddenly appeared near the summit. The steepness of the terrain would help him. He threw balls of food halfway up the mountainside, hoping to lure the goats down and keep them in the area longer. But the objects almost spooked the goats away. And no leopard appeared.

The goats returned the next day, but even with the use of his binoculars, he saw no snow leopards across the vast mountain range. He couldn't last three weeks after all. Xiao packed up, afraid another night would cost him his toes.

In case the mountain ghost had observed him, Xiao decided to wait a week in his cave before trying again.

On the fourth day of his fifth attempt, he caught sight of a female snow leopard standing over two cubs. She would need to feed them, and Xiao felt smug as he prepared his equipment. In less than half an hour he watched a small goat find it hard to keep up with the larger goats in its group. The snow leopard, which easily weighed forty kilograms, sprang across the craggy mountain, causing rocks to tumble under her large fur-covered feet. The goats were fast too. But the smallest goat in the group could not keep its footing; when the leopard lashed out a paw that landed deep into the haunches of its prey, the goat slid sideways out of its grip.

Watching both leopard and goat sliding down the mountain in a hurried life and death chase was exactly what Xiao had hoped for. He raced to the spot near the bottom of the mountain where the goat landed on its side, unable to right itself because of the huge wound made by the snow leopard. Xiao impaled the goat with his spear in one hand; killing it while raising his lit torch higher in the air with his other hand.

The mountain ghost, in a split second, responded by leaping high into the air over Xiao's fiery torch. Flames singed the snow leopard's underbelly. The shock to the leopard slowed the animal's pivot once it landed on the ground, too stunned to understand what had dared to take its prey.

The leopard's slight pause gave Xiao the time he needed to sink his torch into the ground between himself and the leopard. With both hands, he twisted his long- handled spear across a quarter of the goat's leg. The frantic leopard dragged its belly around, stirred by the strong odor of blood. Whenever it hunched up slightly on all fours Xiao threw a rock at it until the leopard moved in half circles behind the torch.

Once Xiao had separated the hind leg, he dropped it into a plastic bag secured around his waist and pulled its cinch shut to close off the smell and prevent a trail of dripping blood. The leopard smelled the remnants of the goat's body.

Light from the torch's flames continued to blind the leopard. It reached out its paws, stabbing at thrown rocks, inching its way closer on hind legs, until a claw caught Xiao's face, bringing him down to the ground. Distracted by the bleeding goat, the leopard leaped into the air, yanking away a piece of Xiao's cheek with it. Xiao screamed! Amidst the pain and bleeding, he managed to pull out another plastic bag and hold it around his head. Xiao hoped to prevent the leopard from smelling him.

Finally, the leopard ran up the mountain to its cubs, the dead goat dangling from its mouth. Xiao knew he had to return to his cave before passing out. Perhaps he could drink blood from the goat's hind leg to replace his? Frantically, he searched his brain for ways to stop bleeding. Suddenly he remembered his first-aid kit and used tape to slow the flow of blood across his jaw. There were no mirrors inside the cave. Small reflective surfaces gave him a hint that his face would forever be different.

Months later, Xiao realized his need to leave the cave, as Woo had. The cave's library contained a finite number of books. Xiao yearned for more. Using the internet was no answer for several reasons. Of crucial significance was his new confidence that he could face fear without the need to kill. Unharnessed fear, Xiao decided, after reading Woo's library of books, was at the root of all he'd done wrong and may have directly led to his mental illness. Exercising courage was a gift given to him by the spirits of the forest. Yet the only way to remain a successful practitioner of courage was to live in the city and face its challenges daily.

The puny young man that Quan and his great grandson, Kee, had easily intimidated was gone. Xiao was all muscle with a damaged electronic device still inside his body, causing severe but infrequent back pain. His memory of Karen, however, remained a constant reminder that mental illness destroys happiness. How long could he live with the knowledge that he'd murdered the only woman who loved him?

More than a year had passed and Xiao had dressed and packed for a long journey. Standing on a makeshift ladder, he pulled the fan away from its housing in the ceiling for the very last time. He crawled through a metal tube with his pack on his back and dragged additional equipment behind him. After twenty minutes of crawling the tube ended. Side walls had partially collapsed. Xiao immediately pulled his backpack over his head until it was in front of him. He quickly reached inside for a folding shovel, hoping to avoid a slow death by suffocation.

He dug up the fallen dirt, easing it behind him, then inched his body forward. An hour later, he reached the round stone he'd kept at the opening of the cave.

Everything outside the cave was different. There was no snow as there had been at this time last year. Autumn was late. He took deep breaths of clean air and saw something out of the corner of his eye. Xiao also heard its hooves against hard ground. A beautiful yet unkempt brown horse with a long thick mane eyed him. It whisked past with its head held high.

Xiao looked around, expecting to see a tossed rider nearby. The horse wore no saddle. Although it was early morning, the air was quickly turning hot and dry. Grass downhill was like straw. Without a rider, he had no expectation of seeing the horse again, but ten minutes after he'd begun his own trek, the horse reappeared, sauntering slowly this time.

It held its head down, as if it longed to communicate. The animal was different from horses he'd seen in the States. Its legs were shorter and its chest narrower. Yet it was quite sure-footed, but skittish whenever Xiao held his hand out. Was it showing off or wanting to show him something?

Not only was the horse not afraid of him, it was not afraid of the mountainside as it raced up to the edge of cliffs. Was he misinterpreting the behavior of a dumb animal because he wanted to ride him? Or was this one of those clever horses that Meng had trained to always return to him? Could this be the animal that had carried him up the mountain unconscious a year ago to Meng's lodge? He had no way of knowing the answers to any of his questions.

With his backpack strapped high on his back, Xiao clumsily mounted the horse, thinking he could pull the animal up short by pulling on its mane. He couldn't bring himself to look back at the small stone slab that hid the secret womb from which he'd been reborn. It had quickly become a part of his past.

Xiao tried to remember all that Meng had mentioned about the terrain a year earlier. The mare sauntered downhill in a slow, even pace under the direct rays of the sun, as if trained to do so. After one kilometer, its rhythmic gait had lulled Xiao into a semi-sleep state.

His eyes closed, he shut out the sunlight completely and yet he didn't like complete darkness—certainly not at age four when his family had been gone from their small San Francisco apartment all day. Evenings brought too many knocks and scrapes against the door he was never supposed to open. There were so many people to fear. Not even the next-door neighbor could be let in. There were also times that weren't so dark, like the time his father got paid in food. The family would sit on the floor and drink lots of black tea with steamed noodles and a piece of fish.

Sometimes their neighbor would come home before dark with Pei Pei, her three-legged dog. Pei Pei played on his own balcony, and Xiao could slide his fingers through the slats of his apartment balcony to pet its fur.

Rarely did Pei Pei stay home all day, but when he did, they were inseparable. Both urinated over the edge of their respective balconies so as not to leave the other alone.

Most days there was nothing to eat. Once Pei Pei tried to bring Xiao something from his bowl, but his mistress caught him and beat him before he got to the railing. Xiao cried softly whenever Pei Pei was beaten but never cried when his own father beat him, not wanting Pei Pei to cry too.

When the dog's mistress became sick and stopped working, Xiao had started first grade and was not home during the day. His father had not yet put him to work at the laundry. The minute Xiao arrived home from school, he would sit on the balcony with Pei Pei, rain or shine, and read to him or share whatever was left from his school lunch.

One day he heard his name called from inside the next apartment.

"Xiao?" the woman asked faintly.

"I am here," he answered, pressed against the wall.

"You think your dad buy Pei Pei for you? He knows you love him. I sell cheap. You ask him, when he come home."

"I will," he promised.

Xiao's face was flush with excitement when his family returned home. His brother Yan, at thirteen, attended school during the day and then worked at the laundry until midnight. It was not until after his father was killed that his sisters were allowed to attend school at all.

Xiao eagerly told his father what their neighbor had shouted through the wall and waited silently for his reply.

"Go sleep," he said.

It was all Xiao could do to stand still. His mother seemed more tired than on other nights, and Xiao could see the color fading from her hair and watched her skin droop around her neck.

Xiao yearned to hold Pei Pei in his arms, but his father never spoke of it again and Xiao was grief-stricken. Days later the woman in the apartment next door died. And the family had a feast on the floor of their apartment with lots of black tea.

"Please," Xiao pleaded, now determined to withstand any consequence his father imposed. "I'll work and pay for . . ."

His father laughed. "I buy Pei Pei already." He held one chopstick high above his plate. It dripped with the warm tea and gravy his mother had prepared. "I like Pei Pei this way."

Xiao's mouthful of dog slid down his chin. His eyes, like bowls of water, became wider and unseeing. He did not breath until someone slapped his back hard. It was his older brother who had done that. Xiao stood dazed but wandered toward his mother who never once stopped eating to look at him. She never wiped the dog or its juice from his face. In that moment of total confusion, Xiao knew one thing well—the woman in front of him was not his real mother.

He could not remember how long he stood beside her wailing, but it was his brother again who carried him into the bathroom and wiped away all traces of his first and only friend.

His eyelids popped open and he inhaled deeply. Had he been floating in space? For one brief moment fear gripped him as he looked straight down the steep side of a mountain from a narrow ledge. Xiao saw no ground on which the horse could stand. But instead of panicking, he shut his eyes once more and let the beast do its job, unencumbered.

Minutes later, Xiao courageously opened his eyes; he noticed strewn bones along the ground, mostly human.

"Whoa," he shouted to the horse and dismounted quickly. Down the mountain Xiao slid. Although Xiao knew his tibia from his fibula, it was no wild guess to rule out Meng's nephews as the owners of the bones. Those young men were almost as tall as he was. However, these bones belonged to someone as tall as—dare he think it—Dr. Woo.

Frantically, he looked across the dirt of the mountain. With bare hands, he searched for cloth fragments, animal skin, equipment, anything he could remember from the day Dr. Woo had left. Xiao couldn't remember much. He'd been given a sedative that day. But he did remember his eyeglasses with ordinary black plastic rims. When he saw something similar next to his foot, he simply stared down without picking them up.

He was finished looking for bones. It was hot against the mountain, and Xiao had to admit that he was not a forensic scientist and had no idea who belonged to any of the bones he found. The horse had no desire to stand and watch Xiao meditate on such issues. With its nose, the animal continuously nudged Xiao's head.

Finally he mounted and let himself be carried along at a rhythmic trot. Once again, Xiao closed his eyes and sank into his past. It had taken many years and several experiments to discover which one of his sisters was really his mother. His search became an obsession, which later turned into a passionate interest in the study of DNA and later in bioengineering.

At eighteen, Xiao discovered what he'd been searching for. Outwardly their father had never shown interest in any of his girls. It was his brother, once more, who unwittingly revealed that their father preferred his oldest daughter, Ching, to his loyal wife. Xiao assumed that Ching had accepted her lot in life and would want to know that Xiao gladly accepted her as his mother. But when Xiao looked into her eyes and told her that, knowing her DNA had confirmed it, she jumped into the San Francisco Bay, her body found that night. Months later, his father died, murdered by an unknown assailant, newspapers had said.

Xiao fell deeper into sleep, guided only by the rhythmic swaying of the horse's rump.

**

The slap of hooves against asphalt woke him. A full moon hung over the peaks of Jade Dragon Snow Mountain. He barely noticed the headlight of a motorcycle that passed with tremendous speed. Quickly, Xiao leaned forward and grabbed the horse's mane. How had he remained on its back for so long, he wondered.

He jumped down to stand on the side of the road, opened his backpack and pulled out a map along with the cell phone Kee had given him from Quan. The phone was covered in tin.

His map told him he was on the outskirts of Lijiang, far below Meng's village. Perhaps Meng had never owned this particular horse. Xiao smacked the hindquarters of the animal that had become his trusted friend and wished it well.

He removed the tin from around the cell phone and punched the only number that hadn't been scratched off. With barely a signal, there was no answer. Just as carefully, he replaced the tin around it and packed it up again.

Xiao flagged down the first men he saw walking and asked directions to the airport. They gawked at the deep hole in his cheek and finally told him it was fifteen kilometers away. One of them offered him a seat on a motorcycle parked not far away and gladly drove him to the airport. Xiao purchased a ticket on a flight to Chongqing with the American Express card he had hidden from Karen. He was on board within the hour.

An hour later, Xiao landed, confident he could escape anyone's notice in the most populated city on the planet. He knew the phone he carried would work here.

CHAPTER 31

"**H**ANK! I KNOW you're in there! You all right?" It was Larry Carmichael's voice as his fist banged louder on the door.

"Shit!" Hank whispered through clenched teeth.

Inez felt her heart pound violently. *They're friends, aren't they? Or was that all an act, too?* Her eyes continued to adjust to the darkness. Knowing it was Larry hadn't calmed her any. Would Shockenaugh put him on their hit list as well?

Hank stood up quickly and opened the door. He saw Larry and the neighborhood boy from around the corner, Teddy Wabley, his bushy red hair matted down. Hank pulled them both inside by their clothing.

"Inez!" Larry shouted, his eyes wide with surprise. "And . . . and Billy. What's going on in here? I heard gunshots and thought . . ."

"You thought of Hank, didn't you," Inez said, "because you knew he probably had the only gun in the neighborhood."

"Hello, Mr. Jeffrey, Dr. Buchanan, Billy," said the boy, "I'm really glad to see everybody in one piece. That's why I came. I was home alone again. 'Course I'm no baby. I'm all of fifteen now, but I heard those gunshots too and wondered whether you and Mrs. Jeffrey were all right. Then I saw Mr. Carmichael running up your walk and . . ."

Larry interrupted the boy as if he weren't there. "So did you pay your electricity bill?" He turned to the wall quickly and switched the lights on.

Agnes immediately switched them back off from where she stood, just outside the kitchen.

"Mrs. Jeffrey!" Larry said, startled. "I didn't see you standing there in the dark. How have you been?"

"Thank you, dear," Hank said to his wife, then turned to Larry. "Larry!" Hank shouted. He wasn't more than a foot from Larry's face. "You trust me, don't you?"

"What kind of a question is that?" Larry asked, backing away from him.

"Well, do you trust me or not, Larry?"

"I trust you!"

"Good, because we're going to need your help. Inez has a story about Gaelen's death that's going to blow you away once you've heard the whole thing. But tonight you've got to trust me. There probably won't be any more guns fired tonight. And no one has gotten hurt. As a matter of fact," he whispered, "I bet you've got the list of phone numbers of all the people on our block. Why don't you give each house a call, particularly if you see their lights on when you get back home? Tell them they don't have to call the police. Tell them that tomorrow we'll discuss everything we know about Gaelen, because tomorrow we could use everybody's help. That's what we'll do. We'll have one of those indoor block meetings we have in the winter. It's too cold to do a block party. And we'll have it at Inez's place, won't we?"

Hank looked at Inez, as if she were an addled child. And she stared back at him, because she was analyzing his every word. Inez knew this was just a glimpse at how Hank controlled his wife.

Inez and Billy said nothing as Hank put his arm around Larry's shoulder, opened the front door, and headed him outside, saying, "You going to be warm enough out here?" He didn't wait for Larry's answer. "You and I'll talk in the morning. I'll call you."

Inez realized she wasn't the only person who didn't know Hank Jeffrey. His best friend on the block didn't know him, either.

"Okay," said Larry. "I can see you're all involved in something serious here, kinda' like my serious stuff with the police."

"That's right," Hank said. "But everything is going to be okay. You'll see."

They all nodded, and Larry reluctantly turned around and left in night air that was colder than it had been minutes earlier.

Hank was quick to say, "Thanks. I appreciate this," and shut the door. "And Teddy," he said while turning around, "I've still got that spare bedroom you're welcome to use. Care to spend the night?"

"Sure thing."

Hank then began shouting orders to his wife. "Agnes, I don't want you up this late or you'll have problems in the morning. You go to bed and I'll tuck you in shortly."

As Hank talked to Agnes, Teddy explained to Inez that his parents always traveled, thereby leaving him behind to take care of himself. Teddy said he enjoyed it but that Hank had done this once before, when there was that terrible lightning storm a year ago. He was glad to spend the night here then.

Inez told him she was so sorry she hadn't known about him being alone so much, that she would have dropped some food over for him if she had.

Hank was visibly becoming more agitated and waved Billy, Inez, and Teddy downstairs to the basement.

Were these precautions necessary? Inez wondered. Yet, Hank had expertise she never imagined. Wren Xiao could have used more expert advice than what she gave him. Could she have done more to help that young man? Perhaps she would tell Hank about him as well. She decided to wait and see what Hank was planning first.

The stairs led to a large basement room with a cement floor that looked like a sparsely furnished second living room. Three TV monitors sat on a table against a side wall, and the two men who had come downstairs earlier were seated in front of them.

"Inez, Billy, Teddy" said Hank, "let me introduce you to Tom and Jerry. That's not their real names. They're a part of a small militia inside Colorado. Right now, they're busy setting up cameras they already placed in trees along Ivanhoe and 17th Avenue Parkway."

The man referred to as Tom said, "We're also hooked up to major intersections along Colfax through the city's internet."

Maybe it was because she was standing close to the furnace that she remembered she still wore her jacket. The basement was warmer than the rest of the house. Inez felt blood rushing to her head as she spoke. "This looks like you're about to wage war."

Hank said nothing.

Inez couldn't contain her fears. "Do you already know who hired Shockenaugh?" she asked. "If we knew that, we'd know who killed Gaelen. Maybe we'd even know if Karen was really kidnapped. Then we could all go home and contact the authorities from there."

"Sit down," Hank said to them. Inez felt he was about to give them instructions on how to invade Iraq. "Billy," he said as he stood looking down at them, "you and I have drawn the first assignment for the night. We'll take the first three-hour shift."

"Fine by me," Billy answered.

Hank looked at Inez. "Billy and I will be escorting you back to your home as part of our shift."

"Thank you," Inez said. "I appreciate it."

"But you'll need to come back here later to do your three-hour shift with Teddy," Hank replied.

"Then Teddy, I want you to curl up in a comfortable chair outside my wife's bedroom for the next half hour or so. You'll need to get some sleep, but I do need you to listen out for Mrs. Jeffrey from time to time."

"Yes, sir. I'll start now," Teddy said and ran upstairs.

"Billy, you're going to be point man. Start out now. Leave by the kitchen door. You're headed for Inez's back door by way of my backyard. Go slow. Keep your eyes open for any anomaly. And use this to contact me if you see something wrong."

Hank threw a walkie-talkie to him.

"I remember these toys," Billy said.

"It's safer than a cell phone at distances like these," Hank replied. "You'll have to climb over some tall fences, but don't let anybody on the street see you. We'll be at her back door in about ten minutes, scoping the place out."

"Got it." Billy was gone in a flash.

"I didn't want to scare anybody who didn't need to understand the seriousness of this mess," Hank said to Inez.

"What do you mean?"

"We don't know who's paying Shockenaugh's bills yet. But we do know Shockenaugh has been reassessing its policies. They're not going to come after you until they've met with their employer; that's another way of saying that they want to make sure they're going to get paid. Maybe their employer hasn't paid them enough so far or maybe something has been compromised that should not have been. We don't know. My personal theory is that Shockenaugh wanted to know just how dangerous you were to their employer before they killed you. They needed to know how much you knew and whether you could ever bite them with it. They wanted information from you, but they also had to give you information in order to sound credible. We haven't been able to verify any of the information they told you."

"Sir!" said a man who sat in front of one of the monitors. His hoodie, she thought was worn to cover his head and most of his face. "There's a lot of wireless chatter all over Park Hill," he said. "If the FBI or CBI were on their toes, they'd be alarmed. There's also more foot traffic than usual on adjacent streets. Some Shockenaugh personnel have been spotted acting like city workers marking off places on sidewalks at this time of night. They're giving the impression the city's planning a big dig around the pipes in this area. I'm sure it's because *we* showed up."

Inez scrunched her forehead in amazement and felt Hank's eyes on her.

He said, "We're on the eve of battle. You should know that the houses of your neighbors and your house have been illegally bugged for alien communication systems. We did that, and we'll take it all down when this is over. You'll have nothing to fear from us."

Her forehead wrinkled even more. "You're suggesting that Shockenaugh may think Billy and I are worth killing after all."

"Yes, that's what I'm saying. You two apparently threaten their employers existence."

Inez took a deep breath and sat up tall, not caring for the moment whether she was lopsided or not. She was proud to be called a threat to Shockenaugh with its obvious mission to murder people. Such a mission could eventually destroy life in America as she'd come to expect it.

Hank took her by the elbow to leave his house by the front door.

"Wait," Inez suddenly said to Hank. "Do you know a man named Gerald Simon?" "No," Hank replied.

She explained how she learned of the name and as they walked down the street, Hank told her he would look into it. He didn't sound convincing, perhaps preoccupied with his observations of everything around him.

The night was chillier than expected. Inez raised the collar of her jacket. Hank wore no jacket. No one else walked along the sidewalk. Hank almost stopped, but not quite.

"Did you hear that?" he asked.

"I didn't hear a thing." Inez kept walking, while he caught up to her in two strides.

Just as she took her first step on the walkway leading to her front porch, Hank grabbed her arm and pulled her back. He was staring along a line of sight beside Inez's fence. In the darkness, she thought she saw a clump of clothing or a pile of something in the distance.

"Go in the house," Hank said.

"No. What is it?"

"Do as I say!" he shouted. He was running to reach the pile on the ground.

He fell to his knees just as Inez wondered if it was a body. She suddenly wondered if it was . . .

"Billy? Billy?" she screamed and ran toward Hank.

Hank turned the body of a young man over to see his face, when Inez arrived.

"I think he's just stunned. A bullet swiped the side of his head, cut his ear."

Billy's eyes opened. "How am I?" he asked. "Thought I . . ."

"They didn't get you," Hank replied. "Consider it a messy scratch requiring a few stitches. Able Voodoo," Hank said into the walkie-talkie he pulled from his jacket pocket.

Just then a man dropped from a twenty-foot tree inside Inez's yard. She jumped back as the man landed on both feet, a rope attached to his waist, about four feet away from them.

"This man," Hank said calmly to Billy, "will walk you back to my place and dress that wound before we do our first shift together. He's got stuff that will work like stitches. You're okay. I'm going to escort Inez inside her house."

Both men pulled Billy to his feet, while blood dripped down the side of his neck. Inez was breathing loudly. This was no playground fight where a school nurse could make it all better with a band aid, but surely, she could do something, she thought.

Inez had a tough time trying to see Billy over her shoulder as Hank held her tightly by the elbow to lead her away from the scene and back to her house before she could say a word.

"Let me have your key," Hank demanded. Her porch light was on, but the nearest streetlamp was across the street in front of Larry's house.

"I can open my own door, thank you very much," Inez replied.

The minute she twisted the key in the lock and opened the door, Hank pushed her aside. He pulled a gun from a holster she'd been unaware of.

"Stay here! I mean it!" he said.

Inez had no intention of entering. She now felt she had reason to take Hank's words more seriously. Hoping to see Billy in the distance around the corner of her house, she walked across her porch to the end of it. Billy was apparently well hidden, because she could see nothing as she looked down the street.

Shortly, Hank reappeared at the doorway, his gun put back in its place. "Nobody's hiding in there," he assured her.

"But shouldn't I go back with you and Billy to see if he's . . ."

"Remember when I said this is war. You've got to stay here and answer the phone. You'll get calls from worried neighbors. Remember, Larry will be directing neighbors to call you. They'll be coming over tomorrow. Besides, Billy and I will return shortly to get some of that food. I know you've got to feed the neighbors something tomorrow morning, so we won't take much tonight. But we'll need to fuel the army of men you've already seen. We're a small bunch, but experienced. It's a good thing you won't have to feed the men you haven't seen. Those men are busy trying to track down Shockenaugh's new owner."

"Thank you, Hank," Inez said softly. "Thank you very much. I'm glad I came to you for help."

He put his arm around her shoulder. But she backed away, smiled politely, then quickly went inside and locked the door behind her.

"Inez," Hank hollered, "I don't believe you're inferior. I'm no Nationalistic Fascist! All of that thinking is behind me. I'm your neighbor.

I didn't know any better in those early days. I mean that." She listened to his footsteps finally run back toward his own house.

Inez pressed her back against the door to her closet in the entryway. She wasn't ready to take her jacket off. This was more than she had envisioned when she asked Hank for help. Was Billy going to be okay? How could he have become a soldier so quickly? What had he heard today that made him so willing to fight? Did he think as she was beginning to think that life, liberty, and justice under law were under attack?

Her landline phone rang. Maybe it was a neighbor?

Timidly, she said, "Hello?"

"I hoped you'd answer this call. This is Trace Mitchell."

"Oh," she sighed, with heartfelt relief. "You can't know how happy it makes me to hear your voice." She carried the phone with its long cord dragging behind her to the nearest living room chair.

"Listen," he said, "Sheila and I were in a terrible explosion."

"Oh, no!"

"Bombs were dropped by jets overhead. Ambulances carried the living to hospitals in Vicenza. The captain in charge was killed. I've already been patched up and most of my hearing has returned. Sheila, however, is in bad condition. She may lose her leg."

"Oh, my God!" Inez said loudly.

"We're in a transport plane over the Atlantic right now, on our way to Walter Reed Army Medical Center. If anyone can help her, it's those surgeons. Listen. I'm calling because you were the only person who had any reasonable speculation about who might be committing these murders and now bombings. Turns out, it's an organization with a funny name."

"Shockenaugh," Inez responded.

"How do you know that?"

"Hank believes Shockenaugh decided to kill Billy and me. That's Hank Jeffrey, who lives down the street. He used to work for military intelligence in South Africa and now he's got my place surrounded with members of his militia."

"Whoa! What did you say his name was?"

"You know how aging men find it hard to retire? Well, I'm not sure Hank retired from intelligence gathering, but he says he's not working with any white nationalist groups anymore. He's a neighbor, and I'm grateful for him at this point."

"From South Africa, you said?"

"Yes. Had me fooled."

"I'll look into it. I'm sure I can get protection for you before the night is over. In the meantime, have you got any ideas who's paying Shockenaugh to do this?"

"Actually, I do. But I haven't had time to do my research."

"We're running out of time before more people are killed," Mitchell said angrily. "Whoever it is uses a racially and ethnically diverse population of people to kill worldwide. And we don't know why. Your guess is as good as anybody else's."

"You mean you didn't think he was trying to put a target on the back of every person of color? Please tell me you thought of that possibility. I'm not going to make guesses. Whoever he or they are, their leader is old enough to have memories of World War II, yet young enough to have an interest in genetic engineering. Young Dr. Wren Xiao mentioned a man named Quan to me. You might try to research that name. I don't know anything about him yet. Haven't had time to look him up on the internet and I haven't had time to learn how receptive the CIA is toward Asian and African Americans. Does our tax dollar buy us the same protections from the CIA as other tax-paying Americans?"

"You've never mentioned these people before and I'm not certain I know what you're talking about, but I'm recording our conversation so I can look into everything you've mentioned. You can reach me at this number, anytime. Leave a message if I don't answer. I'll call you when I have more news about Sheila. I intend to stay with her through her ordeal. I think you were right about her, too."

"And what about Miriam and her son?" Inez asked with trepidation.

"How did you know there was something wrong?"

"It's a long story." Telling him one thing would lead to telling him about the adventure in the UPS truck, and she didn't have time for all of that now.

"Xavier is going to be fine," Mitchell answered. "I've got to stop talking now and get to work. You've given me lots to do," he said.

Inez was anxious to get to her computer before her shift started and yet she continued to hold her cell phone next to her ear after the call had ended. She thanked God for the few people in her life who cared about her. She was happy to have a family of people she belonged to.

CHAPTER 32

FEBRUARY 2007 PARK HILL

OOTSTEPS ON THE front porch startled her. Had she fallen asleep? Inez sat up quickly in her dining room chair. Sunlight seeped through her sheer curtains. Teddy Wabley's head rested on his bare emaciated white arm, which, in turn, lay atop Billy's computer. Hank had explained that the minute Billy's ear was patched, he felt he was far better trained for street warfare than computer research, while Teddy felt better trained for computers. So they switched places.

"Ted, wake up," Inez said gently. "I hear neighbors out front." She looked at her watch. "Five thirty in the morning?"

Teddy's confused eyes darted across the cluttered dining room table and she wondered if his parents were satisfied with the way others had raised their son.

"Could you put a new pot of coffee on for me?" Inez asked.

He rubbed his eyes hard and answered, "Sure thing."

They hadn't changed clothes from yesterday and Inez wanted to brush her teeth in the worst way, but the show had to go on. Maybe later she could excuse herself.

When she opened the door, the Blakes from the corner house were walking away, but they hurried back after seeing Inez at the door. Mrs. Blake seemed eager to come inside where it was warm and help Ted make coffee while Mr. Blake stood on the sidewalk.

"C'm here a minute," Mr. Blake called to Inez. He kept a tight grip on a stainless- steel car mug and looked very pleased with himself.

As Inez walked toward him, she looked up at a tree in her yard. At the very top sat Billy, who waved back, proud as a peacock.

"What are you looking over there for?" Blake asked. "What I want you to see is over here."

As Inez approached him he said, "See that police car at the corner? Larry told us not to call the police last night, but that sounded like hogwash to me. So I called them anyway. Told them I heard gunshots in the area. They sent a car out here to investigate. Said they'd stick around for a while. That's why we didn't hear any more gunshots last night. It wasn't because of anything Hank Jeffrey or Larry Carmichael did, I can tell you that much. We should all have called the police."

"Maybe so," Inez murmured, as Mr. Blake marched up her porch steps and into her house.

Rose Haywood was right behind him, a widow who lived on the corner at the other end of the block.

"Damnedest thing, I tell you," Rose said. "Nice little black girl with a white man carrying a big black camera. Stopped me as I came out of my house just now. You don't mind if I tell you what color these people were, do you?"

It didn't matter to Rose what Inez thought. She kept right on talking.

"They wanted to know if I'd heard about any troop deployment around here," Rose continued. "They'd gotten a tip from some TV station. I can't remember which. Can you beat that? What would the military be doing around here?"

"Maybe we can get to the bottom of this," Inez replied. "That's what this block meeting is for."

She was tired. It had been a long night. Her research had revealed that Shockenaugh had existed under numerous names, since the first U.S. invasion of Iraq. It was now recruiting an ethnically and racially diverse population of agents. What did its new management have in mind? Perhaps it was good a idea to form a think tank of neighbors interested in local and international news. Inez was certain there was a common theme hidden in these murders.

Quickly, she darted upstairs to the bathroom, where she closed the door, brushed her teeth, rinsed, and took a deep breath. Solitude at last.

Inez craved alone time. She wanted time to consider what was going to happen next?

"Dr. Buchanan!"

It was Hank's gruff voice.

"I'll be downstairs in a minute," Inez yelled back.

Before she'd gotten the words out of her mouth she heard heavy footsteps stomping up the stairs. Someone was already turning the knob on the bathroom door.

"Get away from that door!" Inez hollered. Everybody deserved alone time. "I'll be down soon enough, thank you very much!"

She hadn't heard footsteps going down the stairs. Surely Hank knew better than to pull that kind of intimidation on her! As soon as she flushed the toilet, she'd let him have what-for as only a schoolteacher could. If she hadn't been so angry, she would have stayed in the bathroom longer.

Inez jerked open the door. There stood Hank in full military uniform across the hall, in the doorway of her guest bedroom. His bomber jacket told her it was getter colder outside.

"We've got to talk," he demanded.

"Fine. We'll go downstairs."

"No. Tom and Jerry are downstairs explaining to our neighbors what we know already. We need privacy."

Inez could see yet another person behind Hank, standing inside her guest room. He looked African and wore a khaki uniform like Hank's. Her curiosity got the better of her and she finally strolled through the bedroom doorway.

Her love of *Ladies Home Journal* circa 1960 slightly embarrassed her. Ruffled curtains, bookshelves, and an overstuffed chintz-covered chaise lounge reflected a time years ago when she had been married for a short time. The room seemed unusually small with two large men inside of it now who would never be mistaken for the intellectual her ex-husband had been. She sat on the edge of the chaise lounge, while both men stood.

"This is my second-in-command, Commander Yosel. We've worked together both inside and outside the United States."

Inez wondered if Hank brought him along to verify that he was an equal opportunity war-monger.

"You came to me yesterday for help," Hank continued, as he walked to the only window and pushed the curtains aside. "You asked me to help you. Not Trace Mitchell or CBI. You asked *me*!"

He looked across the driveways that separated her house from the mini mansion built where Gaelen's house once stood. Sunlight caught his attention. Seated at an angle behind him, Inez was sure she saw what he saw, a flash of light from atop a thirty-foot tree. She wondered if it was one of his or Shockenaugh's soldiers.

"I want to be sure I understand you today," he said, as he let the curtain fall back to cover the window. He turned to face her and said, "You still want our help or not?"

The men glared at her. Their apparent need to dominate made her wonder about their mental maturity. And who was this new man? Suddenly it became clear what this was all about.

"I used my landline last night, didn't I?" she asked. "That's how you know about Trace. You were listening."

Hank literally snorted before addressing her. "Those Shockenaugh men who masqueraded as CBI agents told you not to use your cell phone because they wanted you to stay home close to your landline. That way they'd know where you were without having to triangulate anything."

Inez was silent, awestruck by Hank's ability to access what the average citizen could not. Unfortunately, her ignorance may have caused Shockenaugh to add another name to their hit list, Dr. Wren Xiao. *Whatever made me think I could be a detective much less a spy?*

She took a deep breath and said, "When I came to you yesterday, I was very afraid, afraid for people like Billy. Death and deception surrounded us. But I wasn't asking for war or an army of men when I asked you for help. I was thinking more about your knowledge base as a former member of what I thought was *our* military intelligence, not another country's. So maybe you have switched sides after all these years. I guess I was hoping we could shake our fists at the right organization to make the evil go away through some group lawsuit."

Hank and Commander Yosel laughed. "What did I tell you," Hank said, "women and knowledge don't mix."

She felt the temperature of her scalp rise until it felt as if a hot weight rested on her forehead. Slowly she stood up.

"Sit down!" Hank shouted.

"Or what?" she shouted back, loud enough for the whole house full of people to hear. How often had playground bullies shouted, hoping to get her attention so she'd come save them from being beaten. She knew what she was doing.

"We're not asking for permission, Inez," Hank shot back. "What we don't want is the FBI or CBI to be called in to arrest us. That would let Shockenaugh work unencumbered. The police will step all over themselves before they realize what's happened here. Don't you understand that the United States government is a client of Shockenaugh?"

Inez shuddered and suddenly Teddy twirled into the room. He carried a stack of papers held close to his rumpled tee shirt and asked, "I'm not interrupting, am I?" He didn't wait for an answer. Into the discussion he jumped, as if the men weren't in the room.

"There's no data on cloning or using DNA from old spit, human hair, dandruff, or sweat, but it is possible that what we're looking for hasn't been translated into English yet. And for good reason!"

Teddy had used a whole ream of paper to print out his findings. He held them up for Inez to see. She glanced through the top few sheets of paper as he waited quietly.

Teddy couldn't wait any longer. "It's an analysis of current data on making a disease-resistant super-intelligent human. India has the same lax attitude toward DNA research, but their scientists are nowhere near as close to fruition as China. Asian scientists would have the same skill set as scientists cloning an Eisenhower or any war tactician, let's say. And it's the Chinese government that fits your profile of who is behind Shockenaugh."

"Look Ted," Hank said, grabbing him by the ribbed neck of his tee shirt, "this isn't a good way to repay my kindness. You *are* interrupting."

Teddy never even looked at Hank. "See, if it's China," Ted continued, "we've got leverage over them to stop murdering. Personally, I don't think cloning war heroes to win ribbons in the 2008 Olympics is what they're up to. My money's on building a super-Asians who can win wars."

Hank tightened dry sun-scorched fingers around the young man's neck, when Inez put one of her hands over Hank's.

"Don't you dare," she said.

Commander Yosel grabbed Teddy by the shoulders and turned him around to face him. "Ted, here," he said with a British accent, "is a very brave boy indeed. He doesn't sit on a fence. No, he has made his decision. I'm proud of anyone so young and so intelligent who can stay the course and not become distracted by others around him. We should all be so diligent in our work."

He looked at Inez and said, "I applaud your influence over him, Dr. Buchanan."

Inez wondered about this man's motivation for intervening. Something about his ability to grab as quickly as he did reminded her of several scary movies she'd seen. He still looked at her while his facial expressions gradually changed.

A barely audible sound came from outside. Inez heard nothing at first and wondered if both men were just screwy warmongers. Both men looked up at the ceiling and then lurched downstairs and through the front door. Inez ran to her front bedroom windows with Ted following behind. They looked down at Hank and Yosel standing immobile in the middle of the street. An overcast sky prevented attempts to see anything above them. A few neighbors followed the two men outside. Others remained on the grass in front of Inez's house.

"Drones," Hank hollered up to the sky. "Maybe four of them. Take cover."

Several neighbors immediately ran home. But most ran back inside Inez's house to seek cover.

Inez ran downstairs where she directed people to her basement. She hollered up to Ted, who'd been collecting papers strewn onto the floor. She asked him to come downstairs and help. Then Hank's voice screamed, "Nooo!" Something about the sound overhead made Hank disappear down the street.

A whole minute passed before a sudden pervasive and vibrating explosion occurred nearby, accompanied by the sound of shattering glass from Inez's living room window. Everyone in her home dropped to the floor in the very spot in which he or she had been standing. As she crouched down,

Inez suddenly remembered Billy. Where was he? Panicking, though careful not to cut herself, she crawled on all fours into the living room, while Tom and Jerry, who had been in the room talking to neighbors, ran past her and out the front door.

Inez scanned the top of the tree in her yard. Billy wasn't there. Her heart formed a lump in her throat as she pondered whether to leave the house and look for him. She decided to stay put until the smoke cleared. It was rising from the street farther down the block.

As smoke cleared she saw Tom and Jerry standing in the middle of the street with the mysterious African soldier, Yosel, who had been upstairs. Maybe they all belonged to the same militia. Two additional soldiers dressed in camouflage came running from Colfax Avenue to join them. One carried a large metal contraption with skinny legs. The other man carried two rockets close to his chest, each a meter long. The four men set up an artillery position in the middle of the street.

"UAV, two o'clock," shouted one of them, who then fired repeatedly with a rifle at something Inez couldn't see. The shots let loose a torrent of screaming people, their voices rising as they shoved past each other and out of Inez's home to get to their own homes.

And poor Rose Haywood. If the legs on that gun the men used had been two inches shorter, they would have shot her head off as she ran past them.

Inez was horrified. Her eyes searched for Billy and Hank until she found Hank getting to his feet with the help of a little girl who, Inez thought, lived a block over. He'd been flattened to the sidewalk across the street from his own home during the last round of gun fire. He barely gained his balance before he dashed toward his house, shouting for Agnes. Inez wondered if his home incurred much damage.

She saw policemen without hats and men in civilian clothing dart between houses. Still no Billy. The sound of sirens was distant.

Just as she got off her knees to go outside and look for Billy, another explosion lifted her feet up from the floor and threw her against furniture at the back wall of her living room. She kept her eyes closed, fearful of flying glass and all other possible horrors. This explosion had been in the opposite direction from the first.

The sirens were much closer now. Slowly she opened her eyes to see her front door hanging on one hinge. She tasted plaster dust and saw people looking back at her from the street outside. A policeman raced through the open door to her side.

"Can you move?" he asked.

Inez was sitting up, her back against an upholstered chair. "Yes, I think so," she answered. Another police officer ran further inside to help others who had not yet left. Two men pulled her to her feet and walked her through her front door. Other neighbors walked out of her house as well. At least that is what she thought was happening.

"Can you tell us what's going on here, ma'am? Did you see the first or the second explosion?"

"No," she said, staring at their badges. She pondered for a moment whether these men were Shockenaugh employees disguised as police. The two men held onto her arms and tried to lead her down the porch steps.

"You'll need to walk to an area on the parkway that we've set up," said one.

"That can't be wise," she replied, "or have you captured the source of those overhead drones?" She was standing at the bottom of her porch as she spoke.

"Drones? Did you see drones?" the policeman asked.

Inez was speechless. When the police officer stepped to the side, Inez could see the front of the house next door to her, the house that had been Gaelen's. The front was gone turned into rubble. Only the back half of the house remained. And to the south of her, further down the street, she could finally see that Hank's house was gone.

"Hank!" she screamed. The horror of what might have happened suddenly dawned on her. She broke away from the police, who called after her. Inez ran at first, then slowed down, resisting the knowledge of what she might see.

Hank stood in the middle of rubble, his head barely above street level. Inez clawed her way over bricks and cinder blocks, until she reached the edge of a large hole in the earth. A furnace lay on its side. Two bodies, each covered by a black plastic cloth, lay at Hank's feet.

Noise from ambulance sirens and people shouting blocked out

everything but what was directly in front of Inez. Police officers stood on either side of Hank, while a third stretched yellow tape across the side of his property.

Hank's head was down. He turned slightly and held out his hand to Inez. He put one arm around her shoulder and said, "Billy went to get Agnes out of the house. He shielded her from the blast with his own body."

With a cracking voice, Inez said. "That's not Billy. Why would that be Billy? Are you sure? Let me see." She stepped closer to the two covered bodies. Realizing she didn't know which body was which, she stood shaking. Hank held her up as she stumbled.

CHAPTER 33

FEBRUARY 2007 PARK HILL

"TED," HANK SHOUTED, "help Dr. Buchanan back to her front porch."

Before taking his hand away from her shoulder, Hank said, "Don't be afraid. The enemy has retreated. They're blending into the crowd behind the yellow tape. They won't try again until the publicity evaporates."

Inez heard strength in Hank's voice and knew this was no time to cave in. She looked into his eyes and knew he meant to kill whoever was responsible for killing his wife.

She hadn't known Ted was nearby, but gradually felt his hand on her elbow. It was the way Billy would have helped. Inez paid little attention to people gathering behind the blockades at each end of the street. She walked head down beside Teddy and tried to imagine a world without Billy.

The noise had increased, and the number of people inside the blockades multiplied exponentially. Paramedics and ambulances were everywhere, putting things down on the ground and picking them up to put someplace else. Inez paid little attention to them and avoided all eye contact.

She and Ted sat quietly on the steps of her porch and watched paramedics patch the scrapes and cuts of neighbors as well as people she thought belonged to Hank's militia. Inez buried herself for moments at a time in memories of Billy. Sometimes she cried out loud, then stared into space. She listened to the loud spats between people over jurisdiction and where to set up a help station. She heard a reporter say two people were dead and fourteen injured, and that five of those injured had been taken to area hospitals.

Sometimes she overheard Ted tell official-looking people to f** off, that she wasn't giving interviews. He told some people that they couldn't tour her home and pushed others off her porch. She vaguely remembered seeing TV cameramen and reporters interviewing people across the street. Familiar faces would stop by to say they were sorry for her loss. And it all had no particular meaning for her.

The house next door to Inez no longer burned. Firemen made sure of that before packing up. Still, she paid scant attention even as the smoke and the air cleared.

Later, two policewomen sat on either side of her and asked questions. The questions seemed superficial as if they thought she didn't know anything about the events that had transpired. Teddy rested against a porch railing a few feet away. Inez caught sight of him out of the corner of her eye. She beckoned to him, asking that he bring her a recipe box from the kitchen, the one with addresses and phone numbers in it. The policewoman wanted Billy's address and next of kin.

After Teddy returned with the box, he quietly waited beside Inez until the policewoman left. Then he said, "I can tell you're feeling better."

"Guess I am," she replied. "I want to thank you for all you've done for me today."

"Aw shucks," he answered. "I learned how to give aid and comfort to someone in mourning. Didn't know how to do that before now."

"You're a very smart boy, and I want you to know that I appreciate every one of those little gray cells you've got." They both chuckled together.

"Poirot, right?" he asked.

"Aha, and you know how to make a teacher's soul sing. Guess I just needed time to ask God why He didn't take me instead of Billy," Inez said.

Without hesitation, Ted answered, "I know why. He wants you to retaliate against the bloody bastards who did all this. You've got to bring them to justice."

From her seat on the porch step, she twisted around to get a better look at him. "Guess I should have asked you earlier," she said. "Could have saved myself a few hours grieving. It's not about me, is it?"

She was talking to herself as much as to Ted. While his words had made her tired, she knew it was time to stand up and smell the coffee. Glancing across the street for a minute, she focused on Larry's house for the first time all day. Where was he? Fire trucks, along with people walking back and forth in front of her, had blocked her view of his place most of the morning. Maybe he'd gone some place and not told anyone. She remembered seeing police knock at his door and then leave when no one answered. But that had been hours ago.

Inez looked at Teddy again. "Aren't you hungry?" she asked. "Every piece of food in my house has your name on it." Her words echoed in her ears, because she'd said the very same thing to a young Billy Needham. She stood up without tears. Her muscles ached, and she remembered Larry again.

"You go inside," she said to Teddy, "and get yourself something to eat, while I look for a policeman. I think it's time I visited Larry."

"Can I go too? I'm not hungry. I've been nibbling on your granola bars all day. I'll even get the police right now." And off he ran.

Teddy cornered a policeman across the street and pointed to Larry's house and then to Dr. Buchanan. Three officers gathered at the curb in front of Larry's house. They told Ted to return to the other side of the street and wait.

Inez and Teddy sat on the porch steps to watch while police walked up the driveway to enter through Larry's back door. No sooner had they entered than a policewoman came outside to wrap yellow tape around the short hedge in front of Larry's house.

With a solemn face, a policeman rushed out of Larry's front door toward them.

"Can either or both of you identify Larry Carmichael?" he shouted.

Neither of them spoke for a moment. Ted helped Inez to her feet.

"Yes," she answered with deliberation.

"We both can," Ted added.

"We only need one person to identify him."

Ignoring him, Ted and Inez grabbed each other's hands. Upon entering the living room behind the police officer, they watched yet another policeman already in the room. He stared at the occupant of an upholstered chair. Inez felt uneasy stepping over newspapers scattered about her ankles and slightly nauseous from the smell of alcohol and urine in the air. Was she ready for this? But as they came around the side of the chair, there sat Larry Carmichael, alive, but handcuffed. Dried blood surrounded a deep gash on his forehead. His entire chin was deep purple. And a gelatinous material glistened on his clothing.

"Knew I'd be rescued." His speech was slurred and his eyes didn't focus.

"What happened to you?" she asked, then turned to the policemen. "Why is he handcuffed? He needs a hospital!"

"Ma'am we had to be sure he was the homeowner. Claims he killed the dead man in the kitchen. Had to make certain it wasn't the other way around. So this is Carmichael?"

Both Ted and Inez nodded yes.

"You wouldn't want to take a look at the other man, would ya'?" asked the officer. "See if you know him, too?"

"You're right, I wouldn't," Inez replied quickly.

"What about you young man?"

"No," Inez said, "he doesn't want to look, either." But Ted had already left her side before she'd finished her sentence.

With both hands in plastic wire, Larry grabbed the bottom of Inez's blouse with his fingers, pulling her toward him. His breath was a combination of spoiled chicken and cheap liquor. Globs of spit rolled down his purple chin from the corner of his mouth. The nearest police officer cut the wrist wires and pushed Larry's shoulder back against the chair's cushions. Inez knelt on the floor in front of him, resting her arm on his knee.

"Sorry, Inez. I never wanted you to see me like this. Got drunk when Hank threw me outa' his house last night."

"No he didn't," she replied sternly. "He was only . . ."

"He woulda' never opened the damn door if you hadn't been there. Hank never spoke to me again after I told you both about Karen and me. Never looked me in the eye again. I thought twice—hell four or five times—before I went to his house last night. I was worried about him, when I heard those shots. So did he send that son of a bitch here to kill me?

Showed him, didn't I? You can't kill a white man that easy, don't matter what his politics are. And I didn't use a gun either. I ain't got one."

Several sets of sirens blasted in the distance.

"Hank didn't send anyone here to kill you," Inez answered. He smelled so bad she had to turn her face to the side as she spoke.

"Sure 'bout that?" Larry asked.

"It's a long story," she continued. "And I'm glad you're alive to hear it. Her voice broke. Listen." Inez could feel herself getting sick from the odor. "I can't tell you everything that's happened, but Hank lost his wife and I lost Billy. Soon as you get looked after in the hospital, I'll tell you everything."

Sirens abruptly stopped at Larry's front door, and two responders entered.

Larry began to yell. "Don't need a hospital! Nothin's wrong with me. I need to find Karen. Where do you think she is Inez?"

He ignored questions from medics.

"He's lost a lot of blood," said one of them, while ripping the side of his flannel shirt open to reveal a deep, long red slash across his rib cage.

Inez gasped and Larry dropped his head back, as if passing out.

"Stay with us, Mr. Carmichael," one of them yelled.

Ted walked into the living room as they put Larry on a gurney. Inez grabbed Ted's arm, worried that he'd see Larry in the worst possible condition, and escorted him outside. She needed the fresh air.

A police officer followed them out, saying there would be men stationed at either end of the barricades all night for the protection of neighbors still on the block. Minutes later, the ambulance left with its sirens blaring.

As soon as it was gone, Ted ran across the street and into Inez's house. She thought nothing of it. The boy had to be hungry. As she got closer, she saw that the front door wasn't dangling on one hinge anymore. Beside her window was her handyman nailing boards across it.

As Inez approached him, he said, "Your assistant called me and said I shouldn't charge you very much, but that you needed my services before dark tonight. I heard about the explosions here in Park Hill on television. Hope they find out what happened."

"Thank you Ben."

"I'll need to call you tomorrow after I get a quote on your window replacement, but you'll be safe tonight. That's quite a young helper you've got there. Where's Billy?"

Inez only nodded and quickly walked inside. Ted was seated at the dining room table with a pencil in his hand, writing feverishly.

"You got my handyman's name and number out of my recipe box, didn't you?" she asked.

"I have to write all this down before I forget it," he said. "But yes. I'm sorry I didn't ask before I did it, but I didn't know when you'd be feeling better and it was getting late when I called him. I won't do it again."

Inez smiled at him, grateful she wasn't alone. "So did you recognize the dead body in the kitchen?" Inez asked.

"Yes, I did," he answered.

Inez was visibly surprised and plopped into the dining room chair across from him. "Well," she asked, "who was he?"

"A member of Shockenaugh maybe? Saw him walking around this block a day ago. Even took a picture of him on my phone. See?" He held it up for her to get a better look. "The police inside Larry's house also let me take a picture of the dead man on the floor so I could compare the photos."

"You're kidding," Inez said angrily.

"I think it was because of the other man who stood in the kitchen. He nodded that it was okay. I could tell he was important," Ted continued. "I think they all thought you were going to follow me into the kitchen. There was a man inside when I got there, who later told me never to describe him to anyone. Although he didn't say who he was, he gave me his card and told me to give it to you. I already read the part that says he's with CIA. He asked me if I knew any of the Chinese nationals he listed very slowly. That's why I had to run over here and write the names down before I forgot them. Here they are: Dr. Wren Xiao, Dr. Woo Lee, Quan Yu, and Kee Yu.

"I didn't know any of them, of course, but I think he really wanted me to ask you. He said he'd like you to call him, only—and he emphasized the word *only*—if you can give him any information about any of them. He said to be sure to tell you that Xiao Wren is still alive and that the man on the floor in the kitchen, the man I'd taken a picture of, was a Chinese national named Bohai."

Ted's information made her heart pound faster. She had no intention of ever sharing information with Ted or jeopardizing this boy's life as she had unwittingly done with Billy.

"Let's get a pizza delivered," she finally said. "You order and I'll pay when it comes. Order all the trimmings and everything that goes with it. Maybe two pizzas. I'm hungry, too."

His face, she noticed, didn't light up as she had hoped it would. While Ted ordered, she got up from her chair and got her broom, walked into the living room, and began sweeping up the mess of glass from around her window.

As soon as Ted got off the phone with the pizza company, he took her broom and swept, while she watched and pondered.

"I know what you're doing," Ted said as he swept glass into a pile. "You're trying to keep me safe. But do you remember the last thing we talked about before the bombs fell?"

Inez had to think for a while. Then she said, "Yes, I do."

Ted continued, "I can't imagine anything more embarrassing to the Chinese government than for the rest of the world to think they used the DNA of white men to fortify their own racial stock. That would be worse than using steroids."

"You're suggesting that the Chinese government hired Shockenaugh to kill anyone who could help connect the dots back to their mission. They needed to save face," Inez said. "And you're right. China can't afford such a rumor, not when they're about to host the Olympics. You know how to contact the Chinese government?"

"Heck yeah! All I need is a computer and my phone. I've even got that photo of the dead man in Larry Carmichael's house. That should make them take us seriously."

"And I'd like to narrate Gaelen's story for them. I want China to know the kind of man they killed."

"That sounds more like a video than an email. But we could do that too," Ted explained, "as an attachment."

"I could end the story," Inez said, "by explaining that YouTube, CNN, *China Today*, may all want to see this video, and that they will see it if China doesn't stop Shockenaugh."

"Couldn't hurt," Ted said.

"I want China to understand that Shockenaugh will cost them more than money. It will cost them prestige."

"And," said Ted excitedly, "it shouldn't take long to send it."

"Good, because early tomorrow morning I've got to go see Billy's mother. We've got to work fast."

"Well, I work even faster when I'm not hungry."

"Delivery!" came a voice from the front door.

CHAPTER 34

JULY 2008   CHONGQING TO BEIJING

"'Y OU HAD US worried, Xiao," Quan said. "But you sound well. Are you in an airport? I hear noise in the background."

Something was different about the quality of Quan's voice. It lacked its aging and sinister tone that boasted of an ability to have anyone killed whenever he wanted. But after all, Xiao thought, it had been a year since he'd heard him speak.

"My mission," Xiao said, "the mission you gave me, required my focused attention. I am happy to report complete success. Perhaps that girl's murder has already come to your attention."

"You certainly took your time reporting the event to me."

"I was certain Kee would keep you informed," Xiao explained. There was a long silence.

"Have you paid attention to Party news lately?" Quan's voice rose slightly. "Kee has been arrested. There's unsubstantiated talk that I too may be arrested soon. It's all a misunderstanding. I can assure you of that."

Xiao made no response. He never imagined Kee or Quan could ever be arrested. Perhaps he wouldn't need to kill them at all.

Quan began speaking again, but only in whispers. "You must understand that I personally gave you no mission to complete, and neither did Kee. After all, you never worked for either of us. And I'm sorry your grant was no longer funded. But your decision to take a year-long vacation must have done you a world of good. You see how well every thing has worked out for all of us."

"Yes," Xiao replied. So the conversation was being monitored.

"I value our friendship," Quan continued, "and hope to converse with you at length about your recent camping trip throughout the Yunnan province. Of course, we do require that you return the government credit card you were issued. Kee may have made a clerical mistake about its use. I'm sure you won't be held responsible for paying the government back for whatever you charged."

"I understand," Xiao answered. What he understood was that something was very wrong.

"Good. Are you in Beijing?" Quan asked.

"No, I hadn't planned to report to you until next week, if that's okay, sir?"

"Oh, there's no need to report anything to me. I merely thought that we might have tea or coffee together. Next week will be soon enough. But things are changing rapidly here in Beijing. My offices are being moved. Perhaps we could meet at a tourist venue like the Drum Tower. How about Thursday a week from today at noon? Bring that credit card with you, and we'll clear that up as well. Traffic will be terrible, but while the Olympic games are underway, there shouldn't be lots of people at our traditional monuments. We'll talk about your future in the Party and bioengineering in general."

"I'd like that," Xiao said.

"Good. It's great to have you back. I'll see you at the Drum Tower a week from today."

**

Xiao sat quietly in the airport, his legs sprawled out in front of him, satisfied that the conversation had gone well. He felt confident that he'd bought himself nearly three days time before Quan's men would seriously attempt to find and kill him. And yet he couldn't be sure it was Quan he had just talked to. The real surprise was that Kee had been arrested. Why? After several minutes of contemplation, he decided not to concern himself with situations that had nothing to do with his own objectives.

He grabbed his backpack, walked quickly to the airport entrance and got into a cab. Xiao told the driver about the Yangtze River Youth Hostel, a place he'd heard of while at Stanford. The driver sped toward their destination, while Xiao squeezed his head and arm out of the window and pitched Quan's cell phone over the bridge and into the Yangtze below.

Chongqing had a foggy, theatrical energy, making the city more nouveau-jaded than Xiao thought any city outside of San Francisco had a right to claim. He quietly hugged his backpack, feeling more like a gangster who had just thrown away his first untraceable gun rather than a cell phone.

"I'm sorry," said a very young blonde with a surfer body from behind the reception counter of the hostel. "You didn't make reservations. We're booked up. But in two days, we should have one or two openings. I can put your name down, if you'd like. There are plenty of places nearby where you can stay up all night, then check back in a day or two."

He thanked her. But if he couldn't get into the hostel, what he really wanted was like a place in Beijing: a park, where people did line and ballroom dances all night long. A place with benches, small tables, and older people who played checkers. It was still daylight but he knew from the parks in Beijing that people would begin to gather early. If he looked around Chongqing, maybe he could find such a park. Wasn't that what the girl meant about staying up all night?

He searched up and down streets near the river. Houses and stalls on the sides of hills reminded him of a drearier Sausalito.

After walking several kilometers from the river, he found nothing that resembled the parks of Beijing. Instead, tall skyscrapers stood on long stone and concrete plazas where people his age paced back and forth in search of excitement.

Places to sit outside were few, but karaoke bars invited people inside for whatever they yearned for. While standing in the middle of a plaza the evening turned cold. Xiao unzipped his backpack to search for his down jacket. He decided not to put it on after all. The air was too humid. Instead, he pulled out a thin and frayed denim jacket with an American flag embroidered on it.

"Hi, man. You from New York?" asked someone behind him.

The words were spoken in English by an Asian man younger than Xiao.

He wore a denim shirt, raggedy Dockers, and was very skinny with a short white apron tied around his waist. He carried a clear glass of something steaming hot and stared at Xiao's scarred cheek. Xiao was hungry and cold.

"No," he said without a smile. "San Francisco."

"Yeah? Well, this is for you." He handed Xiao the glass. "There's a cross between a supermodel and every man's bratty little sister in there," he said, pointing to a plate glass window. "She paid me to bring this drink to you. Said she'd like to meet you, if you're from the United States."

Several people bumped into Xiao as he stared at the glass window about twenty meters away. He drank the liquid down in one gulp and then held his arm high in a salute to the unseen woman behind the building's facade.

"Thank her for me," he said, handing the glass back to the young man.

"Tell her yourself," he shouted over his shoulder.

Maybe he would. Xiao ran to catch up to the waiter, but suddenly remembered his backpack. He turned to get it and his heart stopped. It was gone!

In all directions it was gone. It was gone as if it had never been there. He stopped everyone around him and asked if they had seen someone carrying a backpack. Plenty of people smiled at him but walked away. Had someone planned this theft? Had someone given it to the police? He couldn't go to the police.

A fountain of water, maybe five stories high, suddenly spurted up from beneath a piece of stone on the floor of the plaza. The wind blew the water higher into the air, turning it into a fine mist. Another fountain of water shot up from under another stone and yet another. In minutes the wide space of the plaza was wet and thick with fog.

People dispersed into bars. Others headed homeward. Xiao watched in surprise. He hadn't anticipated a catastrophe. Was an entire city conspiring against him? Was it a crime of opportunity, or was he forever being watched? His money, credit card, even the government card Quan wanted back, his passport and Karen's, as well as two guns were gone.

Laughing voices made him suddenly sad and paranoid. Not wanting to hear any more laughter or be seen by anyone targeting him, he ran and ran and ran until exhaustion made him drop to the ground in an alley devoid of fog. Instead, it was filled with a darkness that swallowed him whole. All the bright lights across the city's skyline had been turned off.

He'd forgotten an important rule, to be observant at all times. He pounded his fist in the dirt. Anger was not his friend. Anger ate up time he'd need to build an action plan.

Still on the ground, he looked up at closed windows throughout the narrow alley. Some were shuttered, others painted, and still others had drapes. He had to be more alert or his life could become as confining as those buildings.

A search of his pockets uncovered one-hundred cui. It wasn't enough to get to Beijing. He folded his money back into his wallet and stood against the nearest wall, ready to absorb information about his surroundings.

Voices from nearby streets slowly entered his world, but one voice was louder than the others. Had his illness returned? Xiao covered his ears for protection. The voice he could hear shouted in Mandarin instead of Cantonese. "Can you tie knots? Can you tie knots?"

With no clue concerning the source of the voice, he decided to answer, "Yes, but what kind of knots?"

A man in a dark suit stepped out of the shadows further down the alley and said in English, "I buy most knots, if they're good. You need work?"

The unknown man had demonstrated courage by stepping into the light. In the past, Xiao's internal chorus of voices would not have permitted him to answer.

"Yes," Xiao answered quickly.

"You from the States?" the same man asked.

Xiao didn't hesitate. "Yes," he replied, while taking a few steps closer.

"So was this factory," the man replied. "It was moved here straight from Missouri. I need somebody, now, to work night shifts. It pays more than the day shift because few young people want to miss what goes on in this city after dark."

Xiao followed him through a doorway and down a long dusty hall. One overhead bulb cast more shadow than light. At the far end of the hall was an open room full of light with about two to three hundred men and women seated in front of sewing machines, automatic staplers, and compressors.

"Wait," Xiao said, holding the man's arm.

The man stopped walking.

Xiao began his story. "I was robbed of everything. I have no passport to register with the police, and I need money to get to Beijing. If you let me work six days, I'll increase your output by sixty percent. I only ask that you pay me fifty percent more than the others for my efforts."

"This is Communist China," said the man. He smiled, as if the joke was on Xiao, then stopped smiling suddenly.

"I know where I am," Xiao replied. "I only ask because we're both Americans."

"And our haughtiness gets us recognized no matter what we're wearing." Xiao's jaw had caught the man's attention.

"What animal did that?" he asked.

"A snow leopard, referred to as the Mountain Ghost."

The man from Missouri was noticeably impressed. He stood closer to Xiao letting his eyes travel over the imprint of a claw where tissue had had been yanked from his face.

"I'll see what I can do when the time comes," he answered.

The man held out his hand and shook Xiao's. The deal was set. They both walked across the large well-lit room until they reached the back doors where the finished products were piling up. Stuffed upholstered sofas and chairs were being hot-wrapped in plastic before they were tossed into trucks. Several men tied knots around wooden palettes on which larger pieces of furniture were tied.

Xiao did the work of two men that first night and each night thereafter he increased his output by one more man. Without shame, he ate whatever workers left from their meals. He slept in the corner of the giant room for no more than thirty minutes at a time between shifts. Most of the workers were women who sometimes left him the best of what they had from their own food. Most workers accepted his disfigured face without asking questions. Others stared at him. After six days of work, he quit.

He had intended to hitch a ride with one of the company drivers delivering wrapped furniture to stores in Beijing. But when he saw an old Suzuki belonging to a fellow employee, he fell in love with it. Xiao wasn't a student of motorcycles but loved them from afar. His work-mate was surprisingly eager to sell him the motorcycle for an agreed-upon low price.

The manager shook his hand and thanked him for the increased productivity without handing him a special envelope of money. Feeling deceived, Xiao turned around quickly to hide his anger. Almost every worker in the room walked up to him with money in their hands to give to him. Three men did not. Xiao counted the money as he received it.

Certainly he was not offended, but did not like this way of being paid a bonus. He swiveled around to the manager and said, "Hold out your hand."

The manager lifted his hand, palm side up.

Xiao gave him two items that looked like small thumbtacks. "I wondered whether to give you these."

"What are these for?"

"They're microphones. Not tacks. Don't hold them up to your eye. People behind me, and particularly the ones who placed them in every piece of furniture you make, will see that you have discovered what they do all day. They are your least productive workers. The ones who didn't pay me."

The manager said nothing.

"If I were you," said Xiao, "I'd return to the States to tell my employer before they find out for themselves. Otherwise, they'll think you did this for China. Surely you can see they're wireless and compatible with 5G technology. I hope I have serviced you well."

Xiao turned and walked to where the motorcycle owner stood beside a massive half-stuffed sofa. Xiao gladly counted out a portion of the money and the worker handed him the keys.

Down the long corridor he walked, quickly, listening to soft footsteps behind him. Perhaps some of the men wanted their money back.

Just as he stepped into the alley Xiao braced himself for what he knew would be an attack. One worker who had not paid him jumped on his back until he was down on one knee. A second kicked his side and Xiao fell flat on his side. Gravel covered his face as he rolled over to get up. Still able to see his motorcycle across the alley in front of him, his pain kept him down.

With every breath, anger from the night he was first robbed returned. He lashed out with his legs and then his fist. He had trained himself in the cave to leap and run quicker than a mountain lion. He was standing again quicker than his opponents could blink. A punch from Xiao's leg knocked one man out as he fell on cement edging. The clicking sound of a quick-release weapon made Xiao even more alert. He hoped it was a retro switchblade—the favored weapon of gangs he'd avoided all his life. Now he was more confident that he could handle that too.

The man with the knife wasted time positioning himself properly. But Xiao bent the man's wrist down until he heard it crack and snatched the knife away from him. A third man came running out of the doorway and into the knife Xiao held waist high. With a push from Xiao, that man fell backwards with a shirt bloodied around the wound.

Xiao gulped down his own adrenaline before running across the alley. He hopped onto his motorcycle, knowing the man with the knife still in him was probably dead. He hesitated for a fraction of a second deciding to leave the knife behind. Then drove mostly nonstop for more than 1,700 kilometers to reach Beijing on the morning of the first full day of the Olympics. As soon as he arrived, he found a large restaurant that satisfied his needs: tea, noodles, spiced fish, and space in the back to clean up before going to the Drum Tower. Would Quan be there? Would he send someone in his place? It didn't matter. Implementing his action plan meant freedom from China once and for all.

Xiao ate hurriedly, not wanting to be late. With no backpack or wallet, he kept his cui close to his body, inside the small pocket of the jeans he'd been wearing since the day he left his dongtian, his cave heaven.

A long line of people waited to enter the WC. When he finally reached a stall, the man in the next one stood beside his very young little boy who cried most of the time.

When Xiao could finally button up his pants to leave, he gladly stepped away from the noise. Once he left the stall, he stopped at the communal sink and heard distinct words between sniffles from the little boy.

The child whispered, "Wanted to play peek-a-boo."

The words were in English and Xiao had heard the voice before, from a very young girl. As he stared into the mirror, he could see the man in the stall behind him trying to look through the crack between the door and the wall of the stall. Xiao kept his head down as he washed his hands, so as not to seem interested. Dr. Woo had called his daughter, what? He couldn't remember.

Suddenly the door to the stall opened. A bareheaded man, holding the hand of a child of five with a Chairman Mao hat over most of its head, slowly walked toward the exit. As the man touched the door latch, Xiao remembered the name and shouted, "Kaitlyn?" The child turned so quickly the hat slid off its head and long dark hair rolled down her back.

With one step and a taut fist, Xiao landed a blow on the side of the man's head. He went down, slapping hard against the tile floor and didn't move. Other men turned their backs on the event and flung themselves into the stalls. Xiao picked up both the girl and her hat and pushed past people crowding the exit, still in line to come in. In seconds, they were out of the restaurant and on his motorcycle.

"I'm a friend of your father's," he said.

"He's dead," she replied with no emotion in her voice at all.

He locked her into his lap with his seat belt and gave her his helmet, even though it was too big. "You probably don't remember me."

"Oh, but I do," she said, taking the helmet off her head. "You were in bed for a long time in our dongtian."

He told himself he didn't have time to smile. He had to stay focused, to get away from the restaurant before police came. Reaching the Drum Tower in time to meet Quan was his most important concern. But admittedly, Kaitlyn was a distraction.

In his heart, he was certain that both Quan and Kee were too powerful to have serious problems inside the government of the People's Republic of China. If anything, their power had probably increased over the year he'd been gone from Beijing. They would certainly try to end his life if he didn't end theirs first.

As soon as he parked his motorcycle in the parking lot of the Drum Tower, he carried Kaitlyn in his arms to the nearest monk in front of the small prayer drums just outside the huge building.

"Please help me," Xiao pleaded in Mandarin. "I have come here to plead with the mother of my little girl. I need her to come home with us. Will you take my daughter for only a few minutes, maybe thirty minutes?" Xiao held out his arms with Kaitlyn in them. "Sit with my daughter and I will donate to your mission as soon as I return. And please don't leave this spot. I need to see her from the top balcony of this tower."

Xiao placed her in his lap, bought the appropriate tickets, and ran up the narrow steps inside the building before the monk could object. Fewer people than normal were taking the climb up, although it was midday. The bird's-nest arena was likely packed with Olympic spectators.

On the steps he passed a woman with a little girl, a man with wild, uncombed hair, and three male tourists, who climbed separately. Two of them carried more than one camera, as if determined to convince the public they were harmless.

Xiao had visited the tower many times before and remembered being told that it was 46.7 meters tall. Once on top, he loved listening to different languages spoken at once, just as he would hear them in San Francisco's Chinatown. But today was a new experience. He walked across the top floor of the building as a gladiator would walk into a coliseum, alert and expecting to be attacked from all sides.

Today he listened to tourists complain about hotel accommodations and their worries over seeing all the events at the Olympic stadium. He looked for Quan. Trained drummers had not yet begun their demonstration.

The Asian man with the uncombed hair walked up to Xiao and asked in Cantonese, "You are from the United States?"

Xiao didn't answer but stepped aside, not wanting to be seen next to someone so disheveled. He noticed a tall man behind the Asian. His back was towards him, but Xiao knew who he was immediately. Xiao stepped sideways to avoid altogether the man who spoke to him in Cantonese and grabbed the shoulder of the man behind him. He turned the man around. It was Dr. Woo. Happily surprised, Xiao opened his mouth wide, a smile already engulfing his face.

But Woo spoke first. "Quan sent me to kill you in order to free my daughter."

Instinct told Xiao of the blade Woo carried below his waist.

"No," Xiao yelled. "I have Kaitlyn!"

Just then Woo's head snapped backward with a loud gasp. A woman screamed. Xiao watched Dr. Woo fall on his back. A long blade slowly and silently protruded out the front of his chest as his back squarely met the floor. Now standing in front of Xiao was Woo's killer, the Asian who spoke Cantonese. The hint of a smirk sat on his face.

The two men exchanged glances for less than a second before the man ran in the opposite direction. But in that moment, time had stood still. Was that a madman, a friend, or an enemy? In that moment, Xiao realized that the man and his clothes looked more American than Chinese. And the man was gone.

Blood slowly spread outward from Woo's body as Xiao sadly stepped back to avoid it. He backed directly into a man walking alone. Startled, Xiao jumped away.

"It was you, wasn't it" said an American tourist wearing the type of white collar worn by priests and ministers. Xiao hadn't noticed him on the steps, which meant he had to have been on the top floor waiting. His black suit had no dust or lint on it. "*You're* the man from the States. That man with the knife was asking about you, wasn't he?"

The priest's face suddenly became distorted as he backed away from Xiao. He turned to dash out the side entrance but kept looking back at Xiao like a man avoiding the plague.

Someone hollered, "STOP! STOP!"

Xiao flexed on the balls of his feet, ready to kill anyone he could identify as Quan's emissary with his bare hands. Suddenly he thought of Kaitlyn waiting for him below. He followed the American man with the white collar to the balcony outside, just in time to see the priest, if he really had been one, bend backwards. A small hole, unnoticed before, now produced a trickle of blood that oozed down his face, as he fell over the railing to the ground below.

Xiao leaped down several steps at a time, knowing he had be out of there before the police arrived. Upon reaching the bottom, sounds of people running greeted him. Large navy-blue police trucks had parked close to the entrance. Luckily he was past their barricades as large numbers of police swarmed the entrance. Several people whispered, "three dead bodies," and Xiao wondered who the third body was.

Slowly he walked outside and down the steps. Adrenaline made the veins on his face, neck, and hands pop. The monk continued to pray, while

Kaitlyn ran toward him to take hold of his hand. She smiled and his heart began to slow down. Xiao dumped money into the monk's pot and continued walking toward his motorcycle.

He thought of Dr. Woo and became more determined that Kaitlyn should have her chance for the life her father hoped to provide. Xiao wondered about the men in the tower. Had any of them been CIA agents? Had Quan sent additional men besides Dr. Woo to make sure everyone was killed off?

Gradually, out of the corner of his eye he noticed that the police were spreading out in all directions, about 150 meters in a sparse circle. Were they circling him? How long did he have before they took his freedom?

A few men on motorcycles were parked beside his own bike. They were yelling something. Another group on electric bikes rode up to him and called out, "Glad you made it." Some reached out and slapped his back and more drove up waving frantically. Xiao walked more cautiously, while analyzing how he would protect Kaitlyn. Who were these guys? Some had dark skin and some looked familiar. They quickly surrounded him.

"Xiao Wren, right?" one man asked in English. "Friend of Inez Buchanan?"

Gathering Kaitlyn into his arms, he stared at the group, who now surrounded him. "Yes," he replied.

"We've been looking for you in every major city from Beijing to Taiwan. Hurry," said another.

"You don't remember me?" asked a black young man, who cut in front of Xiao's bike.

"I do now," Xiao answered. "Didn't you receive a grant, too?"

"Yes. Dr. Buchanan contacted expats on Facebook," he answered. "Said you could use an escort. That Russian guy over there, Serge, suggested we use our own bikes or rent one. We didn't know you had your own. Been away for a while, haven't you?"

"Yup," Xiao replied. He couldn't help smiling, as he sat Kaitlyn on his lap and strapped her in.

"That's okay. We gotchou' back, man."

Xiao knew he'd return to the States one day; if not today then tomorrow, if not tomorrow then the day after. Saving his mentor's daughter from a fate worse than death was a deed he would always be proud of. She'd been his first chance to put others first. Being a Chinese American was different from being an American. But what American had no ethnic or racial background to flaunt? Was that even possible? He looked at the faces of the men around him. Being a Chinese American was a lot different from being a Chinese adult from China. He was tired of being used.

He could forget Quan and Kee for now and concentrate on a new action plan, one that said he'd be a crazy Chinese-American forever.

ONE YEAR LATER

CHAPTER 35

WINTER 2009   NEPAL, KATHMANDU

I T WAS FIVE o'clock in the morning in Nepal, when a vesper transport taxi carried Inez to a small family-owned storefront just above Kathmandu. Dust rose from asphalt streets below, but Inez didn't care. She'd travelled a long way, shedding fears of being ridiculed with each mile she took. Setting her aging eyes on such a spectacular view of the Himalayas was a good thing. This had to be God's reward for the faithful, those who saved their traveler's miles for decades, thinking they'd die before they'd have any place to go.

Inez carried a nylon tote bag in one hand and a Styrofoam cup in the other, full of what the store's proprietor swore, in broken English, was fresh Florida orange juice. She said nothing to refute his claim but knew the color wasn't right. What Inez really wanted, and what she was in the act of fulfilling, was to simply sit outside the store alone among the rickety sets of rusty iron tables and chairs to watch the sun rise over Ganesh Mountain. The scene was worth every lie she'd told her tour guide in order to leave her group for just this one day, all day, and to meet them later in New Delhi.

Halfway down the hill stood a recently painted cinderblock orphanage run by the Sisters of Mother Teresa. Apartment buildings, houses, and businesses surrounded it on all sides, as if the orphanage held some importance to the community.

Although she wasn't in the middle of downtown Kathmandu, traffic on the outskirts was just as astonishing. Loud trucks and cars carried construction materials to rebuild the city. Communities of people had come together to help restore what was salvageable after a combination of earthquakes and political upheaval.

She watched clouds change the shadows across the mountains in the distance. As she sipped her drink, Inez watched a scooter turn onto the street near her, slowing just outside the orphanage before resuming its speed toward the juice bar and stopping beside the outdoor table Inez occupied.

"Is this seat taken?" asked a big man, shouting from his scooter. He'd already removed his helmet as he swung a leg over to get off. He turned a chair right side up and waited beside it.

The minute she saw his head, Inez was speechless. She fumbled through her daypack for her reading glasses to verify her suspicions. She hadn't heard another American voice since she'd left her tour group.

It was Hank Jeffrey! The last time she'd seen him he had been standing over two bodies. Her eyes began to tear up. They both stood and embraced for a long time. She pulled away and caught him looking at her chest. She turned away to sit down again. He'd never done that before, a gesture that simultaneously made her quiet with melancholy and angry at his rudeness.

"I thought I should get a hug," Hank bellowed. "After all, I was your neighbor for fifteen years. Not as long as Galen perhaps, but certainly long enough to get a hug . . . no matter what our politics."

Inez took a deep breath and put her anger away. "You're right," she confirmed.

"Wow! Never thought I'd hear you agree with anything I said. You must be lonely. Better find out where the ex-pats meet. I'm sure there's a North American Social Club around here somewhere."

"Stop," she insisted. "You act like it's normal to see me here. I'm not lonely. I haven't been here long enough to be lonely. And you probably know why I'm here."

He nodded.

Inez felt stupid. Of course an intelligence officer or whatever he really was would know what she was doing in Nepal.

"But I found out you were here maybe a couple of days ago," Hank continued, "and since I've been wanting to talk to you for some time now, I . . ."

"Never thought I'd hear you say that," she countered.

"You're right. I'm exaggerating." He chuckled slightly at his own attempt at lightheartedness.

"I wanted to congratulate you," he continued. "I've already congratulated our little Teddy. Emailing the Red Chinese Government that same night with your video was just brilliant! What the hell were you two thinking? 'Course, I can forgive the boy. What would he know? But you're the adult in the room." There was no smile on his face.

Inez silently stared at him with defiance equal to his look of disapproval. Calmly, she replied, "I had to stop the Chinese from continuing to hire Shockenaugh assassins or I wouldn't have had a single neighbor left alive. If you were being paid per body, what would stop you from killing? They knew they'd never save face if any country found out they were going to use the DNA of white American leaders to build future Chinese warriors."

Hank leaned further back into the wrought-iron lawn chair. His chair's arms had grabbed him around his middle like an inflatable life preserver. "What's that you're drinking?" he asked.

"You won't like it. It's too sweet."

"Don't go away," he said, forcing his chair down past his hips.

"You're doing it again," she said. "Giving orders." Inez could feel her shoulders become rigid.

"Okay. Go away then. I'll catch up with you this time next year. Maybe by then we can talk to each other with civility." He stomped off into the neighborhood store, while Inez seethed.

He was interfering with her enjoyment of a breathtaking range of mountains, more rugged than the Rockies. Who gave him permission to show up? A few minutes later he returned with a cup of something hot and sat down hard into the snug chair. He started talking immediately, as if determined not to let Inez interrupt again.

"We intercepted your video that same night. Didn't take anything out of it, but we attached a video of our own, the autopsy of a man named Bohai."

Her anger made her face wrinkle.

"Hey!" Hank said, noticing her grimace. "At least he was dead when we dissected him. So they got our combined videos a day or two later than you originally emailed the thing. What the hell difference does that make? Shockenaugh killed him, by the way, not Larry. Bohai was the guy in Larry's kitchen, remember? We dug out three hollow-point bullets on our video, to prove our collective points. Don't worry. I was given the 'go ahead' to tell you this. Actually, some of your skills have caught the eye of more than a few important people in Langley. But I'll get to that later."

Inez spoke as clearly as she could. "I have no skills whatsoever in your field."

Hank continued talking. "Shockenaugh wanted him dead because they hadn't trained nor hired the guy. To them, he was a loose canon playing war games in their house. Quan sent him over. Shockenaugh knew who Bohai was. Quan had bought the company you see, and Shockenaugh hoped Bohai would be counted as just one of their hits.

"I think Shockenaugh figured it all out before the CIA did, that Quan was spending money for things his government hadn't sanctioned. We think Shockenaugh had bills that weren't being paid. Quan gambled that his government would back him eventually, and maybe they would have. But he got way too cocky and spent way too much money. He messed up when he ceased to operate in absolute secrecy and when he thought his man could do a better job than the men he hired Shockenaugh for. You know, don't you, that Bohai was supposed to kill you? He traveled with two other men who carried parts of the drones they used."

"That's what I figured," Inez said.

"Hey now, you can't take all the credit for this. Quan Yu was playing this game as far back as when Chiang Kai-Shek was in the picture. Quan survived Mao. That in itself is impressive. But they quietly executed him six months ago. Red China doesn't play with people who embarrass them. They have to save face, you know. Hey, I remember hearing that that's what tipped you off. China could only save face if everyone who knew anything died.

"Anyway, Quan was the only one who had personnel able to track Gaelen down and kill him for his uniforms. Nobody in China is going to reveal what Quan had planned for the United States but we think maybe several dirty bombs. Quan was able to track Asian Americans through bank accounts, social security, and credit card numbers.

"I was part of an envoy invited to verify Quan's death, months after he'd been executed. That's what brought me to China last week. Even then, the Chinese wouldn't answer how many of Quan's protégés they had arrested or executed along with him."

Inez hoped Hank hadn't seen her jump slightly.

Hank had taken a swig of whatever was in his cup. "Gruesome, huh?" he finally said.

"What is?" Inez asked. "The stuff in your cup or all the executions?"

He took another gulp and continued talking. "Interpol is certain Quan had more than a hundred U.S.-born counterspies working for him. Question is, will these people become spies for the U.S. now that Quan is dead or have they been killed off too? I'm trying to track some of them down."

Hank smiled broadly at Inez, who could only imagine what he was thinking. "Sounds like you've joined the CIA," she said. "I thought you were retired." She was being facetious.

"Pay's good. Why not? So there I was last week in Beijing, thinking about you," he said. "When I couldn't reach you by phone, I called Larry Carmichael. Told him I forgave him for fucking Karen Drisco."

Inez winced.

"Isn't forgiveness incredible?" he continued. "So he told me where you were and the name of your hotel. After all, I'm a single guy now."

For Inez, any idea she ever had of becoming a spy just evaporated.

Hank picked up his cup. "Let's drink to that. To Agnes, forgiveness, and being single."

He reached over and gently bumped his cup against hers. Both took tiny sips.

"So isn't this a little off the main highway for a vacation?" he asked.

"Perhaps," she answered, thinking that Larry apparently hadn't told him everything after all.

"I hear you don't attend those China Scholar dinners in Washington anymore. You don't pass out those little cards that look like tiny hands. Creepy, if you ask me."

Inez felt her total dislike for the man return. "I'm still astounded by your access to people's personal data."

"Still don't trust me?"

They looked at each other in knowing ways. Inez realized she'd need to send him away with some feeling that they were not enemies.

"I simply felt I wasn't competent to help students with the kinds of problems they might typically face in China," she answered.

"That's not true. The Denver Post gave you and Teddy all the credit for shutting down Shockenaugh for good. The entire organization has disbanded. But if you're in the intelligence community you know they've already reorganized under a different name. Besides, you're able to look through people, observe patterns of behavior, come up with a reasonable hypothesis. You juggle all these things and come up with the right answer."

Inez refused to smile or say thank you. Maybe he'd leave soon.

"My brother lives in Tucson," Hank continued. He changed the subject, she thought because her face couldn't hide her discomfort. "So I've moved there with him. Agnes loved Colorado, not me."

Inez sighed, disappointed that he hadn't left yet. "Your house is going to be gorgeous when contractors are finished," she replied.

"Thank you. Wanna' buy it? I'd need a good excuse to return to Colorado."

Inez returned his stare, while sipping her drink. He was one stupid cowboy if he thought she was going to bite on that apple.

"Did you know, they plan to tear down that monster mansion next door to you, the one they built over Gaelen's house? Apparently, the foundation was destroyed by that drone's missile meant for your place."

Of course she knew. "Hmm," she replied. "Reminds me of the one thing that troubled me. What made those drones hit the wrong house? They're usually so accurate, aren't they? They go where someone sends them."

"Those things happen, Inez. It's all a part of waging war."

Hank had one thing right; she still didn't trust him. If she thought he'd had anything to do with manipulating those bombs that killed Billy and his wife, she would hound him until the end of his days, until she'd brought him to justice. It must have been written on her face, she thought. Why was he sweating?

Finally he said, "What I wanted to talk to you about was the CIA."

"No need. I have their phone number."

"Democracy is still in jeopardy. I thought we might work together from time to time."

"Oh, heavens no. All those years I thought you were just the neighborhood bigot. Then I find out you were a drum majorette for South Africa's countrywide bigotry. Why, you're so powerful, you can monitor traffic anywhere in Denver. Or should I have said you can monitor traffic anywhere? You can shut down a fourth of an entire metropolitan area. But more important, you can successfully lie to friends with a straight face and a bogus accent. I don't know who the hell you are. And I don't care. I'm on vacation. How's that for being cryptic?"

Hank immediately got up from his seat without any trouble and carried his empty cup into the store. He came out without it. Never looking at Inez, he mounted his scooter, put on his helmet, and said, "Until the next time you need me," then drove off down the hill toward the center of Kathmandu.

Inez had no stomach for the rest of her fruit drink. She poured it into the road and prayed that wouldn't get her locked up in a Nepali prison.

She was afraid of men like Hank, capable of complete deception and able to exterminate anybody from the human race whenever they determined it necessary. Was that the downside of being a spy?

She got up from her seat and brushed away the street soot from her clothes. Her decision not to mention Xiao's name to Hank was deliberate. She feared Hank's ability to use him as Quan had, if he was still alive.

"C'mon Billy. Walk with me. Keep me company," Inez said out loud.

She walked across the street and down the middle of the block to the orphanage. Entering through tall, unlocked, wrought-iron gates, she looked at her watch. She was early. Beyond the gate was a courtyard. A large building, by Nepali standards, stood behind a second set of locked gates. Although there was no ceiling over the yard, sounds from the street had vanished. She was amused by the acoustic miracle, realizing she was about to enter a world saturated in religious belief.

"Inez, Inez." Karen Drisco's voice broke the silence. Her face, surrounded by a white linen habit looked even younger than Inez had remembered her. Ancient-looking keys jangled loudly in Karen's hands, as she ran toward the remaining gate. Squealing toddlers scurried behind her, and by the time the gate was opened, the little ones imitated the two women by hugging the only parts of Inez and Karen their little arms could reach. The two women held each other like mother and daughter.

"Praise God, He let me see your face again," Karen said. Tears streamed down her cheeks, making Inez cry as well.

Inez had known in her heart all along that Karen was alive. The signs had been there from the beginning. In the condo Karen shared with Sheila, the poster of Kathmandu was positioned at the very top of the stairs, as if it was the heaven she had hoped to attain. Missionary pamphlets strewn over the coffee table had phone numbers scribbled on them, some of which Inez had quietly stashed in her purse. But it had been Sheila's words that made Inez the most suspicious; that Karen wasn't the same after her father threatened to take her out of St. Anselm's school.

"I was afraid at first," Karen said, "that none of you would ever forgive me."

"Forgive you for becoming a nun?" Inez asked.

"No one wrote, and no one called me. Years ago I thought Dad hated me because of my dream to become a nun. I know better now, but then I thought maybe all of you hated me for letting him down, even after death."

"So you sent your closest friend, Jane Plane, to the restaurant, the young woman who worked at the Red Cross with you. She was supposed to tell us what you had decided to do with your life and where you were. Am I right?" Inez asked.

"I know it was cowardly, but honestly, I didn't know that I was going to do this until Jane and I lost our jobs. When the Red Cross said we had to leave because they had no way to pay us, I was ecstatic; I took it as a sign from God. But my best friend was planning suicide. She was pregnant with no husband, money, or family. So I gave her my car and all the money I had. Inez, I just know something has happened to her, because Jane would have written or called me. She knew exactly how to reach me." Karen's eyes searched her face.

Under that scrutiny, Inez couldn't hide her sadness for a girl she'd never met.

"From what little I've learned about her," Inez explained, "she's never been seen since that night in the Tiffany Plaza parking lot. Police think she could have been kidnapped at gunpoint. I refused to believe it. Remember, we all thought it was you."

"Let's go in here to talk," Karen said. She unlocked another gate at the top of a flight of stairs just inside the courtyard. A train of toddlers followed her up the stairs and down a corridor into a long room where hundreds of plush toys were piled up to the ceiling in one corner.

"This was once a government building with a prison in the basement. The Nepalese government gave it to us. We take care of more than a few of their welfare issues in exchange.

The children crawled over the mountain of toys giggling and laughing, while the women sat huddled together on primary school-sized chairs in an opposite corner.

"I'll continue to look for Jane," Inez said, "but the fact that not one piece of your car has turned up makes me think she and the car were taken out of the country."

"Lately, I've not been as worried about her as I was when I first got here," Karen said. "Perhaps God has given her the peace she's looked for. I pray for her a lot.

"I also see," Karen went on, "that God has given you the grace to sound more like a detective, Inez. Have you left the world of fixing education fraud to become a criminal investigator? I used to love to stuff fliers under people's doors for you when I was younger. And as I got older, I remember thinking that praying to God for the right outcome was probably just as statistically successful as trying to influence voters with fliers."

"I wish you'd shared that insight with me," Inez said. "It would have saved me a lot of money."

Both laughed. Karen wrapped her arms around Inez as they sat close and watched the children. They looked as if they had come to the orphanage from all corners of the planet.

Inez said, "I don't want to be a detective, but I can't stop being curious. I'll always want to know how I can fix things. I had to fix a few things about myself in order to come to Nepal."

A little boy with droopy eyes rubbed against Inez's leg. She picked him up and set him on her lap.

"Then how about becoming a global detective," Karen said laughingly, "but only if you visit us here in Kathmandu every time you're in the neighborhood."

"You mean become a spy?" Inez asked. "I wish I had that kind of courage."

"I've seen you stand up to gang members before. You've got as much courage as my . . ., as my . . .," Karen couldn't finish.

"As your dad?" Inez said. "You blamed yourself for your dad's death, didn't you?"

She buried her face in her hands and cried.

"I came," Inez continued, "to explain what happened the night you found your dad on the floor."

Karen used a handkerchief to wipe her face, made the sign of the cross with her rosary, and then kissed the crucifix, as if fortifying herself for the story to come. Inez watched her with reverence, realizing that Karen could just as ceremoniously have wrapped herself in a prayer cloth to begin a reading from the Torah. That wanting to understand the will of God was the hope of many people all over the world.

Inez began with Miriam and Gaelen's lie about his heart problems and continued with Gaelen's attempt to sell World War II uniforms on eBay.

"I don't want to hear any more Inez. Telling me about my dad's death isn't going to teach me how to stop being naive. Dad was worldly and a better man than most because he used what he knew to help others, and I'll be eternally grateful for having him in my life for as long as I did, no matter how he died. Unfortunately, nothing he did kept him from getting murdered. All I can do is make sure Dad and Mom's influence on me rubs off on the people I serve."

Quietly Inez listened to the things she said, while children played leap frog over her shoes. Telling Karen about Billy Needham and Agnes Jeffrey could wait. She also had to tell her why the Denver Police Department wanted proof of life from her before they would exonerate Larry. The fact that there was no body helped him, but he still wasn't totally cleared.

"I love you, Dr. Inez Buchanan," Karen said. "You've never laughed at my stupid questions or treated me like a baby. I admit that my pride made me think I was responsible for Dad's death, but I knew better. I thought I had caused his heart attack."

Two more children, tired of stuffed animals, ran to the seated women.

"Do you know how to play peek-a-boo?" asked a girl in English.

"You speak English!" Inez answered. "That's marvelous. So do I."

"Her name is Kaitlyn," Karen said quickly. "She's been here only a few months. A very nice Chinese-American man dropped her off, explaining how her parents and brother had been killed. Hopefully she's too young to remember any of that. He was an interesting man, though. Said he planned to visit her next year. Somehow he was . . . he was very handsome and yet he had a gruesome scar. You could almost see the imprint of an animal's claw that must have ripped through his cheek."

"Yes, I know how to play peek-a-boo," Inez said to the little girl. "But you look awfully tired. How about a nap first?" Inez sat very still and let the girl climb up, content that her prosthetic could also be a child's pillow.

Inez whispered to Karen while the children slept. She felt herself wanting to teach her last lesson before leaving. "I believe Gaelen's cleverness survives inside of you Karen. His cleverness is waiting to help whenever you need him. What I'm trying to say is, never entertain the false notion that you're totally safe anywhere. Stay alert. God's keeping his eyes on you."

Karen smiled, grateful that Inez had arrived in time for the evening's ceremony. Softly she said, "I intend to change my name from Karen Drisco to Sister Inez tonight. And I'm so glad you could be here to witness it."

Inez was speechless.

ACKNOWLEDGEMENTS

I want to thank all of the critique group members I met going back to 2007. Thank you for sitting through this novel for so long.

I can't thank Mr. and Dr. Stirling enough for making themselves available to me at the last minute and for all the work they did to help this novel get born.

I'd also like to add Mrs. Carole Adelstein—she is known for giving the shirt off her back—to my list of marvelous supportive people. As my neighbor, she has unselfishly answered my call to come out and play when I'm not writing. But most of all, and for which I am most grateful, she was my beta-reader. Thank you.

ABOUT THE AUTHOR

CORDY FITZGERALD lives with her family in Denver, Colorado. The first thirty years of her life were spent in Washington, D.C. A graduate of Dunbarton College of Holy Cross, she received her Masters' from Catholic University of America and a PhD from The University of Colorado in Denver. She has written short stories for children, *The Nubie,* and *Shopping Cart Annie.*

Printed in the United States
By Bookmasters